SCREW

Hell's Handlers Book 8

Lilly Atlas

ISBN-13: 978-1-946068-33-0

Other books by Lilly Atlas

No Prisoners MC

Hook: A No Prisoners Novella

Striker

Jester

Acer

Lucky

Snake

Trident Ink

Escapades

Hell's Handlers MC

Zach

Maverick

Jigsaw

Copper

Rocket

Little Jack

Joy

Screw

Join Lilly's mailing list for a **FREE** No Prisoners short story.

www.lillyatlas.com

Table of Contents

One biker in denial.
One woman with secrets.
One enforcer with something to prove.
Three parts of one uncertain future.

Jazmine lives with secrets she buries beneath conservative clothing and avoidance of relationships. Those secrets are just one reason she spends months resisting the advances of the Hell's Handlers' resident flirt, Screwball. Mostly, she can't stand Screw's constant parade of one-night stands and inability to be serious. But the man is charming, and her resolve is only so strong. When Gumby, a romantic interest from Jazz's past, returns to her life, she suddenly finds herself stuck between two men who hate each other on sight yet seem inexplicably drawn together.

As the new enforcer for the Hell's Handlers Motorcycle Club, Screwball faces a challenge he's avoided his entire life: the heavy weight of leadership. Now he's in charge of protecting his club as threats from an enemy MC mount. Even though he doubts himself, Screw wants the opportunity to prove his worth to his brothers. Meanwhile, he also finds himself attracted to Jazz in a way he's never experienced. When Jazz's eye-catching biker from Arizona shows up in town, Screw finds himself wondering if a future full of commitment might be worth leaving his comfort zone.

Having grown up with a brutal father who spoke with his fists, Gumby learned early to suppress certain sides of himself. When he crosses the country in search of a woman he can't shake from his head, he not only finds her in danger but the object of one very appealing enforcer's desire. He soon discovers denying his true identity can be impossible when faced with real temptation.

Can three wounded souls overcome their baggage in time to save the Hell's Handlers MC and their relationship?

SCREW

Lilly Atlas

PROLOGUE

Gumby – 1997, Arizona

"The fuck you doin' boy?" Will's dad demanded a second before his meaty palm smacked against the back of Will's head. The soda that had been an inch from his lips sloshed over the sides of the cup, sending a spray of sugary liquid all over the paperback in his lap. "Thirteen-year-old boy at a goddammed football game and he's fucking reading." His father shook his head, clearly disgusted.

Nothing new there.

"It's homework, Dad. I've got a test on the first three chapters Monday morning." Why did he bother explaining?

"Pay some fucking attention. Maybe you'll learn how to start acting like a fucking man." His father belched as though backing up the statement with action. As though the putrid, beer-tinged burp somehow set him a level above the rest of the men in the stands.

Speaking of…

As Will turned the novel over on his lap, careful to keep the wet pages flat, he did a quick scan of the crowd. Sure enough, more than a few disapproving glances and whispers were directed his and his father's way.

Nothing new there, either.

Will's family was trash, plain and simple. Last year, when the school district re-zoned during the summer months, he went from living on the wrong side of the tracks and going to a crappy public school to still living on the wrong side of the tracks but now attending a public school across town.

Where the rich kids went.

The middle school he now attended was chock full of the snobbiest kids he'd ever met. Kids who were dropped off by Lamborghinis and Ferraris. Kids who wore jeans that cost more than his entire family's monthly food budget.

His father fucking loved it. Felt the fact his rundown two-bedroom shack somehow ended up in a new school district meant *his* status in life had elevated.

What a joke.

His dad still got up at four every morning to make it to the chicken factory by five where he worked a line, inspecting the packaging of the birds. He earned himself a few pennies above minimum wage. By two in the afternoon, he was home with his flabby ass planted in his fraying recliner where he remained until the six to ten beers he downed each evening finally put him to sleep.

Oh, yeah, that was a man Will wanted to be like. Fuck if he'd allow himself to end up like that. If reading and getting good grades got him a better life than his old man, he'd read every fucking chance he could get.

"You paying attention, boy?" his dad asked, gaze on the field.

No. "Yes, sir."

"Good. You should be out there playing instead of always fucking reading." His dad lifted the glass Snapple bottle he'd set between his feet and spit into it, adding to the muddy liquid already half filling the bottle.

Will's stomach turned as it always did and he gazed at the field. Look at that, all it took was a nasty bottle full of tobacco spit to make him interested in watching the game.

Football, sports in general, just weren't his thing. Never had been. He was a book worm, much more interested in learning the way things worked than running around outside. Lately, he'd been gobbling up books on car engines. Why couldn't his father praise him for that? Didn't men like cars?

"You're tall enough to play this shit," his dad went on as though Will was actually engaged in this conversation. "Or maybe basketball. Gonna be really fucking tall, like me."

God, he hated any kind of similarity between them, even height.

His dad lifted one of Will's arms and shook it. "Too bad these fucking things are all gangly and limp." He snorted—a sound full of revulsion. "Long fucking arms and legs without any muscle. Guess you could be the fucking kicker."

"Stop it," Will said, yanking his arm free. His gaze caught one of a woman sitting a row down and a few people over. She wasn't even pretending to hide her frown as she observed and probably listened to the interaction between Will and his father.

As the game clock ticked down way too slowly, he let his mind wander. At thirteen, he still had years of living with his father before he could get out of the house. When he was younger, he'd had dreams of leaving their shitty dust trap of an Arizona town and heading to a prestigious university. Leaving this life behind and making something of himself.

Recently, he'd read this account of a man who bought a motorcycle and traveled across the country, settling wherever he felt a connection. Sounded amazing. Perfect really. To be that free. He hadn't been able to get the idea out of his mind.

College probably wasn't a realistic goal. So far, he made good grades, but probably not good enough to get a full ride anywhere. And his family didn't have two pennies to rub together. Even if they did, it sure as hell wouldn't be given to him to use on an education. Maybe it was time to change his goals. To be realistic about what his life would be.

"I gotta take a piss and I'm gonna get something to eat. I'm fucking hungry," his father said.

Will blinked. The game clock no longer counted down. Halftime.

He gazed around the bleachers which had really cleared out now that everyone was running off to grab a snack or use the restroom. Of course, his dad didn't think to ask if Will wanted anything.

Just as he was about to turn over his book and try to read despite the wet pages, his attention snagged on a football player nodding along to his coach, who spoke with his hands and seemed to be giving some kind of pep-talk.

His school was up, but only by three points. A lead easily lost.

Number twenty-seven shook his head then the coach slapped him on the back and sauntered off. Twenty-seven, Carson Hills, if Will remembered correctly, set his foot on the bench, then bent forward to fix the laces. The guy was a senior. Quarterback of the football team and dating the lead cheerleader. A total cliché, but he seemed to have it all. His father was some world-renowned plastic surgeon, living in this gigantic mansion on the lake.

Carson switched feet and as he did so, his ass flexed, and Will felt a twitch and thickening between his legs. He knew what it was. Same damn thing happened when Carson's girlfriend Lacy wore those low-cut shirts that showed off her boobs. Same thing that happened when he looked at those Victoria Secret catalogues that still came for his long-gone mother.

Wasn't like his dad had any kind of birds and bees talk with him but the kids at school talked about sex enough for him to know exactly what it was. And he'd started jerking off recently, so…

He knew what it was to be turned on.

And Carson's ass was turning him on.

Wasn't the first time it had happened when he looked at a guy, either. No, that was a few weeks ago when he'd been watching some movie on TV. The star had stripped down to dive in a pool and as soon as his stomach muscles had been revealed, Will popped a boner. He'd nearly thrown up on his potato chips when he figured out what was happening. Instead, he came up with a bunch of excuses and reasons it was just a one-time thing. The leading actress had just been running around in a bikini. He was tired and not fully paying attention to what he was watching.

Whatever.

But then it'd happened again. And again. And by that third time, Will had admitted to himself what he refused to acknowledge out loud.

Both men and women turned him on.

And wasn't that just great.

Why him? He had no problem with people being gay or bisexual. Made no difference to him at all. But his dad? God, if he ever found out—

"The fuck you lookin' at boy?" his dad turned and sidestepped his way down the aisle. His gut nearly took the head off some oblivious spectator a row below.

Shit.

"What? Nothing." Will straightened, and immediately tore his gaze away from the round male ass fueling his current fantasy.

"You were fucking staring at that guy." His father's gaze shifted between the field and Will.

With a roll of his eyes Will said, "You're crazy."

This time, the smack to the back of his head nearly knocked him off the bench. "Watch your fucking mouth, kid. I know what I saw."

The stands were filling once again, so Will stared at his feet. Maybe his dad would lay off if he didn't react.

"Better not be staring at some fucking guy, boy. Didn't raise no fucking fag, did I?"

A few gasps came from the surrounding spectators. Will kept his gaze fixed on his worn sneakers as shame burned in his cheeks. "No, sir," he whispered.

"What?" his dad said, seeming to only get louder. "Can't hear you. Said I didn't raise no fag, did I?" He didn't care one bit that his offensive slur was not only overheard by dozens, but that it cut like a knife into his son's soul.

"No, sir," Will said, louder this time. Nothing would be better at that moment than if the bleachers would crumble, sending him crashing to the ground twenty feet below. Probably be the only thing to distract the horrified people wondering how trash like them ended up at this school.

"That's right." His father nodded before shoving a handful of nachos into his pie hole. "I find you looking at a dude's ass again and I'll show you how we deal with fags in our family. You hear?" he said with his mouth full, crumbs spraying with each word.

"Yes, sir."

"Good. Look at her over there. That's what you should be staring at."

Will shifted his gaze to the woman his father ogled. She was a brand-new teacher in her early twenties, and she was gorgeous. With those short jean shorts and tight tank top, she did it for him just as much as the football player.

"A hot one, ain't she, boy," his dad said with a lecherous chuckle.

"Yeah."

Thank God he didn't have to lie.

Chapter One

"Hey, brother, talk to you a second?"

A heavy kick to the bottom of Gumby's foot had him grunting and rolling the creeper out from under the vintage Mustang he'd been fighting with for the past few hours. He stared up into the laughing face of Acer, one of his brothers in the No Prisoners MC.

"What's up, brother?"

"Jesus, you're a fucking mess. What the hell happened?" Acer asked with a raised eyebrow. He folded his arms across his chest and took a step back as though the grease would magically jump off Gumby's coveralls and onto Acer's ninety-dollar Ralph Lauren shirt. The boujee fucker.

"Let's just say squirters aren't good in all instances."

"Take your word for it," Acer said with a wink.

"You do that." Gumby dropped his feet to either side of the creeper and curled to a sit. Using a rag almost as dirty as his skin, he massaged his left hand. An old injury made the damn thing ache from time to time. "So what's going on? You need me for something?"

Acer studied him for a moment before fishing a piece of paper out of his pocket. Slipping it between his index and middle fingers, he held the slip out. "I found her."

Gumby's stomach dropped straight to the floor. "Come again?"

"Found her, brother. She's in Tennessee. That's the address where she works."

Unable to formulate a response, Gumby unfolded the paper and stared at the written address as though he'd somehow know how to get there.

Tennessee.

Tenne-fucking-see. A good chunk of the way across the goddammed country.

Why?

"A diner?" he finally said, looking up at Acer.

His brother shrugged. "Looks like it."

With a slow nod, as his brain tried to process the information, he said, "You sure it's her?"

"Yeah, brother, I'm sure. She's been using her father's last name."

That news had Gumby's spine straightening. "Her father?"

Being a Sunday afternoon, the club-owned auto garage was deserted except for Gumby, who'd decided to get a jump on this impossible project he was working on for a buddy.

Another shrug from Acer. "Yeah. That's why it took so long to find her. No hits trying her last name, or her stepfather's. I figured she musta made something up. Then last weekend, I tracked down her stepbrother. Remember that fucker?"

Gumby nodded. Jazz's mother remarried when Jazz was just a kid. The guy had a son who had to be a good ten plus years older than Jazz. He popped up from time to time, usually got in some trouble with the law, misdemeanors mainly, then jetted back out of town not to resurface again for a year, sometimes more. Usually he came around when he needed his daddy to fork over some money. "Has to be two years since I've heard he was around. Weird motherfucker."

"Yeah, that hasn't changed. He's in lock up." Acer pushed away from the cabinet.

"No shit?"

"Yep. Some kinda psych institute for criminals. Apparently, he attacked some girl in Chicago about six months ago. Fucked her up good. He'll be locked up for a good few years. Anyway, I asked if he knew anything about where Jazz might be. The guy laughed and said, and I quote, 'That fucking bitch wouldn't call me if she was on fire. But she should. I'm the only one who can help her.'"

What the fuck? "Seriously?" Was that why she left? Was she in some kind of trouble the club hadn't known about?

"Told you. Still weird as fuck. But he did say if I was looking for her, I should check under Jazmine Barnes. Apparently, her sperm donor's last name was Barnes."

"How did we not know that?"

Acer lifted a shoulder. "It's not on her birth certificate. Not anywhere on paper. I'd have found it if it was."

"Huh," Gumby said, staring back down at the scrap of paper. Went to show how much he'd still had to learn about her before she left town.

"You gonna call her?"

It was Gumby's turn to shrug. Resting his forearms on his knees, he let the scribbled note dangle between his legs. "Don't know."

"Seriously? You've had me looking for her for over a year and now that I finally found her, you don't know if you want to call her."

"Clearly, she doesn't want to talk to any of us."

"Well, you got a point there."

They fell silent until Acer walked over, clapped him on the shoulder then said, "I'll leave you to it, brother."

Gumby nodded but didn't bother to glance up as his brother walked out of the garage. Instead he stayed where he was in the quiet garage, staring at the paper as guilt and uncertainty pricked his skin.

It'd been this way for more than a year. This unexplainable feeling that somehow Jazz's leaving had been his fault. His brother's wife, Marcie, had rolled her eyes and called him egocentric when he'd voiced the concern to her, but still, he couldn't shake the feeling that he'd somehow been responsible for her fleeing Arizona.

Maybe because she'd vanished the day after they were supposed to go on a date. The day after he'd canceled their date last minute.

But she'd understood, or so she'd claimed. Canceling the date had been unavoidable. Club business interfered, and he was required to put his MC first. Jazz knew that. Jazz understood that. Hell, she'd been working as the receptionist in the garage owned by the club for years.

Why then, had she vanished without a trace the following morning?

The club had been stumped and fucking worried as shit. Hell, when she hadn't shown for work, his prez, Shiv, had been ready to send out a fucking search party. And then Lila, his VP's ol' lady, had finally admitted to receiving a text from Jazz. Three fucking sentences that had everyone scratching their heads but calling off the blood hounds.

Everyone except Gumby, who couldn't let it go.

I needed to leave. I'm fine. Please, please, do not let them look for me.

They hadn't been a thing. Hadn't so much as kissed. But he'd liked her. And she'd liked him, or so she'd said when she agreed to a date. Every time he'd laid eyes on her, his dick hardened to the point of painful. He'd lost count of the number of times he'd spilled on his shower floor with her name rushing from his lips. Jazz was fun, edgy, kind, spunky, sexy…

Okay, maybe it was more than like on his part. He'd been pretty much infatuated with her for a while but had never taken any steps to make her his.

There were things about him she didn't know. Things very few knew, and he feared no woman would understand. Hell, he didn't understand it.

So he hadn't made a move.

Not until the day he walked into the lobby of the garage and found some forty-five-year-old accountant drooling all over her.

That was the day he'd lost his mind and practically ordered her on a date. He'd never forget the look on her face that day. Her short hair had been studded with pink highlights that matched the pink on her lips. God, they'd looked so fucking delicious. To this day, he got hard recalling the way they'd quirked up into a smirk. Then there was that mesmerizing sparkle in her dark eyes. She'd been on to him. Known he'd finally asked her on a date because of the asshole leaving a puddle of slobber on her desk.

They'd been planning to keep it casual. Dinner, drinks at a local bar, maybe some dancing, and if he was lucky, headboard-banging sex to top off the night.

But fucking club business had derailed the plans. And no one from the MC had seen Jazz since.

Finally, after more than a year, he had a way to contact her. She'd changed her cell number and her email addresses as well. The few messages he'd sent were kicked back immediately. Would she speak to him if he called her at this diner or would she slam the phone down?

Had her feelings for him been stronger than he realized?

Did his canceling the date hurt her that much?

Was he the catalyst that made her run from Crystal Rock? From her friends, from her family?

His stomach churned as his most pressing fear pushed its way to the forefront of his mind.

Had she discovered his secret and been crushed? Shocked? Revolted?

There was only one way to find out and a phone call wouldn't cut it.

With a sigh, Gumby pulled out his cell and swiped the screen, ignoring the streak of grease he spread across the surface. Wouldn't be the first time he'd gunked up the thing.

Three minutes later, he was booked on a flight that would have him in Tennessee by six o'clock in the evening in less than one week.

Jazz very well might throw him out on his ass the second she laid eyes on him, but he wouldn't be leaving until he got some answers.

Chapter Two

Jazmine – 2001 - Arizona

"Jazzy, I'm going to work. Your dad will be home in an hour. You sure you're okay here by yourself?" Jazz's mother called from near the front door.

Jazz rolled her eyes. She was thirteen, not three. "Yes, mom," she yelled back. "Pretty sure I can survive by myself for a whole sixty minutes." Especially when all she was doing was the stupid essay, she'd put off for the past few days. Three pages on Greek mythology.

Yuck.

"Watch that sass, missy."

She rolled her eyes again.

"You know not to open the door for anyone, right?"

"I know." Jazz set her pen down and stared at the open door to her room, waiting for the next order. Always the same.

"No friends over."

"I know."

"Especially not boys."

Jazz giggled as her gaze shifted to her favorite poster. The five guys in the popular boy band beamed at her with their perfect hair, white teeth, and adorable faces. "I know!"

After shouting a final goodbye, Jazz turned on her music app full blast. Pop music filled her room, shaking the walls and drowning out the usual house noises that seemed so much louder when she was home alone. She'd never admit it to her mother, but being home by herself freaked her out. Every creek and rumble of pipes made her jump out of her skin. On the flip side, having no one around to yell at her over her loud music was always a great thing.

Half an hour later, she'd actually made significant progress on her paper. Tapping her pencil against her desk in time with the music, Jazz scanned her textbook. All she needed was a solid conclusion and this paper was done.

As the verse ended and the chorus kicked up, Jazz belted out the lyrics alongside Taylor Swift. Just as she opened her mouth to sing her favorite part, the music cut, plunging her room into immediate silence. With a loud shriek, she spun around.

"God, Paul, you scared the crap out of me." With her hand over her chest, she tried to keep her heart from bursting through her rib cage. "I, uh, didn't know you were coming here. Your dad will be back in a little bit."

Her words didn't seem to click with her wide-eyed stepbrother. He scanned her room with frantic jerks of his head as though expecting the boogey man to appear at any time. A ten-year age gap wasn't the only thing that kept them from being close step-siblings. Something was off with Paul. He was twitchy, always rubbing at his arms and legs with his eyes darting around. And he stared at her. A lot. A few times, she even caught him rummaging in her room. He seemed to have some fixation with her she'd noticed shortly after meeting him three years ago, and no amount of denial from his father or her mother would change her mind.

The guy gave her the major creeps. Luckily, he'd never lived in the same house as her, and didn't come around often, but when he did, he hardly left her alone. At least she didn't have to worry about him hitting on her. Paul was gay, despite his father's many attempts at changing that situation. Supposedly, he'd sent Paul to one of those horrifying conversion camps when he was a teenager. At least that's what her mom claimed.

Poor guy. Must have been awful. And it probably explained why he spouted so much religious talk.

"Paul?" she asked as his haggard appearance finally registered. "You okay?"

His hair was a rat's nest of unkempt brown curls, sticking out in all directions as though he'd slept on it wet and hadn't bothered to tame it when he woke up. A wrinkled T-shirt and baggy jeans covered his slight frame. The look didn't appear to be a style choice, but just clothes that were too big. He'd always been a slim guy, but now he was practically skin and bones.

Wide eyes met her gaze. "Huh?" he asked, then was back to scanning all around her room. "I'm not here to see my dad. I'm here for you."

The hairs on Jazz's arms stood straight on end. In the years she'd known him, they'd hardly spent any time alone. She made a point of it. "What?" she squeaked. "Me?"

"I'm here to save you. He's coming. He might be here already."

Okay, this was weird even for Paul. Sure, she'd caught him talking to himself a few times and he always seemed to be spouting one conspiracy or another, usually religiously based, but someone coming for her? "Uh, who, Paul? Who's coming? Your dad is on his way home, but he's the only one coming here."

He looked her straight in the eye. "The Devil." Were this any other time, Jazz would have laughed and rolled her eyes, but a frigid shiver ran down her spine instead. Paul's gaze portrayed just how much he believed the two words that just fell from his lips.

His head jerked to the right as though he'd heard something coming from near her bed, then he took three steps toward it which finally moved him from her doorway. Keeping one eye on him, Jazz tip-toed toward the door.

Paul lifted her pillow, peeking under it as though Satan might actually be hiding there.

Blood rushing in her ears, she took another soundless step toward the door.

"Where are you going?" he shouted like she was across the house instead of five feet away.

She froze, then looked over her shoulder. His bloodshot eyes were wide as saucers, staring at her with true panic. Was he on something? "Um, maybe we should go out into the living room and wait for your dad. He should be here very soon."

Paul's body went still, but his eyes still scanned the room. "He's already here."

"Your dad?" She hadn't heard his motorcycle pull in and that thing usually rattled the windows.

"No," he said, voice taking on a chilling note. "The Devil."

Jazz's hands began to shake the longer Paul stared at her. "Uh, m-maybe, maybe uh, we should just like um, go ch-check, uh check for, for your dad." She started for the door again resisting the urge to break into a sprint.

"No!"

The command was so sharply issued, Jazz stopped on instinct.

Paul grabbed her upper arm. "He's here and he wants you. We need to keep you safe," he said as he dragged her back from the door with a rough yank.

"Ow! Paul, stop. There's no one here." She twisted, trying to free herself from his surprising strength. Beneath his bruising grip, the skin of her arm pulled and burned like his hands were made of fire. "Please, Paul, stop."

"Shh." He threw her against the wall, holding her there with a hand on her chest. "I know where he is." His sunken face leaned in so close she could smell the smoke on his breath.

"P-Paul, listen to me, please."

"I know where he is."

This wasn't working. She needed a new plan. Maybe… "W-where, Paul? Where is he?" Maybe by playing along she could steer him out of the room.

He looked into her eyes and she swallowed as dread filled her. "He's in you."

Jazz's knees buckled at the cold look in his eyes and had he not drawn her in for a bone-crushing hug, she'd have fallen to the floor.

"Don't worry," he whispered as he squeezed her. "I know what to do. I have to get him out."

"W-wh, uh, like an exorcism?" She asked, voice trembling. "O-okay." The room began to spin.

Breathe, Jazz. Stall him.

"L-let's do that in the l-living room." Hopefully that would give her some chance to escape. His father should be home within the next ten minutes. She could do this.

She could keep him going until his father got home. She had too. No matter how scared she was, no matter what he did to her, no matter how hard it was to breathe. She couldn't panic. She could do it.

"No. I have a better idea."

Or maybe not.

Paul released her then shoved her against the wall once again. Her back hit hard, knocking the breath from her lungs. As she sucked in a painful gulp of air, a clicking sound made her focus on Paul's hand. Her heart slammed against her chest. "No!" she shouted but it came out in a harsh cough. "No! Paul, no!"

He held an open switchblade way too close to her shoulder. His mouth turned down in a frown and she could have sworn those were tears forming in his eyes. "I'm sorry, Jazzy," he said. "It's the only way."

She couldn't breathe, couldn't think, could only see that sharp blade as it moved closer and closer to her skin.

"No. No, no, no, no, no!" she screamed again and again, finally finding air. Jazz thrashed, flailing her limbs and using every ounce of her strength to break his hold. "Please, Paul, let me go. Please don't do this. The devil isn't here. It's just me. Jazz. Your sister. Please." Tears fell from her eyes in giant drops.

"It's not her," he whispered to himself as he used his entire body weight to keep her anchored against the wall. "It's not her. You have to save her. He'll kill her."

Bucking against the wall, Jazz sobbed. "Please. I'm just Jazz." She'd be covered in bruises tomorrow from where her elbows, spine, and head banged into the wall repeatedly. None of it mattered. "Please!" She continued to struggle even as she ran out of steam and her body fatigued.

"It's all right, Jazz. I know it will hurt, but you'll be saved. I won't let him have you." He said.

He placed the tip of the knife against the pale skin covering her shoulder. Jazz shrieked. "No! Don't! Please!"

And when the first sharp slice tore through her flesh, she screamed.

And screamed. And *screamed.*

Chapter Three

"I need to start having the prospect warm up my car before I leave," Jazz grumbled as a full-body shiver ran through her. Though this was her second winter out of the toasty Arizona desert, she hadn't gotten used to the cold.

At all.

And the seven-minute drive from work to home wasn't enough time for her car to warm up. At least not when the day's high never made it out of the thirties. Even with a hat, scarf, gloves, puffy down jacket, and wooly socks, she felt the chill. And not in a brisk, refreshing sort of way, but in an I'm-buried-under-an-avalanche-and-about-to-freeze-to-death way.

When it came to the cold, Jazz was a complete and utter wuss.

The good news was she only had half a mile left until she reached her home. The bad news was that it had snowed a good three inches while she'd been at work, so she now had to shovel the driveway, a task she loathed. Shell and Toni had laughed when she'd whined, telling her to make the prospect do it, but that felt all wrong. The poor guy was stuck watching her boring ass all day when she wasn't even someone's ol' lady. How could she ask him to do manual labor on top of it? No, she'd suck it up and shovel her own driveway like the big girl she was. And if the prospect jumped in to help, well…she wouldn't turn him away.

She wasn't stupid.

As she turned onto her street, a smile lit her face. There in the driveway of her little rented house stood her next-door neighbor, Jeremy, using his snow blower to rid her driveway of her white nemesis.

What an angel.

She pulled into the snow-free driveway just as Jeremy was powering down his snow blower. After giving a little wave to the prospect as he parked next to a mound of plowed snow, she exited the car. "Seriously, Jeremy, you are the best. How has some lucky girl not snapped you up yet?"

He snorted as he set down the blower. Dressed in a leather jacket, biker boots, and black jeans, he looked like he'd fit right in at the Hell's Handler's clubhouse, but for some reason unknown to her, he'd been denied the opportunity to prospect.

"Been waiting on you, Jazzy, you know that." He winked, then walked her way. "But you keep breaking my heart at every turn." The words were spoken with a lightness to them, but the gaze that held hers conveyed a sincerity that had her face heating.

Thankfully, her cheeks had already reddened from the cold. Otherwise her blush would be obvious, and she'd hate to give the guy the wrong idea. Even if she'd been interested in Jeremy, dating him would have proven way too awkward, considering how close she was to the men of the MC. Supposedly, he'd attempted to prospect more than once and hadn't made it through the door. "Flattery will get you everywhere," she said with a wave of her gloved hand and an airy chuckle. "But I see the parade of chicas you've got coming and going from your bachelor pad over there. Pretty sure you're loving your freedom."

That made him smile. Teeth, a little on the yellow side gleamed at her. Overall, he wasn't bad looking. Somewhat attractive, with buzzed brownish hair, a smooth-shaven jaw, and eyes on the greener side of hazel. His muscles were real as was his passion for motorcycles and desire to join the Handlers. The problem with Jeremy was how he always seemed to be trying just a little too hard, which often came off as needy. At least in Jazz's opinion. She'd never say it aloud, but Jeremy was a beta male and Jazz was the kinda girl whose head only seemed to turn for alphas. Was it a good thing? Perhaps not considering she was twenty-nine and pathologically single.

"What can I say, Jazz? The ladies like what they see."

She cocked her head, studying him. Were his neediness the only issue, perhaps she could have overlooked it and gone out with the guy, but it wasn't the only problem. She had mountains of her own issues holding her back.

"Of course they do," she said with a wink. "You're a stud. Anyway, thanks for taking care of the driveway for me. I really appreciate it. I've dreaded the thought of shoveling out since the first flake fell."

"Why shovel when you can blow?" Jeremy said wagging his eyebrows.

Jazz laughed. "I'm sure there's a naughty joke in there somewhere, but I'm not gonna dig too deep for it." When Jeremy groaned, she laughed again. "See what I did there? Shovel? Dig?"

"Unfortunately. Your comedy game needs work." He slung an arm around her shoulders and propelled her toward her door. "Better get that sweet ass inside before it freezes off, Arizona-girl."

Jazz dug out her key. "Thanks again, Jeremy."

"My pleasure, babe. Long as I'm not out of town I'll take care of your driveway, okay?"

God, why couldn't she be attracted to this guy? He was so damn sweet. "You're seriously the best, Jeremy," she said before giving him a peck on the cheek. "I think Mrs. Sampson might actually have an old snow blower out back in the shed," she said of her land lady. "I went out there once and found a snake staring at me so that was the last time I ventured back there. And I won't ever be going again." She shuddered and it had nothing to do with the chill for once. "I'd rather die than find another snake. That shed is off limits to me."

Jeremy laughed. He kissed her back then started down her driveway, calling, "Don't worry, I got your back. Unless I'm out of town, you won't have to shovel or battle the snakes to look for the snow blower." With a wave of his hand he reached the sidewalk and turned right toward his own home.

Monty, the prospect who'd been tasked with following her for the day, stared at him from his truck while chatting away on his phone. For his part, Jeremy glared back then flipped Monty the bird before making his way up his own snow-free driveway.

Interesting. Jazz would be lying if she said she wasn't curious why the MC didn't seem to care for Jeremy. Though she could see how he wouldn't be such a great fit, she had a feeling the rejection came from more than just the fact Jeremy was a bit… weak. Ugh, just thinking the word made her feel like a bitch.

Well, none of it was any of her business. Time to get inside and get some coffee brewing to warm herself from the inside out. Just as she shoved the key in the lock, her phone rang. After digging it out of her overstuffed purse she held it to her ear without looking at the screen.

Her mistake.

"Crawly, really?" Screw's disgusted voice entered her ear, stopped at her nipples to perk them up, then continued straight to her pussy which fucking fluttered at the sound.

Damn him.

Key still sticking out of her door, Jazz sighed. "What are you talking about, Screwball?"

"You put your fucking lips on Crawly. Let him put his lips on you."

Jazz pinched the bridge of her nose as an ache began to form between her eyes. Of course the pain, it did nothing to squash the arousal brought on by his voice and the memory of another pair of lips on her. A set of lips that she'd given into in one very needy moment a few weeks back.

Another mistake because now that memory popped up at the most inconvenient times.

Like now.

"Okay, buddy, first of all where and on who my lips land is none of your business. And second of all, what the fuck are you talking about? Who the hell is Crawly?"

Screw practically growled as he said, "Jeremy Crawly. That pansy-assed mother fucker who was on your doorstep five fucking seconds ago."

What the…

Jazz spun, scanning the street for an annoying biker. "You spying on me now?"

"That the kind of man you're looking for?"

He wasn't on her street. At least not in sight. Screw wasn't subtle enough to be hiding in the bushes or some nonsense like that. He was too loud and too proud to hide from anyone. Had he actually been there, he'd probably have stormed out the moment she kissed Jeremy's cheek and laid some ridiculous claim on her.

Your stomach did not just flutter at the thought of being Screw's, you stupid silly girl.

She continued to scan the street, consciously ignoring Screw's question, and as her eyes passed over the navy truck in front of her house, she scowled. "Really, you traitor?" she yelled at Monty.

When the prospect shrugged through the foggy windows, she flipped him off then stormed into her house. "Not that I owe you any explanations, asshole, but it was a kiss on the damn cheek to thank him for getting the snow off my driveway before I got home from work. He didn't want me to do it myself and freeze my tits off. I didn't see *you* out there actually doing something for someone else."

"I was on my way with my blower when I got called into Copper's office. He wanted to meet with me but was fine with waiting until I was done at your house. I called Monty to tell him to either sit on you so you wouldn't shovel or get his lazy ass out of the truck and start shoveling until I got there. He let me know Crawly had already completed the job."

If she were in a movie, the background noise would be a whistling sound as the wind left her sails. Every time she put Screw in the box called *careless womanizer,* he went and did something to surprise her.

Of course, ninety-nine-point nine percent of the time it was with the end goal of getting laid, which kinda negated the whole good deed thing.

"Damn you, Screw," Jazz said as she sagged. Her back hit the closed door with a heavy thud she'd have felt if it weren't for the thickness of her puffy jacket. "How many times do I have to tell you—"

"I know you're not gonna fuck me if I shovel your driveway, Jazzy."

"But you thought I'd fuck Jeremy for it?"

"What? No, shit." He actually sounded frustrated with himself. "Look, I may like to fuck and it's no goddamn secret that I want to fuck you, but I'm not an asshole. You hate the cold and live by yourself. You don't have a blower and there's about four inches out there. It'd have taken you all goddamned day to shovel, and who the hell knows if Monty is worth anything."

"He's been prospecting for two months."

Screw snorted. "That don't mean shit. The fucker's got a long way to go before patching in."

True enough.

Jazz sighed and the silence between them grew heavy.

"A thank you kiss on the cheek, huh?"

Jazz stared at the ceiling, willing herself to end the call. Just a quick goodbye and the push of one button and this conversation would be over and she could focus on not thinking about Screw for the rest of the day. But did she do that?

Nope.

Of course not. That would be logical. Healthy, even.

"Yes. I'm not interested in Jeremy." What the hell was wrong with her? Maybe the cold has frozen all the parts of her brain responsible for rational thinking.

"Good to know," Screw said.

Was that relief in his voice?

Once again silence fell.

As he said, he'd made no secret about wanting to sleep with her and had been turning up the heat big time lately. Screw was exactly the type she went for. Arrogant to the point of cocky, built as hell, a take charge man who would no doubt act that way in the bedroom. Screw fucked any and everything that walked, male or female. He made no apologies about the quantity of temporary lovers he had, instead wearing it like a badge of honor. He'd take them one, two, hell, three at a time in any combination of genders, and while the fact he was bisexual didn't matter to her—okay that was a lie, the thought of him getting it on with another man mattered, but only because she'd had one or two hot as hell fantasies of him and another man going at it—the cavalier attitude he had toward sex did matter.

Jazz wasn't naïve. Nor was she a prude or a virgin. She liked sex as much as the next girl, maybe even more, and she'd had a one-night stand or two, okay, maybe five in her day. But things changed. Life had thrown her one big curveball that dried her sex life up cold. But even when she'd been in a position to be free with her affections, the men she'd been with didn't have such a who-gives-a-fuck attitude about sex. Nor were they in her inner circle. Sleeping with Screw would be disastrous in the sense that she'd still have to see him every day. She knew herself, and one time with him would never be enough. He was too potent, too charming, too magnetic. Despite her best intentions, she found herself inexplicably drawn to the man and it would only worsen if she let him touch her.

Hell, one kiss two weeks ago and she couldn't get the damn man off her mind. What the fuck would happen if she let his cock inside her?

Maybe it was a good thing she had a concrete reason to say no.

"You hang up on me?"

"No."

"Jazzy?"

Her eyes fell closed. "Yeah, Screw."

"Take your jacket and your boots off. Unwind from work. I'll let you go."

It was those times when he spoke to her as though he cared that she weakened in her resolve to keep him at arm's length.

"Can't have you falling asleep when I finally get inside you, now can we?"

And then he killed it.

Every. Damn. Time.

"Goodbye, Screw."

His inability to remain serious with her was probably for the best. Kept her from doing something stupid like forgetting her own problems. If the idiot ever realized all he had to do to get her was to drop the act and show her the real man, she'd be screwed.

No pun intended.

"Bye, Jazzy."

"Hey, Screw?" she said, cursing herself for giving into curiosity.

"Yeah, babe?"

"Everything okay? With the club…I mean with Copper wanting to talk to you?"

His heavy sigh was so unlike him, she frowned.

"Guess we'll find out, won't we? Bye, babe."

He disconnected the call and it was a full two minutes later that Jazz realized she was still in her coat and boots. Still leaning against her front door.

Still frowning at the empty foyer.

No. *He* would see. She needed to keep out of his business and not ask how the meeting went next time she saw him.

As she finally pushed off the door, a flash of heat shot through her alongside the memory of Screw's lips on hers. His strong hands at her waist.

"Get out, get out, get out," she said, hitting the heel of her palm against her forehead. Maybe a hot bath and an early glass of wine would scald him from her memory.

Chapter Four

Screw – 2004, Tennessee

"Do you understand what we're saying here, Lucas?" Principal Kavanaugh asked. The old dinosaur stared at him with his sausage fingers folded on top of his messy desk. His two chins wiggled like Jell-O when he tilted his head to the side as though he actually gave a fuck. As though Luke was too stupid or too oblivious to notice the way ol' Kav's gaze drifted at least a dozen times toward where Luke's mom sat next to him, no doubt staring at her tits.

What a fucking joke. He pretended to act all concerned about Luke's education and shit, yet he was the same as everyone else who tolerated him, hoping for a shot at his mom.

"Yep. Got it." Luke slouched in his chair, causing his baggy jeans to ride up, but he didn't bother fixing them.

"So you understand this is your last opportunity to turn yourself around?" Kavanaugh's gaze slid to his mother again before focusing back on Luke. The old bastard seemed nervous. Like he really didn't want to make the adoring smile Missy—the fucking mother of a student—aimed his way disappear. Hell, the bastard probably had a puddle of rancid sweat pooling between his chins. Was his stubby little dick hard too? Probably.

"Of course he understands, *sir*," Missy said in her sugary voice, so sweet Luke's teeth were near rotting from hearing it his whole life. For once, wouldn't it be amazing if she actually meant it? If she was the type of mom who'd take him home, read home the riot act, then ground him for a month? He nearly laughed out loud. What kind of kid *wanted* to be grounded?

One craving a parent who loved them.

"We both understand how generous you've been to give my Luke this extra chance to prove he can behave. And we're so grateful. You must really care about my son." She leaned forward, giving Kavanaugh an even more prime view of the tits nearly spilling out of her shirt. Luke swore she borrowed her tops from his six-year-old cousin.

Somehow, he resisted the urge to vomit and kept his face neutral. He could pretend this conversation bored him instead of sickened him.

Kavanaugh smiled and out popped a third chin in front of the others. The bastard's wide red nose seemed to spread even farther, those spider web veins becoming even more prominent. His cheeks and the shiny bald spot on the top of his fat head flushed, nearly matching that Rudolph nose.

"Well, that-that's just great. I'm glad to hear it, Miss Roulette."

Jesus, if this went on any longer, Luke would need to find a fucking drool bib for the guy.

As though finally remembering the one he was actually supposed to address, Kavanaugh focused on Luke. "This is the fifth time you've been in my office this year, son."

Son? Jesus fucking Christ. Luke gripped the edge of the armrests to keep from launching out of his chair and slapping the patronizing grin off his principal's face. *Son*. Like Missy was gonna see this prick as some sort of fatherly figure for him. What a joke.

"Per district guidelines, I should have expelled you by now. But I'm giving you another chance. One last chance." He shook his finger.

Christ, was this guy for real? Was he supposed to thank him now? Maybe nudge his mom in ol' Kav's direction?

"You humiliated those boys. I can't keep letting this stuff slide, Lucas. Detention, even suspending you doesn't seem to be enough. Parents of the other children are starting to get involved. If you do something like this again, I'll have no choice but to expel you. Do you understand?"

Luke ran his tongue over his teeth. Had he brushed them that morning? Huh, he couldn't remember.

"Lukey?" his mother said, sounding like the most concerned mom to ever have walked the planet.

Complete horseshit.

And he understood all right. He understood Kavanaugh was dumb enough to believe giving Luke an extra chance was going to increase *his* chances of getting his hands on those tits Missy was teasing him with. What Kavanaugh didn't understand was that Missy was a look-but-don't-touch kinda gal. She flaunted what she had all over town, leaving a trail of slobbering losers in her wake, but it was nothing more than the ultimate tease. The principal was just another in a long line of horny morons to fall for her shit.

What a stupid fuck.

Why the hell would he want a father figure anyway? The last one to grace their lives bailed after stealing Missy's hard-earned tit-shaking money. Probably went right up his nose.

"Lukey?" his mother said again, still sounding like she gave many shits about her son, but his time, she dug the spike of her fuck-me heel into his toe. The action occurred under the desk, hidden from Kavanaugh's sight.

Jesus, fuck that shit hurt. No wonder men bowed at her feet. Forget the tits, platinum hair, and peek-a-boo shorts, she probably threatened to pop their balls with those spears.

Well, he had to give them something if he didn't want to spend the rest of his day in the office. "Yeah, yeah. No more shit. Got it."

She narrowed her eyes at him before turning those baby blues —contacts of course, not much on her was real—back on his principal. "There you go, Mr. K. You won't have any more trouble from him." She stood and held out her hand, neon blue nails and all.

"Well thank you, Miss Roulette. I appreciate your involvement. It's obvious how deeply you care about your son."

Oh, gag me with a dick. Missy appreciated one thing and one thing only.

Attention.

Well, cash too. Look at that, she cared about two whole things. Progress.

Kavanaugh stood and took his mother's hand, holding it far longer than a normal handshake. Her slender cigarette-stained hand nearly disappeared in the giant mitt his principal had. What were the chances that same hand would be stroking the guy's dick to thoughts of Missy later?

Pretty damn high.

"Let's go, Lukey."

Luke stood, slung his worn backpack over his shoulder and got the fuck out of that office without a backward glance. Two days of suspension meant nothing beyond two days of freedom. He could use it. He hadn't been laid in a few days and the college guy he'd been fucking on the sly had his girlfriend in town for a visit. He claimed she was up for anything including a threesome with a high school junior.

Perfect way to spend his new free time.

"Hey, wait up, you little shit," Missy growled from somewhere behind him.

Luke rolled his eyes but slowed to a stop before turning to face her. Missy trotted down the hallway, tits bouncing and jiggling all over the place as she teetered on those fucking stilts. The sparkles on her silver tank top nearly blinded him as they caught the florescent lights in the hall. Her red leather mini skirt rose so high, she practically showed off her twat, not that she would have given a shit. It's what she did for a living, for fucks sake, only with a pole and some seriously bad disco lighting.

"What?"

By the time she reached him, she was panting like she'd run a few miles instead of twenty feet down a hallway. Guess shaking it on stage for horny scumbags didn't do much for the cardio. "G-give me a m-minute," she said, placing a hand on his shoulder as she sucked wind.

Luke just shook his head. As he watched her catch her breath, a memory drifted into his brain. He'd been four, maybe five, right before his old man took off. The three of them had been playing outside their trailer. They'd run around, chasing his mom, laughing their heads off. When Luke finally caught her, she'd let him tackle her to the ground. She was panting, just like today, but laughing as she did so. What he really remembered was the happiness. The love. The free playfulness of childhood.

And it was the last time he'd felt it because his dad ran out two days later.

Shit, where had that come from?

"Okay, I'm good." She removed her hand and propped it on her hip, which only served to thrust her breasts forward. Thankfully, school ended an hour ago, but the few students still in the hallway stared as they walked by like she was a fucking car wreck no one could avoid gawking at.

After winking at a group of losers, she said, "Streaking across the football field wearing nothing but pasties you stole from me. Seriously, Luke?"

When he did nothing but stare at her, she huffed and rolled her eyes like an actress in one of those stupid soaps she loved. Since she worked night, she was free to watch that garbage all afternoon.

"Why do you always have to be such a fucking screwball?" she asked, with a sneer as she grabbed his arm and dug her talons into it.

He yanked free, smirked, then started backward toward the exit. "It's all part of my charm, Missy." As he continued to walk, he lifted his arms in a flourish. "Besides, what the fuck do you care? It's your fucking work uniform. You should love it. I think you'd be proud I'm following in your footsteps"

Just as he was about to hit the push-bar to open the door with his ass, it opened and in walked Kevin fucking Murphy. Captain of the football team and Luke's number one tormentor. Behind him Jeremy and Ted, Tweddle Dee and Tweddle Dumb came through the door. Those two couldn't find their dicks without Kevin guiding them. Their eyes widened at the sight of Missy then they glanced at each other with excited grins like they won some jackpot.

"Hey, Luke!" Kevin said with a huge smile as though they were fucking bros instead of mortal enemies. The evil gleam in his eye made up for the grin.

"Asshole," Luke said in greeting.

"Lukey!" his mother said on a gasp. "What is wrong with you?" She strutted over and slid her arm around Kevin's shoulders, physically unable to avoid seeking the attention of every male in her presence. Even those her son's age. "I'm Luke's mother."

Of course, Kevin couldn't do anything but gape at Missy's tits. "Hey, Miss Roulette. Nice to meet you. I'm Kevin, a *good* friend of *Lukey's*." He smirked now, wagging his eyebrows as he looked Luke's way. Jeremy and Ted snickered like the idiots they were.

"Oh, that's so nice." She squeezed him close, mashing her tits against Kevin's side. The fucker didn't even try to disguise his boner. "And what a handsome young man you are. I'm so glad Luke has such nice friends in his life."

Where was that dick he'd wanted to gag on earlier? Cuz he needed it now even more than before.

Kevin moved his leg until he was practically rubbing his jean covered cock on Missy's bare thigh.

Skilled in this game, Missy pretended not to notice.

Luke didn't bother with that shit. "Have at her," he said to Kevin, whose jaw dropped in shock.

Didn't think I'd call you out, did you?

Kevin's face flamed and he started to step away, but Missy held him close. "I'd love to get to know Lukey's friends better. He never brings anyone home."

Ha, wonder why?

"Seriously," Luke said. "Go for it." He grabbed his crotch and gave it a good heft. "Might as well. It'll make us even since your mom sucked me off last night."

With that he turned and slammed through the door barely catching his mom brushing off his behavior to Kevin as his typical *screwball* behavior.

Maybe if fucking mother-of-the-year back there spent more than five minutes giving a shit about her son, she'd see that fucking screwball behavior for what it actually was.

The only way for a teenage boy to survive the horror of being in a small-town high school where his mother was the headlining act at a sleazy strip club known for looking the other way when underage teens walked through the door. If their fists were full of dollar bills, they were admitted. And every day at school, Luke got to hear all about the quality of his mom's lap dances. Or how she twirled her nipple tassels like a fucking pro.

Because she was.

And he was nothing more than an annoying screwball the law required her to feed and shelter.

Chapter Five

Screw rapped his knuckles against Copper's closed door. The moment his president's gruff, "Come in," sounded, Screw nearly hurled.

There he was, a twenty-six-year old biker who had no problem beating the shit out of anyone requiring a life lesson and he was about to piss himself. All because his president requested a meeting.

A three-person meeting.

Just Screw, his VP, and the top guy himself.

Fuuuck.

For the two hours, sixteen minutes, and a few seconds, since this meeting had been requested, he'd been racking his brain to figure out how and where he'd fucked up. That had to be it, right? Why the hell else would the two top dogs in the club want a private meeting?

Fuuuck.

Thing of it was, he couldn't think of a single damn thing he'd done to piss off the prez. This shit had him so spun up, he'd turned down an easy blow job from one of the newer Honeys, the MC's club girls. First time in his goddamned life he'd missed out on a fucking blowie. And he'd heard this one had some serious suction, too.

He would have said yes. Never mind he hadn't done so much as shake anyone's hand since he'd kissed Jazz. He would have said yes if it weren't for Copper. Copper was the only reason he'd turned the Honey down.

Fuuuck.

"Said come the fuck in," Copper yelled, frustration clear in his voice.

Shit. Caught daydreaming to top off whatever ass chewing he was about to receive. Making the president wait. Great idea.

He opened the door and walked in to find Copper behind his desk and a grim-faced Viper in a chair opposite the prez. The third and empty chair might as well have had a giant cock sticking out of it because he was pretty sure he was in for an ass fucking.

And not the kind he liked. This would be un-lubed and violent.

"Have a seat, Screw," Copper said.

"You know, if you guys wanted me for a third, you coulda just said so. Am I the lucky one who gets to be the cream filling in this cookie?" Screw asked as he dropped into the seat with a grin.

When neither man so much as cracked a smile, he swallowed.

Fuuuck.

Over the past year, he'd been working his ass off to keep the sarcastic quips, pranks, and general nonsense in check. Being patched into the club was serious business and he tried to treat it as such despite the natural tendency to fall back on jokes and tricks. Something he'd be doing a helluva lot of if these two booted his ass out of the club in the next few minutes.

This club had become his life. What the hell would he do if they dropped him?

"Screw," Copper said in a tone that had Screw seeking his president's gaze immediately. "Chill the fuck out, brother."

He blinked. "Huh?"

"We ain't here to ride your ass about anything."

Viper snorted. "He'd probably like that."

What the fuck? Had he walked into an alternate universe or something? Granted, as one of the newer patched members, Screw hadn't spent a ton of one on one time with the heads of the club, but really? Not only weren't they gonna kick him out, they were gonna make sex jokes?

As he stared at Viper like his VP had grown a few extra heads, Copper chuckled. "Think we had him sweating, V."

"Gotta get our fun somehow," Viper said with a shrug. Clearly these two had been enjoying his anxious misery.

"Well, I'd be lying if I said I didn't nearly shit myself before coming in here. Thought for sure I'd fucked something up."

"Nah," Copper said with a wave of his hand. "Nothing like that. Actually, we got an opportunity to present to you."

An opportunity? "Okay…"

"You heard about, Mamma V, right?"

Of all the ol' ladies, Cassie, or Mamma V, Viper's ol' lady, was the one Screw had spent the least amount of time with. She and Viper were old enough to be his parents, and Cassie acted as a sort of mother hen for the club. The other ol' ladies were her chickadees and she clucked over all the guys as well. The clubhouse's kitchen never lacked for delicious food thanks to her. Well, until recently. For the past few weeks, since before the holidays, she hadn't been around much at all.

And, three days ago, they found out why. "Yeah, shit, Viper, I'm sorry, brother. Can't believe Cassie has cancer. How is she feeling?"

Viper sighed and ran a hand down his face. The defeated sound held the weight of the world "Pretty wrecked right now. She had chemo yesterday and it fucks her up for a few days."

"Jesus, I'm sorry. Goes without saying, anything—"

Viper held up a hand. "Know it, brother. Thank you."

Screw meant it. Every word of it. Any damn thing Viper or Cassie needed, he'd make it happen. The three of them fell quiet for a moment. It was a heavy thing, a loved one having cancer.

Through the silence, Screw studied his vice president. Most wouldn't recognize the anguish flowing just below the surface, but to those who considered him a brother, his torment was obvious in the sunken cheeks, smudges under his eyes, and missing smile.

True and deep despair over the suffering of the woman he loved. What was that like? Loving another person with such ferocity, their illness and potential death affected every aspect of your own life? Screw couldn't imagine it. Couldn't imagine letting someone touch him on an emotional level. Touch him physically, fuck yes, he would and did seek that out as often as possible. But nothing fucking more than that.

His thoughts drifted to one little pixie-haired beauty. The one who'd eluded him for nearly a year. Never before had he worked so hard to get a woman in his bed. Never had he worked at all, but stubborn Jazmine turned him down at every pass.

It only made him want her more.

He'd get her. And her eventual surrender would be sweet as fuck.

But even that, all the effort he put into bedding her, it was just sex. Nothing more and certainly nothing less.

"Anyway," Viper finally said with a shake of his head as though trying to shed the sadness for a few moments of business. "I need to step down as VP. It ain't fair for me to keep the position when I'm unable to give the club as much attention as needed right now."

Well, shit. That sure as fuck wasn't what Screw had expected walking in the door. "Fuck, Viper." He shifted his attention to Copper. "You ask this of him?"

One of Copper's rust-colored eyebrows rose.

Okay, yeah, questioning his president wasn't the smartest move. "Sorry, prez, that news fucking threw me."

For a moment, Copper's scowl had nerves hopping around in Screw's stomach. Was he about to be tossed from the office on his ass? He'd deserve it for speaking to his president that way.

Instead of ripping him a new one, Copper scratched his beard. "It's all right, brother. Viper and Cass came to me with this. Fucking threw me too," he said with a small smile for Viper. "But it's the right decision for them, so we'll make it right with the club."

A glance at the relief on Viper's face had Screw nodding. He may not understand that kind of commitment to one person, but he understood loyalty to his brothers and if this was what his VP needed, he'd have Screw at his back.

"What do you need from me?"

"Glad you asked, brother," Copper said as he leaned back in his chair. He steepled his fingers, tapping the pads together a few times. "About thirty minutes ago, I asked Zach to step into the role of vice president. He agreed, which leaves me without an enforcer."

Holy shit.

Screw's palms grew damp and his tongue dried right up.

Zach would be assuming the role of VP.

The club needed an enforcer. Since he'd patched in, Screw had been working with Zach. Learning the role, basically operating as Zach's number two. Did that mean…?

"You okay there, brother? You hear me?"

"What? Huh?" Fuck. Screw blinked, clearing his vision and returning him to the present. "Sorry, I thought the surprises were done for the day."

Viper chuckled. "Hope you're ready for one more."

The out of control pounding in his chest almost made him miss the next words from Copper's mouth. "Think you're up for filling Zach's shoes?"

When Screw did nothing but stare, both men chuckled. "Hello?" Viper asked, knocking on the top of Screw's head. "Anyone in there? Think you might have exploded his brain, Cop."

"You're asking if I…"

With a nod Copper said, "Yes, Screw, we'd like you to become the club's enforcer. I'll be honest with you, I didn't have high hopes for you when you prospected. Your name alone gave me pause, Screwball. You lived up to it at first, never taking shit seriously, always fucking around, but you've proven me wrong. Zach raves about you and basically demanded you take over for him. From what I've witnessed and from his endorsement, I don't think there's anyone better for the role."

Jesus, there he was being asked to take on the baddest role in the club, and all Screw could do was sit there with his mouth hanging open like some kind of living flytrap.

"Think he's gonna cry?" Viper asked on a laugh.

Copper shrugged. "Maybe. But if he does, the job's going to LJ. Can't have a pussy as an enforcer."

That finally drew a laugh from Screw and pulled him from his stupor. "Fuck, you trying to give a guy a heart attack today?"

"Gotta admit, this is more fun than I thought it'd be," Viper admitted as he slapped Screw on the back.

"So what do ya say?" Copper extended a hand. "You in?"

His smile hit so fast it nearly made his cheeks ache. Screw stood and clasped Copper's hand. "Yes, fuck yes! Shit. I'm the fucking enforcer."

The other two men cracked up and Screw didn't even give a fuck that it was at his expense. They'd blown his mind today both with their offer and their faith in him.

"Uhh, so what now?"

Releasing his hand, Copper shrugged. "Now we party. Tomorrow night. Send off for Viper and a big fucking congrats to you and Z."

Hell yeah, he could get down with that.

"Pretty sure you don't need it from what I hear, but think of all the pussy you'll get now that you can drop the E word."

They were right, he didn't need it. Depending on what he was in the mood for that night, the women and sometimes men flocked to him. He had a reputation as being a damn good fuck and that alone brought them in droves. What could he say? Everyone had some kind of gift. He was a master at bringing the O's and there were hordes of smiling fans out there willing to give him a glowing recommendation.

"Won't hear me complaining about that."

"Didn't think so." Copper rolled his eyes. The guy was stupidly in love with his ol' lady, Shell.

Monogamy. Shit, the word was nearly enough to kill the high of Cop's news.

"All right. Get the fuck outta here. Viper and I got shit to do." Copper picked up a pen and flipped open a file folder. At least being enforcer didn't require paying the bills or dealing with attorneys.

Screw stood. "All kidding aside, prez, thank you. Promise to do you and this club fucking proud." It had taken until well into adulthood for him to find a place in the world where he didn't have to rely on being a fucking court jester.

The instinct remained, hovering just below his skin. Every day, he put actual energy and effort into remaining real and not fall back on his childhood patterns.

Huh, looked like he'd grown the fuck up at some point in the past year. Well, kinda.

"There's not a doubt in our minds, Screw."

With that, he bumped his fist against Copper's then Viper's and made his way toward the bar, feeling like he was on top of the fucking world. "Gimme a shot of tequila," he said to Thunder as he slid onto a stool.

Before the prospect had a chance to grab the bottle, a body appeared on the stool next to Screw.

"Well, what has you looking so happy?" Darla, a girl who'd been hanging around the club for the last week asked.

She was cute in a schoolgirl sorta way. Long blond hair often in pigtails that hung to her tits. She loved to wear these pleated skirts and crop tops showing off her long legs and flat stomach.

Nothing wrong with any of that. From what he'd heard she was pretty much up for anything any time.

His kinda girl.

"Make it two, Thunder."

The prospect smirked at him and winked at Darla before grabbing a second shot glass. "Here you go." He set the full shots in front of them.

"Thank you," Darla practically purred. "What are we drinking to?"

"To me," he said. "Just to fucking me."

"Well, I'll certainly drink to *fucking you*." She picked up her shot and downed it. As the liquid slipped between plump lips that no doubt caused many a man to moan in pleasure, a flash of black hair caught his eye.

Immediately Darla was forgotten as he turned to face the newcomer. The black hair he'd assumed was Jazz ended up being Amelia, the woman who delivered liquor to the club once a week. Aside from the same color hair, Amelia didn't look a damn thing like Jazz. She was shorter, rounder, and much darker skinned than Jazz.

Shit, who knew what that little brain fart was about.

"Should we do another, or is there something else you had in mind?"

"Huh?" What? Who…Oh, Darla, right.

Her eyebrows drew down as her lips stuck out in a glossy pout. The action he'd usually use to his advantage only annoyed him for some reason. "You forget I was here or something?"

With a chuckle, he signaled for Thunder and pointed to the Tequlia. "Of course not, darlin'. Who could forget you?" Yes, he had, he'd completely spaced out about the woman he'd been talking to three seconds before simply because he thought he'd caught a glimpse of the woman who'd run from him for an entire year.

Now that Jazz was on his mind, one thought bounced around his brain. What would she think of his news? Would she be proud? Would this finally be it? The thing that tipped the scales and drew her to his bed?

Only one way to find out.

"Sorry, Darla, I gotta run. Thunder, you'll take care of her?"

"Sure, Screw," Thunder called from the end of the bar.

"You on a tight schedule or something?" she asked, voice all sex. She wasn't gonna let him go until she made sure he knew what he'd be missing out on.

"No."

Darla stepped close, pressing her ample tits to his chest. He'd be lying if he said he didn't appreciate her assets. "So how about before you run, we hit one of those rooms and I send you off with an even bigger smile on your face."

"Take a rain check?"

"Promise?" There was that pout again.

"Sure thing, sweetheart." He kissed her cheek, then made for the exit.

When he was halfway to his bike, Screw stopped cold. Did he just turn down a sure thing in favor of a woman who'd probably give him a handshake at most?

Never once since he started fucking at the tender young age of fourteen had he walked away from a guaranteed orgasm. Now he'd done it twice in one day. Oh, hell, who was he kidding, he'd been doing it for the past two weeks.

What the fuck was wrong with him?

Had to be the stress of the holidays and the shock of all Copper and Viper had thrown at him that afternoon.

Couldn't be the gorgeous pixie who'd become a near obsession.

Nope.

Chapter Six

Jazz tugged on the sleeves of her tight gold sweater as she made her way to the bar. They ended about five inches above her wrist which was a little higher than she was comfortable with, but Toni had threatened her life if she didn't purchase and wear the sparkly thing to tonight's party.

When she'd left Arizona, fled really, she'd been in such a dark place, she'd anticipated spending the rest of her life hiding from the world. Her body and mind had been so messed up, she'd needed to leave her life behind and start fresh—alone. But the women of the Hell's Handlers MC had a way of sucking you in with their warmth, fun, and sisterhood.

The party was for Screw—at least in part—because he was now the club's enforcer. An honor for sure, and a huge show of faith from Copper and the other members of the exec board. They'd held church right before the party where they'd all obviously voted in agreement with Copper's choice.

The clubhouse was nuts tonight. Wall to wall people packed the place, drinking, dancing and causing the usual mayhem. Jazz loved the energy of it all. The happiness of her friends and even the guests she didn't know letting lose, forgetting their stress, and partying the night away. Even the depressing news of Viper stepping down from his position as VP hadn't killed the mood.

Could be because he threatened to slash the tires of anyone who moped or bitched, or so she'd heard from Cassie earlier that day.

Just as she'd finally wormed her way close enough she could actually see the bar, some giant man's knuckles collided with her cheek. "Ahh, shit," Jazz cried as she doubled over, cradling her cheek, or what was left of it. God, it felt like he'd crushed all the bones on the right side of her face.

"Fuck, lady, you need to watch where the hell you're walking." The words were spoken slowly, as though the speaker had to think extra hard about what he wanted to say. Their pace didn't matter though, the message came through loud and clear, firing Jazz's blood.

"Excuse me?" she said as she straightened and looked up… and up…and up.

Shit, this guy was huge. Dressed like a lumber jack just off the job, in fitted jeans, a red flannel, and tan work boots, he scowled down at her with brown eyes and a very bushy beard.

"Ever think you shouldn't wave those big ape arms around in a room this crowded?" For crying out loud, how was she supposed to know the lug was gonna be flinging those things all over like they were tentacles instead of arms? Man, her cheek stung. Probably gonna leave a mark too.

"What did you say to me, bitch?" The big guy moved in front of her, blocking her path. His beer sloshed out of its long neck as he used the bottle to point at her.

She jumped back with a yelp. It was one thing to slap her across the face, and quite a another to spill beer on the two-hundred-dollar suede boots she'd treated herself to for her birthday last year. Some crimes were unforgiveable.

A few of the partiers had taken notice of the drama and backed up, making a small circle around her and moron over there. So much for anyone jumping in to help. Drunk people certainly had their priorities straight. "Look," she said, forcing her stance to relax. It wasn't as though she could convince this guy to do anything with her physical stature. Not when he towered over her by a good foot. She lifted her hand from her face, holding it and the other up in surrender. "Let me pass and we'll forget all about it. I'm just trying to get myself a drink."

Or ten.

"Don't think so," he said crossing his arms over that massive chest. The beer bottle dangled from his fingers, swinging like a pendulum.

Jazz sighed.

"Maybe you don't know how shit works around here, but bitches show respect to the men in the club."

Was he for real? Jazz laughed. "You're not in the club, asshole."

His eyes narrowed, practically shooting darts her way. "The fuck you say to me?"

She rolled her eyes. Was he this dense? "You're not wearing a cut," she said with exaggerated slowness as though speaking to someone of lesser intelligence. "That means, you. Aren't. In. The. Club." As she spoke, she used her forefinger to punctuate each word.

Just as the guy reached out, a growled, "What the fuck," came from her right side. The asshole dropped his arm at once, and Jazz's eyes fell closed in a combination of relief and resignation. Couldn't someone, anyone else have come to her rescue?

"I asked what the fuck is going on here?" Screw asked, getting up in the guy's face despite the fact he had a good five inches on Screw.

"Screw, it's nothing," Jazz said, reaching for his arm. "Just a misunderstanding. Let's forget it and enjoy the party." Her hands closed around his bicep, or at least tried to. It was too big to circle. She tugged him back toward her. As Screw resisted being dragged away from the conflict, his muscles flexed, nearly popping her hands right off him.

Dayum, when had he bulked up so much?

"This bitch don't know how to respect members of the club," the guy said as though he had the right to comment on anything Handlers related.

Jazz groaned. Here it came.

"You ain't in my fucking club," Screw said, his voice more lethal than she knew he was capable of.

"Not yet, working on it. Supposed to meet with Copper tomorrow about prospecting."

With a snort, Screw turned, and finally looked her over. Apparently, the accidental slap did leave a mark because his face went from pissed to murderous in a fraction of a second. Nostrils flaring and fists clenched, he started to turn back toward the asshole.

"No! Screw, wait!" Jazz grabbed the open flaps of his cut and yanked with all her strength. He didn't budge forward, but he stopped turning which was enough of a win. "It was an accident, okay," she said, speaking quickly. "He was flailing those big arms around when I walked by and he clocked me. Just a little red mark"—she hoped—"No permanent damage, and nothing to get worked up about."

Time stood still as Screw's hand lifted and settled against her sore cheek. "Don't give a shit," he whispered. "No one fucking touches you without bringing you pleasure."

"Ahh," her eyes widened as her jaw fell to her knees. Being momentarily stunned allowed Screw to break her hold and turn back to the now snickering asshole.

Despite being smaller, Screw charged the guy, shoving him back with both hands against his massive chest. The hang-around's back hit the bar, bending in what had to be an painful angle. "I'll tell Copper your meeting is canceled," Screw growled.

All around them gasps and curious questions flew as more and more people clued into the drama unfolding.

Jazz's face heated, but not because of the slap. God, how she hated being the center of attention. As she moved toward Screw, she tugged the too short sleeves of her sweater down in vain.

"Screw!"

"Everything okay, brother?" LJ asked as he appeared inside the circle of doom.

At six foot six, he was much closer in size to the asshole.

"Just taking out the trash," Screw said, yanking the asshole to a standing position.

"The fuck?" the guy said. "You can't throw me out. I'm meeting with Copper tomorrow. Who the fuck do you think you are?"

"Oh, shit," LJ said. "I'll get rid of him for you, brother."

"Thanks." Screw leaned in closer and said. "I'm the club's fucking enforcer and I sure as fuck can toss your ass outta here. As for respect? You don't fucking deserve it, but the lady does. I want to hear a fucking apology."

"S—" Her mouth snapped closed at the deadly look Screw shot her.

"Let's go, fucker," LJ said, shoving the guy forward.

With fists curled and face so read it bordered purple, the guy stepped into Jazz's space. Though she wanted to cower, she held her ground.

"Sorry, ma'am," lumber jack said. "Be more careful next time."

"T-thank you," she said, feeling every single eye in the place on her. Goddamn Screw.

LJ shoved and the lumberjack stumbled but regained his footing, hoofing it toward the door. With Screw's attention on the retreating back of the asshole, Jazz escaped toward the bathroom. She hadn't run into any of her girlfriends yet, though she'd spotted most of them clear across the clubhouse. Too far with the blaring music to notice what had just gone down.

After checking that her face was still intact, if a little angry, and reapplying her lipstick in a pointless attempt to draw attention away from the cheery red mark on her cheek, she exited the bathroom. If she'd thought she needed a drink before, she'd been dead wrong. Now she *needed* a drink.

"Fucking Christ, woman," Screw said as he grabbed her arm and towed her down to the end of the hall, ensuring privacy. Before she had the chance to react, her back met the wall and Screw's hand cupped her cheek once again

"It's really all right. Just red and sore. Probably won't even notice it by tomorrow night."

"Doesn't matter," he said, gaze on her cheek. "Shouldn't have happened. And he sure as fuck shouldn't have spoken to you like that."

"While I agree on both counts, the first part truly was an accident."

"Hmm," he said as he leaned forward.

Her breath caught. *Danger! Danger! Sexy man way too close.* "W-what are you doing?"

Suddenly his hand disappeared from her face, replaced by the soft brush of his lips. "Kiss to make it better."

Jazz trembled. Her breath froze in her lungs. Why did he have to feel so good? How could the simple stroke of his lips across her cheek have her more fired up than her last lover ever did? His mouth was soft, but firm at the same time. When he did it again, this time closer to her ear, a run of goose bumps erupted down the side of her neck.

"Screw," she whispered, more of a plea than anything else.

But for what?

To stop, of course. It had to be for him to stop. It was the only smart choice.

"Screw," she said with some force this time.

He drew back. Their gazes locked, and for several seconds the rapid *thump, thump, thump* of her heart was the only sound in her head.

"Congratulations," she finally said. A safe topic though it came out hoarse and strained. "Looks like that meeting with Copper was a good thing."

Screw cocked his head, studying her. She held her breath. What did he see when he looked at her?

"It was," he said with a nod before taking hold of one of her wrists and lifting it to his mouth. "Showing forearm today, huh, Jazzy? Pretty flashy for you."

She yanked but couldn't break his gentle but iron clad hold. "Let go," she said through clenched teeth. She should be grateful he'd ruined the charged moment as usual, but all she felt was annoyance.

"Not yet." He nipped her flesh then, the bare skin of her forearm right where her sleeve ended.

Jazz fought the urge for her eyes to roll back as her knees threatened to buckle.

"Hey, what's this?"

Shit.

Shit, shit, shit.

Screw rubbed his thumb over a two-inch-long raised scar peeking out from her sleeve. This time when she jerked her arm away, he released her.

"It's nothing," she said, rubbing her wrist. "Cut myself on a nail sticking out of my parents' fence. Happened years ago."

If he noticed she didn't make eye contact as she spoke, he didn't say it, just watched her as though peering through her head to all her secrets. Jazz shivered and she couldn't say if it was arousal or unease. The two seemed to run side by side where Screw was concerned.

He leaned in and as if by reflex, Jazz's hands went to his chest.

Push or pull?

The theme of this game they'd been playing for months.

"What are you doing?" she whispered as his mouth once again moved toward her face. Only this time, instead of kissing her or the red of her cheek, he turned his head, presenting the side of his face.

"Waiting for my thank you kiss. Now that I know you like to give them out."

She should shove him away. Needed to make him leave. But his face was so close. The new beard he'd been working on the past few weeks had started to fill in. That rough texture would tickle her lips and be so warm against her mouth. Before her brain even had time to tell her to stop, she leaned forward and pressed her lips to his cheek in a long peck.

"Mmm," he hummed. "That's nice."

Jazz let out a slow, shaky breath as she leaned away from Screw. He turned to face her, and their gazes met before his shifted to her mouth. He was close. Too close. Dangerously close. Movement over his shoulder caught her eye, drawing her attention for just one split second, but it was enough to have her heart skittering to a dead stop in her chest.

"Oh, my God," she whispered on an exhale.

"What?" Screw turned, immediately stepping in front of her when he saw the newcomer. "You know him, Jazz?"

Battling the intense urge to run, she stared unblinking and unable to speak.

"Jazz?" he asked as he stepped closer.

"Who the fuck are you?" Screw asked, his voice growing hostile.

She needed to do something before he went on the offensive.

Placing a hand on the center of Screw's back, right over the Hell's Handler's insignia on his cut, she said, "It's okay, Screw. This is Gumby. I know him from when I lived in Arizona." On legs that felt like weak twigs, she stepped around Screw and in full view of Gumby.

He looked good. Handsome. Not wearing a cut, which wasn't surprising since he was in another MC's territory, he still looked like a cross between a badass and a bookworm. Black rimmed Clark Kent glasses sat on the bridge of his nose giving him the studious look she'd always loved. Such a contrast between the leather jacket, heavy biker boots, torn jeans, and mop of sandy hair. At some point over the last year, he'd filled out or maybe bulked up, as he didn't look quite as rubbery as his name would suggest. Gumby would never be brawny like Screw, but he looked damn good with those long, lean muscles.

Neither said anything, both taking in the changes to each other's appearance. No doubt Gumby was wondering why she wore long sleeves and pants when he'd been so used to her in edgy little tops and short skirts.

Finally, after what felt like hours of silent staring, Screw'd had enough. "Someone gonna tell me what the fuck is going on here?"

Gumby's gaze shifted to Screw, then back to her. This time, his focus stayed on her face.

And his eyes narrowed. "You fucking hit her?" he asked in a voice so deadly Jazz gasped.

"What? Gumby, n—"

Gumby charged.

Screw nudged her aside and shot forward toward a raging Gumby.

"Guys! Stop! No!" Jazz yelled.

Gumby's back hit the wall with a bone-crushing thud, but it didn't seem to faze him. He wasn't as brawny as Screw, but he'd been boxing for years. He brought a sharp elbow up, knocking Screw's chin. Screw's head flew back with a grunt, giving Gumby the second he needed to free himself. Just as he was about to reverse their positions and attack Screw, Jazz dove between them.

"Stop it!" she screamed. Thank God the music was louder than a stadium concert and this time her drama didn't draw a crowd. Twice in one night? What the hell were they putting in the booze around here?

Standing between the two huffing and snarling bulls, Jazz said, "That's enough." One hand rested on each man's chest and she couldn't help but notice the difference in thickness of the muscles beneath her palms. Screw's were large, bulky, the kind that could hold a girl still while he pounded her into oblivion while Gumby's were leaner, ropy, the kind that spoke to stamina and extended bouts of bone-melting passion.

Jesus, what the hell was wrong with her?

"Gumby," she said, turning her back on Screw. "He did not do this to me. Some drunk asshole out there was waving his arms around like an idiot and accidentally knocked me upside the head."

She let that process for a moment, until the set of Gumby's shoulders relaxed, and he nodded once. He could always be counted on to be reasonable, thank God.

Though she wanted to run to her car, drive away, and bury her head for the rest of the night, she had to face this. Had to face Gumby and find out why he was there. All of a sudden, visions of death and destruction bombarded her mind. Oh, God, had he tracked her down to tell her some horrible news? Bile rose halfway up her esophagus.

"Screw," she said, shifting her attention to the man who had her head fucked up, down and back again. "I've known Gumby for years. Can you please give me a few minutes to speak with him alone?"

"No fucking way. You're stuck with me whether you like it or not."

Those words should not have sent a thrill through her.

Chapter Seven

Thirty minutes after he walked into another MC's clubhouse and found Jazz with some fucker's hands all over her, and a bruise on her cheek, he was seated in a booth at a closed diner, pretending he wanted the piping hot coffee she'd made. What he really wanted was to smack the smirk off the douche bag with his arm resting on the back of the booth behind Jazz.

Though it'd be immensely satisfying, Jazz probably wouldn't appreciate him bloodying her man's lips. Especially since they looked so soft and full. They'd stretch to make a fucking perfect O shape as he slid…

Oh, fuck.

No.

Not no; hell-fucking-no-way-on-this-mother-fucking-earth.

Gumby may give in to that side of himself on occasion. Usually in dark corners of some seedy club, but he refused to feel even an ounce of attraction toward this man.

This smug fucker clearly enjoying his advantage.

After a few minutes of an intense stare down with the meathead, Jazz broke Gumby's eye battle with the other biker by looking up from her coffee with a sigh.

Gumby relented first, shifting his attention to Jazz.

Fucker.

If he couldn't use physical violence to take the guy down a few pegs, maybe there was another way. "You look good Jazz. Gorgeous."

And she did. A bit thinner than she had the last time he'd seen her, which could be concerning because she'd always been very trim. She still had the pixie haircut she preferred. The one that made her look chic and sassy at the same time. For some reason the hot pink highlights stirred his cock the same way they always had. Jazz was this incredible combination of sweet and edgy that just fucking revved his engine.

"Thank you," she said giving him a soft smile as her cheeks turned only a few shades lighter than her highlights.

"Damn, I sure have missed you." He made sure to add a little intimacy to his voice. Let the brute beside her wonder about that.

Sure enough, the guy's face twisted into a sneer.

"Don't you think it's time to properly introduce me to this asshole, Jazzy?"

The nickname grated on Gumby's nerves like steel wool, but he fought to keep his expression neutral. They were playing the same passive aggressive game; injecting little digs and subtle jabs in their words and he'd be damned if he lost.

Jazz sighed again then rested against the back of the booth. Almost instantly, Screw's arm dropped, coming to lay across her shoulders. She shot him a death look and he removed the offending limb with a chuckle.

Interesting.

"Screw, this is Will. He goes by Gumby. Gumby, Screw." As she spoke, she waved her hand between the two of them unnecessarily. It wasn't exactly brain surgery to figure out who was who since they were the only two men in the place. She had no idea what Screw's real name was, so she went with the handle.

When neither made a move to greet the other or shake hands, Jazz rolled her eyes. "Jesus," she said, disgust filling the space between them. Then she rolled her eyes again and mumbled,

"Stubborn fucking bikers." Straightening her shoulders, she made eye contact with Gumby and his stomach fucking flipped. She was just so damn pretty. Sharp angles, big dark eyes, long thick lashes as dark as her hair. So damn pretty. And he'd never had her. Never been granted so much as a taste.

And God did he want one. Maybe now more than ever.

"Screw is the enforcer for the Hell's Handlers MC."

When Gumby nodded, she shifted her attention to Screw whose suspicious stare hadn't left Gumby since they sat down.

"Screw, Gumby lives in Arizona, where I came here from."

The guy didn't even blink.

"Screw!" Jazz snapped. Finally, Screw turned to her.

"Yeah, babe?"

She rolled her eyes. "When I lived in Arizona, I ran the front desk for an auto body shop owned by the No Prisoners Motorcycle Club. Gumby worked there and is patched in the club."

"Huh." With one eyebrow raised and a shitty fucking grin, Screw said, "Never heard of 'em."

At the rate Jazz was rolling her eyes, the things were gonna start spinning in her sockets. "And you know every MC in the country?"

Laughing probably wasn't the smartest move, but Gumby couldn't help the bark that left him. At least until Jazz turned that disapproving frown his way. Damn, that thing was lethal. "You his ol' lady?"

Her shouted, *"No!"* came so fast and strong, Gumby had to bite back another burst of laughter.

Jazz didn't stifle hers though. Instead she nudged Screw with her elbow, but it did nothing to quell the expression of absolute horror on the man's face. "You about to break out in hives over there? I know you're allergic to the phrase ol' lady. I think I have some Benadryl in my office."

Screw's jaw ticked and his eyes glittered with the promise of retribution. But not directed at Jazz, no, that was all aimed

Gumby's way. He wanted to tell the guy to bring it. Sure, he didn't have the muscular bulk of Screw, but he could damn well hold his own and cause some damage.

"The fuck you want with her?"

Gumby shrugged. "Just here for a visit. Want to catch up. Been a long time."

She bit her lower lip and wouldn't meet his gaze. Guilt? Regrets? Or discomfort over his presence?

Leaning forward, Screw rested his forearms on the table. "She's lived here for over a year. Not once has she mentioned you or anyone else from *Arizona*."

He said the word as though she'd allegedly moved from there.

"Pretty sure she's not interested in catching up," Screw practically snarled.

Man, this dog was in full-on junkyard mode.

Jazz put a hand on his arm. "Look, Screw, I can promise you Gumby is no threat to me. He's not here to hurt me. No, I haven't talked much about my life before I moved here, but it's not because of him. I'm completely safe with him. Could you please give us some time alone to catch up?"

ABSOLUTELY NOT.

The words hovered at the tip of his tongue, but Screw bit them off. It fucking hurt though, and he swore he could taste the metallic flavor of blood in his mouth from restraining himself so hard.

He had no logical reason to stick around and witness their sappy reunion. No right to be a part of their private conversation that would no doubt involve some emotional crap.

Screw didn't do emotional crap. He had no claim on Jazz and didn't want one.

He wanted to fuck the woman. Long, hard, and deep, but that was it.

And yes, he wanted her safe, but she assured him she was and so far, nothing about this Gumby asshole—what the hell kinda name was Gumby, anyway—so far nothing about him screamed threatening.

"Sure," he said, sounding much more flippant than he felt. After scooting out of the booth, he stood and looked at Gumby. "She doesn't leave your sight. Had some shit going on in the area lately and she's protected by the club."

Though concern crossed his features, Gumby nodded. "Got it."

"And you," he said staring down at Jazz. "You do not leave here without a tail. Either this fucker follows you home, then you text me, or you text before you leave. Someone will come. Got it?"

Jazz rolled her eyes but nodded. "Yes, sir," she said with sass, but goddamn she had no idea what that did to his cock.

Gumby did though. His nostrils flared, and pupils dilated. Was he imagining Jazz calling *him* sir? Maybe while he fucked her? Maybe while Screw fucked her.

He nearly laughed out loud. That'd be something. Since he'd been shooting death glares at Gumby from the moment the guy walked into his clubhouse, he hadn't taken the time to really look at the other man. Now that the dust had settled, he did just that.

The guy was a looker, no doubt about it. Taller than Screw by a few inches, he didn't have the mass or brawn that Screw had, but he had strength. Long, lean, runner's muscles. Just the kind that Screw liked to run his hands or tongue all over. An image of Gumby naked and spread out in his bed flashed though his mind, only Gumby wasn't the only star of this show. No, Jazz was there too, between his legs, sucking him off. She was on her knees, bent forward with one hand on either side of Gumby's hips as she bobbed up and down on his cock. The position left her wet pussy open and perfectly lined with Screw's cock.

Would she gasp and pop off Gumby's dick as he pushed into her, unable to continue with her task as the pleasure ramped? Or would she clamp down, sucking harder and stronger as she took his cock?

Shit. Now he was hard as a fucking stone and turned the hell on by the two people at the table. Well, he might as well enjoy the fantasy, because that particular one would never come to fruition.

"Screw?" Jazz asked with a frown.

"Sorry," he said. "Just thinking. You'll text, right?"

She nodded, forehead wrinkled.

"Say it."

"I'll text."

"Okay." Thankfully, she seemed oblivious to the predicament in his pants.

He turned to Gumby, who was clearly not oblivious because his gaze was directed straight at Screw's crotch, which twitched under the visual attention.

Interesting.

"Not out of your sight."

Gumby jerked his gaze up to meet Screws, a flush coloring his cheeks. Embarrassment at being caught? Or something else? Dare he hope…arousal?

Not that it fucking mattered.

"Not out of my sight." Gumby stood and extended his hand.

His leather jacket fit him like a glove, and those dark jeans sat low on his trim hips. Jesus, he needed to get fucking laid.

"Promise I'll take good care of her." This time there wasn't any innuendo, just a genuine promise.

"Yea, I just bet you will." Screw slid his palm across Gumby's, clasping the frowning man's hand. The second their skin touched; electricity fired up Screw's arm. Gumby's hands were large with long, strong fingers and calluses. Fuck if that wasn't one of the things Screw liked best about being with a man. Sure, a woman's soft silky hands were amazing, but sometimes he just craved the rougher touch of a man who worked with his hands.

"You going back to the party?" Jazz asked.

Was he? He should. The party was partly in his honor after all, yet the urge to let loose had long fled him. Still… "Where else would I go?" he asked with a wink. "That's where all the willing women are gonna be tonight. Think I'm in the mood for something short and red headed." He wagged his eyebrows.

If he hadn't spent so much time over the past few months studying Jazz, he'd have missed the flicker of sadness that crossed her features. What did she expect? He was gonna pine after her while she walked down memory lane with this guy?

Not his fucking style.

"Right," she said. "Well, have fun."

He winked. "Always do. 'Night, babe." The insane urge to bend down and take her mouth in a searing goodbye kiss almost knocked him to his knees. Instead, he nodded and left. Walked straight out to his SUV without another word.

But as he reached for the door handle, he turned and gazed through the window at the pair sitting in the booth. Gumby's hand now reached across the table, covering Jazz's. A soft smile tilted her lips as she reconnected with a man she hadn't seen in more than a year. A man she clearly had history with.

Something dark and ugly twisted low in Screw's gut. He felt murderous and ill at the same time, wanting to smash through the glass and rip Gumby away from Jazz all while dropping to his knees to vomit the drinks he'd consumed earlier.

The only problem was, he couldn't decide if he wanted to beat the shit out of Gumby or shove him against a wall and fuck the shit out of him while Jazz watched.

And waited for her turn.

Chapter Eight

Jazz woke the next morning to the same knot of guilt she'd fallen asleep with. It'd caused her to toss and turn for hours, eventually falling into a dream-filled sleep that felt completely inadequate. At least she didn't have to work today. Though she did have a house guest to entertain.

God, why had she offered him her guest room?

Oh, right, the guilt.

They'd talked for quite a while. After Gumby had reassured her everyone she cared about back in Arizona was safe, healthy, and happy, he'd jumped right in and asked why the hell she left without a word and cut off all contact.

So she'd lied.

At least partially. She'd told him she needed to break out on her own. Get away from the small, shitty town she'd grown up in and experience more of the world. If he thought it weird she'd settled in another small town with an MC, thankfully he didn't voice it. Nor did he say whether he'd bought her bullshit answer.

She hadn't left to find herself. She'd left for one very serious and specific reason.

Fear.

At the time, she'd felt she had no other option and informing the MC would not only have exposed her shame and humiliation but would have set off a chain of events that could have ended in a death.

At the time, and for months, she'd placed a huge portion of blame on Gumby. He'd canceled their date which ended up being the catalyst for events that had altered her life permanently. He'd become the focus of her hatred. Had he kept the date, she'd never have been home, never have suffered. But he'd had club business. And he'd bailed on her.

It'd been so easy, giving him her anger. And perhaps for a time, it'd been necessary. The rage and hatred she'd harbored enabled her to leave despite the terror of venturing out into the world all on her own. She'd fed the anger, nurtured it until it grew into full-on hatred of a man she'd had very strong feelings for.

A man who did not deserve any of her ire.

At some point, maybe seven months ago, when she'd realized she'd found happiness in Townsend, Tennessee, her mind released some of its anger, replacing it with guilt and shame. Because Gumby was in no way to blame for what had happened to her. He'd just been an easy outlet for the jumbled mess of ugly feelings born from trauma.

At that point, she'd convinced herself that Gumby, and everyone she'd left behind in Arizona, must hate her, which made it easy to continue to avoid contact. But now she knew the truth. They'd all suffered when she'd fled. All worried about her. All missed her.

But none more than Gumby, or so he'd said.

"I've had Acer looking for you since you left. I've never felt right about it. Always felt I'd done something to drive you away." He'd stared at his hands, flat on the table as he'd said that. Something about the familiar grease stains under his blunt nails had tears forming in her eyes. Showed some things stayed the same even after the passage of so much time. Even after her life had completely changed.

She owed him a lot. An apology. An explanation. The truth.

The first two she'd given willingly, even if the explanation was a lie because the third was impossible.

Jazz blew out a breath just as her phone buzzed from her night table. Probably one of her girls wondering what the hell happened to her last night. She'd shot Holly a text as she was leaving so her friend wouldn't worry, but didn't exactly clue her in to what had gone down

God, she needed some coffee and fast.

Raking a hand through her short hair, she grabbed the phone.

Nope. Not Holly.

Screw. Of course.

I'm outside. Didn't want to startle you by knocking. Open up.

Jazz stared at the screen. No one confused her more than Screw. The man embodied contradiction. So sweet and caring at times then completely apathetic and full of nothing but raunchy suggestions the next. Now, she didn't mind the suggestions being raunchy, just that he flung them around to anyone and everyone in a ten-mile radius.

Come on, Jazzy.

With Gumby still asleep in the next room, this seemed like a terrible idea.

I have coffee.

Or maybe it was a wonderful idea.

With a groan, Jazz forced her tired body off the bed and shuffled down the hallway to her front door. It was seven a.m. on her day off, and she'd yet to have a hit of caffeine. Those were the only two excuses she had for opening the door without even thinking of putting on a bra or running a brush through her wild hair.

The minute Screw's lips curled, Jazz wanted to sink into the ground. She may not have been blessed in the boob department, but she still had 'em and they were reacting to the sight of the sexy man in a leather jacket and skull cap standing on her doorstep holding out coffee. The new beard made him look even more roguish than usual.

"Fuck me, you look goddammed adorable," Screw said with a chuckle.

Her face heated.

"Come on in, you're letting the heat out." She stepped back, allowing him entry. Screw strutted in her house, because he couldn't walk like a normal man, then set her coffee and a small brown sack on her gray wooden entry table.

After shutting the door, Jazz took a breath and turned to face him, not at all ready for the questions he'd most likely have. Instead of grilling her straight away, he cocked his head, grinned and strutted once again, this time into her personal space. As though on instinct, she crossed her arms over her chest to hide her nipple's response to the clean, cold, wintery scent of Screw.

He lifted his hand, ran it through her hair, and she nearly freaking purred like a damn kitten. "Love the way this sticks out all over in the morning."

She narrowed her eyes. Was he mocking her? "Screw—" She tried to take a step back but his fist closed, holding her captive with a firm but gentle hold on her hair.

"Looks like you spent the night being well fucked. Also love how I can grip all your hair like this. Gives me so many ideas."

Jazz shivered and Oh, how she wished she could blame it on the chilly press of his leather jacket against her thin pajamas.

"Screw," she said, hoping he caught the weak warning she tried to convey.

"You fuck him?"

Her eyes flew wide. "What? Who the hell do you think you are?"

His eyes shot sparks and her fucked-up, neglected libido soared. "Did. You. Fuck. Him."

Jazz seethed. He had some fucking nerve questioning her about her sex life. "Please, you've probably fucked a hundred people since you started trying to get in my panties. I don't owe you a damn thing."

The grip he had on her hair tightened. Instead of freaking her out, the sharp tug on her scalp sent need straight to her pussy. "That may be," he whispered before dragging a thumb across her lips. She had to clench her teeth to keep from licking his finger or worse, sucking it into her mouth. "But I haven't fucked a single one since I tasted these lips."

"Wha—" She stood, mouth agape and mind in compete disbelief.

Screw took full advantage, crushing his mouth to hers while she tried to process his statement. His hand shifted, releasing her hair, only to cup the back of her head, holding her at his mercy. His tongue invaded her mouth with wet, aggressive, downright dirty kisses. Last time they'd locked lips, almost two weeks ago, she'd been in a vulnerable mood and shocked at the gentle and sweet way he'd manipulated her mouth. This time, well this was exactly what she'd have expected from a man as experienced as Screw.

He teased her, stroking that clever tongue over hers then retreating the second she followed. Then he'd nip her lip and plunge back in again. She never knew what was coming and it caused a weak-kneed response that had her grabbing the lapels of his jacket to ground herself. It was that or completely melt into the warmth of his body.

His free arm banded around her back, pressing her against his hard body. And hard it was…everywhere. It amazed her how incredible it felt to be in his arm. His warmth, his strength, his talented mouth had her feeling safe, desired, free. If this went on much longer, she'd give in. She'd break a promise to herself and beg the man to fuck her stupid.

It'd been so damn long…

Eventually, he stepped back, capturing her lower lip between his teeth and giving a firm tug as he left her. To her everlasting shame, Jazz stood there for long seconds, eyes closed, mouth parted and waiting for him to return. Only the heavy trod of booted feet on her wood floor had her eyes fluttering open and her hands releasing his jacket.

Instead of the arrogance of a victory smile, Screw watched her with undisguised lust. The man was more potent than all booze in the world.

"Guess I got my answer," he whispered.

"What?"

"There's no way he fucked you. Only a fool would let you out of their bed within hours of getting you there. And I may not like the guy, but if he has your interest, at least we know he's not a fool. See you later, Jazzy."

With that, he stepped around her and opened the front door. Jazz followed him with her gaze. Who was that man?

"Bye, Gummy Bear," he called over his shoulder right before pulling the door shut behind him. Ahh, there he was. The Screw she knew. Not the confounding version of Screw who'd seemed to have been replaced by some sincere and genuine body snatcher.

Turning back around, Jazz met Gumby's stare. She pushed a hand through her hair, aware once again she wasn't wearing a bra. And if she thought her hair messy before, it had to be a complete rat's nest now that's Screw had run his fingers all through it.

She shivered at the recent memory.

"Uhh, sorry about that," she said, pushing past Gumby into the kitchen. "You sleep okay?"

When he didn't speak, she spun to find him in her kitchen holding the coffee Screw had brought her. "You forgot something."

So much for ignoring the elephant in the room. "Thanks." Had he seen Screw kiss her stupid? If so, what the hell was he thinking? His expression didn't reveal much.

Gumby crossed his arms over his chest and propped his hip against the door frame. The position had his black T-shirt riding up, revealing a strip of chiseled abs and of course, that goddamned V all women went bananas over. Arousal sparked by Screw's mouth and hands reignited at the sight of Gumby looking all delicious and...hungry.

Holy crap, did she need to get laid. Aside from the few times Screw had touched her in the past few weeks, it'd been close to two years since any man had his hands on her body. Clearly, she was having some kind of adverse reaction to strictly self-induced orgasms if two different men in the span of five minutes had her fired up.

"I'm gonna, uh, take a shower," she said, jerking her thumb in the direction of her bedroom. "I can make some breakfast when I get out, or you can just help yourself to whatever if you don't want to wait."

Gumby walked toward her, stalked was more like it, stopping when he was close enough to touch. Jazz had to tip her head back to meet his gaze. "Not your ol' man, huh?" he asked, smoothing his thumb over her swollen lips.

Shit, he had seen them.

"No," she whispered, fighting the desire to close her eyes and lean into the caress.

"Missed you, *Jazzy*." No one in Crystal Rock had ever called her that, but the moment Screw added that *y* to the end of her name, it'd taken off here. She had to admit she liked it. The little nickname made her feel like family.

Guilt swirled through her, settling in her core. How did she tell him she hadn't missed him? First because of misplaced anger and then because she hadn't allowed herself to think of him and the feelings he'd evoked for so long.

Self-preservation.

But now that he was here, standing in her kitchen, his thumb stroking the fluttering pulses at the base of her throat, a longing she'd buried came rushing back to the surface with surprising ferocity.

She swallowed hard, feeling his hand stroking her sensitive skin. God, how would those hands feel coasting all over her? It'd been so long since she'd been touched on the skin she hid beneath her clothes. And it would continue that way, so she needed to get out of her head and stop these ridiculous musings.

"Go shower. Then how about we take a drive through the mountains and find a place for breakfast."

"Uh, sure," she said with a nod. Going to the diner was out of the question. She wanted to be alone with him when they continued their talk. If they went to her place of business, the curious stares and nosy questions from her friends would make her nuts. At this point, she wasn't ready or willing to talk about many of the things they'd want to know.

Gumby released her then stepped back, keeping his gaze locked with hers. It smoldered, hot and needy, causing a ripple of excitement to run down her spine. Everything she'd felt for him, everything she'd wanted from him came rushing back, including the physical desire.

The same physical desire she'd had for Screw not five minutes ago.

Shit.

As if life wasn't complicated enough.

"I'll be fifteen minutes tops," she said then did the only thing she could think to keep her sanity.

She fled into the bathroom.

A cold shower would do her well, but with forecast in the low forties again, burning hot was what she'd be choosing. After flipping the shower on, she stripped out of her clothes, averting her gaze from the mirror in a dance she'd perfected over the last year and a half. As the steam of the warm water wafted from behind the curtain, fogging the mirror, she relaxed in the knowledge she didn't have to stress about where to focus her gaze.

In the span of a few hours, the stable life she'd created for herself seemed to have flipped upside down and been given a vigorous shake.

Screw was wearing her down. She hated to admit it, but his constant attention and efforts combined with his irresistible freaking sex appeal, and he was well and truly getting under her skin. Or he had been until Gumby walked back into her life reminding her of all she'd wanted and been so close to having.

A man who wanted her for more than just a few hours with her body.

Not that any of it mattered. No matter how weak Screw made her or how many old desires Gumby stirred, neither would get a shot at her body.

She glanced at her blurry form in the hazy mirror.

No man would.

Chapter Nine

Gumby pulled into the parking lot of the cabin Jazz assured him was actually a hole in the wall restaurant about forty-five minutes from where she lived. The place was apparently owned by a James Beard-winning chef who'd grown tired of life in busy city restaurants and moved to the mountains of Tennessee. He now owned a cozy but eclectic restaurant in the Smoky Mountains.

"It's really beautiful here," he said as he stepped out of her SUV. Had it been summer, he would have seriously considered taking his sweet time and riding his bike across the country, but he'd known crossing the US in January would have been a miserable and sometimes dangerous endeavor.

"It is. I never realized how much I would love the mountains." She reached for her door handle, but he'd jogged around the vehicle, then pulled it open before she had the chance to do it for herself.

"Thank you," she said, cheeks pink.

He extended a hand, holding it still. Would she take it?

After hesitating a second, she placed her gloved hand in his. Gumby drew her up from the car. Without releasing her small hand, he started for the restaurant. Surprisingly, she didn't try to free herself from his hold. Instead, she curled her fingers around his.

The scene he'd walked in on, Screw practically devouring her, had been on his mind all morning as they'd driven through the gorgeous snowy scenes of the Tennessee mountains.

Jazz had clearly been into it. Her glossy eyes, swollen lips, and pointed little nipples didn't lie. Then there was Screw. He hadn't so much as glanced Gumby's way, but the raspy, lust-laden voice he'd whispered to Jazz in might as well have been a tight fist around Gumby's cock. In that moment, he couldn't have said who he was more jealous of. He'd wanted to be the man who'd kissed Jazz stupid, but he'd also have killed for Screw to whisper to him with that fucking sex voice.

When they reached the door, Gumby held it open for Jazz who shot him a small grin as she slipped inside the door.

"Welcome!" a middle-aged woman with a tight bun of silvery hair and snowflake apron greeted them. "Cold one today, huh?"

Gumby chuckled. "Yes, ma'am, it is."

"Well, come on in. We're not busy right now so I have an open table right by the fireplace. Sound good to you two?"

"Sounds perfect," Jazz answered as she pulled off her gloves then hat.

Gumby trailed Jazz who followed the woman to a wooden table directly in front of a roaring fireplace surrounded floor to ceiling by stone. Heat immediately permeated his chilled skin. Jazz let out a little moan of pleasure as she held her hands open in front of the flames.

"That feels amazing."

Jesus, was she trying to kill him? All he could think of were those words falling off her lips as he pleasured her with his tongue.

After being seated, a menu was placed in front of each of them and they fell into silence as they scanned their options. "What are you thinking?" Gumby finally asked. They needed a way to break free of this disconnect. Despite chatting at the diner, sleeping in her home, and spending the morning together, they hadn't begun to slide into a comfortable place, and it sucked.

"Their Crab Eggs Benedict is to die for. I'll probably get that." She kept her gaze fixed on her menu.

"Sounds good to me. Let's make it two."

A minute later the waitress appeared and took their orders. Once she'd left, quiet ensued yet again.

Enough was enough.

"Jazmine?"

"Yeah?" She asked, attention on the crackling fire.

"Look at me. Please."

With a sigh, she turned her head. The profound sadness in her pretty eyes had him reeling back.

"Make me understand," he said.

Further clarification wasn't necessary. Jazz wasn't the type to play games and pretend she didn't understand what he meant.

After a nod and a small smile that didn't reach her eyes, she reached across the table and placed her hand over his. Without giving it any thought, he flipped his palm, interlacing their fingers.

"Something…uh, something happened that night. The night we were supposed to go out."

"Okay…" His forehead scrunched. What could have happened? As far as he'd known she hung out at home after he'd canceled their date.

She blew out a breath fiddling with a button on her blue cardigan. "It was something that wouldn't have happened if I'd been out that night." She shook her head, looking again at the fire. "Or maybe it still would have. I don't know. But it made me realize I needed to leave Arizona. To start fresh. To cut ties," she whispered.

"Fuck, Jazz, were you…" He couldn't even say the word rape. And how would it have happened? Did someone break into her house?

Thankfully, she put him out of his misery quickly. "No," she said, squeezing his hand. "It wasn't that. I'm not…I don't really want to talk about it, but I'm fine. Now. I'm okay and I'm happy here, Gumby. But afterward, I was angry. Furious, really, with the club…with you." She met his gaze and he didn't see any anger, but regret was written all across her somber face.

Gumby tried to mask his mounting frustration. They were supposed to be clearing the air. She was supposed to be explaining, and instead of clarity, he was more confused than ever. "So angry that you didn't tell anyone where you were going? So angry that you completely cut us out of your life? So angry that you gave up on us having a chance at something?"

"Yes." Her small whisper cut him to the core.

The waitress returned with two mugs and a pot of coffee. With her cheerful smile and sunny delivery of their beverage, she seemed oblivious to the tension at the table. It was Gumby's turn to stare at the fire.

When Jazz squeezed his hand again, he turned back. "I'm sorry," she whispered. "I was in a dark place and needed to leave Crystal Rock for my own reasons. After a few months, when I had some distance and perspective, I realized my anger was misplaced and entirely unfair. By then, I'd been gone so long without speaking to anyone I thought you'd have all forgotten about me. I thought it was better to just continue on as things were." She cast her gaze downward, staring at their joined hands.

"You thought wrong."

Her eyes widened. Sitting near the heat of the fire had an adorable flush warming her skin. He could see the flickering flames dancing in her dark eyes. "What is it that you want? Why did you come here?"

Gumby sipped his coffee, giving himself a minute to formulate his thoughts as he enjoyed the strong brew. "It's been bothering me the entire time you were gone. Lila told us you were safe, but I couldn't help but feel your leaving was somehow connected to me. Jester told me I was just an arrogant asshole, but I couldn't shake it. The feeling of being responsible."

"So you tracked me down."

He nodded. "So I had Acer track you down. Took this whole time since you led us to believe you landed in the north. Gotta say, Jazz, you haven't cleared up too much."

"I know." She added a generous amount of cream to her coffee.

"I think I feel more responsible now, knowing you held me accountable in the beginning. It's like I owe you an apology, but I don't know what for."

She shook her head. "No. Please don't think that way. I promise you, you were not the cause of anything. You owe me nothing. If anything, I'm the one who owes you. I'm truly sorry to have made you worry and doubt yourself." Her gaze met his. "So, now that you've found me, what do you plan to do? Are you heading right back?"

He held her stare and gave a slow shake of his head. "I'd like to stick around for a bit."

Her throat moved as she swallowed. "Why?" The squeaked word had him chuckling.

"You know Marcie had a baby? And Lila's knocked up?"

The way her mouth popped open told him she'd had no idea.

"Wow," she breathed with the first full smile he'd seen from her. "That's incredible."

As he nodded, Gumby said. "Over the past few years, I've watched them all find it. That thing we're all searching for. The person that just fits. I've tried." He shrugged. "Tried to find it. I want it. And every time I think about it, your face is there."

"Gumby…"

He held up a hand. "Look, I'm not here to profess my love like some psycho stalker. I know we hadn't even been on one date, and know we haven't seen each other in ages, but I feel like we were robbed of a chance. And after all this time, your face is still the one I see when I think about a future. I'm here for a chance to…well, I'm here for a chance."

Jazz blinked rapidly as though chasing tears from her eyes. "I don't know what I have to give you, Gumby. I wanted it, wanted you so bad before I left, but there are things…" She got a faraway look in her eyes.

"Baby, I have *things* too, trust me." The main thing being his attraction to men. And how it'd always been far stronger than his attraction to women, until Jazz. Was it unfair of him to ask her for more? Could he do it? Commit to a life where he'd never feel another man beneath his fingers?

He didn't know. But he had to try, because the alternative was continuing a life of dirty hookups in dark corners with nameless, faceless men he didn't give a shit about and who didn't give a shit about him. Because though he'd given into his desire for men many a time, he sure as fuck didn't plan to settle down or even begin a relationship with one. No matter how bad his cock craved it.

"I've changed in this past year. I'm not the same. My life's not the same. I live in Tennessee for fuck's sake," Jazz said, throwing up her free hand. The other she kept connected to his. "I'm not sure I'm capable of what you want anymore."

Their food arrived at that moment and they dug in, quiet for a moment as they each processed what the other had said.

"How long were you thinking of sticking around?" Jazz asked after about five minutes had passed.

"Up to you. I've got three weeks off from the shop."

She rested her fork on her plate. "Three weeks? Wow, Hook must have been feeling generous," she said speaking of the club brother who managed the garage.

"Been ages since I've taken any time."

Jazz picked up her fork, speared a baby potato, then ate it delicately. After chewing slowly and swallowing, she licked her lips. Gumby groaned as that pink tongue swiped over the mouth. The mouth that fucker Screw had feasted on while Gumby still hadn't had so much as a taste.

"I think I'd like you to stay."

He nearly dropped his coffee mug. Did she say she wanted him to stick around? Her fingers trembled as she reached for her own coffee.

"I can't even tell you I'll try, Gumby. I'm just not in that place. But I've missed you. And I'd love to reconnect as your friend. If that's not enough I underst—"

"It's enough," he said. "It's everything." Then he stuck a fork in one of Jazz's potatoes. She scowled at him, pointing her own utensil in his direction.

"Watch it, mister."

And just like that they fell back into their old groove of teasing, laughing, and enjoying each other's company. If he'd had known her hatred of sharing her food would be all it took to melt the ice, he'd have swiped from her plate before now.

On the way out, they held hands again, this time without the thickness of tension and awkward silence. Though Jazz hadn't done much to explain what had happened to run her off, at least she hadn't chased him away.

Friends. He could do friends. It's what they'd been before.

What would Screw think of their friendship?

Instead of opening her door, he backed her against the car and boxed her in with his hands propped on the window on either side of her head. "He's not your ol' man, huh?"

"No, he's not. And he never will be. That's not what he wants from me."

Too bad she didn't make eye contact when she said that.

Gumby resisted the urge to narrow his eyes at the obviously unspoken words. Screw may not want her for an ol' lady, but he sure wanted to fuck her. Probably would have gotten the chance too, if Gumby hadn't come to town.

Well fuck him.

Gumby's chance with Jazz had been ripped away by forces he still didn't fully understand. Nothing would keep him from reconnecting with her—as a friend of course. Not even a jacked and moody enforcer.

He leaned down, brushing his lips against hers in a barely there kiss. When she sighed a soft sound of wonder and her lips parted, he took her mouth. She fit against him so perfectly, he couldn't stop himself from nudging his hardening cock against her soft stomach.

"Good," he whispered in her ear. "Because I plan to enjoy the next few weeks with you." Then he kissed her again because now that he'd had a taste of her sweetness, he didn't think he'd ever be able to stop sampling.

Eventually, Jazz placed her hands on his chest, giving a gentle push. "F-friends," she said, eyes shining and chest heaving. "Just friends, Gumby."

"Sure," he said, and she narrowed her eyes at the easy capitulation. "Just friends."

There was nothing friendlier than a kiss.

Chapter Ten

It'd been a good day. Incredible day, really. As she drove them back to her house, she wasn't ready for it to end.

After the awkward, tension filled morning they'd been able to fall into a pattern that was as comfortable as it was exciting. An oxymoron, but somehow it worked. It was as though she was meant to be there, with him, feeling the buzz of happiness and excitement.

Gumby was the perfect combination of gentleman and rogue. An alpha, take-charge man, and an outlaw biker who had another side. An intellectual, caring, compassionate side that spoke to her.

Unlike Screw, who may have more layers to him, but fuck if he'd let anyone uncover them.

Heat shot through her as the memory of Screw's kiss charged to the surface. Dammit, all it took was the mention, the thought of his name to have her recalling their chemistry. A physical connection like that wasn't something one found every day. Maybe she could have given into it. It wasn't as though she *had* to take all her clothes off to have sex. She could get hers and leave a good majority of herself covered. Even knowing physical was all it'd be, she could get behind it, if Screw respected it. But he didn't. He'd be out the door and onto the next conquest before the aftershocks finished rolling through her.

And there would be aftershocks. Probably multiple orgasms, too. Hell, maybe he could even break her record of three in one night…

Shit! Why was she thinking about this? Gumby should have all her thoughts. Gumby had traveled across the country after searching for her for a year. Gumby was kind, patient, sexy as hell, and wanted her for more than a quick romp. Gumby was the kind of man she should be interested in. He was the only man who should be on her mind.

Even though she'd put him in the friend zone.

But goddamn Screw had wormed his fucking way into her psyche. Wormed, hell, he'd bulldozed through her goddamn skull.

Jazz dropped her head in her hands. What was she doing? She had nothing to offer either man. Even sex. Especially sex.

Suddenly, the walls of the car seemed to shrink around her, nearly crushing her with their confinement. She threw open the door and stumbled out, sucking in large gulps of air.

Gumby startled, looking across the top of the SUV at her. "You all right?" he asked, turning away from the gas pump.

"Uh, yeah," Jazz straightened before glancing over her shoulder. "Just feeling drowsy. Must have been the wine at dinner." She started walking backward, thumbing in the direction of the gas station market. "I'm just gonna run in and grab a coffee. You want anything?"

He flashed her a grin that had her knees weakening. Something about those Clark Kent glasses combined with his leather jacket and mussed blonde hair was damn potent.

"Yeah, babe, coffee sounds perfect." He winked then rested his arms on the top of the SUV. "Don't mind me, I'm just gonna stare at your ass as you walk away."

With a roll of her eyes and a chuckle, Jazz turned. What ass? She'd always wished she had more of one. More of everything really. Hips, ass, tits…everything was just slightly…flat. A quick peek over her shoulder revealed Gumby didn't seem to have a problem with her backside. As advertised, his gaze was riveted to it.

So sue her if she didn't stick it out a bit and try to exaggerate her strut.

"Good evening," a bored sounding attendant said as he sat behind the counter, flipping through a car magazine. The guy didn't so much as flick a glance in her direction when the bell jangled, indicating her arrival.

"Good evening." The warmth of the market heated her skin instantly, making her almost too hot with her thick winter jacket. Jazz headed to the center of the store where an island held multiple coffee machines and options to doctor it up anyway she'd like.

For herself, she added some sugar and too much vanilla creamer, and for Gumby, plain black coffee as he'd taken it during breakfast that morning.

She popped the lid on the second coffee as the doorbell rang. A smile curled her lips. Probably Gumby, considering they'd been the only car filling up. Still smiling she turned just as the attendant said, "Good eveni—" then cleared his throat.

Jazz sucked in a breath.

The attendant seemed to have a similar reaction to the newcomers. He sucked in a breath and straightened; magazine forgotten.

"C-can I h-help you?" he asked. Poor kid couldn't have been much more than nineteen. With trembling hands and the way he gnawed his lip and stuttered, he looked seconds away from pissing himself.

Jazz could relate.

Spreading throughout the market were six men, mostly large, mostly bearded, mostly grim faced. They grabbed some forties of shit beer, bags of chips, and a few sodas, remaining largely quiet.

Nothing out of the ordinary for a late-night gas station run, except for one very significant factor.

Each man sported a worn leather cut, boasting Chrome Disciples rockers. None wore jackets, just cuts and dirty T-shirts or wife beaters as though it wasn't currently thirty-eight degrees. If it hadn't been for the quiet when their cars pulled up, she'd have guessed they'd rode in on their bikes too.

Such tough guys.

Not that it mattered, the problem was their presence. They'd popped up a few weeks ago, riding into town with their one-percenter cuts in a territory already claimed by an outlaw MC.

A blatant show of disrespect and a giant fuck-you to the Hell's Handlers. Worse, they'd bragged about settling in the area and made it clear the Handlers were to either join them in their arms dealing endeavor or they'd be fast enemies. In the week or so they'd been in town, they'd caused an immense amount of drama for the Handlers. Crank, their enforcer, had shown up at the diner, stalked Chloe one afternoon, and even went so far as to lure Toni and Shell into a trap. One that nearly ended in death for her friends, and had got Zach shot in the process.

After it all went down, the club up and disappeared. No one thought the reprieve was permanent, but it at least gave the Handlers some time to figure out what their next move was.

What the hell was she supposed to do now? Leave the coffee and slink out the front door? Waltz up to the counter and pay the terrified attendant?

Instead of either of those options, Jazz held her breath as though that would somehow make her invisible to the bikers.

"Well, well, well, who do we have here?"

So much for that.

Jazz stood, rooted to the floor, a sixteen-ounce coffee to go in each hand as a man with a crooked nose and cauliflower ears sauntered up to her. His hair, wavy and dark, nearly reached his shoulders. Across the left side of his chest a patch read Crank, with another stating Enforcer right below it.

Shit.

"Excuse me," she said, finally finding her voice and ungluing her feet. She took one step only to have her path cut off by Crank.

"Now, where ya running off to?"

Did he know her? How she was connected to the Handlers?

She swallowed as she lifted the coffees. "Excuse me, I need to pay for these."

He cocked his head and studied her with surprisingly shrewd eyes. She could practically see the wheels turning in his mind as he figured out how to work this situation to his advantage.

But the main question remained. Did he know she spent her free time hanging with the Handlers? Did he know she considered the ol' ladies her honorary sisters?

"You're a pretty little thing, ain't ya?" Crank asked as though she hadn't spoken.

Jazz shifted under his perusal but didn't respond.

"Ain't she pretty?" Crank called to a much larger man with a beer gut and straggly blonde beard.

"Ehh, she's a'ight. Little scrawny. Ain't got a lot of hair. What the fuck you gonna hold on to while she's sucking you off?"

And that was her cue to get the fuck out of there.

His words served as fuel, firing her blood and kicking her ass in gear.

"Get out of my way," she said, shoulders straight, head high.

"You don't want to suck his cock?" Crank asked, laughter in his voice. "Hey, Ollie, don't think she wants your meat, man?"

He snorted. "Fuck if I care what she wants."

Jazz's gaze caught that of the wide-eyed attendant. The poor kid now stood holding his phone as though trying to decide whether he needed to call in some help.

She probably had about two seconds before Gumby came in to see what the hell was taking her so long. That would only fan the smoldering flames.

"Get the fuck out of my way," she said through gritted teeth this time.

Crank's head fell back on his shoulders and he let out a loud laugh, but he stepped to the side.

Jazz didn't waste any time getting the hell out of there, but as she passed him by, he stopped her with a hand on her chest.

Could he feel the erratic drumming of her heart? Fucker probably fed on her fear. Staring straight ahead at the attendant, she tried to control her breathing. His hand was way too close to her breasts and she swore it felt like a sticky slug, even through her many layers.

He leaned in, so close his hot breath wafted across her ear. It took everything in her to resist the urge to shudder.

Her gaze locked with the attendant's. The kid lifted the phone as if to ask whether he needed to call the police.

"Tell the ginger I'll be seeing him," he whispered.

A cold chill ran down her spine.

He knew who she was.

Jazz pushed forward, keeping her gaze fixed ahead. Crank didn't move his hand. Instead he let it slide from her body and had she not been wearing a sweater and bulky coat, he'd have copped a good feel. As she walked past the checkout counter, the kid said, "On the house."

Only then did Jazz look down at the coffee still in her hands. She'd completely forgotten. Stirring it hadn't been necessary as her trembling hands shook it all up.

"Thank you," she mumbled as she hurried to the exit. One of the men opened the door for her, a leering grin on his face.

"Be seeing ya, sweetheart," he said, slapping her on the ass as she walked by.

Jazz yelped, and one of the coffees flew out of her hand, landing with a steamy splatter across the sidewalk.

Gumby, who was halfway between the pumps and the market frowned and began to jog toward her. "Hey, what the fuck was that?" he yelled to the biker who'd hit her.

Chaos was seconds from ensuing.

Fuck the coffee.

Jazz dropped the remaining cup in the parking lot, jumping sideways to avoid the splatter. She ran toward Gumby, hooking her arm in his as she reached him.

"What the fuck was that?" he said as he tried to pull free. "He just hit your ass? You know him? That wasn't a Handlers cut."

"I know," she said, tugging him with all her might. "We need to go. Now."

"Wait, I can't let that shit slide, babe," he practically growled.

"Yes, you can. I'll explain everything, but we need to get the fuck out of here, now."

Finally, he relented and let her tow him to the car.

"Remember how to find the clubhouse?" she asked.

"Yeah…"

"Good." She tossed him the keys, shaking too hard on the inside and outside to focus on the road. "We need to go straight there." She fumbled through her purse as she spoke.

Gumby started the car and drove away from the gas station but pulled over on the side of the road only seconds later. "Jazz," he said in a commanding tone she'd never heard from him.

Phone in hand, Jazz stared at him, mouth open.

"I need to know what the fuck is going on. We up shit's creek here?"

"I don't know," she whispered, no longer looking into the eyes of the guy who wanted her, but the dangerous biker he hid well beneath the often sweet exterior. "I promise to tell you everything that's going on," she said. "But I need to tell them first."

Jaw ticking, Gumby nodded once then hit the gas, hard. He may not like it, but he got it and knew she wouldn't betray the MC by spilling their business to anyone, even him. His hand curled around hers, tapping a nervous rhythm on her thigh.

Not only would he understand, he probably respected her for it.

Though she could tell by the hardening of his jaw and the severe frown that he hated the fuck out of it.

Jazz lifted her phone to her ear. "Shell?" she said when her friend answered.

"Hey, Jazzy! Where the hell have you been all day. We miss you."

"I—" She cleared her throat. "I need to talk to Copper."

Immediately, Shell went on full alert. "What's wrong? Are you okay?"

"Yes, I just need to talk to Copper."

"I can put him on the phone if you need him right this second, otherwise, we're all at the clubhouse."

Shit. She didn't want to do this in front of the whole club. Not with Gumby in tow. Too many questions she didn't want to and couldn't answer. But it looked like she had little choice. Gumby sure as hell wouldn't wait out in the car.

"I'll see you in ten."

Chapter Eleven

"The fuck is wrong with you, brother?" LJ asked as he watched Screw with a raised eyebrow.

Shit.

Fuck.

"Huh? What? Nothing. What do you mean?"

"Seriously, Screw, you're all…agitated," Holly said swiping her hand through the air in the direction of the pile of scraps he'd peeled off his bottle and left on the bar.

Agitated didn't begin to describe it. Felt like his insides were trying to claw their way out of his body.

"My dick is agitated," he said reaching between his legs. "You wanna help settle him down?"

"Ugh, Screw!" Holly covered her eyes with her forearm making him laugh. "Can you be serious for one second? You're all jittery and weird."

"It's all good, sugar. Just got some extra energy," he said, then chuckled when LJ scowled. Sugar was the nickname the big guy used for his pastry making goddess of an ol' lady and he got his fucking panties in a wad whenever anyone else called her by his name. Especially Screw.

So, of course he called her sugar almost exclusively.

With a roll of her eyes, Holly patted LJ's giant bicep in a mostly patronizing gesture as she said, "It's okay, baby. You're the only man for me."

LJ turned his scowl on his woman, only she didn't seem to notice because she was still fixated on Screw. "Is it the enforcer thing? Are you nervous about it?"

Seriously? He turned his attention back to LJ, who now wore a smirk and had an arm across Holly's shoulders. "This what it's like having an ol' lady? Always asking you shit you don't want to talk about."

LJ opened his mouth, but Holly beat him to it. "Yes," she said, completely unaffected by his insult. "Now stop being a dick and tell Auntie Holly what's wrong with you."

LJ coughed to cover up his laugh, earning him a swat from his woman. Ever since Izzy had a baby and named her after Holly's deceased sister, Joy, she'd been calling herself Auntie Holly.

"Auntie Holly, huh? Isn't there a porn star called Auntie Holly?" He grinned at LJ who was back to scowling. "You know the one I mean?" Screw held his arms out in front of his chest. Huge ti—"

"Okay, buddy, how about this," she said, pointing a finger at him. "You haven't gotten laid since before Christmas. That's more than fifteen sex-free days. Probably a record for you. By now, you'd normally have slept with a dozen people. You're cranky, fidgety, and annoying the hell outta me. So what gives?"

Screw felt like he was naked, and not in the good way. Not in the about-to-get-sucked way, but in the bug-under-a-microscope way, as though Holly could see through the thick layers he had surrounding his soft core.

"Well, shit, sugar, you're keeping pretty close track of where my cock's landing. The big guy not satisfying you these days?" He clucked his tongue with a shake of his head. "Hear that's what happens when you get monogamitis."

Holly didn't take the bait, though LJ sure did. He grunted and began to rise, but Holly stopped him with a squeeze to his clenched fist.

Okay, yeah, he was being a first-rate jerk, but fuck if he was gonna let anyone see under the hood. Even his best friend's girl.

"Make whatever jokes you need to, Screwball," she said with a sad, almost pitying smile. "Doesn't change the fact that you haven't had sex in fifteen days."

Actually, it was seventeen. Seventeen long days and nights where his dick wouldn't perk for anyone but the one woman who didn't want him.

"So I figure," Holly went on. "Either you got dick rot, or something's weighing on that twisted maze of a thing you call a mind."

Screw scratched his chin. "I'm sorry, did you just say dick rot?"

"I did. And you're *still* avoiding the issue. God, a therapist would have a field day with you."

She had no idea.

Just as he was about to tell her exactly what he'd do with said therapist, the door opened causing a rush of frigid air to blow through the club house.

A bunch of the guys and their women had stuck around after church, drinking and hanging out. A few Honeys mingled around with the single guys, lining up their nighttime plans. Usually the first one claiming a girl, Screw had hung back, choosing to chat with LJ and Dr. Freud.

Clearly, he'd made the wrong choice.

He shivered, "Jesus, Thunder, close the fucking door already," he yelled. Thunder had gone out to unload a few cases of beer from his truck a few moments ago.

"Uhh, not Thunder," Holly said, pointing over Screw's shoulder.

He turned and nearly fell off the stool at the sight of a pink-cheeked Jazz holding the hand of the fucking light-haired Clark Kent lookalike.

The room went quiet as Jazz squeaked, "Uh, hey, guys." When her gaze landed on Screw, she dropped Gumby's hand immediately, but the guy scooped it right back up, smug eyes on Screw.

Motherfucker.

Screw hid his mounting distress behind a wink, and he swore interest flared in Gumby's eyes. In response, Screw's dick twitched. What a sight it would be to have the guy on his knees, mouth full of his cock as he stared up at Screw through those sexy lenses. Fuck, he clenched his fists, allowing his short nails to dig into the skin of his palms to keep his hips from punching forward as though being pleasured by Gumby.

A few of the ol' ladies, Holly in particular, appeared ready to bust out of her skin as she was forced to hold back the millions of questions she no doubt had for her friend.

Who was the guy?

Why was he holding her hand?

Were they in a relationship?

Had he fucked her?

Would he fuck Screw?

Even better, would he fuck Screw while Screw fucked Jazz?

Damn that was a fantasy.

Okay, maybe those last few questions wouldn't fall from Holly's lips but came from Screw's own kinky fantasies.

As everyone sat there surrounded by a thick cloud of awkward, Copper stepped out of his office, a smiling Shell plastered to his side. Her eyes went wide as all heads swiveled her way and she immediately began smoothing her hair down.

Screw snorted. If they hadn't all picked up on the fact their prez was fucking his ol' lady in his office before, the quick 'n dirty hair fix was a dead giveaway. On a normal night, Screw would have been the first one in there with a quip about joining in or position recommendations. Especially since Mav was away on an impromptu honeymoon. But tonight, he just couldn't conjure enough energy to give a shit about shocking them with a crude joke.

"Uh, I forgot to tell you Jazz was coming by," Shell said, face cherry red.

Jazz stepped forward. "Yeah, I need to talk to you about something, Copper."

If he'd been a dog, this was where Screw's ears would have perked up. Over the past few months, he'd become somewhat of a Jazz expert as far as her mannerisms, moods, and emotions. Came from staring at her so goddamn much. He pretty much had each of her facial expressions nailed down.

All except her *O* face, of course.

Something in the tone of her voice had him and from the looks of his brothers, most of the gang going on high alert.

"This a conversation for my ears only?" Copper asked as he rubbed thick fingers through his beard.

"Uh, no," Jazz said with a shake of her head. "I mean, I'm not sure you'll want everyone to hear it, but it's something the club needs to know. It's important."

Basically, club shit that wasn't for the motherfucker's ears.

With a muttered, "Fuck," Copper waved Jazz his way. "Come on into the chapel. I'll have the guys join us if you don't mind."

The way her eyes bugged at the invitation into the chapel should have had Screw laughing, but his stomach had already begun to cramp with anticipation of what he just knew was about to be bad news. Five minutes into being the enforcer, hell, they hadn't even gotten him his patch yet, and his gut was screaming. He was about to be tested.

As the ol' ladies climbed off their men's laps and gathered together at the bar, Jazz whispered something in Gumby's ear. He shook his head and spoke back to her, deep grooves forming between his eyes as he frowned. Screw had the strangest urge to press his lips to that very spot.

Shit, his head was fucked tonight.

Jazz shook her head, also frowning, then started to turn, but Gumby grabbed her and hauled her back.

She pushed against his stomach and Screw jumped to his feet.

Did she not want the fucker's hands on her?

Before he had a chance to barrel that way, Gumby's gaze met his. A fuck-you smirk tilted his lips exactly one second before those goddammed things landed on Jazz's. She allowed it for a second, but quickly pulled her head back with a shake. When she turned this time, her eyes immediately landed on Screw and the guilt was clear.

Interesting.

She ducked her head and preceded him into the chapel.

Any other time, Screw would have taken a seat next to Jazz and flirted her ears off. Tonight, with the sour taste in his mouth and too much shit bouncing around in his head, he found himself not in the mood to banter with her for the first time since he'd met her. So instead of sitting at her side, he chose a spot opposite her. Not only would he not have to smell the motherfucker on her, but he had a clear view of every emotion that crossed her face.

Like now, with her rigid shoulders and wringing hands, she was nervous as fuck.

Screw sighed. "Hey," he said across the table.

Her head snapped in his direction.

"Take a breath and sit. It's just us."

As though he'd given her permission to finally exhale, air whooshed out of her lungs. Then she nodded and slid into the seat.

"All right, Jazzy," Copper said, keeping his tone light and friendly. Though rough, gruff, and often impatient, Copper was a damn good leader who know how to put people at ease when necessary. "What's up?"

Which was now for sure.

"All right." She drew in a breath as though fortifying her courage. "About half an hour ago we were getting gas—"

The word *we* hit him like sandpaper scraping across his skin, but he bit back the caustic and snarky comment on the tip of his tongue.

"—I went inside to grab coffee and while I was there, a group of bikers came in. They were wearing Chrome Disciples jackets."

"Fuuuck," Zach muttered, as he shoved a hand through his hair.

"Motherfucking shit," Jigsaw murmured.

Then there was Rocket, who in rare outburst slammed his palm against the table as he bit out a curse.

Copper lifted a hand, effectively ending the eruptions. "As much as it sucks," he said, "none of this is a surprise. We knew they'd be back and to be honest, I'm surprised they stayed away this long."

Screw froze as the implications bombarded him. As enforcer, much of this would fall to him. Not alone, of course, as the club functioned as a team first and foremost, but alongside Copper, he'd be expected to not only carryout his president's orders, but help devise a plan to keep the club safe.

Christ, what had he gotten himself into?

He glanced up to find Jazz's gaze on him. She gave him a small smile and a nod and damn if it didn't bolster his confidence. Was it meant to? Was she silently lending her support and belief in his ability to keep his brothers and their women safe?

Jesus, why the fuck did he even care?

He'd worked his entire life to not give a shit what anyone thought about him.

"Thanks for letting us know, Jazz," Copper said. "We're gonna talk for a few, then we'll be out, okay?"

She nodded but didn't move to get up. "Uhh, there's actually more."

"Of course there's more," Jigsaw said, slumping back in his chair.

"Okay, let's have it." Copper folded his arms across his massive chest.

"They spoke to me, well one in particular."

Once again, Screw felt like a hound on the trail of a scent.

"I assumed they wouldn't know who I was, so I'd planned to just buy my coffee then get the fuck out of there, but Crank stopped me and told me to tell you he'd be seeing you soon."

Copper's chest rose and fell with the force of his sigh. "Anything else?"

Jazz shook her head with a snort. "No, just your standard inappropriate sexual comments and a near groping."

As though her words were the crack of a whip against his flank, Screw shot to his feet and leaned across the table. "They fucking touched you?" Suddenly leading an attack on the Chrome Disciples seemed like the perfect way to spend his time.

Mouth in an O, Jazz leaned back in her chair. Her head moved back and forth in a rapid clip. "Uh, no, not really. It was nothing. I'm fine, Screw."

"No and not really aren't the same thing, Jazmine. We'll be chatting about this later." He stared straight into her flared eyes as he spoke.

If the guys were surprised by the intensity of his reaction, none showed it.

"Okay," Copper said. He sounded heavy, as though the weight of leading the club bled out through his voice, "Let's do this. Collect your women and head home for the night. Tomorrow I want you all here for church at nine. Bring the women. We'll meet, then have breakfast."

After some goodbyes and fist bumps, his brothers filed out of the room leaving him and Jazz alone at the table. For a few charged seconds, they stared at each other until Jazz rose then came to sit by him.

"Can I talk to you about something quickly?"

"Sure, after you convince me nothing more happened at the gas station."

"Screw they just made some crude comments. Nothing I or any woman hasn't heard before. Sure, it skeeved me out, but I'm fine. Promise." She shrugged, and he tried to see through her skull to determine if she was as *fine* as promised.

With a slow nod, he finally relaxed. "All right. What'd you want to talk about?"

Jazz sighed then took one of his hands in hers. As always, a surge of electricity shot up his arm at the contact. If the quick dilation of her pupils was any indication, she felt it too.

"We've had fun, Screw, playing our little cat and mouse flirting game."

He narrowed his eyes. Where the fuck was she going with this?

"I need to ask you to back off a little…actually a lot. This isn't me being coy or playing the game. This is me seriously asking you to stop trying to get me in your bed. I know we kissed a couple times, and it was hot, but we can't do it again. I'm not going to sleep with you. It isn't going to happen."

When she was done speaking, she released his hand and folded hers in her lap, watching him expectantly.

As her words registered, each one seemed to prick his skin with a sharp pain. "So you and the tall guy, huh?"

"What? No." She shook her head. "We're friends." With a shrug, she bit her lower lip. "That's not the point. The point is that this game between us needs to stop. I'm not trying to be a bitch here, Screw, but I need to ask you to respect my decision."

"Hmm." He tilted his head and stroked over his bottom lip. "You know, the best way to keep me from flirting with you is to keep my mouth occupied. So, if you're not gonna make use of him, maybe you could gag me with that tall drink of water out there. Bet he's got a niiice cock." He waggled his eyebrows while licking his lips. Though the taunt was meant to get under her skin, just the thought of sucking on Gumby's cock had Screw's own cock throbbing.

Jazz's face fell, causing an odd twist in his gut. Maybe he needed to eat something. Or get some sleep. His stomach had been fucking ridiculous all day. Probably just the stress of using nothing more than his hand to get off for the past few weeks.

A situation he needed to remedy immediately if he was going to be forced to watch Gumby and Jazz slobber all over each other. Friends. Yeah, fucking right. This was clearly the I'm-interested-in-someone-else brush off.

She rose, sending him a look of pity that rankled like nothing else. "You just can't do it, can you?"

He frowned, his boner deflating somewhat, until she put her hands on her slim hips, pulling the material of her fitted shirt, tight over her small breasts. Then he came back to life quick. "Can't do what?"

"Can't take anything thing seriously. Can't give me five seconds of respect and actual consideration. If it doesn't benefit your dick," she said waving a hand wildly toward his cock, "then you just don't give a shit about it. And that right there is why you never stood a chance with me."

Screw's skin seemed to shrink around his muscles, nearly suffocating him in his own body. She thought he didn't give a shit about her? Christ, she had him losing his fucking mind. He hadn't fucked anyone in weeks. He thought about her morning, noon, and night. "Jazz—"

"No!" She held up a hand, eyes shooting fire. "I don't give a shit how many people you've fucked, Screw. I don't care if they're women, or men, or any combination of the two. I care that you forget the name of each and every one of them the second you come. I care that it's nothing more to you than masturbating with a flesh and blood body. This is done! Today." She slashed an arm through the air, then stormed out of the chapel.

Screw stared after her, his gut churning. The things she'd said...well she'd hit the nail way too close to its goddammed head.

A light knock had his head swiveling toward the open door. "You all right, brother?" LJ asked.

"Pssh, of course I'm all right." He winked then waved a hand up and down his body. "She'll be back. Who the fuck could resist all this? It's a fucking masterpiece."

As LJ backed out of the room, Screw's head fell back against the seat.

Fuck.

She was motherfucking wrong. He took shit seriously. Just chose to enjoy his life and laugh his way through it. What was he supposed to do? Cry into his whiskey because Jazz didn't want him? That the kind of man she was looking for?

No Jazz didn't want weak. Apparently, she didn't want him though, either.

Christ, it was all too much. Jazz, this Gumby fucker, the Chrome Disciples. How the fuck was he supposed to manage this shit coming at him from all angles? And she wanted serious? He'd fucking combust if he didn't have humor as his outlet.

The looming issue with the Chrome Disciples pressed down heavy on his soul. Some things he couldn't joke or tease his way through. Those things he tended to fuck up.

Like his shot with Jazz, apparently.

Would he fuck up his club the same way?

Chapter Twelve

His second party at the Hell's Handlers' clubhouse. This time as an invited guest. And maybe he'd even get to stick around for more than fifteen minutes. Though with the way it'd been going so far, he wasn't sure he wanted to.

Jazz walked up to him with a drink in each hand. "Here you go, sir." She mock curtsied while smiling, but it all seemed... forced.

"Thanks," he said as he took the beer from her. He planned to have a few, but not much more. Keeping his wits about him seemed wise tonight. Though the clubhouse was rockin' in full party mode, he'd noticed he wasn't the only one avoiding the hard stuff tonight. With their rival club back in town, many of the Handlers seemed on edge. A little tense. Security around the perimeter had been beefed up tenfold since last week's party.

"So, you ready to meet my girls?"

Finally, a genuine glow of happiness from her. Whatever had gone down between her and Screw a few days ago had killed her a little inside. She'd been subdued ever since. A shell of the woman he'd traveled so far to see. That woman still existed. He'd seen her the day they went to breakfast, but Screw had messed with her head, sending her into a minor depression. For that alone he hated the Handlers' enforcer.

"Of course. Bring on the ladies."

She bounced on the balls of her feet, grinning as she towed him across the crowded room where a gaggle of females had gathered. They didn't even try to hide their curiosity as he and Jazz approached.

Each and every one of them greeted Jazz with a hug and a complement on how good she looked. Clearly, she'd found a sisterhood she loved, and they seemed to hold her in just as high regard.

"So who do we have here?" A long haired curvy blonde asked. She looped her arm through Jazz's, openly assessing him.

He had no problem with that. Getting Jazz's friends in his corner couldn't possibly be a bad thing. So let them gawk.

"Ladies, this is Gumby. Gumby, this is my girl posse. We have Holly, Toni, Chloe, Stephanie, Shell, and…is Izzy here?"

The red-haired beauty she'd called Chloe shook her head. "She stayed home with the baby tonight."

Jazz nodded. "She has a newborn. You'll meet her soon, though."

"Ladies," Gumby said with a dip of his head. "Nice to meet you." They were a gorgeous group, all dressed in similar attire. Tight denim, skimpy tops, high heels. Nothing overly flashy or revealing, but a bit of skin showing. All except for Jazz, that was. She wore a fitted sweater, covering every inch of skin on her upper body. While she looked stunning, of course, Gumby had a hard time reconciling the woman he'd known in Arizona with this version of Jazz. She'd never been trashy or skanky, but she'd loved to dress up and flash a teasing hint of skin. Since he'd arrived, he hadn't seen so much as a bare elbow. For whatever reason, she'd taken to keeping herself one hundred percent covered, even in her own home. Hell, even while she'd been working out yesterday.

"He's a cute one," Holly said, nudging Jazz with her elbow. Her blue eyes shone with mischief.

Pink-cheeked, Jazz nodded. "He's all right." Then she winked.

Gumby clutched a hand to his heart. "Just all right. Damn, woman, you wound me."

Jazz giggled. The sound lifted his spirits.

As he chatted with the women, answering their rapid-fire questions, he couldn't help but catch a glimpse of Screw out of the corner of his eye. The guy had downed three shots in five minutes and was working his way through a glass of whiskey. Guess he wasn't worried about getting shit-faced. Irresponsible ass. One of the Handler's club whores, someone had called them Honeys, hung off his arm laughing like he was the funniest man on earth.

Every few seconds, Jazz's gaze drifted Screw's way and the light in her eyes dimmed a little more. The guy had to realize his behavior would bother Jazmine. Just a few days ago, Gumby had caught them in a heated lip-lock. Now he flaunted some bimbo right under Jazz's nose. What the hell was the guy thinking? Was this all a game to him? Did he get his kicks watching Jazz dangle on the end of his line?

No matter how much she protested, Jazz had some level of attraction for Screw. It was the why he hadn't quite figured out yet. Sure, the guy was hot as fuck, but couldn't Jazz see past that to the selfish asshole beneath?

Okay, fine, the man also loved his club, had the full trust of his brothers, was pretty damn funny, and seemed respected by the women of the club as well. Maybe he wasn't a total fucker, but he sure seemed to be on a mission to wound Jazz tonight.

And fuck if he was gonna stand by and watch the guy hurt her. A sexy ass, swagger, and that soft looking beard didn't give him the right to stomp all over her. No matter what went down between them the other day.

"Well, welcome to Townsend, Gumby," Shell said, drawing his attention back to Jazz's friends. "Let any of us know if you need anything while you're here," Shell said with a sweet smile. If he wasn't mistaken, she was the president's ol' lady.

"Thank you. Your town is nearly as gorgeous as Jazz is."

A collective, "Aww," came from the ladies, making Jazz blush and roll her eyes, but some of her sparkle returned.

Point, Gumby.

He dangled his empty beer bottle, giving it a shake. "I'm gonna grab another. Anyone want a refill?"

The ladies shook their heads.

"Want me to come with?" Jazz asked, flicking her gaze again to Screw who hovered near the bar. Sweet of her to offer to be his back up, but Gumby actually hoped to catch the guy alone for a minute or two.

It was time to clear the fucking air.

"Nah, babe, I'm good. Enjoy some time with your girls."

She looked ready to protest, but he winked and rushed off before she had the chance. After asking the barman for another beer, he felt rather than saw Screw sidle up next to him. How he'd known it was Screw and not anyone else on earth was a mystery he'd rather not delve into.

"Well if it isn't Townsend's newest resident," Screw said as he signaled the Honey lending a hand behind the bar. He held up two fingers. "Tequila."

Gumby wanted to refuse, but it seemed like a challenge, so he accepted. "Not a resident. Just visiting an old friend," he said as he turned toward the man and leaned against the bar.

"Hmm," Screw said, facing Gumby as well. His grin was a little sloppy but no less confident.

"You're upsetting her." Why beat around the bush.

Screw laughed, slapping his palm on the bar. "*I'm* upsetting *her*? Shit, had I known you were funny as well as hot I'd have brought you coffee the other morning."

What? Screw thought he was hot? Was he…did he…

"What is it that I'm doing to upset the queen? Breathing?"

"Don't be an asshole. You're acting like she doesn't exist. You're flashing your whores in her face." No, Screw wasn't really coming on to him. He was just trying to get under Gumby's skin.

"You jealous?" Screw bobbed his eyebrows.

Now it was his turn to laugh. "That you have a harem? Nah, been there, done that. Ready for something with some depth." God, why did the man have to be so goddammed good looking? A plain black T-shirt stretched across his broad chest. The thing barely contained his biceps. The men Gumby had been with tended to be on the smaller side. Less dominant, twinkier, he might say. Someone who wouldn't be looking for acts Gumby wasn't interested in now or ever. Screw was the opposite. Dominant, aggressive, powerful and it ticked every one of Gumby's closeted buttons.

"Actually, I meant jealous of them. You know, cuz they get a piece of all this." He winked and lifted the hem of his shirt revealing a set of abs that would make any interested party beg.

As Gumby was about to refute the claim as ridiculous, the Honey delivered their shots. "To…friends." Screw said as he lifted his glass.

Gumby met the man's chocolate gaze. It was the best way to describe his eyes. The exact color of milk chocolate whereas Jazz's were far more the bittersweet variety.

Still holding up his full shot glass, Screw raised an eyebrow. His mouth was canted up in a cocky grin that shouldn't have made Gumby want to suck on his lip. But it did.

Shit. The shot…right.

He lifted his glass. "To friends. New and old." He could toss out an olive branch. They may not become best fucking buddies seeing as how they both wanted Jazz, but they could be cordial. Friendly.

They tossed back their shots at the same time. Screw licked a lingering drop off his lower lip and Gumby was helpless to do anything but track the movement. Fuck, those plump, kissable lips…

"So," Screw said, smirk back in place. "Jazz know you like cock?"

Gumby coughed as the last bit of liquid slid down his trachea. He glanced around. Thank fuck, the music was deafening, and no one seemed to be paying attention to them. No one but Jazz, who watched with a frown from across the room. He tried to give her a reassuring smile, but she began walking in their direction.

Marching more like it.

"What the hell are you talking about? You're crazy. I'm pretty sure I like pussy. Always have. Always will."

"That may be," Screw said, tilting his head. "Doesn't mean you don't like cock too."

He could barely fucking breathe. Some asshole was going to out him and ruin his life. His family was far more important than his enjoyment of dick. Christ, he could lose his club, his job, his…everything. He cleared his throat. "Sorry, man, but I don't. You musta misinterpreted something."

Screw's laugh held a bitter note. "Like what? The way you stared at my mouth just now? Or how about the way I keep catching your gaze on my ass." He stepped close and dropped his voice. "Trust me, I know when someone wants me."

Sure, when everyone wanted him, it was pretty easy to catch on. Arrogant ass.

"Tell me you're not hard, right now," Screw whispered.

Gumby shook his head. "You're out of your goddammed mind."

"Aw come on. You owe me. Jazz told me to fuck off and get the hell out of her life because of you, so—"

"You're fucking unbelievable."

Oh, shit.

Jazz stood two feet away, hands on her hips, eyes blazing. "You can't even fathom that I just don't want to sleep with you, can you? It's not totally impossible for someone not to want you, Screw. It's called real life and you need to fucking grow up and live in it." She tossed her hands up, turned, and stomped three feet away before coming back and getting right in Screw's face.

He kept the arrogant grin, but his jaw ticked. The man wasn't nearly as unaffected as he wanted them to think. Interesting. A small layer of the onion that was Screw had been peeled back.

"I said that shit to you the other day because of me. Not because of him." She jammed her finger into Screw's chest, probably breaking the digit in the process. "Ow, dammit." She stepped back, shaking out her hand. "I said it because I'm more than a dumb fuck you can forget about five seconds after you come. I'm worth more than that even from a fucking hook-up. So I asked you to back the fuck off for *me*." She pointed to Gumby. "Leave him the hell out of it."

Jazz stormed off, walking past her girlfriends with a few mumbled, "I'm fines." Holly tried to catch Jazz's arm but she jerked away and continued toward the restrooms. Toni held Holly back from running after her.

For just a split second, so fast Gumby almost missed it, Screw's expression crumbled, and his eyes followed Jazz's path across the clubhouse. But as quick as it came, it vanished, and he was back to being a smug fucker.

"Huh," he said with a shrug. "She looks pretty fucking hot when she's pissed. Bet she'll ride you damn hard. Better go get you some of that before her mad wears off." He turned back to the bar and ordered another shot.

If he hadn't seen the flash of anguish, Gumby would have believed Screw was as callus and unfeeling as he wanted the world to believe. But pieces of the puzzle were beginning to fall into place. Screw wasn't a heartless, unfeeling asshole. Quite the opposite.

Still, it didn't excuse him acting like a compete jackass at every pass. And it didn't simmer the mad he'd worked up at seeing Jazz so undone.

Screw's shot arrived and he lifted it to his lips. "To angry fucking," he said.

Quick as a whip, Gumby lashed his hand out, smacking the shot away from Screw's mouth. It sprayed across the bar and down Screw's shirt.

"What the…"

"Hurt her again and I'll end you," Gumby growled before storming away.

He needed a few moments alone to gather his thoughts and this fucking party was not the place to do that.

"Hey," he said to Holly as he walked up to the ladies. "There a quiet room I can hide in for a few minutes? I need to…uh…make a phone call."

Smooth, Gumby.

The pitying looks he received let him know not one of the ladies bought his story.

"Head up the stairs. Third door on the left."

"Thanks."

Gumby took the stairs two at time. The whole way, the hairs at the back of his neck stood on end. When he reached the top, he risked a glance Screw's way.

Sure enough, the infuriating and sexy man stared straight at him.

And damn if his traitorous cock didn't love it.

Chapter Thirteen

If she'd been smart, she'd have left an hour ago. Before the dramatic confrontation. Now, she'd lost track of Gumby, lied to her friends with the classic *I'm fine* bullshit, and been a grade-A bitch to Screw. Not that he didn't deserve every word out of her mouth, but that wasn't her. She wasn't anybody's doormat, but she didn't lose her temper and lash out, either.

In her defense, the two men at odds had completely fucked with her head, making her question up from down and right from left. Any woman would have snapped.

That counted as a solid defense, right?

Now she had to apologize to the man who'd probably twist her remorse into a sexual innuendo, leaving her angrier than when she'd started.

Damn Screw. None of this would even be an issue if the man wasn't so…potent. She could have shrugged off the flirting, let him down gently, and gone about her life.

But he was. So goddammed potent. He had this magnetism about him that drew men and women willing to shed their pride for just one taste of him. It's what kept her trapped in his sticky web for all these months. Sickest part of it was she'd miss the attention if it disappeared. Being the focus of Screw's sexual desire was…exciting. More than exciting, it was intoxicating.

With a sigh, Jazz trudged up the stairs, heeled boots clunking with each weighted, dejected step as she headed toward one of the bunk rooms where visitors often stayed. Bikers crossing the country or ones popping by to party for a few days who needed a place to crash were given the bunk room. The place had six no-frills bunk beds and a bathroom attached you couldn't pay her to venture into. Thankfully, the Honeys took care of cleaning that place, though from what she'd heard, they did a half-assed job at best.

As she wandered her way down the deserted hall, she took a second to soak up the silence. Or quasi-silence. A heavy drum beat still pounded from below, but it was muffled and not nearly as overwhelming as it seemed just sixteen steps down.

A loud thump followed by an oomph had Jazz picking up the pace as she rushed to the bunk room. Finding Screw and Gumby beating each other to a pulp would be icing on the shit cake of the evening. Copper didn't tolerate that nonsense in his house. They wanted to take it outside, no one cared, but tearing the place up drove the president nuts. Just her luck, she'd have to be the one to find them and tell him the two morons were battling it out in the bunk room.

Maybe she could put a stop to it herself before it got out of hand and men needed to be brought in to break it up.

Just as she was about to burst into the room and make sure the guys were still breathing, a low-pitched, growly voice rang out. "Now, tell me again how fucking straight you are."

What the fuck?

Jazz peeked through the slit of the partway open door. Immediately, she lifted her hand to her mouth to stifle a gasp of shock.

Directly in her line of sight stood Gumby with his back against the wall, Screw's body flush against him, trapping him in place with a hand on the wall by Gumby's head. The other hand lay between them—Jesus, was he massaging Gumby's cock?

Gumby's eyes held a note of panic as he stared at Screw. He shook his head back and forth.

He didn't want this.

Though she should scream out for Screw to back the fuck off, her throat constricted so tight, she felt like she couldn't draw in air. What the hell was Screw doing?

"I said, tell me how this hard cock means you're straight." The raw sexual command in Screw's voice sent a shiver down Jazz's spine.

Gumby's head hit the wall with a dull thud as he moaned into the quiet room.

Wait…that was not a sound of protest. It was one hundred percent a sound of need.

Did he want Screw's hands all over his body? And why the fuck did that thought make her hotter than she could remember being in ages?

"Thought so." Screw said. He removed his hand, planting it on the wall alongside Gumby's shoulder. Though Gumby was taller, Screw appeared so much larger in that moment, having the position of power. "You like cock," he said in a ragged whisper as he rolled his hips into Gumby's.

After another tortured moan, Gumby shook his head. "No. Back off."

"Seriously? Even as I'm grinding my hard as fuck prick all over your hard as fuck prick, you won't admit you want my cock?"

"Fuck you," Gumby said.

Jazz stood there, heart hammering and feet rooted to the ground, unable to tear her gaze away. Gumby was gay? No, she'd noticed a bulge in his jeans more than once back when they'd been flirting constantly. So he was bisexual? Like Screw. Holy shit, how had she not known this? Was she that oblivious? Or was that part of him not public knowledge?

As much as Gumby denied his attraction to Screw, he hadn't pushed the other man away. In fact, he was shoving his pelvis forward, thrusting against Screw's erection.

A harsh chuckle left Screw's mouth. "I'd sure as fuck let you."

Her eyes nearly fell out of her head. Somehow in all the times she imagined Screw with a man, she'd never thought he'd give up control enough to be on the receiving end. And yes, she'd imagined it. Quite a bit. An embarrassing amount, really. And now, as the thought crossed her mind once again, it was Gumby's face she saw, contorted with pleasure as he pushed his cock into a writhing Screw.

Gumby.

Jesus. She should leave. Walk away from both of these men. This road led nowhere but confusion, jealousy, and heartache. Yet she couldn't even blink for fear of missing what came next.

"Okay, fine, you don't want my cock," Screw said without backing off even one inch. In fact, he leaned in even closer, lips near Gumby's ear. "Bet you want my mouth."

"Fuck," Gumby muttered sounding absolutely tormented.

"Say it," Screw ordered.

Eyes squeezed tightly closed, Gumby shook his head. Against the wall, his fists curled into tight balls. If she wasn't mistaken, he ground his knuckles into the rough concrete surface of the wall as though working his damnedest to keep his hands off Screw. He'd be scraped and bloodied if he wasn't careful.

"Say it, and I'll suck you so good." Screw jammed his hips forward and Jazz swore she felt it deep inside her pussy, the hard-pulsing drive of his shaft. "Gumby, say it and I'll make you come so hard the roof'll blow off this fucking clubhouse."

Say it. Say it.

Shit, not only was she a voyeur, she was apparently an all-around perv. Her sex clenched and time seemed to stop as she waited for Gumby's response.

"No." Gumby said.

She bit her tongue to keep from screaming, "Nooo," into the air. Shit, when had she become such a creeper?

"No, you don't want me to suck you or no you won't ask for it?" When Gumby didn't reply, Screw laughed, but the sound held a bitter note to it. He began to lower Gumby's zipper keeping his gaze on the taller man. "Won't ask for it, but I bet you won't fucking push me away, will you?"

Again, no answer.

As Screw worked the bulging zipper down, Gumby's hands remained fisted at his sides. His chest heaved and his mouth parted with the force of his breathing.

Was this something he'd done before? Had he been with other men? Was he bisexual or had he just fallen under the erotic spell of all that was Screw?"

Her thoughts had taken her so far away, she'd somehow missed the fact that Screw had dropped to his knees in front of Gumby. Gumby's head still rested against the wall, tipped back as though staring at the heavens for mercy. His chest rose and fell too fast to be anything other than turned on. Then there was his lower half.

Jutting straight out from his body, long, and damn near purple, Gumby's cock bobbed only inches from Screw's mouth.

Jazz's mouth watcred at the thought of taking that flesh into her mouth and making Gumby cry out in pleasure. Was it the same for Screw? Was he just as eager to taste the man before him?

"You gonna imagine I'm her?" Screw asked, and for the first time, Gumby opened his eyes and stared down at him.

Holy shit. Were they talking about her? She held her breath. The answer to Screw's question suddenly became the most important thing in Jazz's world.

"Maybe." Gumby finally spoke, his voice a gravelly rasp. "Maybe I'll scream her name when I come."

Screw growled as though that turned him on.

Between her legs, her panties grew damp. Oh, who was she kidding, they'd left damp behind five minutes ago. She was soaked, aching, and dying for release. What the hell was wrong with her? Screw was about to blow Gumby, who'd threatened to scream her name when he came.

She should be sickened, not because it was two men but because of the convoluted way they'd involved her in their twisted game of lust and hate. But instead, she was one puff of air away from coming.

"Since you don't like dick, you might wanna close your eyes again. I'm about to suck this monster, and I've got one helluva cock myself."

"Jesus." Gumby's head fell back once again, and he slammed his eyes shut.

Screw circled his thumb and forefinger around the base of Gumby's cock drawing a grunt from the taller man.

Just when Jazz thought he would open his mouth and take Gumby inside, Screw lifted Gumby's cock and dipped his head, nuzzling his nose against Gumby's balls.

"Fuck," Gumby said on a breath. His fists opened; palms flat against the concrete. The knuckles were streaked with blood from the way he'd abraded them against the wall.

Next, Screw's tongue snuck out, licking over Gumby's sack a few times.

Jazz pressed her legs together as the ache intensified to nearly unbearable. Her heart was beating so hard, she feared it'd out her as the voyeur she'd become.

"You're so fucking hard," Screw mumbled as though to himself. He shifted, spreading his legs somewhat as he ran his tongue up the side of Gumby's shaft. Against the wall, Gumby shuddered right before a harsh shout ripped from his lips. "Jesus, fuck!"

Screw appeared to have taken Gumby all the way to the back of his throat. His nose disappeared into the well-trimmed hair surrounding Gumby's cock while his fingers dimpled into

Gumby's hips. Would they leave marks? Would Gumby carry small bruises from the force of Screw's grip?

And why was that so hot?

Gumby's hips punched forward once, then twice, but even Jazz could see how he held back, not wanting to ram down Screw's throat.

Sitting back on his heels, Screw pumped Gumby's wet cock twice before giving it a firm squeeze. "Hey," he said, causing Gumby's eyes to open once again. "I ain't a fucking princess."

The two men stared at each other and Jazz swore she could see the electricity crackling between them.

"Fuck my goddamned face," Screw growled.

Something shifted in Gumby then. As though his control had finally snapped, his hands left the wall and he grabbed fistfuls of Screw's light hair as he jammed his hips forward. His long cock entered Screw's waiting mouth with a ruthless thrust.

Jazz gasped and squeezed her thighs together. Her eyes burned from how long she'd kept them wide, but she refused to blink and miss a second of the most erotic show she'd ever seen.

Instead of gagging at the powerful intrusion, Screw groaned around Gumby's length as though he loved every inch being forced down his throat.

Gumby showed him no mercy, hammering Screw's mouth again and again. Screw took it all, grunting and groaning the entire time. His hands held Gumby's hips, encouraging the brutal fucking. Though Gumby's eyes remained closed, Screw kept his gaze cast upward on the man he was pleasuring.

Never in her life had Jazz seen anything so beautiful, so captivating. Or so she thought until a moment later when Gumby let out a surprised shout and buried his cock down Screw's throat. His body jolted with the force of his climax as he emptied himself into the other man.

God how she'd wished both men were naked. Gumby would be gorgeous with his lean muscles corded and straining while the heavier, thicker Screw would be the picture of power, even on his knees.

When Gumby's body stilled, Screw stood. They now maintained an intense eye contact. The air grew so thick with tension, Jazz felt it in the hallway.

What now? Would Gumby freak? Had he done this before?

Jazz bit her lower lip.

"Um, I can return the favor," he said as he reached for Screw's zipper. Though the words came from Gumby's lips, he sounded hesitant.

With a harsh chuckle, Screw stepped out of Gumby's reach. "No thanks."

"What?" Gumby frowned.

"What are you offering?" Screw folded his muscular arms across his chest.

Still frowning, Gumby said, "What do you mean."

"Tell me what you're gonna do to me?"

"I'm gonna…return the favor."

"What? Suck my cock? Jerk me off? What?"

"I…uh…"

Screw snorted. "I just swallowed your cum and you can't even fucking say it." With a shake of his head, he took another step back, then another.

He spun toward the door, kicking Jazz into gear. With a sharp inhale at the look of fury on Screw's face, she darted farther down the hallway, pressing herself into a dark corner. Screw yanked the door open so hard, it slammed against the wall.

Jazz held her breath, but he didn't emerge into the hallway right away. Instead, he must have turned back to Gumby. The silence weighed a thousand pounds. She didn't dare exhale and within seconds, dizziness swamped her. But it didn't last for long because the moment Screw spoke, she sagged against the wall, a deflated balloon.

Nothing had changed between the two men who seemed to hate each other despite their attraction.

"I'll take care of myself," Screw said in the most caustic tone she'd heard from the man. "Not in the mood for pussy tonight."

Chapter Fourteen

What the fuck had he just allowed?

Gumby leaned heavily against the wall, alone in a room where Screw had just sucked him off like his life depended on it. He'd had his share of blow jobs from both men and women, but fuck if he'd ever had one like that. Seemed as though Screw couldn't get enough of Gumby's cock. The man appeared to derive as much pleasure from sucking Gumby as he got from the hot suction of Screw's sinful mouth.

Maybe he'd been right about that angry fucking.

Any time in the past he'd gotten a blow job from a guy, it'd been in a dark corner of a seedy club or out in a back alley behind the place. Also dark. And always far from his hometown, where no one would recognize him. No one would stumble upon him and discover his secret. And no one would get hurt. Traumatic memories tried to worm their way into his sluggish thoughts, but he forced them away.

He'd fucked a few guys over the years too, but once again, no eye contact. Hell, he just bent them over the nearest surface and went to town. If he couldn't see their face, he didn't have to acknowledge the fact he was fucking a guy.

Which was utterly stupid. Men felt different. The strong contours of their back. The lack of curve in their hips. Strong, hairy thighs against his. All the traits that attracted him to men were the things he pretended to ignore.

Yeah, he was a damn head case.

The need he had for men never went away. No matter how much he denied it. Ignoring it never worked either. So he managed it with the occasional encounter, but soon after, the urge to feel a man beneath his fingertips would rear its head once again, causing him to drive hours out of town to find a nameless, faceless man to slake the lust.

Lust he couldn't even admit out loud. Lust he always wrote off as some physical anomaly born of stress or some other bullshit excuse.

Didn't take a trained psychologist to figure out he couldn't admit he was bisexual because of his upbringing. Because his piece of shit father pounded his own disgust into Gumby both verbally and physically.

You want a cock, you reach down and yank your own like a normal fucking man.

If I see you look at that faggot one more time, I'm gonna make you wear a fucking fairy costume to school.

I find out you're on your knees for some pansy and I'll shoot your fucking knee caps off myself.

That last one had been accompanied by a brutal beating responsible for two missed days of school. Over and over, Gumby's father drilled into him his hatred for homosexuals until Gumby shoved that part of his life so deep, he'd sworn it'd never see the light of day.

Little did he know at that time, his body had a way of making its needs known. Now, in his mid-thirties, five years after his father's passing, he still couldn't find his way out of the closet. Some lessons lingered.

Screw was right. He really was a fucking pussy. His left hand cramped up, making him realize his fists were clenched at his sides.

With a sigh, he shook out his hand, then tucked his spent cock back in his pants and pushed off the wall. As he stepped out of the room and turned toward the stairs, he froze.

Jazz stood in the hallway, halfway between the staircase and where he now stood. He swallowed as nerves tickled his throat. Had she run into Screw on her way up? Though he barely knew Screw, the guy sure seemed like the type to brag about his conquests. And after Jazz told him to back the fuck off? Yeah, he'd probably rubbed her face right in it.

"Hey…" he said, taking a slow step forward.

She gifted him a small smile but didn't advance toward him. Though she didn't run screaming either, so maybe she hadn't witnessed the man who'd been trying to get in her pants sucking him off only moments ago.

Jesus what a clusterfuck. A twisted triangle of desire, denial, and now…secrets.

"Hey."

"So, tonight…" She shifted then rubbed her upper arms over the glittery long-sleeved sweater she wore.

"Sucked ass?"

Jazz laughed and some of the heaviness in his gut dissipated. "Think I've had enough for the night. I wasn't sure if you wanted to hang out longer…"

The quiver of uncertainty in her voice had his chest tightening. Regret, remorse, frustration…desire. Such a pool of powerful emotions, and none of which he felt comfortable voicing to Jazz.

To anyone.

"Nah, I'm more than ready to take off."

"Ok, great," she said on a rush of exhaled air. She stood and waited for him to reach her in the hallway. The tight set of her shoulders and missing smile were all he needed to see to understand how much the night had affected her. From what he knew of this new version of Jazz, she loved the men and women of this club and they loved her. For her to be lying to them had to be killing her.

And she had lied. She wanted Screw just as much as he wanted her.

Even if she refused to reach out and grab him. He should have been excited about that prospect, except she'd turned him down as well. A little prickling at the back of his neck had him wondering if she was steering clear of all men.

And if so…why?

As she started to turn for the stairs, Gumby snagged here by the back of her neck and drew her gently to him. Without protest, she wrapped her arms around his waist, and rested her cheek against his chest where his heart still beat out of control. The feel of her, soft and warm against him, smelling like a juicy fucking orange, had his well-used dick twitching back to life.

Jesus, he was a sick fuck.

But then she sighed, a soft sound of contentment, and sex no longer dominated his mind. Now he wanted nothing more than to chase her demons from her life.

"I needed this," she mumbled against his chest, sounding sleepy.

"Makes two of us." After indulging in a few more moments of having Jazz in his arms, Gumby said, "Come on. Let's get moving before you pass out right here."

A soft chuckle was her only answer, but she let him wrap his arm around her shoulder and walk her down the stairs side by side.

With each step, the music grew louder. For the long moments while he'd been upstairs, driving his cock down Screw's throat, the rest of the world had ceased to exist. Somehow, he'd completely forgotten a party waged on right below him. In true MC style, men and women drank and danced in various stages of undress, some well on their way to needing a room in the next few moments.

Of course, standing in the thick of it all, directly in their line of sight as they descended the steps was Screw. His head was tipped back as he drained a beer. The muscles of his throat worked rhythmically causing his Adam's apple to rise and fall, and Gumby could think of nothing other than running his tongue over that very spot.

Beside him, Jazz tensed.

Was she having similar thoughts? Or did her mind stray to the disagreement they'd had earlier?

With just three steps left until they reached the first level, Screw glanced up, making direct eye contact with Gumby. When his gaze caught Jazz as well—or more accurately, Gumby's arm around Jazz—his eyes narrowed with undisguised hatred. The glare didn't last long though as a bimbo in a scrap of fabric and five-inch heels flounced into Screw's peripheral vision. Almost instantly, his frown flipped into a deadly smirk. He snaked his arm out, tagging the Honey around the waist. She let out a window-cracking screech then giggled like a little girl as her body crashed into Screw's. He leaned in, whispering something in her ear that had her rubbing her fake tits and no doubt well-used body all over him.

Jazz's steps faltered and had Gumby not had an arm around her, she'd have tumbled the last few steps.

"Thanks," she said with a phony sounding chuckle. "Musta drank more than I realized."

Or you just saw a man you want setting up his next conquest. "No worries." *I know how you feel.* Not only was he looking at a man he wanted planning his next fuck, it was on the heels of a spectacular blowjob. The lead pipe tenting Screw's jeans was courtesy of Gumby, and he'd be giving it to some two-brain-celled bitch in no time.

Not that Gumby cared.

Fuck.

He was here for Jazz. To work his way back into her life and eventually her bed. Not for Screw, or any man for fuck's sake.

The mountain air must be fucking with his head. Now, he couldn't even blame it on the prolonged period of celibacy, since it had ended fifteen minutes ago.

With a resigned sigh, Jazz said. "Get me the fuck out of here, Gumby."

He released her shoulders, grabbed her hand, and propelled them toward the exit. There they went, walking hand in hand away from a man they both wanted.

A man who'd be balls deep in some club whore before they reached the car. One peek over his shoulder had his eyes locking with Screw's. The other man's mouth was drawn in a grim line of displeasure, at least until the tits-on-a-stick licked a long stripe up the side of his neck. Then his expression morphed into a smart-assed smirk.

Gumby's stomach soured and he turned away. He didn't give a shit whose mouth licked or sucked on Screw and that's the way it would stay.

"Fuck this night," he mumbled under his breath.

"Couldn't have said it better myself," Jazz replied as she pushed the door open, allowing a rush of cold air to smack them in the face.

The car ride home was mostly made in silence with Jazz staring out the window while Gumby navigated her SUV through the winding mountain roads. Though he'd committed no offense she was aware of, he couldn't shake the feeling he'd somehow done something to upset her.

He steered into her narrow driveway, and Jazz was out of the car in a shot, neither waiting for him to kill the engine nor come around and open her door. She practically marched to the front door, then preceded him into the house without bothering to close the door behind her. Guess the move meant he was still a welcome guest.

The girl moved fast, he'd give her that. By the time he made it inside and shed his leather jacket, she was sitting on a bar stool at the small kitchen island with red wine filled near to the brim of a generous-sized glass.

"Want some?" she asked without turning.

"Nah, wine's not really my thing. I'll grab a beer." He circled the island, heading for the fridge where she kept a stock of Hatch Chile Gatos. Gumby couldn't help but grin. She must have the brew imported from Arizona as it came from a craft brewery outside of Phoenix. All the ol' ladies in his club had been nuts about the stuff. It was brewed with chilies, leaving a subtle heat on your tongue. Lila, his VP's ol' lady, said they liked their beer like they liked their men. Smooth, with a little kick at the end.

"Haven't been able to shake my love of that beer," Jazz said from behind him.

With a small smile, he shut the fridge and popped the top with the magnet bottle opener on the front of her refrigerator. "I'm glad. It's good shit." As he turned to face her, his eyes widened. "Wasn't that glass full about two seconds ago?"

With a shrug, Jazz lifted the wine glass and poured the final drops into her mouth. Gumby watched, transfixed as her delicate throat worked the liquid down.

Delicate throat? What the fuck was wrong with him? First he let Screw give him the blow job of his life in a place anyone could have walked in on and now he was waxing fucking poetic. Maybe sticking around Townsend for any period of time was a shitty idea.

"I was thirsty," she said, reaching for the bottle. "Still am."

"Whoa, hold on, babe. Maybe you shouldn't have anymore." Gumby placed his hand over hers where it wrapped around the dark bottle. Such an innocent touch, but still, a ripple of electricity shot up his arm. With a small gasp, Jazz met his gaze. Had she felt it too?

"You got a problem with me drinking a second glass of wine in my own house?"

Well, when she put it that way. He released her. "No, ma'am. Knock yourself out."

She filled the glass again, not quite as high as the first one, but more than halfway. "Don't mind if I do." After setting the bottle down, she took a healthy gulp, though didn't down the entire contents like she had the first go around.

"You want to talk about it?"

She snorted. "Fuck no."

He set his bottle down directly across from her on the island, then braced himself on his palms. "You want him." It wasn't a question.

Once again, she snorted, but this time, couldn't meet his eyes. "No," she said with a surprising amount of vehemence. "I don't want him. I want him to stick to his whores and leave me the fuck alone."

Why he pushed this, he couldn't have said, but he also couldn't stop himself from saying. "No. You want him to forget the whores and just be with you."

I get it. The man's potent as fuck.

Her eyes widened as her head moved right and left. "You're wrong," she whispered.

"I don't think so."

Suddenly Jazz straightened. "No!" she said with force, slamming her glass on the granite. Dark purple liquid sloshed over the rim of the glass and down her hand, splashing on the counter. "You're fucking wrong," she said. "What the fuck is this, Gumby? I thought you came here for me. I thought you wanted me, and now you're trying to push me toward him. Toward a man who thinks it's his mission to fuck as many people as possible. Would *you* want to be with someone like that?" Her tone seemed almost accusatory.

Ridiculous. She couldn't possibly know what happened between him and Screw. How the other man proved beyond a shadow of a doubt why men and women shed their pride to be with him for just a few moments time.

"Shit," she said looking down at her wet hand as though only now realizing she'd spilled the wine. With a huff, Jazz moved to her sink, grabbing a wad of paper towels from the countertop holder. Her shoulders stiffened then slumped.

Fuck. He'd jacked that up, making her crappy night even shittier.

"Babe," he said, moving in behind her. "I did want you." Fitting his front to her back where she stood at the single sink, he continued, "I *do* want you." It shouldn't have been possible for him to be as hard as he was, not after the epic orgasm less than an hour ago, but there he was, hard, throbbing, and nesting his erection in the small of Jazz's back. "But you said just friends."

"This is so fucked up," Jazz whispered, breathy.

She didn't know the half of it. What was his plan here? To fuck her? Here in her kitchen while his cock was coated in dried saliva from Screw's mouth?

Fucked up didn't begin to cover it. Yet still, as though of their own accord, Gumby's lips moved to Jazz's neck at the same time his arms closed around her. When he kissed the side of her throat, a shuddered sigh left her. He took that as consent to move forward and nipped at her jaw before kissing a path up behind her ear. With her short hair, he had perfect access to what was clearly an erogenous zone. Jazz trembled in his arms.

Paper towels forgotten, she shifted her hands to cover his where they rested against her flat stomach. "Gumby," she said when he licked the shell of her ear. Fuck, his name said in that low, near moan shot a spike of lust straight to his dick.

Jazz craned her neck, turning her chin until their lips were just millimeters apart. Despite the voice of reason whispering just how fucked up he was for kissing a woman while the memory of Screw's mouth devouring his cock still played on a loop in his mind, Gumby captured her lips in a searing kiss.

Nothing gentle came from the meeting of their mouths. Without breaking the connection, Jazz turned in his arms, wrapping hers around his neck. She stood on her toes and with a little growl, tried to get even closer to him.

Gumby chuckled as he lifted her ass then settled her on the edge of the sink. Her legs went around his waist as though they'd done this a thousand times before. Jazz tasted of wine and frustration; the aggravation of the night having caught up with her. Gumby had no problem being the man she took that stress out on, especially if it turned into sexual aggression as it seemed to be.

They ate at each other's mouths, fighting for control of the kiss. When he nipped her lower lip, Jazz whimpered and for some un-fucking-known reason, Gumby got a flash of Screw on his knees sucking him like his life depended on it. The combination of that image with Jazz's mouth on his and her body beneath his hands sent him to a level of desire he'd never experienced before.

The need to fuck nearly consumed him. As his tongue battled Jazz's and she moaned into his mouth, he slipped his hands under the hem of her long-sleeved T-shirt. Fuck, all that soft, warm skin felt like heaven beneath his fingertips. His thumb ran over a tiny ridged line, peeking up from the waistband of her jeans, a scar perhaps. The little bump barely registered because at the same moment Jazz rocked her hips, causing her denim covered pussy to grind directly into his dick.

Fuck, this was happening. He was going to fuck her until they were a hot, sweaty mess of satisfaction and all thoughts of a cocky, muscle-bound biker had been pounded out of his head.

As Gumby began to work Jazz's top up, he coasted over another ridged line and she tensed beneath his hands.

"Stop!?" Jazz screamed with such force, he immediately released her and stepped back.

"What's wrong?"

She scrambled off the counter, yanking her shirt down with such force the fabric stretched and gave him a peek of her lacy black bra. Panting, and blinking as though fighting tears, she backed up and wrapped her arms around her midsection.

What the hell was going on? "Jazz—"

"Sorry." She held up a hand. "I can't do this. It's just too..." She shrugged. "Too fucked up."

Because even though she wouldn't admit it, she had... something, whether feelings or just a physical attraction to Screw. And Gumby had let the man suck him off.

Then he'd almost fucked her an hour later.

Fuck.

Thank Christ, she didn't know, she'd toss him out on his ass.

"I'm sorry," she whispered.

"Don't be." He exhaled, running a hand down his face while thinking of the steps to replace a car's oil. Anything to help kill the boner.

What a fucking disaster. The man he couldn't admit he wanted was more than willing to fuck or be fucked at any time and the woman he'd shout from the mountains for refused anything more than a friendly kiss. "This was my fault." As he took a step toward her, she held up a hand.

"Not now, okay? I'm just gonna go to sleep." With that, she turned and started down the hall toward her bedroom. A place he wouldn't be welcome tonight, if ever.

"Fuck," Gumby muttered as he walked toward the front door. Jazz didn't even think to check the locks. They'd be chatting about that tomorrow. With the potential for danger from a rival club, she needed to be vigilant no matter how distracted or upset.

He locked the deadbolt, frowning at the inefficient protection it would afford her home should someone really want in. Tomorrow he'd get on that.

A flicker of light from the street caught his eye. His hand went to his back where his pistol often lived, before remembering he'd left it at home. Bringing a gun into another clubhouse wasn't exactly the best way to make friends.

Narrowing his eyes, he stared out Jazz's window at the pick-up truck parked across the street. The light he'd seen turned out to be the glow of a cell phone.

Screw may hate them both right now, but he'd still ordered protection for them. Gumby didn't know whether to be insulted the other man didn't think he could protect Jazz on his own or thrilled he could sleep without worry, knowing the Handler's had his back.

Either way, the fact the man wanted them covered sent and odd surge of warmth through his chest.

Just one more log on the raging fire of fucked-up feelings.

Chapter Fifteen

Screw let out a low whistle as he scanned the shiny bike in the bed of a brand spankin' new black pick-up.

Being out and about in town without his cut felt…unnatural. So disturbing, in fact, his stomach churned with guilt. Combine it with the suit and tie, something he hadn't donned in a good few years, and it was no wonder his skin felt too tight for his bulky body. Maybe it was just the damned jacket he'd borrowed from Zach. The restrictive material stretched across his traps, pulling with every movement. So sue him, he didn't own a fucking suit of his own. This would hopefully be the last time he'd ever put one on.

"Hey, don't even think about touching my fucking bike, man." An average sized guy with a blonde fauxhawk strode over, chest puffed and eyes narrowed. But what was most telling, and the reason Screw had spent most of the morning staking out the gas station, was the Chrome Disciples cut the guy wore.

He lifted his hands and took a step back. "Wouldn't dream of it, man," he said biting back his natural urge to be snarky. "Just admiring. She's a beaut."

The prospect sized him up and dismissed him as a threat in about two seconds flat. Foolish asshole. He'd learn not to judge a book by its cover or an enforcer by his benign suit and tie.

"Thanks man. Worked my ass off to afford her. Just picked her up last week. Finished driving her up from Alabama this morning." He opened the driver's side door and tossed a bag of potato chips on the front seat before rounding to the back to stand by Screw. "Just pissed it's too fucking cold to give her the ride she deserves right now. You ride?"

It'd been a risk, sure, encountering a member of the Chrome Disciples face to face, but he'd gone with it. So what if he hadn't mentioned it to his club. It was called taking the initiative. This fucker was just a lowly prospect. If he knew any of the Handlers by sight, it'd be the big players. Exec board members. And sure, Screw was one now—fuck if that didn't still feel surreal—but he'd bet the CDMC didn't know about the shifting of positions in the club.

"Nah, got a cousin down south who does. I don't really know much about bikes, but I was walking by and the sun caught the chrome. So shiny it nearly blinded me. I don't need to ride to know a nice piece of machinery when I see it."

The guy, who had to be about five years younger than Screw preened like a proud fucking peacock.

"So, you uh, part of a motorcycle club?" Screw said, pointing toward the guy's cut.

"Yeah." He opened the tailgate then hopped into the bed to make sure the bike was still strapped down securely.

"Huh. Hell's Handlers, right? I live in Knoxville but have a house I come out to here so I can escape the city. I've heard you guys mentioned a few times."

The prospect snorted. "Don't fucking think so. I ain't one of those pussies."

It wasn't in Screw's nature to let being called a pussy slide. Normally, he'd pop this douche bag's head off with one good punch, but the asshole was more useful to him conscious and talking than out cold on the ground. He lifted his hands. "Sorry, didn't mean to offend you. I'm just curious since I know nothing about that world. Isn't it weird to have two clubs in one town?"

The guy grunted then sat with his legs dangling off the edge of his truck. After pulling a circular tin out of his pocket then shoving a wad of dip in his lower lip, he spoke. "Depends," he said. "Some clubs coexist well, but not us." With a shrug, he spit a stream of brown liquid on the ground. "Guy in charge of the Handlers is Copper. Arrogant fucking asshole. Thinks he owns this town and everyone in it. They ain't straight, but they ain't exactly badass either."

"Huh." Screw leaned his hip against the guy's truck and when he didn't get his head blown off he said, "Some of the stories I've heard about them are downright crazy. Seem pretty badass to me. You guys have some kinda turf war or something going on?"

With a shake of his head he jumped down. "Not really. Well, maybe. We wouldn't give a shit about them, but my prez said there's no way they'll let us stick around even though our clubhouse is a town over."

The Handlers sure as fuck didn't want these gun runners operating on their turf. His MC may not run drugs, guns, or women, but they sure as fuck could still end up in prison for many of their business ventures. Loan sharking, muscle for hire, the occasional gambling ring. A few of their members fought in an underground MMA ring as well. Then there was murder plain and simple. Fuck with the club, come after an ol' lady and you'd find yourself six feet under. They may view it as justice, but the cops sure wouldn't. So, no, a gun trafficking club that would undoubtedly bring the feds sniffing around at some point wouldn't work. Not to mention Copper just didn't want all those weapons running through the club's territory. That business inevitably turned messy and by messy, he meant fucking bloody.

"That sounds fucked up."

"Yep," he said as he slammed the tailgate closed. "Told you, they're a buncha pussy bitches."

"You guys gonna do something about it?"

The prospect eyed him for the longest few seconds of Screw's life. Shit, stupid question for him to ask. There wasn't any way to make a question like that sound innocent. Had he just outed himself? Was he too eager? Crank confronting Jazz had lit a fire under his ass. Screw wanted the CDMC gone. And fast.

Screw held his breath, working to ignore the sweat soaking into the collared shirt beneath his wool jacket. How the hell men wore this shit everyday he'd never know. Forty-two degrees and he was sweating like a fucking married dude caught eating out a club whore. Or so he imagined one would feel. He sure as fuck would never find that shit out.

"Let's just say my prez doesn't let anything fuck with his profits."

"I hear that."

"Hey." The prospect approached him, and Screw froze, poised and ready to defend an attack. "You in town through the weekend?"

He nodded. "Yeah, got off work early and drove out here. Spending the rest of the week in my cabin." It'd be foolish to throw away whatever opportunity this prospect was gonna present.

The prospect spit on the ground, his brown teeth bared. "You should come party with us this weekend. Gonna be fucking epic. Guarantee you've never seen shit like this is your buttoned-up suit-wearing world. Whatdya say?"

Screw's heart started to pound. No fucking way Copper would okay this shit. Too much risk of it being a trap. "Sounds like just what I need to shake things up."

The guy's head fell back on his shoulder and he laughed. "Oh, it'll do that. Here, gimmie your phone." He motioned toward Screw's hand.

Well fuck, he had Handler's shit all over his phone. A bead of sweat trickled down his spine as he began to lift the device.

"Actually, scratch that. Just gimmie your number and I'll text you the address. Tell 'em Squirt sent you."

"Squirt?"

The guy rolled his eyes. "Youngest prospect. Hoping to change that shitty name once I patch in. Come on, I got shit to do. Your number?"

Screw rattled off the number and seconds later a text from Squirt buzzed through.

"Sweet, man. See you Saturday. Sure as fuck hope you ain't a prude," he said with a laugh as he strode toward the driver's door once again. "I can promise you a pick of women who'll do shit you've only dreamed of."

"Not a prude," Screw said, but it was pretty much to himself as Squirt slid into his truck. Any other day, even being an intensely stupid reaction given the danger, he'd have gotten hard at the thought of those club whores ready and willing for whatever he could drum up. And when it came to fucking, his imagination was off the charts. Today, however, he couldn't even muster a flicker of interest. Whether it was the memory of Gumby's groans as he shot his load down Screw's throat or the disgust in Jazz's eyes as she left him to his Honey last night, didn't matter. His dick was deader than Kurt Cobain.

After watching Jazz and Gumby leave the clubhouse hand in hand, he'd sent the Honey on her way with a few caustic words the poor girl didn't deserve. She couldn't be blamed for Screw's shitty mood. How the hell was she supposed to know he couldn't get it up for anyone but Jazz lately—well, Jazz and apparently Gumby, because he was sure as fuck hard after blowing the man.

The truck roared to life, causing Screw to jolt and hop out of the vehicle's path. Fuck, he needed to be more alert than that, especially if he planned to hit the Chrome Disciples party this weekend. There, he'd need to be at the top of his game, ready for a potential ambush.

Twenty minutes later he sat in a booth at the diner across from a scowling Copper. "You've got to be fucking kidding me," Copper roared despite the complete lack of privacy.

A hush fell over the diner as all eyes turned their way. Being eleven-thirty in the morning, the place was bustling with the early lunch crowd.

A wide-eyed Toni glared daggers their way.

As Screw turned his gaze back to Copper, he caught sight of Jazz emerging from her office with a worried expression. She avoided looking at him—no surprise there—instead focusing on Copper.

With a wince, Copper lifted a hand Toni's way. She just rolled her eyes and resumed refilling coffee cups to her counter customers. Within seconds, the dull roar of happily munching and chatting patrons kicked up once again.

Copper leaned in. "Look, Screw, I get you want to take the initiative and be proactive here. And I appreciate you taking this shit seriously, but there's no fucking way I can allow this. It's just too goddammed risky. Crank's been one step ahead of us, so we have to assume this is a trap." He'd dropped his voice so low, Screw had to lean in to hear him.

"What the fuck has you two looking so serious?" Zach said from the side of the table. Standing next to him with a frown on her make-up free face was Lindsay, the-thirteen-year-old girl he and Toni had recently taken in.

"Hey, sweetie," Screw said giving her a chin lift.

She blushed an adorable shade of pink, casting her eyes to the ground. The guys had been teasing him about her schoolgirl crush on him, so he tried to be sensitive of her feelings. Fuck if he didn't know how rough it could be being a teenager, and how it scarred a person for life. This girl had already been through so much having been used as a pawn by the Chrome Disciples MC.

"Hi, Screw. Hi, Copper," she said before glancing up at Zach. "I'm gonna go help Toni."

"Sure thing, hon."

She gave Zach a quick hug before jetting off, which had a goofy grin appearing on the new VP's face.

"She seems to be settling in well," Copper said as Zach slipped into the booth next to him.

Z's gaze tracked the girl where she got to work behind the counter, taking over Toni's task of refilling coffees. "Yeah, all things considered she's holding up. The nightmares break Toni's heart, but hopefully we can move past those once she really starts to believe she's safe."

"Nightmares?" Screw also watched the girl who'd seen way more than any thirteen-year-old should. He knew the feeling. Maybe he could pick her brain about the new Chrome Disciples clubhouse. She'd most likely been there a time or two.

With a nod Zach said, "Yeah, same one every time. She's back at that campground with Shell and Toni, only they hate her for her role in tricking them. When we show up to rescue our women, we leave her to the Chrome Disciples. She wakes up screaming in terror every time. It's fucking wrecking Toni."

"Shit," Screw said. Damn, his heart went out to that girl. Her brother had been a prospect for the Chrome Disciples when their parents died unexpectedly, leaving her in his care. The guy was a piece of fucking shit, who got himself booted from the club before he patched in. As payment for their time and trouble, Lindsey was left with the CDMC. As far as Screw knew, she wasn't sexually assaulted, but she sure as hell wasn't treated well either. They'd knocked her around and pretty much used her as a servant, including making her cozy up to Toni with the end goal of fucking with the Handlers. Their plan worked. Toni's soft spot for troubled youth had her falling hard for Lindsey. She and Shell nearly ended up kidnapped by the CDMC when Lindsey called Toni stating she needed help. The women ran to her aid, falling into the CDMC's well laid trap. Zach got shot during the rescue effort and all three women were treated for hypothermia after being out in the elements for far too long. In the end, they liberated Lindsey from the club and the kid now had a permanent home with Z and Toni. No wonder Copper suspected foul play with this party business.

"How's the shoulder, bro?" Screw asked Zach as Toni meandered over with a fresh pot of coffee. She poured a cup for her ol' man before topping off Screw and Copper's mugs.

"Sore, but not too bad," Z answered as he slipped an arm around his woman's waist. "Toni takes good care of me."

"Sure do." Toni leaned in and gave her man a kiss Zach quickly took advantage of. After a few seconds of tongue tangling, a flushed Toni gently pushed him away. "I may own the place," she said with a chastising grin for Z, "but that doesn't mean my patrons want to see me sucking face."

After shooting them a sassy wink, she sauntered back toward the counter.

"Damn, I love that ass," Zach said in a reverent tone.

It was a pretty good ass.

"Hey, eyes front, fucker," Zach snapped.

With a smirk, Screw shifted his gaze. "You're the one who drew my attention to it."

"I'm also gonna be the one to gouge your eyes out of your head. Enough of this shit. What had you two looking like you wanted to go at each other's throats when I walked in?"

The glower reappeared on Copper's face, and he jammed a finger in Screw's direction. "This fucker here staked out the gas station where Jazz ran into the Disciples. Sure enough, one of their prospects showed up, and he fucking talked to him. Got himself invited to a party this weekend."

One of Zach's blonde eyebrows took a trip into his forehead. "You shitting me?"

"Nope," Screw said with a shrug. If Copper wanted him to apologize, he'd be disappointed.

"That why you're wearing this shit? Why you wanted my suit?"

With a nod, Screw said, "Yep. Figured he wouldn't get suspicious of a businessman who didn't live here permanently. Guy had a shiny new Fat Boy in the back of his truck. Chatted him up about it and before you know it, I got an invite to their housewarming party this weekend. Squirt warned me I better not be a prude." He chuckled. "Claims their women will do pretty much any fucking thing I want."

With a grunt, Z rolled his eyes before shifting to face Copper. "It's not a bad idea, boss," he said earning him a death glare.

"You're right. It's a shitty-assed-terrible-fucking-dicked-up-motherfucking-bad idea." Copper dropped his voice which had begun to rise again. "He's out of his fucking mind if he thinks I'm gonna okay this bullshit," he said, pointing a finger at Screw.

Zach sighed. "Might be our best shot at some serious intel."

Shaking his head, Copper said, "No. Not happening." His face fell into a stony mask. "It's not worth the risk. They put serious time and effort into the kidnap attempt on Toni and Shell. What makes you think this is any different? What makes you think they don't know what each and every one of us look like? Right now, they're sitting in their clubhouse, hands on each other's dicks giving each other a jerk for a job well done."

"Huh," Screw said as he scratched his chin. "Actually, that sounds like it might be right up my alley. Sure you won't reconsider?"

The look Copper shot him had his hands raising in surrender. "All right. I hear ya, prez. Consider it dropped."

At least for the moment. There was no way Screw planned to let this opportunity pass him by. He may not be able to fully turn off his jokester ways, but he sure as fuck took the fate of his club seriously. If the only way to help his brothers was to go behind enemy lines, he'd do it in a fucking heartbeat.

President's approval or not. Even if he got his ass kicked out of the club, keeping his brothers and Jazz safe would be worth it.

Chapter Sixteen

Though the diner had closed an hour ago, Jazz still lingered at her computer, finalizing the week's payroll. Employees were paid biweekly, and in order for that to happen, she was required to have the numbers submitted to their payroll company Friday before pay week. Today, she was taking her sweet time, mostly due to the fact both Gumby and Screw sat out in the dining room, waiting—for her. Gumby had dropped her off that morning with a promise to pick her up again once she was finished, and Screw got stuck with guard duty as Copper needed the prospects for an even more menial task.

So now both men, who as far as she knew hadn't spoken a word to each other since the blow job she wasn't supposed to know about, sat in the dining room. Were they on opposite ends of the room glaring at each other? Were they close and working hard to avoid eye contact? Were they all over each other, maybe fucking on the counter?

Okay, clearly, that wasn't happening, but she'd be lying if she said the idea didn't get her motor revving. In fact, thoughts of Screw and Gumby going at it had become her go-to fantasy for the week. One that fueled more sessions with her vibrator over the past six days than the past six months.

Ugh.

With a groan, she let her head clunk against the desk.

She needed help.

As though it wasn't bad enough her days were consumed with fantasies of the two bikers, her nights had been overtaken with dreams where they turned their hungry eyes her way. Just the thought of both men touching her at the same time was nearly enough to make her come. She'd never had a threesome before, and certainly wouldn't now, but the idea of it kept her hot and bothered more often than not.

If only things were different…

She lifted her head an inch before letting it bang back down on the desk.

"Hey, can you do me a favor before you give yourself a brain injury?"

Jazz popped her head up to find Toni hovering in the doorway, her mouth tilted up in a half smile. "Sure, what do you need?"

"I ordered some different style uniform shirts to try out with the new logo, and even though I ordered all mediums, they sent a few extra smalls." She held up a long-sleeved crew neck shirt with Toni's Diner and their logo on the back.

Jazz rose and held out her hand. "Yeah sure, that's no problem. They look great by the way."

"I think so too. Just come on out when you're ready so I can see it." She tossed the shirt across the few feet separating them.

Jazz caught it one handed. "You got it, boss."

With a laugh, Toni said, "You got skills, Jazzy." Then she left, pulling the door closed behind her.

As the door clicked shut, Jazz blew out a breath. Thank God, the shirt in question had long sleeves. So far, no one had questioned her always being fully covered up. She'd have thought they'd at least tease her, considering most of the women associated with the club liked to bare it all, but everyone seemed to be satisfied with her explanation of always being cold. That probably wouldn't last forever, especially the more summers she spent in Tennessee, but so far, so good.

Jazz pulled off her shirt, turning her back on the oval wall mirror hanging behind the door. She closed her eyes as she slipped the new garment on. Overkill maybe, but the habit had become second nature by now. She just couldn't look. Couldn't bear to see what had become of her body. What would keep a man from wanting her. What would ensure long years of loneliness. Even in the shower, she refused to look at her naked body. Shaving with her eyes shut had been quite the treacherous chore at first, but now she could shave without sight like nobody's business.

And Toni thought her only skills lay in the T-shirt catching arena. What would she think about the blind shaving?

She'd think you were certifiable.

Opening her eyes, she glanced down at the black shirt with teal lettering. On the front, over the left breast was Toni's name, natural, seeing as how she'd thought she was ordering shirts to try herself. She craned her neck to check out the back. The diner's logo sat in a big circle between her shoulder blades. More fitted than she'd originally thought, the shirt hugged her body and actually made it look like she had some breasts. Not bad.

"This came out nice," she said aloud. Jazz pulled the door open and strode out into the main dining area. "I look pretty damn good, if I do say so my—oh, hey." Somehow in the two minutes she was donning the shirt, she'd forgotten about the two men waiting on her.

Toni sat at a booth with both Gumby and Screw. The men were on opposite sides of the table. Had Toni been the one to draw them together or had they overcome their silence and gravitated toward each other? After all, there was a pretty strong attraction there.

"Damn, woman, that shit makes your tits look stellar." Screw said.

Immediately, Gumby's mouth turned down, but he too had his gaze glued to her chest.

It was such a Screw thing to say, such a normal reaction from the jokester that Jazz couldn't do anything but laugh. He hadn't spoken more than two words to her since the night she asked him to back off and the moment of normalcy felt so damn good, she nearly teared up.

Gumby tore his gaze away from her body to glare at Screw who shrugged. "What? It does. I'm not blind."

"Shut it, you two," Toni said as she rose from the booth to circle Jazz.

Heat rose to her face under Toni's perusal. She'd made it her mission to blend in and not be stared at over the past year and change. Being the subject of such blatant scrutiny was uncomfortable to say the least.

"I love it!" Toni clapped her hands together and bounced on the balls of her feet. "I'm so glad Zach finally convinced me to officially put my name on there. Toni's Diner. Simple, but it makes me so happy."

"I think it's perfect," Jazz said looking down at herself. "Too bad this one doesn't have my name embroidered on it."

Laughing, Toni waved her hand. "I'll order you a few of those. Oh, wait." She moved back to the table, then rifled through the box. "The shirts rock, but I'll have to have a chat with the company before we make a big order. I can't have them sending incorrect sizes like this. Here, another extra small." She tossed a shirt Jazz's way. "Try that one on for me too, if you don't mind."

Once again, Jazz snatched the shirt out of the air. This one was teal with black lettering, a reverse of what she wore. "Yeah, sure. I'll be right back." She held it up to get a better look and her stomach sank to the floor. "Uh, Toni?" she said unable to keep the tremor out of her voice. "This is a tank top."

Refolding a few of the shirts, Toni said, "Yeah, I know. I'm not sure I want to go the sleeveless route. The neckline is low, maybe too low even though it's squared. But I figured if I was ordering a bunch of different styles, I might as well get a few so we can make a decision on it. I just need to see you in it for a second." She lifted her head and smiled, oblivious to the turmoil raging through Jazz.

"Uhh, maybe you should model this one."

Toni snorted. "Sorry girl, an extra small I am not."

An invisible hand wrapped itself around Jazz's throat, squeezing tighter with each excuse Toni knocked back. Her next words came out a strangled whisper. "H-holly could—"

"Holly left about ten minutes ago, and you think her boobs are gonna fit in that thing? Come on, girl, it'd be downright pornographic."

"I'd pay money to see—"

"Shut it, Screwball," Toni said, holding her hand in front of his face.

Jazz stood frozen to the spot like a helpless animal caught in the high beams of a semi-truck. Memories assaulted her. Events she kept in a tightly sealed box in her mind broke free.

The smell of blood.

The sound of her own screams.

The terror.

The pain. God, the pain…

"Just try it for me, please. I promise you only need to keep it on for a minute. You won't get too cold." Toni still glared at Screw as she spoke. She'd yet to notice her employee's internal freak-out.

Jazz rubbed over her arms as the sensation of a thousand bugs crawling across her skin grew in strength. The thought of standing before her friends in the low-cut tank brought with it a paralyzing dread that kept her feet rooted to the ground.

"No!" she yelled with far more force that the situation called for.

Toni, who'd resumed chatting with Screw, whipped her head around. Her eyebrows narrowed. "Seriously?"

"Yes. I'm not putting this on." Jazz threw the shirt back to her friend and boss. Never before had they even come close to arguing over a business decision, or a personal one for that matter, which could be why Jazz felt the urge to vomit. Or it could be the horror of imagining herself walking out of her office in the tank top.

A look of concern crossed Gumby's handsome face and he began to rise. "Jazz, you okay?" he asked but his question was overshadowed by Toni's huff.

"Jazz, just put the goddammed shirt on. I can't believe you're giving me a hard time about this." Toni threw up her hands, then planted them on her hips.

The walls of the diner began to close in on her as the three of them stared. This was so out of character for her, this blatant refusal to help her boss without any kind of explanation, but what could she say?

I have horrifying scars all over my body.

No, she'd rather die than admit the truth. They could never see her shame. Never discover what had been done by her own family member. What her parents hadn't prevented. What she hadn't been strong enough to stop.

"I'm not putting it on."

"I don't—"

"Toni…" Screw circled Toni's wrist with his hand, halting her tirade. When she turned toward him, he whispered something to her that had her frowning for a different reason. She turned back, assessing Jazz and the expression of concern grew.

"Jazz, you're shaking. What's wrong?" Toni took one step forward, but Screw prevented her from drawing closer.

She needed to run, but her damn feet just wouldn't move.

He slipped out of the booth and slowly walked her way, Gumby hot on his heels.

"Jazzy?" Screw said. "You really are shaking. And you're sweating. Why don't you sit down, babe?" He reached for her and the second his fingertips made contact with her arm, she yanked it back with such force, she stumbled and would have fallen if it weren't for the counter behind her.

"I'm fine," she said, working to play it off though her heart jack hammered in her chest and her skin itched as if those bugs from moments ago had bitten her in a hundred spots.

"Why don't I drive you home?" Gumby asked, holding up her keys.

"Jesus, what the hell is wrong with you people?" She suddenly screamed, completely aware she was melting down in spectacular fashion, but unable to stop the train wreck. With a shake of her head, she snatched her keys from Gumby's grasp and marched toward the door. "I said I didn't want to wear the goddammed shirt, not that I was dying. Back the fuck off. I'll get myself home."

Then, with that stunning display of freak-out, she ran to her car.

The drive home was made with tears streaming down her face. God, what must her friends think of her? Words like raving lunatic or psycho bitch were the first that came to mind. Before she knew it, she was pulling into her driveway, having driven the last few miles completely on autopilot. As if screaming at her friends wasn't bad enough, now she was risking lives by driving while far beyond distracted.

She killed the engine then flopped back against the leather seat. It was then she realized she wasn't just crying, she was full on sobbing, complete with choking gasps, snot, and gallons of tears. A knock on her window had her jumping so hard her hand whacked the steering wheel.

Shit.

Jeremy stood on the other side of her window, jiggling her door handle. "Unlock the door, babe," he said.

Great, another witness to her humiliation. All she wanted was to crawl under her covers and sleep until the memory of this day faded into oblivion. Maybe following a few glasses of whiskey.

Instead, she lifted a trembling hand to the panel on her door, hitting the unlock button. Jeremy opened the door, and immediately pulled her out into his arms. His touch only intensified the creepy-crawly feeling on her skin, but before she could pull away, another voice rang out.

"I'll take it from here, man," Screw said, all but ramming Jeremy out of the way with his shoulder.

He scooped her up into his arms and tromped straight toward her front door, leaving her neighbor in the driveway, jaw hanging open. Somewhere inside, Jazz knew she should protest. Should demand he put her down. Later, being carried like some sort of damsel in distress because she was too zoned out to get into the house herself would only amp up the mortification. Not to mention leaving Jeremy in her driveway without any kind of explanation after he'd only tried to help hit new levels of rudeness.

But for the first time since holding up the tank top, Jazz didn't have the urge to claw her flesh off. Instead, held protectively against Screw's chest, she felt nothing but warmth against her skin. With that warmth came a sense of safety she hadn't felt in too many years to count.

He carried her into the house, and had she been thinking straight, she'd have wondered how he got in without the key. As it was, her brain was clouded with a mix of embarrassment, vile memories, and regret.

Screw set her down on the couch so gently, a fresh round of tears fell. What the hell was wrong with her? She didn't cry. Tears didn't solve shit as she'd learned long ago, so she never bothered with them. All they did was leave her puffy-eyed and exhausted.

Before Screw even had a chance to fully release her, a glass of what smelled like whiskey was pushed into her hand. "Drink," Gumby ordered.

Gumby?

Where had he come from?

Jazz blinked, trying to clear the cobwebs from her brain. Gumby's presence explained how Screw got in the house. But wait…since when did those two get along?

"You heard the man, baby, drink," Screw said, lifting the glass toward her lips. He sat next to her on the couch while Gumby perched himself on the edge of her coffee table. The thing couldn't be more than eighteen inches high, and the poor, tall guy's knees were practically in his nose.

As ordered, she took a sip of the whiskey. Then another, then…fuck it, she downed the entire contents in three healthy swallows. It did the trick, burning her esophagus and bringing her back to the moment.

Her actions of the past half hour came crashing down around her as though an earthquake crumbled the house. "Shit," she said, glancing around. "I need to call Toni and apologize."

Gumby took the glass from her and set it next to him before capturing her hands in his. "You don't need to call her now. She told us she'd check in tonight to make sure you're okay. She's not mad."

His warm hands completely engulfed hers, making her aware of just how cold she'd grown. Apparently, during her tantrum at the diner, she hadn't thought to grab her jacket.

"I'm sorry," she said, head dropping forward. Someone rubbed up and down her back. Had to be Screw since Gumby still held her hands.

"It's all right, Jazz," Gumby said, giving her hands a squeeze. "Can you tell us what that was all about?" His voice held no recrimination, just compassion.

She shook her head. No, she couldn't tell them. She couldn't tell anyone. Not only was the story horrifying, but humiliating, and would no doubt change the way these men looked at her forever. No man would want her once they found out what happened to her. How could any stand to look at the mess of her? But knowing it and having it confirmed by two men she felt wildly attracted to were two very different things. The first kept her from seeking physical intimacy. The second could destroy her.

"Hey, Jazzy?"

She turned her head, locking gazes with Screw. The man with the solemn expression and eyes swirling with worry didn't resemble the Screw she knew. He was barely recognizable as the womanizing sex fiend who couldn't take anything seriously. Right then, he looked as grave as could be.

"That was about a lot more than a shirt. There's no judgment here. Not from us." He shifted his gaze to Gumby who nodded. "We all know you've cut ties with your past, babe. You never speak of your life before you popped up in Townsend, alone. None of us have pried because you've always seemed happy, but I know you keep secrets. And now I know they're painful ones. I just want to help you. *We* just want to help you."

He stroked a finger across her cheek, making a shiver run down her neck. It'd be so easy to get lost in those crystal blue eyes, that handsome face. So easy to beg him for pleasure. To use physical ecstasy to chase away the emotional turmoil.

But the aftermath, the inevitable rejection would only destroy her. And where would it all leave Gumby? She wanted him just as much as she desired Screw. It was high time to admit it to herself. No more denying, no more blaming it on her subconscious fantasies. She wanted two men. And wanted them together.

But she couldn't have even one of them.

"Jazz, did someone hurt you?" Screw asked.

As she shifted her gaze between the two men, she swallowed. She had to give them something. A morsel to satisfy them for the moment.

"Yes," she whispered, revealing more to them than anyone beyond hospital staff knew.

"Is it why you left Crystal Rock?" Gumby asked.

She nodded.

"Was it…oh, Jesus." Gumby dropped her hands and shot to his feet, a palm pressed to his stomach. All the color had drained from his face, leaving him a sickly pale shade. "Was it one of my brothers?"

Chapter Seventeen

He was gonna be sick.

Just the thought that one of his club brothers, men he loved as family and trusted with his life could have hurt Jazz had a pain he'd never experienced crushing his chest. If she confirmed his worst fear, his entire world would implode.

"No!" Jazz grabbed for him, but he scooted from her reach. Her touch would break him, sever the thin thread holding him together. He wanted, no *needed* to know what happened to her.

Out of character, Screw remained silent and watchful on the couch next to Jazz.

She stood, following his path across the room. "Gumby, I promise you, it wasn't one of your brothers. No one associated with the club hurt me. They would never have cu—" She caught herself with a shake of her head. "They'd never have hurt me."

The relief at her declaration did nothing to mitigate the ache in his chest. Each heavy thrum of his heart felt like a hammer hitting his ribs. They stared at each other until Screw finally had the balls to ask what Gumby couldn't.

"Jazz, were you…" He cleared his throat. "Were you raped?"

She turned her sad eyes on Screw. "No," she said, though Gumby didn't think either of them believed her. It wasn't the first time she denied the claim, but sexual assault seemed the most obvious reason Jazz would be terrified to reveal her body, especially in the presence of men. It'd also explain why she hadn't pursued anything with Screw, Gumby, or any other man since coming to Townsend.

Yeah, he'd asked around.

With a resigned sigh, her shoulders slumped, and she walked back to the couch, gesturing to the cushions. "Please come sit," she said. "I can tell you don't believe me. I'll tell you what happened."

He did as she asked, taking a seat beside Screw. Though their bodies weren't touching, in fact a good foot separated them, something about having the other man nearby provided a sense of comfort. Jazz's story was going to be brutal; he knew it in his bones. But having someone else experience the devastation alongside him eased his dread.

Strength in numbers.

Jazz didn't return to the couch. She didn't sit at all. She almost appeared lost in her head as she began to pace the length of her small den, hands wringing.

Pressure against the side of his boot had Gumby glancing down. Screw's foot rested right against his own, having crossed over into his personal space. Gumby glanced at the other man who watched Jazz like a hawk. Even though Screw made no acknowledgment, Gumby knew the move was an intentional lending of physical support. And he appreciated it so much more than he could say. Something shifted in him, something more than just the sexual desire he felt for Screw. He was drawn to the other biker in a way he'd never allowed himself to be drawn to another man. In fact, the only experience he could compare it to, was the pull he felt to Jazz.

Unacceptable.

He couldn't be drawn to a man in such a way. Had to be the high emotions flying around the room. Regardless, the confusing reaction was something to be analyzed later. Not now. Now they both needed to focus on Jazz. And if he needed Screw's presence to get through her tale, so be it.

A worry for another time.

"I'm not sure where to start," she said without glancing their way.

Gumby shared a look with Screw. The other man sat perched at the edge of the couch, bouncing one knee and gnawing his lower lip. From what he'd gathered, Screw didn't do serious often. In Gumby's experience, those kinds of people were often using jokes and teasing to deflect, to keep from feeling deep emotions. Here and now, the man was denying his nature. Allowing Jazz to reach in and wound his insides with what would no doubt be an agonizing story.

If he could protect Screw from the pain, he would, but the man deserved to know as much as Gumby did. So he reached out and placed a hand on Screw's arm. Screw jumped, then seemed to get the message. He scooted back, settling against the cushions of the couch though his leg still twitched.

"Start where you feel comfortable," Gumby said.

She snorted and it was good to hear a little spunk from her. Glancing their way, she said, "Well, I'll start a little way back since Screw doesn't know much about my history."

"Start anywhere, I'll keep up," Screw said.

"Okay, well, Gumby knows all this, but my dad passed when I was really young. A little over three. My mom didn't remarry until I was seven."

She was right, he already knew all this, but the refresher helped and Screw nodded along, riveted to every word.

"My stepfather was all right. A bit of an ass, but fine, I guess." She shrugged.

The guy was an ass. A sanitation worker for the town of Crystal Rock, he'd grown bitter with his station in life, becoming a general douche.

"He had a son, Paul…" Her gaze drifted before focusing back on them. "He's ten years older than I am. P-Paul never lived with us in the house, at least not officially. He'd pop up every now and again, stay for a while, then disappear. As a kid, I always thought he was odd, but hadn't spent enough time with him to really get a handle on it. My mom complained to my dad that Paul did drugs and would steal from the medicine cabinet or her purse when he was around, but my stepdad always denied it. Paul could do no wrong in his eyes. Though looking back on it now, I think he may have been partly afraid of his son." She bit her lower lip as she shook her head, probably lost in memories.

Paul? Paul was the one who hurt her? That motherfucking bastard. Did Jazz know he was locked up? Until Acer had mentioned the incarceration, he'd never thought Paul could be a threat to anyone. The guy was thin, scrawny really, jumpy as fuck, and had those shifty eyes of someone always on the lookout for an attack.

"He always thought people were out to get him. He'd scan the street ten times in an hour, freak out if the phone rang, or talk about outlandish conspiracy theories." She chuckled but the sound wasn't one of humor. "When I first met him as a kid, I wondered if he was some secret spy. A James Bond type."

With a heavy sigh, she stopped pacing and walked around the coffee table. She sat where Gumby had been seated before. He almost offered her his spot on the couch but didn't want to interrupt her thought process.

"You're doing great, Jazz," Screw said. He hadn't moved his foot, in fact his hand now rested on the couch, right next to Gumby's. The urge to hook their pinkies together overwhelmed him.

Ridiculous.

"Thanks, but that was the easy part." She took a deep breath, straightened her shoulders and continued. "One night, when I was thirteen, my mom had to leave for work, and my step-dad was running late. They didn't like leaving me alone; we didn't live in the greatest area, but she really had no choice. She couldn't miss her shift, and my step-dad was on his way home. I should have been alone twenty minutes maximum. But thirty minutes later, when I was in my room doing my homework, Paul came in. It'd been a solid year since any of us had seen him. He didn't come around much. Paul was gay and before I knew him, his parents sent him to one of those religious camps where they try to pray you straight or some nonsense. Anyway, he hated his dad for it and only really came by when he needed something. I'm not sure where he spent the rest of his time. I never wanted to know."

Gumby tensed but forced himself to keep from reacting further. He supposed he'd been lucky to have been spared that fate. Though if his old man had gone that route, maybe he would have been the only one hurt…

"Paul looked awful. Sweaty, and jittery, with circles under his eyes. He kept saying that someone was coming, and we needed to get away."

Jazz began rubbing her left upper arm, over and over. She rocked back and forth, staring straight ahead though not actually seeing anything.

"With each passing second, he grew more and more frantic until he suddenly froze and said it was too late to get away. 'H-he's here,' he said." She swallowed. "And when I asked who he told me, 'The Devil.'" Jazz's voice cracked and she shook her head. "Sorry, I just…I need a minute."

God, his heart was going to split in two. Screw's too if the anguish in his eyes meant anything.

"Take all the time you need, Jazz. We're not going anywhere," Gumby managed to say around the lump in his throat.

She gave him a nod then took a deep breath. "It was then I knew something was seriously wrong with him mentally. He often talked with fire and brimstone religious undertones, but this was out there even for him. When I asked him w-where the devil was, he turned on me and said… h-he was in me, and it was his responsibility t-to get him out. Uh, to save me." She cleared her throat, seeming to use the act to buy herself another second. "I remember thinking he meant some kind of exorcism so I said we should go in the living room. I was trying to buy some time for his father to get home. I thought he'd say some prayer and that'd be it. I was wrong."

She fell silent. Gumby's throat felt tight. He knew the next words out of her mouth would be awful. Knew he should say something comforting, but words failed him.

"What did he do to you, Jazz?" Screw asked, voice ragged.

"He c-cut me. Right here." She pointed a trembling finger at her left shoulder. "Said I had to bleed to get the devil out of me." A tear rolled down her cheek, followed by another, and another. "It wasn't deep, but it hurt so bad. I remember screaming until my throat was raw. That's how my stepfather found us. Paul holding a bloody knife to my injured arm. He dropped it and ran. We didn't see him again for three years."

Jesus Christ. He wanted to gather her in his arms and press his lips to that spot. But he held back because this was about Jazz purging the poison, and her story wasn't over. "What did your parents do?"

Her laugh was bitter. "Brushed it under the rug. Said he must have been high and not acting rationally, but it was so much more than that. I think they were just relieved when he vanished again. The next time he came back, I was sixteen and terrified of him. My parents let him stay for a month and I hid from him as much as possible. He was always watching me with this distrustful gaze. A few times he made comments about the devil, but I never stuck around long enough to hear him out. He cornered me once, but I got away. After that month, he was gone for another year. The pattern continued, where he'd show up then disappear. He cut me a few more times, nothing that required medical attention, but it was always so painful."

She shrugged as though it was no big deal, but Gumby thought he was going to be sick. Her family hadn't protected her. Just let some strung out head case torture her. There had to be more she wasn't telling them. Her recounting was growing too… clinical. What about the daily fear? What about all the nights she had to go to sleep wondering if and when Paul would show up and what state he'd be in.

"The last time I saw him was Memorial Day weekend in twenty-eighteen."

Gumby froze, unable to draw in a breath. Memorial Day weekend. Jesus Christ, the Saturday he'd canceled their date had been two days before Memorial Day.

She flicked a glance in his direction but that was all the indication she gave that the specific date held any other meaning.

Clueless as to the added tension, Screw reached out and grasped Jazz's hands, stopping her from ripping off her thumb nail. "You're going to ruin your nails."

She didn't seem to notice, just barreled on with her story. "I was in my apartment, alone. I didn't even think he knew where I lived. After I moved out of our parents' house at twenty, I made sure I never saw him again, at least not if I was alone. Anyway, that night, there was a knock on my door. I answered without checking the peephole. I thought it was…" Her gaze flicked in his direction before she shook her head. "I thought it was someone else, so I answered without looking. Didn't matter what I thought. I should have checked. I always checked. But that night I made a decision I will forever regret."

She'd thought it was him. Had she thought he'd finished his club business early and decided to surprise her? He'd had the shit beaten out of him countless times as a kid, but nothing compared to the internal pain of her admission.

She took a shuddering breath.

"Do you need to stop?" Screw asked.

Thank God for him. Gumby couldn't speak to save his life.

"No. I just…it's hard to relive. And I've never told the story to anyone. But I need to finish now that I've started." She trembled. "I need to get it out."

As though he could no longer stand the separation, Screw drew her off the coffee table and onto his lap. She struggled for all of two seconds before relaxing against his broad chest.

Gumby turned so he was facing the two of them. They made a beautiful picture. Jazz with her short dark hair, creamy skin. Screw with his longer, brown hair, scruffy face, and tanned skin.

Gorgeous.

Instead of feeling jealous, feeling like Screw was poaching his woman, he felt satisfied seeing them together. It seemed right, but because he was present too. He wrapped his hand around her calf, giving a squeeze in support.

"P-Paul pushed his way into my h-house and just…attacked." She choked out a sob. "S-same thing as always, I was p-possessed. He was the only one who could save me. He shoved me, and I fell. For a moment, I was stunned, and he managed to drag me into my kitchen. As he started to yank my clothes off, I really did think he was going to rape me, but he wasn't remotely interested in that." The words tumbled out one right after another, so fast he almost couldn't make them out.

She blinked, tears coursing down her face. "H-he pulled out a knife, same one he'd used in the past. As soon as I saw it, I nearly passed out, I was so t-terrified. I'll never forget the feeling of being truly paralyzed by my fear. He o-ordered me to get up and sit in one of my kitchen chairs."

Screw's big hand coasted up and down her back. Gumby met his gaze. Rage simmered in his eyes, much the same emotion Gumby was experiencing. Paul was a dead man. Somehow, someway, the man would pay for every mark he put on Jazmine.

"I didn't get off the ground. I couldn't move. Couldn't think. Could barely breathe. My hair was a little longer then, and Paul yanked me up by it, dropping me onto a chair. Before I had a chance to process what was happening, he had my arms and legs tied to the chair with…with this gold ribbon I'd used to decorate Fia and Acer's wedding gift."

Gumby's heart couldn't take much more, yet she hadn't even finished.

"H-he, he cut me. Bad. Deep. So much deeper than ever b-before," she said, choking on the words. "A-and he didn't s-stop. So many times. Over and over." She shook her head back and forth against Screw's chest. "I was screaming." Her voice dropped to a whisper. "Just screaming and screaming. I'd never screamed so much in my life. And Paul just kept repeating, 'I have to save you. I have to save you.' He truly believed he was bleeding some kind of evil spirit out of me." She'd gone from whispered words, to near shouts of hysteria in a few sentences.

"Jesus, Jazz," Screw said. He stopped stroking her back and just held her. "Breathe, baby."

She did as instructed, sucking in a few shuddered breaths before speaking again. "H-he cut my arms, my stomach, my chest, my, my b-breasts," she said, whispering the last part.

A low, deadly growl came from Screw.

With each word from her mouth, Gumby felt the prick of a knife scoring his own skin. The words *your fault* throbbed through his head over and over in time with his pulse.

She wouldn't have been home.

If he hadn't canceled on her, she wouldn't have been home. Wouldn't have been brutalized by a very ill man. He didn't know how she could even stand to look at him, let alone have him under her roof for weeks.

How would he look himself in the mirror, knowing what his actions had caused? He deserved a punishment as bad as what Paul earned.

"How did you get away?" Screw asked, bringing him back to the conversation at hand.

"I'm not, I'm not really sure. Some of the details are hazy. I passed out at some point, probably from the blood loss. There's this murky memory of someone knocking on my door. I'm guessing they heard me scream. I came to on the floor." She shuddered and Gumby would have done anything in that moment to erase those horrifying memories.

They were the kind that never left. The kind that snuck up, wrapped a hand around your throat, and squeezed until the air stopped flowing. The kind that took over, clogging the mind and destroying confidence, relationships…lives. Somehow Jazz hadn't let that happen. Yes, she'd suffered and continued to suffer, but she'd survived and made a life for herself. A life where she was safe, happy, and loved.

"Two things came to me even before the pain registered. And, God, was there pain. I tried to sit up, but my hands slipped on the ground. It was so damn slippery." Her throat rose and fell as she swallowed down what was probably hysteria. "So much blood. The smell hit my nose at the same time I realized what had caused me to lose traction. This metallic, sickening smell I still wake up to in the middle of the night. I kinda freak out at the sight of blood these days." She gave them a sheepish smile.

"Christ," Screw said, his voice thick. The other man blinked as though struggling with his emotions.

Gumby understood. Keeping himself in check took everything he had. But now wasn't the time to make this about him or Screw. Jazz needed to purge the toxicity she'd held onto in silence for so long.

"Did you go to the hospital? I mean…no one heard from you after that day. It was as though you vanished until you sent Lila a text saying you'd left town and didn't want to be contacted."

She flushed as she nodded. "I drove myself to a hospital in the next county."

"Jesus, Jazmine." Gumby pushed off the couch and stalked through the den. As his blood boiled, he turned on her. "Do you know how stupid that was? What if you'd passed out on the road?"

Screw also stood after setting Jazz on the couch. With a much calmer expression, he walked to Gumby. Two strong hands landed on Gumby's shoulders nearly making him shiver at the warmth. "Hey," Screw said. "She's good. She's here. She's strong. Let's let her finish the story."

Shit, he was an asshole. "Yeah, of course. Sorry, Jazzy."

She gave him a weak smile. "You're right. I know that, and if I heard that any of you did the same thing, I'd flip out on you. But I was desperate. Humiliated, scared he'd come back, terrified of what I looked like. I didn't want to risk Lila seeing me in the Emergency Room, so I went elsewhere. I was too ashamed. And two days later when I got out, I stayed in a hotel until my affairs were in order. Then I left."

The thought of her, broken, scared, alone, leaving all she knew behind...

Gumby caught Screw's gaze and the agony there reflected what he felt deep inside.

Something passed between them. A non-verbal agreement, a truce, maybe a cease-fire. Jazz was what was important tonight and neither man would be leaving until she knew what a goddess she was.

Screw walked over to her, gently taking her tear-stained face between his hands. "I'm in fucking awe of you, Jazmine."

She snorted. "You really are crazy."

"No," he said, so serious, Jazz's eyes widened. "I've known you were gorgeous from the moment I laid eyes on you. I knew you were funny the first time you shot a witty comeback at my flirting. I knew you were compassionate when you offered to babysit Beth that time Shell was in a jam. You'd known them for all of two days but jumped right in to help. I knew you were sweet the first time you brought food to the guys at the clubhouse. And I knew you were selfless when I watched you wink at a customer who couldn't pay their bill as you told them it was covered. The moment you turned your back, I watched you dig through your tip money to take care of their check."

None of this surprised Gumby. He'd known for years the kind of person Jazz was. They were all reasons he'd pursued her. Her face was bright red and adorable as she listened to Screw extol her virtues.

"But I had no idea the core of steel that lay beneath this beautiful exterior. And I'm in complete awe of it."

"I'm not beautiful. Not even close. And strong?" Her harsh laugh gutted Gumby. "Don't even go there. I'm so far from strong it's not even funny."

"Bullshit," Gumby growled it out as his anger began to bubble to the surface. "Is that how you see yourself? As ugly and weak? Because if so, the only problem you have is poor eyesight."

Jazz frowned as silent tears streamed from her red rimmed eyes. "It's what I know. Not how I see myself." She looked him straight in the eye and gave him the saddest smile. "I-I haven't been able to look at myself without clothes in a year and a half."

And if that wasn't the most tragic thing he'd ever heard, he didn't know what was.

Chapter Eighteen

Jazz had never felt fatigue like she did just then. This deep, emotional exhaustion that consumed her and made her want to sleep until the memories disappeared.

But they'd never leave her. No matter how hard she wished them away or how long she slept, that horrible night would always be a part of her.

She trembled under the intense gazes of the men she'd just spilled her most private shame to. For so long, she'd feared someone would catch sight of her scars, find out what had happened to her, and she'd be forced to admit the demoralizing tale.

She'd been unprepared for today to be that day, but standing there, the sole focus of Screw and Gumby's attention, she felt a degree of relief among the draining emotions. A small measure. As if the knowledge that she no longer hid a massive secret from the entire world lightened her.

Even though she'd confessed what happened, she hadn't meant to let them know just how deep her body image issues ran. It was one thing for them to know she didn't want others to see her scars, and quite another to learn she couldn't stand the sight of her own body.

Leave it to Screw to pounce on the admission. "What do you mean you haven't looked at yourself?"

With a laugh that sounded forced, she waved away his concern. "Nothing, I was just being dumb."

He cupped her shoulders with his big hands, fingertips digging into the muscles at the base of her neck. Jazz nearly moaned as the knots gave way to his talented massage. Nothing, not even tension was a match for Screw when it came to touch. "It wasn't nothing. It's exactly why you lost it today in the diner."

She tried to avoid his gaze, but he wouldn't allow it, taking her chin in his hand and tipping it up.

"Are you trying to tell me you haven't looked at your body since you were injured?"

If only she could sink through the floor right now.

"Jazz," Gumby breathed. "I'm so…God, I'm so sorry." He sounded as devastated as she felt. As though his insides had been pulverized by a meat grinder. The apology wasn't just for what she went through, but what he perceived as his part in it. The words were so laden with guilt. Her story must have wrecked him especially since she'd alluded to harboring undeserved anger toward him for so long.

Oh, God, why had she opened her big mouth? He was going to blame himself. She shifted her gaze from Screw to Gumby.

The man seemed to have shrunk before her eyes, sinking in on himself with the weight of her account. Why the hell had she blabbed the story? Why now of all times? "Gumby," she whispered.

"Is it true? How is that even possible?" Screw asked, oblivious to the extra reason for Gumby's agony.

With another light laugh she didn't feel, she said, "Guys, it's no big deal. I just avoid mirrors and close my eyes when I'm changing or showering. You'd be amazed at how good I am at blind shaving." She gave them a sunny grin.

When neither man so much as cracked a smile, her bravado deflated.

"Don't play it off, Jazzy," Screw said. "You need to look. You need to see that you haven't been destroyed. That you're beautiful." He cupped the back of her neck. "You can't live your life afraid of your own skin. What about men? What about sex?"

Her damn stomach began to quiver, and her breath felt stunted. She rolled her eyes. "Leave it to you to turn this into a sex thing."

Screw didn't take the bait. The compassion and understanding in his gaze edged too close to pity to be tolerable, so she pulled away and put a few feet of distance between them.

"He's not making it a *sex thing*, Jazzy."

God, now Gumby decided to take Screw's side?

"It's a legitimate concern. Are you going to close yourself off from relationships, from pleasure for the rest of your life?" Gumby reached for her but she stepped back.

"I pleasure myself just fine," she said, placing her hands on her hips. "Not that it's any of your business, but I don't need to stare at a mess of scars to use my vibrator."

She didn't miss the way Screw's nostrils flared and his jaw tightened. "What about comfort? What about connection? What about sharing a life with someone?" he asked.

Jazz's head fell back on her shoulders as a genuine laugh bubbled out of her. "Oh, that's rich. That how you view the future, Screw? Pretty sure you think that's all a load of bullshit. You don't need any of it to get off, so why the fuck would I?"

"Because you're a better person than I am." He got in her face. "Because you deserve what Toni and Shell have. What Izzy and Chloe and Holly have. You deserve it fucking all." His voice rose to a yell, and she fought the urge to run and hide.

"Screw, come on, man." Gumby pulled him back with a hand on his shoulder. It lingered far longer than acceptable before stroking a path down Screw's back. The men shared a look, heated and full of longing. The connection between them took her right back to the scene she'd observed in the bunk room the other night.

She'd much rather focus on that than the mess of her own life. Time for a subject change.

Jazz cocked her head. "You know, I saw you two."

Both men froze, but Gumby's was the only face she saw as Screw had turned his back to her. He cleared his throat. "Saw us?"

"Mm-hmm. At the clubhouse."

Gumby paled.

Screw turned, wide-eyed. "And what is it you think you saw?"

"Your mouth. His cock." She nudged her chin in Gumby's direction before noticing the man looked ready to throw up.

Shit.

Making him uncomfortable wasn't the point here. Was he worried she'd be angry? Jealous? Or worse, was he ashamed of his desires?

A smirk tilted Screw's lips. "Yeah, I sucked his cock. Fucking loved it too. And he's lying if he tells you he didn't fucking love it. Guy came like a geyser."

Even though Gumby appeared ready to bolt, she plowed on. "Saw that too." Jesus, what the hell was wrong with her? There she was again, pushing because she felt cornered, just as she'd done in the diner only this time her words were cutting a man who didn't deserve harshness from her.

"You know this won't work, right?" Screw said, slowly stalking toward her.

She was trapped, pinned by his piercing gaze. "I don't know what you mean," she whispered.

He circled behind her, placing his lips at her ear. "You're trying to shock us. Make us forget what happened to you. It won't work. Look at him." She glanced at Gumby, who now wore a look of understanding, though an underlying current of guilt and maybe even shame still flowed from him.

"He wants you," Screw said. His warm breath tickled the sensitive skin of her ear, making goose bumps erupt all over her skin. "Wants to touch you, taste you, feel you. And so do I."

Her breath hitched. "Oh, my God," she whispered as moisture pooled between her legs. This had to be a dream. How could they want her, knowing what they'd uncover once she was bare to them?

A change came over Gumby. His eyes smoldered and he seemed to grow before her eyes. He appeared to communicate with Screw over her shoulder without words before stalking toward her with a gait that could only be described as a prowl. "He's right," Gumby said. "And this bullshit stops now."

"Wha—"

He grabbed her hand and pulled her down the hall toward her room with Screw hot on her heels.

"Gumby, what the hell are you doing?"

His long legs ate up the distance to her room in no time. To keep from being dragged along, she was practically jogging. When he reached her room, Gumby propelled directly over to the vintage floor mirror that had come with the home. Most of the time a spare bed sheet covered the mirror, but she'd taken it down when Gumby arrived so he wouldn't think she was crazy.

"No, Gumby, no. I can't—"

"Shhh," he said wrapping a long arm around her chest. "Breathe."

She squeezed her eyes shut, shaking her head.

"So you saw us?" he asked.

"W-what? Uh, yes."

Where was Screw? He'd been silent since Gumby started his caveman routine but hadn't been far behind in the hall. Was he also in her bedroom?

"Did you like it?"

What?

"Um..."

He let out a soft chuckle. Warm air tickled her ear. "Well, it sounds like you watched for a while, so I imagine you weren't repulsed."

Christ, had she liked it. She still thought about it at least ten times a day. "N-no. I wasn't repulsed. Surprised, but not repulsed. Never that. You two were…beautiful together."

"Did you wish you were in the room? Had a closer look? Maybe you wished you could touch too. Did you want to be between us, Jazzy?"

Her breath caught in her lungs as her heart began to pound hard enough to make her shirt quiver. Between them? With both sets of hands on her? Both mouths…

Her nipples tightened to near painful points at the thought.

"Jazmine?"

"Y-yes," she whispered, eyes still closed. "I wanted to be between you. I wanted to touch you. Both of you."

A sharp inhale came from in front of her.

Screw.

Her eyes flew open to find him only a few inches from her, gaze like fire as he stared at her mouth.

She was between them.

Holy shit.

"He looked good, didn't he?" Gumby asked. "Sexy as fuck down on his knees with my dick in his throat. Yes?"

Where the hell had this dirty talking man come from?

She whimpered as she nodded, afraid if she opened her mouth, she'd beg one—or worse both—of them to take her.

"Can I tell you a secret?" Gumby asked.

She nodded. Her gaze stayed on Screw as he listened with flared nostrils and blown pupils to Gumby's words.

"Screw may have looked good on his knees, but he felt un-fucking-believable. Sass is not the only talent that mouth has."

As Gumby spoke, Screw lowered himself to his knees so slowly it seemed to take an hour. She couldn't tear her gaze away from the captivating man.

"Do you want to feel him?" Gumby nipped at her earlobe.

Did she want to feel it? She craved it.

"Do you want to feel him right here, between us?"

Holy fuck. Was she about to do this? It was a mistake, that was for damn sure. But her mind was so tired after unburdening her soul, she just didn't have the energy to think of all the reasons she should say no. It would feel so good and she wanted that right now. Screw was right. She missed this, needed it. Physical connection, comfort, pleasure.

"Yes," she whispered. "I want it."

"One condition."

Her gaze met Gumby's in the oblong mirror.

"Eyes stay open the entire time."

The knee jerk reaction to scream, "No," nearly won, but she managed to keep the word in her throat. Just went to show how aroused they'd made her. "I don't know..."

"Trust me, baby, you do not want to miss this because you're worried about a little mirror," Screw said from the floor.

As she peered down at him, he slid the side zipper on her flat ankle boot down.

"Lift."

In a near trance-like state, she did as ordered for one foot then the other. Once her feet were bare, Screw rose to a tall kneel and reached for the zipper of her jeans. One eyebrow arched into his forehead.

She would regret this. No doubt. Screw's serious, caring, almost loving persona would disappear the moment he got his. And a threesome? Sure, the fantasy rocked, but reality had a way of being too...real.

But maybe, even if she woke up tomorrow alone and appalled by her behavior, maybe the pleasure would have been worth it. She'd have memories of feeling cherished, desired...whole.

Only one way to find out.

"Please," she whispered, and Gumby's mouth latched onto her pulse point, sucking until her knees wobbled. She stared into the mirror, trying to take it all in at once. Gumby's mouth on her neck, Screw lowering her jeans over her hips, his longish hair in a sloppy ponytail at the base of his skull. It'd been so long since she'd been touched, and here she was with two sets of hands on her. The sensations bordered on overwhelming and they'd barely even started.

Though for her, what made this moment so powerful was the fact these men held her secrets. She wasn't going to have to hide. Wouldn't need to keep herself covered as she'd always imagined would happen when she gained enough courage to take a lover.

She stepped out of the jeans when asked, and once she was clad in only her silky purple bikini panties, Screw pressed his nose to her mound and inhaled. "Fuck me, you smell good."

Jazz gasped, and Gumby took that moment to grasp her chin, turn her head, and dive into her mouth. His tongue met hers in a hot and possessive kiss that had her head spinning. When he released her, her panties were around her ankles, and Screw was watching them with a look of abject hunger. "I could watch you two make out for hours."

Jazz gazed down at Screw who shifted his attention to the tiny thatch of dark hair between her thighs.

"He's gonna blow your fucking mind," Gumby said. She lifted her gaze back to the mirror in time to see him wink. His lips were swollen from their kiss, eyes glazed and just as hungry as Screw's. "Trust me. I speak from experience."

Jazz's entire body tingled with anticipation. She felt so primed and ready, one flick of Screw's tongue was bound to have her erupting like a volcano. Hopefully, this experience wouldn't burn them all to ash.

Screw and Gumby shared a heated look. What did it mean? So much of this was beyond her control and understanding. She had to either let the storm sweep her up or bow out now before the seas became too rough to navigate.

Screw kissed her right thigh, just above her knee and that light touch alone sent a current of sparks straight to her pussy.

Fuck it.

Jazz spread her legs, kicking her panties off in the process.

With a chuckle, Screw kissed her again, two inches higher than last time. "Someone's getting a little eager."

Gumby laughed along with him. "Well, I did make her some big promises just now."

"Guess I better get to work then."

Their playful banter chased away any lingering doubt.

The moment Screw's teeth grazed her inner thigh, Jazz cried out.

"Fuck, this is gonna be fun," Screw muttered before going in for the kill. He licked a slow, torturous path through her folds, starting near the bottom of her pussy and ending with a swirl around her clit.

Jazz yelped, her head falling back against Gumby's chest. For his part, Gumby ran his hands all over her upper body, outside of her clothes. He never lingered, stroking over her shoulders, stomach, breasts, making her desperate to feel skin on skin.

But did she dare?

No, she couldn't. For all their bold claims of wanting her despite the scars, they'd yet to view the marks on her body. Once they did, there'd be no going back. No unseeing the horror show that was her ruined skin. And there was a very real possibility they could be repulsed.

How could she blame them? She couldn't. Men were visual creatures. The sight of a woman's body turned them on. The display of hers might make them run.

Screw placed a hand on each of her thighs, nudging her legs farther apart. He licked her again, this time groaning when his tongue gathered her wetness.

"How does she taste?" Gumby asked in a near growl.

Screw looked up, and Jazz could have come from the sight alone. The strong, self-confident man, staring up at them from between her spread legs.

Jesus, he was sexy.

As slowly as he'd knelt the first time, he rose, keeping his focus on Gumby. "You tell me," he said when he'd reached full height.

His hand shot out, catching Gumby by the neck before pulling him into the hottest, dirtiest kiss she'd ever witnessed. They ate at each other's mouth with a near animalistic ferocity. And knowing they did so to share her flavor? It was the hottest thing she'd ever conceived, let alone been a part of. If it weren't for the light groans of pleasure coming from both men, she'd worried they were trying to injure each other.

They broke apart, both panting like they'd run there from the clubhouse. Jazz didn't know what to do. Should she say something? Kiss one of them? Both of them. She was so far out of her realm of experience.

None of it mattered when Screw dropped back to his knees.

"Fucking delicious," Gumby said, as he resumed touching her while Screw set about teasing her with flicks of his tongue.

She soaked it all up, fighting to keep her heavy eyes open. Screw squeezed her ass, pulling her even closer to his hungry mouth.

She jolted with a yelp and an, "Oh, my God," as extreme pleasure shot through her. It was then she realized Gumby had slipped his hands under the hem of her long-sleeved shirt. Both his huge palms rested on her abdomen, over the lowermost scars. His fingertips played with the ridged skin beneath them. She knew from right after the attack, when she was forced to clean the wounds, they were two of the smaller ones, but it'd been so long since she peeked, she wasn't sure what they even looked like anymore.

Breathing in a shuddered breath, her gaze met Gumby's in the mirror. With his focus locked on her, he gathered the end of her shirt in his hands, lifting only a couple of inches. Jazz's stomach muscles jumped and clenched beneath his touch.

This was it. The moment she exposed the deep, dark, core of herself to not one, but two men.

"I guarantee neither of us will think you are anything less than beautiful, Jazzy," Screw said from the ground. "It's just not possible."

He kissed her then, straight over her clit, making her sigh in pleasure. The sweet words, which sounded so sincere, bolstered her confidence.

She could do this. If nothing else, it'd be an indicator of how her life would play out. Hiding wasn't her style and yet she'd done it for so long, even from herself.

After blowing out an exhale, she nodded at Gumby in the mirror.

He lifted the shirt slowly, as though she were a wounded animal he worried about startling. Instead of resuming his task, Screw stroked through her drenched folds, rimming her opening before dipping just the tip of his finger in. He repeated the action again and again until she was trembling beneath his touch. In a high kneel position, he was too close to the skin being revealed. Too close to the part of her she hated, but she just couldn't muster the strength to ask him to back off.

Inch by inch, Jazz became more and more exposed. The raised lines scattered all across her stomach came into view. All so ugly she couldn't look. By the time Gumby had the shirt to the underside of her breasts, she was shaking, but no longer in pleasure. In fact, the strangling fear overrode all the pleasure Screw's hand had been wringing from her.

"Wait!" she yelled, grabbing Gumby's hands. "Th-that's high enough. I can't...they're...they have scars," she whispered.

And there, right beneath her shirt, so close to Gumby's hands was the part of her she detested the most. Her breasts had never been big or even average sized, but her nipples had been sensitive, and she'd loved having them touched, pinched, sucked, and generally played with during sex.

Now?

Now she didn't even touch them herself. Paul had cut them, leaving her with scars on the mounds and deformed nipples.

Gumby stopped moving but didn't lower the shirt back down. "Look," he said.

Jazz shook her head keeping her teary eyes focused on his face in the mirror.

"Look, Jazmine. See how strong you are. How beautiful. What a survivor you are. See how your body made itself whole again. See what we see."

How was it possible for them to see all that when all she saw was a damaged mess? A sob broke free, but she bit her lower lip, not allowing any others to escape.

With nausea rising in her gut, she lowered her gaze just in time to see the back of Screw's head move toward her stomach. He blocked most of her view, but she still saw a few raised, light lines. Some were thin, small, and others gnarled, twisted, and much thicker. His lips landed on one of the large ones, applying a light suction. Then he moved on to another, sucking harder this time.

Hard enough to leave a mark.

Her heart clenched so hard, it missed a few beats. He wasn't disgusted. Didn't find her ugly or disfigured. He still wanted his mouth on her.

She wasn't sure she deserved this gift they were giving her, but she planned to hold tight to it with both hands so the memories of feeling beautiful would persist.

On and on Screw went, kissing each and every scar, sucking the biggest ones and replacing what she saw with a love bite. Tomorrow she'd have multiple hickeys on her stomach, something she'd actually want to see.

As he loved on her ruined skin, Screw sank a finger into her pussy. Jazz's head fell back, bumping against Gumby as her eyes fell closed.

He tsked. "Nuh-uh-uh," he said with a chuckle. "You know the rules."

"It's too good."

"I know, baby. Trust me, I know."

She smiled, then cool air wafted across her breasts, stealing her ability to think and driving her to a near panic attack.

"No," she whimpered, grabbing for the shirt.

Gumby pushed her hands down. "Shhh," he whispered. "It's okay. Keep your eyes closed and let me tell you what I see."

Screw circled his thumb over her clit.

God, when he touched her that way, she could barely make sense of up from down. How was she supposed to form a rational argument and fight Gumby on this?

"I see two tits that aren't huge, but they'll fit nicely in my hands." He demonstrated by closing his palms over her breasts and giving a light squeeze. All the while Screw continued worshiping her scars and fingering her.

"Yes, Jazz, your tits have scars like the rest of your torso."

"And m-my nipples?"

"Scarred, baby."

Tears leaked out of the corners of her eyes.

"But I bet..." He brushed his thumbs over her neglected nipples and the unexpected jolt of pleasure was so sharp she shouted. "Yeah, that's right, still so damn responsive."

"Holy shit," she said.

"None of this detracts one bit from how fucking gorgeous you are, Jazmine. Not one of your scars makes me want you any less. And I'm pretty goddammed sure they don't make Screw want you any less either. He's practically fucking drooling. You want a taste of these beauties, don't you, Screw?" he asked as he played with her nipples.

"Fuck yes," he said on an exhale.

"I don't know. Pretty sure you're already in the middle of something down there. Maybe if you're a good boy and finish Jazz off she'll let you suck her gorgeous tits."

Screw growled and Jazz couldn't help it, she giggled. These two had done the impossible. They'd made her smile when she'd been so sure this moment would be fraught with nothing but sorrow, tears, and shame.

It was time. Beyond time.

After a few more seconds, she finally mustered the courage needed to believe their words. Jazz let her eyes flutter open and forced herself to stare straight into the mirror and take in the sight before her.

Even before noticing the scars, her attention was drawn to the two men making her body sing. Gumby's long, tanned fingers stroked all over her naked skin while Screw still worked his finger slowly in and out of her body. Now that the initial fear had worn off, she began to feel the pleasure all over again. Gumby circled his thumbs over her nipples until she was squirming between the men.

He'd been right when he said the scars on her body hadn't diminished their desire for her. Screw's eyes were heavy lidded, his lips swollen and shiny from her arousal, and his muscles bunched with tension. Gumby also looked ready to attack at any moment. There wasn't anything feigned about their responses.

Finally, she shifted her attention to her own body. The scars were…everywhere. Tons of blemishes. Big, small, thin, thick, raised, flat, they were all there in a random scattering across her torso and breasts. More marred her arms, but those remained hidden by her shirt which bunched above her breasts.

The men gave her a moment to study herself, gently stroking her but not driving her toward orgasm. As unconventional as this had been, she couldn't have imagined surviving this any other way. These men took something she feared and made it happen in a way that didn't involve getting drunk and breaking the mirror as she'd often imagined would happen.

To her, the scars were ugly, but knowing that these two men, who could have anyone they wanted, male or female, still desired her went a long way toward rebuilding her shattered confidence. Maybe tomorrow, once alone, she'd feel differently, but for now, she believed them when they said they weren't disgusted. That she was still beautiful. Still desirable as a woman.

"Thank you," she whispered.

"Don't thank us yet," Screw said with a wink. "As Gumby said, I've got a job to get to. Then I'll take all the thanks and praise you want to give me."

With a laugh, she rolled her eyes and shoved his head down.

"Ahh, I see how this is gonna be," he said, before tonguing her clit.

Had she any brain cells left, she'd have quipped some witty remark, but it was impossible with the things he was doing between her legs. After pulling her shirt and bra the rest of the way off, Gumby pinched her nipples, hard this time, making her arch into him with a low moan.

Suddenly, the urge to deepen the connection to these men became a sharp, clawing need she couldn't ignore. She tilted her chin up, offering Gumby her lips and he needed no additional encouragement. He kissed her, sucking her tongue into his mouth as he worked her nipples with agile fingers.

Screw ate her like he was fucking starving, lashing her clit with his tongue before shoving it deep inside her. She could barely process the onslaught of sensations coming from so many parts of her body.

When Screw sucked her clit into his mouth at the same time Gumby twisted her nipples, she cried out into Gumby's mouth and fisted both men's hair. She swore they groaned in unison at the rough tugs on their scalps.

Her legs trembled and her stomach coiled tighter and tighter with each new sensation. Never before had she been so soaked, so needy, so willing to beg for release.

But she didn't need to because Screw's fingers were back inside her—two this time, stroking her toward a hard and fast finish. His other hand squeezed her ass hard enough to leave marks as he held her gyrating hips against his mouth.

"Fuuck," Jazz moaned as electricity fired through all her limbs. "I'm gonna come," she shouted against Gumby's mouth. "Jesus, I'm gonna come so hard."

"Fucking do it," he growled in her ear right before sinking his teeth into her neck as he pulled her nipples. Screw sucked her clit and rubbed furiously over that extra sensitive spot in her pussy.

Jazz screamed as her entire body stiffened then exploded. She shoved her hips forward, drawing any extra sensation she could from Screw's insatiable mouth. She shook and groaned, still fisting both men's hair. Who knew how long it went on before she realized she was practically balding them as she chanted, "Holy shit," again and again?

As the orgasm faded away, leaving her a sated blob, she sagged against Gumby.

Screw rose, going straight for her breasts. He sucked one nipple into his mouth than the next.

"Jesus," she cried. Her entire body felt so sensitive, like a live wire popping and buzzing with energy. With a weak effort, she shoved at Screw's head while he laughed.

Gumby wrapped his arms around her from behind, supporting her limp body. Once fully standing, Screw pressed a chaste kiss to her lips. Her own flavor lingered on his mouth and she couldn't resist reaching out to run her thumb across his swollen lips.

"Kiss him," she whispered.

"Don't have to ask me twice." Screw wound an arm around Gumby, trapping her between them as the two men shared a passionate kiss over her head.

Her sex clenched as though she hadn't just had a monster orgasm.

"Come on," Screw said after the kiss ended. "Let's get some sleep."

Huh?

"Sleep?" she asked. "Really? But what about—"

"We're good, babe. We wanted to take care of you this time."

This time. As though there'd be a next time. Nice thought, but she wouldn't hold her breath. Besides, there were so many questions, so much to talk about. Until a few days ago, she hadn't even known Gumby was attracted to men. Not that it mattered, but…shouldn't she have known?

He gave her a little nudge and she followed Screw toward the bed. As though he belonged, he slid under the covers and scooted to the far edge. "It's just a queen," she said with a laugh. "Not sure we'll all fit."

"Guess we'll have to sleep close," Gumby said in her ear. He gave her a playful slap on the ass. "Come on girl, get that sweet body under the covers before you freeze."

"Let me just put something on."

"Fuck no," Screw said. "Get in here."

She stared at the bed for a moment before shrugging and climbing in, naked.

Turning, she watched Gumby slip in next to her. Screw wrapped a muscled forearm around her waist and pulled her flush against him. Gumby wiggled close, pressing up against her front.

Sleep would never come. Not after such an emotionally charged afternoon. But perhaps she could find a measure of peace for a few hours, tucked between the two men who'd gotten her to finally share her story.

Though shaken by both confessing her darkest secret and the intensity of the physical encounter, her soul felt…different. Lighter, maybe. The acceptance they showed her of the story and her scarred body provided a balm to her aching psyche.

When it came down to it, being shunned for the way she looked proved to be the greatest fear. Though solitude, keeping herself covered, and avoiding relationships gave her control over her isolation, she still faced the same end result. Revealing herself to a man who had the power to crush her with rejection robbed her of her power. So, she'd lived in self-imposed relationship exile. But they'd accepted her. More than that, they'd wanted her, desired her sexually, and had given her indescribable pleasure. For the first time in ages, confidence filled her.

Was this a one off or would it happen again? And did she even want it to happen again? Screw certainly wasn't known for sticking around, so the smart thing would be to expect nothing and if she was gifted another experience like this one, take it and revel in it. And if she woke alone in the bed, the knowledge that for a little while they'd truly wanted her would have to be enough.

God, it felt perfect surrounded by the two men who'd been stuck in her head these past few weeks.

Warmth from the two strong male bodies blanketing her seeped into her bones. Strength too. Along with someone's intoxicating cologne. In a matter of seconds, her eyelids grew heavy and she was pulled into the lull of sleep.

Too bad perfection was nothing more than a beautiful illusion.

Chapter Nineteen

The moment Screw opened his eyes, events of the afternoon came rushing back like he'd been hit with a fire hose spray. His body, especially the part that had gone to bed hard and aching, wanted to recall the most erotic encounter of his life, but his brain couldn't shake the horrifying ordeal Jazz had been through.

The scars…Christ, the scars. So fucking many of them. He hadn't been lying, and didn't think Gumby had either; the scars didn't detract from how much he wanted her. Wanted to touch her, taste her, fuck her silly. But they fired a rage in his gut like never before. Those marks were a constant physical reminder that she'd suffered unimaginable pain at the hand of someone who should have loved her and wanted to protect her.

Paul would pay for what he did to Jazz. Screw vowed that down to the very core of his being. Perhaps he should be more sensitive to the man's unstable mental state, and maybe empathy would come later, but right then with Jazz's dried tears on his skin, he wanted nothing more than to fuck the guy up in the worst way.

Running a hand down his face, he glanced to his left where Jazz lay, curled up on her side, facing him. Her features had relaxed in sleep, giving her a peaceful appearance.

In a matter of weeks his life had gone away from carefree hookups—and a fuckton of them—easy living in the MC, and little responsibility over heavy shit he wasn't prepared to handle. Keeping his head in the game and not falling back on flippant habits sucked, but now he had serious shit in his life he couldn't avoid. Jazz, Gumby, his position as enforcer, the Chrome Disciples. From one extreme to the other.

Would he drown under the weight of responsibility? Would he fail in a spectacular way, letting down everyone important in his life?

Would someone suffer because of his inadequacies?

Fuck, one issue at a time.

The usual urge to run from the bed hadn't hit him yet. In fact, all he wanted was to wrap his arms around Jazz and continue sleeping until morning. A glance at the clock on a nightstand adjacent to the bed let him know it was only eight in the evening. They'd slept for quite a few hours, but there were still many more until the sun came up again.

Enough to wake his bedmates for a *real* threesome.

With a sigh, he forced himself to roll to his back. He should leave. It's what they'd both expect of him, so there shouldn't be any hard feelings. He peeled himself off the bed. After taking a few seconds to convince himself this was the right decision, he rose.

Jazz shifted and murmured in her sleep, which had him smiling. As he turned to get one final look at her soft and sated form, he frowned.

They were the only two in the bed.

Where had Gumby gone?

And when had he left?

Screw padded out of the room and down the hallway. A quick peek in the empty guest room had his frown deepening. Had Gumby left the house?

Would he do that? Seemed like quite the dick move for a guy so interested in Jazz.

Hello pot, may I introduce you to my pal, kettle?

Fuck.

Just as he was about to search for his boots, movement from the front porch caught his eyes. Was someone sitting on the loveseat? What the fuck? It couldn't be more than forty degrees outside.

Boots abandoned, he shoved the front door open and stepped outside onto the lit porch. Immediately, bitter cold assaulted his uncovered arms and the freezing concrete beneath his bare toes had him wanting to hop around on alternating feet.

Gumby sat on Jazz's whicker loveseat with a Sherpa blanket wrapped around his shoulders. His hair stuck up all over the place from sleep and, like Screw, he wore what he'd fallen asleep in, jeans and a Henley. The glasses that gave him such a Clark Kent look were absent. He didn't even flinch as Screw came outside, instead sat staring into distance, lost in his head.

"Hey, man," Screw said, rubbing his chilled arms. "Jesus, it's colder than Elsa's twat out here."

"Who?" Gumby asked not taking his attention away from whatever his gaze had latched onto.

"Elsa." Damn, thirty seconds was too long to be out dressed as he was. With the state Gumby appeared to be in, sharing the blanket was probably out of the question.

"Yeah, I heard you. Who the fuck is Elsa?" He shifted, pulling the fabric tighter around his shapely shoulders.

Really? Was there a person alive who didn't know Elsa? "You know, the queen from Frozen. Has that ice power and shit."

"Frozen?" Gumby finally turned toward him, a ghost of a smile tilting his lips.

Mission accomplished.

"As in the animated movie?"

Screw shuffled closer, resting his back on a column opposite Gumby's chair. "That's the one. Can't believe it took you this long to catch on."

Gumby snorted. "Sorry I'm not up on my Disney princesses."

With a laugh, Screw said, "You will be. Give Beth another week and you'll know all their names, ages, birthdays, cup sizes —"

"Cup sizes?" Gumby said with a raised eyebrow.

"Okay, maybe I researched those on my own." He shrugged. "Sue me."

Gumby chuckled, then fell silent.

"So what has you out here in the dead of night freezing your balls off? You thinking about Jazz's story?"

"You could say that."

Hmm, something was off. His tone too flat, lifeless, guilt ridden. Fuck. He hadn't even thought twice about kissing Gumby multiple times during their encounter with Jazz. That what had the guy freaking out? Clearly Gumby had reservations about admitting his attraction to men. Was he out to anyone? His own club?

Well, if he hadn't been, he was now, to at least two people.

"You wanna share what's goin' on in that dome of yours, or you hoping my dick'll freeze so you can break it off."

No response.

With a sigh, Screw nudged Gumby's foot with his own. The thing felt like a block of ice. How long had he been out in the cold? "Hey."

Gumby shifted his gaze.

"We can play this however you want. However you need. Okay? I'm not gonna run to the clubhouse and start spreading our private shit around. You want this to stay on the down low, I can do that." He gestured between them with his hand before tucking the cold appendage into his armpit.

"Fuck," Gumby said as he leaned forward to rest his elbows on his thighs. "Haven't even gotten that far in my freak-out yet. But don't worry, I'll get there."

After huffing out a small laugh, Screw tilted his head and waited. With each passing second, his body grew number, except his toes. They burned like fucking fire.

Eventually, without making eye contact, Gumby said, "We had a date." It sounded as though those four simple words had sliced his insides as he spoke them.

"What?" Screw frowned. "Who? When?"

"Me and Jazz. We were supposed to go out. First time alone. Fuck, I'd been looking forward to it. For fucking weeks. But some shit came up with the club." He shrugged and he finally looked at Screw.

The self-hatred in his eyes had Screw's insides clenching.

"You know how it is. Club comes first. Especially over someone who isn't an ol' lady. I had to cancel on her. She didn't get pissed though. Jazz doesn't do drama like that. We said we'd pick another day." He fell silent again as he shook his head.

Dread began to twist Screw's stomach in a large knot. "When was your date, Gumby?"

So much time passed, he wondered if the other man had heard him but then Gumby said, "The Saturday of Memorial Day weekend. Twenty-eighteen."

Jesus Christ, it was as though he'd been punched in the gut. All the air whooshed out of Screw, leaving him weak-kneed and shaking. Fuck, the guilt of that would be enough to destroy anyone. Add it to confronting his sexuality, and Gumby had a lot of shit on his plate.

"Gumby, you have to know…"

Gumby lifted a hand. "Don't say it, Screw. Don't say it's not my fault. She wasn't supposed to be home. There's only one reason she was home, and it's me. She even told me she struggled with my part in it. She told me something happened that weekend and for a while she was mad at me."

"Gumby, she was scared, hurt, traumatized. What happened once she had some distance? Does she still harbor ill feelings toward you?"

He shrugged.

"Pretty sure she wouldn't have let you get your hands all over her tits tonight if she had a problem with you."

"Doesn't matter if she forgives me. Doesn't mean I didn't fuck up, Screw."

With frustration rumbling through his chest, Screw pushed off the column. When he reached Gumby, he threaded his hand through the man's short hair, catching the strands in a hard grip before tilting his head back to ensure Gumby's focus. The pain and self-hatred in Gumby's eyes gutted him. This man fully blamed himself for Jazz's trauma.

An overwhelming urge to comfort this hurting man swamped Screw. He was so far out of his element here, being the one to ease another's burdens. Gumby had obviously stepped out of his comfort zone to be with him and Jazz tonight. Screw wanted to give the man something in return. Something to prove he wasn't just an asshole out for a good time. Something to show he cared. "It's Luke," Screw said with a growl, giving the name no one but his president even knew. "Say it."

"Luke..."

It wasn't quite the sexual plea he'd been hoping for, but fuck if the name didn't roll off Gumby's tongue straight to Screw's dick. "Listen to me and listen fucking good," he said, giving Gumby's head a light shake. "You fucking know this ain't your fault. If you've been with your MC for any amount of time, you know shit happens. Bad fucking shit we could 'what if' and 'if only' for the rest of our lives. Playing those games doesn't do shit for Jazz. She doesn't need the stress of making you feel guilty on top of all she's dealing with. So take another minute to feel how you need to feel then put it away. It ends right fucking now because it's not your goddamn fault she has a psychotic and strung out brother who never received the help he needed. Get me?"

By the time he finished his tirade, his chest was heaving, he no longer noticed the freezing temperature, and he practically shouted the words. Oh, and his dick was harder than a fucking spike.

With a single nod, Gumby said, "Yeah, I get you."

"Good." Now that the lecture had ended, what remained was Screw's tight grip on Gumby's hair, their faces inches apart, and one—he glanced at Gumby's lap—two hard cocks. Neither had come earlier in the evening, and while he'd loved giving Jazz the attention, he'd been left with one helluva case of blue balls. Gumby didn't seem to be faring much better.

"What the fuck do you do to me?" Gumby asked, voice strained as though he knew resisting would be a wasted effort but hadn't quit yet.

"Hopefully, I get you off, fucking hard."

A grunt was the only response.

Screw released Gumby's hair then positioned himself in front of the other man. With their gazes locked, Screw slowly undid his belt. Then the button on his jeans. And the zipper. When he started to lower it, Gumby tracked the move like a hawk. It was too fucking cold to get naked and Screw wasn't about to risk the moment by suggesting they relocate inside, so he just pulled his swollen shaft out of his black briefs.

Gumby licked his lips and Screw swore he felt that fucking tongue on his sensitive skin. "Jesus," he whispered. "You may not know what the fuck I do to you, but I know you make me fucking crazy. Take yourself out."

Glancing around into the quiet night, Gumby hesitated.

"Do it," Screw barked. If he didn't get off and get Gumby off in the next few minutes he was going to self-destruct.

Gumby's eyes flared at the order. Hmm, looked like the other biker on the porch enjoyed being bossed around a little.

File that under *Useful Info*.

Yes, he was pushing Gumby out of his comfort zone and maybe that made him an ass, but he had no patience for closeted hookups. Hiding his sexuality had never been a thing for Screw. If it felt good, he did it. Why the fuck not? He got one go around on earth and didn't plan to waste the time worrying over whether others approved of his sexual practices or not. Basically, he was game to try anything once, and if it felt good, he'd add it to his bag of tricks. More than one of his male partners had been surprised when he'd asked them to fuck him, assuming his whole alpha biker persona would make him a strict top.

Stupid assumption. Getting nailed in the prostate felt fucking amazing. One of the best things in life. Why the hell wouldn't he want it as often as he could get it?

He couldn't tear his gaze away from the sight of Gumby unveiling his dick. The man did basically the same maneuver Screw had done, making only enough room to free himself from the tight confines of his navy boxer briefs. Access to their cocks was all Screw needed. They wouldn't fuck tonight. Not here on Jazz's porch while she snoozed away inside. No, the first time they fucked she'd be present, right there with them, maybe between them.

Guess that confirmed he wasn't ready to leave.

Fuck, getting any further involved with these two would be a huge mistake. Jazz would end up hurt when Screw inevitably bailed. He didn't do fucking feelings and Jazz would want that at some point.

But she'd have Gumby to catch her when Screw let her go. Maybe this could work. Could be the best of all worlds. For a little while, he'd play their third. Have some fun. Fuck. Then, once emotions crept in, he'd jump ship leaving Jazz and Gumby to the relationship garbage.

If it was so easy, why did the idea of his two lovers comforting each other in his absence make him want to spit nails?

"Hey," Gumby said. "Where'd you go?"

Screw blinked then shot Gumby his patented sassy grin. "Nowhere. But I'm about to climb onto your lap."

Gumby moved his hands aside. "By all means."

Once again, Screw sifted his fingers through the other man's hair. Gumby's eyes fluttered closed as a groan left his lips, but they popped back open when Screw gave a firm tug on the short strands.

One at a time, Screw brought his knees up on the bench, on either side of Gumby. As he settled in, their dicks bumped, and sharp pleasure zapped him.

"Fuck," Gumby said through clenched teeth.

"Yeah." It'd been a while since he'd been with a man, and Screw had nearly forgotten how damn good it felt to rub his cock against another one.

"You gonna jerk us off?" Gumby asked, his breathing growing erratic.

"Nuh-uh. You are," Screw said before nipping Gumby's lower lip. His lover reacted as he'd hoped and fused their mouths together. Just as their kiss earlier had been, this was animalist in its intensity. They fought for dominance, for control, for anything to increase the pleasure. Every stroke of Gumby's tongue against his might as well have been against his cock with the way it drove him higher.

Was it a test? Maybe. Perhaps Screw needed to know Gumby was willing to touch him, pleasure him, be as lost in the wanting as he was. Because if Gumby couldn't even fist their cocks, then it was over before it started. Gumby could pretend to the rest of the world that he didn't like dick, but he sure as fuck would admit it to Screw.

Within seconds, Screw was so desperate for release, he found himself grinding down on Gumby's length to increase the friction. When the other man broke the kiss to let out a tortured groan, Screw said, "Wrap your hand around us. Jack us, Gumby, before I fucking die."

"Christ, Luke…"

His name at that moment nearly brought the entire scene to an explosive and premature finish. Holy shit, who would have known hearing his given name could be such a fucking turn-on?

Gumby brought his hand to his mouth and spit before bringing it down between their bodies. Why that act was so hot, Screw might never know. Maybe because it was so raw, primal, carnal. A product of their impatience and unwillingness to run inside and grab the packet of lube Screw had in his jacket pocket.

Gumby's wet hand curled around them. Both cocks fit perfectly in the cradle made by those long fingers. He wasted no time giving a firm tug to their aligned cocks.

Screw's head fell back on his shoulders. "Jesus," he whispered.

"You approve?" Gumby asked, humor in his ragged voice.

"Fuck yes. Give me more. Work us, Gumby." He bracketed Gumby with his hands holding the top of the bench on either side of his head.

With a little rumble in his chest, Gumby started to stroke them in earnest. As his fist coasted up and down their cocks, Screw kissed him, fighting to keep his eyes from crossing at the power of the pleasure.

They alternated between wild, unrestrained kisses and breaks filled with groans and curses. Gumby's strokes sped up, calluses rasping over their tender skin in a way that had Screw thrusting into the man's hand as he sought even more contact.

"Goddamnit, I'm gonna fucking come," Gumby said as he began to ease up on the pressure.

"Don't you fucking stop," Screw warned. "I'm right there with you." He closed his hand over Gumby's, increasing the pressure to near strangling as he rocked back and forth in their grip.

They strained against each other, hands flying over their cocks as they humped into their joined fists.

"Now, now, now," Screw yelled. "Fucking give it to me."

The muscles in Gumby's neck corded as his head fell back on his shoulders. He let out a horse shout then warm liquid spilled over their hands. The sensation was all Screw needed to propel him into an orgasm so powerful his vision blurred. "Fuck!" he yelled, coating their fingers with even more cum.

It took a few moments for the tremors to cease, but when they did, Screw once again became aware of the cold. Might have had something to do with the cooling cum all over them.

"Shit, Luke," Gumby said as he ran his clean hand through his hair. "That was…"

"Yeah." He paused as they took a second to stare at each other then said, "I like it when you call me that."

The almost shy smile Gumby gave him had him chuckling.

"You gonna blush, biker?"

"Nah. Don't think it's possible after that." Gumby grabbed the blanket he'd been enveloped in. The one that slid from his shoulders the moment Screw climbed in his lap. With a serious expression, he used the covering to clean both their sticky hands. "We probably need to talk about all this with Jazz."

Blowing out a breath, Screw nodded. "Yeah. You know if she's working tomorrow?"

With his own nod, Gumby said, "She is. All day. Maybe tomorrow night we can meet here. Grab a pizza, have some beer, and just chill."

Fuck that sounded domestic. But it also sounded…nice. A night to just hang with the two people who turned him on the most and whose company he actually enjoyed. There were worse ways to pass an evening.

"Sur—aw, fuck, I can't tomorrow. I've got a…thing I gotta take care of."

"Club shit?"

Screw turned his head, gazing at Jeremy's dark house. The guy was bound to pop over with questions after the way they gave him the supreme brush off earlier. "Something like that."

He must have done a shitty job of keeping the guilt out of his voice because Gumby said, "What the fuck's going on, Luke?"

Damn him for using Screw's true name. Made it seem more than a hookup. His own damn fault for giving the name to Gumby in a weak and sex-crazed moment.

"This have anything to do with what Copper was ranting at you about the other day?"

Fuck. Sharing club business wasn't allowed, Gumby would know that, but since he already planned to break the rules…

Fuck it. He trusted Gumby. Stupid perhaps, but true.

"I got invited to a party at the Chrome Disciples clubhouse tomorrow night."

Wide-eyed, Gumby straightened. "What the fuck? That's the club Jazz and I ran into at the gas station, right? The fuckers who almost kidnapped your president's ol' lady."

Screw raised an eyebrow. "You've been paying attention."

"This shit affects Jazz. Fuck yeah, I'm paying attention. Don't tell me you're thinking of going against Copper's wishes."

"Fair enough. Look, they don't know who I am. I ran into a prospect and chatted him up. He thinks I'm some businessman who has a hard-on for bikes. Guy told me about the party. This is the perfect fucking way to get inside and see what the fuck their operation is, how big they are, how serious they are about fucking our shit up."

"And Copper shot you down."

"Copper blew me out of the fucking sky."

Stroking his face, which looked like it hadn't been shaven in a day or two, Gumby stared Screw straight in the eye. "You're going anyway?"

"Thinking about it." He ran his hand over the enticing stubble. Rough against his palm, he'd love to feel it on the ultra-sensitive skin of his balls. Too bad that would probably never happen. Usually men who were terrified to admit they liked cock weren't sucking it every other day.

"Fuck."

"You ain't gonna try to talk me out of it?" He gave Gumby a half smile.

Gumby shook his head with a smirk. "Pretty sure it wouldn't do any good. Besides, I agree with you. It's your club's best chance at getting some serious intel."

"Okay, so you'll keep Jazz company tomorrow?"

He shook his head. "Actually, she's got a thing with her girls. I forgot about it when I made the offer to hang."

Excellent, that would keep him off her radar. "Good, that's good. Just make sure you get her there and take her home."

Another headshake. "They're meeting here. And I'm coming with you, so we'll need to make sure the girls are covered by your club."

"What? No, Gumby—"

He lifted a hand. "Shut the fuck up, Screw. No way in hell are you walking into enemy territory on your own and without the backing of your club. Have you considered you might be walking into a trap?"

There they were talking while he sat on Gumby's lap, their dicks still out, lying limp and sated between them. The scene was entirely too comfortable, entirely too…relationshipy. If Screw hadn't known better, he'd have thought Gumby actually cared about him. "Of course I've considered it's a trap. We need to move on these guys before they get another chance to fuck with us, so it's a risk I'm willing to take."

Gumby's chest rose and fell as he sighed. Too bad it was winter and freezing. Screw would have loved to peel Gumby out of his clothing and lick the man all over. All those long, lean, ropy muscles.

"Then it's a risk we take together."

"Why? This isn't your club. Isn't your problem. I know you care about Jazz, but—."

"This isn't just about Jazz. It's about you, Luke. *You* need someone at your back. You know it. Don't be stupid. Let me be that man. I mean, let me be your backup at the party. Two sets of eyes are always better than one," he rushed on, but it was too late, Screw hadn't missed the emotion in Gumby's voice.

Let me be that man.

The words touched a part of Screw he kept hidden under a heavy pile of jokes and sarcasm. Just when he needed that part of himself the most, to keep from letting Gumby's words worm their way into his heart, it failed him. Instead of making some shitty comment, he fucking kissed Gumby.

"Couldn't think of a better man for the job."

Chapter Twenty

Gumby navigated the increasingly familiar roads, racking his brain for something to say. Unfortunately, all he could do was recall the two mind-blowing sexual encounters of the previous night, and it certainly wasn't the time for that discussion. He didn't even know how he felt about what happened between the three of them and then between him and Screw on the porch. Shit, just the memory of it had him at half chub. Clearly his body knew where it stood. His brain on the other hand...yeah, a big fucking mess.

Then there was his heart. The damn confounding organ that had suffered with each word of Jazz's story only to be soothed and mended by Screw. Now, his heart clenched with a warm yet terrifying feeling whenever he thought of either of his two lovers.

Not the time.

Instead of coming up with anything profound to break the tension, he risked a quick glance at the man seated beside him in the cab of the truck. Though the truck belonged to Screw, one glance at the man when he'd arrived had been all it took for Gumby to realize he'd need to drive.

Screw was...antsy to say the least.

After another few minutes of maddening silence, he pulled over to the side of the darkened road. They had another three miles to go until they reached their destination.

"Hey," he said.

Screw blinked and swiveled toward Gumby. "Huh? Why'd we stop? Something wrong with the truck?"

Wow, he really had been out of it. "Nah, just checking in. You seem…" How to say it without offending the man or sounding like a concerned boyfriend.

Which he was not and never would be.

"Seem what?"

"Off." Gumby shrugged.

Screw looked smokin' hot in dark black jeans, a nicer quality than he seemed to typically sport, and a charcoal Henley. No leather, chains, or rings. The outfit hovered somewhere between biker and plain casual. Perfect to portray the persona of someone curious about the MC culture but not quite part of the in crowd. Gumby had dressed similarly in dark wash denim and a simple black T-shirt. Biker boots completed both of their looks.

"Just getting my head in the game."

"Nah, it's more than that. You're…"

Screw raised an eyebrow as though daring Gumby to insult him.

"I don't know you well, but you're a big personality. Always laughing, joking…inappropriate. Tonight, you're just…" He lifted a hand from the wheel with a shrug.

"Oh, well, that's clear as fucking mud. You're real smooth with the words. If I were fucking you right now, we wouldn't even need lube, you're so fucking slick."

Shit, the thought of being pinned down while Screw fucked him had him clenching the steering wheel until his knuckles whitened. He'd never gone there before but couldn't deny the interest.

"There you are," Gumby said with a smirk. "Nice of you to finally join me, but how about you get real and tell me what's fucking your head up."

Screw grunted. "You complain I'm too serious and now you're saying I'm too much of a smartass. Make up your goddamned mind."

"I don't want to make up my mind so you can act like you think I want you to act."

"So what the fuck do you want?" Screw slammed his hands on the dashboard then left them there as his head dropped to meet them.

"I guess I want you, the real you to tell me what's going on in your head. We're taking a risk tonight. I'm here, and I've got your back. I need to know you've got mine too, cuz if shit goes south…"

If shit went south, they were fucked, and not in the way he'd been fantasizing about seconds ago. In a shit-they're-going-to-pull-out-my-toenails kinda way.

"So, you can't admit you want me, even when your dick is in my mouth, but you want me to spill my guts to you?" Screw spat the accusation across the interior of the truck.

Was this fucker for real? Gumby shifted the car into drive. Here he was risking his ass to back Screw up and the bastard wanted to talk about why Gumby didn't look in his eyes while Screw was blowing him. "You know what? Fuck you, Screw."

Before he could take his hand off the gear shift, Screw's closed over it. Though the other man stared straight out the windshield, Gumby knew where his attention lay. With a sigh, he shoved the car into park.

Screw removed his hand, still looking out into the dark night. "My mom was a stripper. Sometimes a whore when money was tight. We grew up not far from here in a town even smaller than Townsend. Her strip club was a real seedy joint. Fucking sad-ass, has been strippers with droopy tits and drug habits. Velvet carpets probably loaded with cum from years of nasty fuckers jacking off right there in the bar. Shit lighting, shittier acoustics."

As his heart clenched for the difficult childhood Screw must have endured, he nodded. "I know the type."

"Yeah. Well, the bouncer was the uncle of a kid I went to high school with. By the time we were thirteen, he was letting the fucker and his buddies sneak in the back and watch the shows. Made my life at school…uncomfortable."

Having kids at school know what your mother looked like naked and shakin' her tits on stage? Yeah that'd make life for a high school boy difficult. Add in the fact said boy was bisexual, and Screw musta had a time of it.

"Fuck," Gumby said.

His passenger huffed out a laugh then finally turned his head, looking straight at Gumby. "I was into boys and girls with a mom giving lap dances to my classmates. Yeah, it fucking sucked." He shrugged as though it hadn't shaped his entire adult life. "But I survived it."

Tilting his head, Gumby said, "By never letting anyone think you took shit seriously. By making them think it wasn't possible to get to you."

With a nod, Screw chuckled. "I was such a shit. Pranks, mouthing off to everyone, even more of a smart ass than I am now. I dedicated my teenage years to not giving a fuck and making everyone laugh with my outrageous behavior."

"Screwball," Gumby said as the meaning behind the name became obvious.

Another nod. "My mom's favorite thing to call me when she was pissed over my antics."

An unexplainable urge to pull Screw into his arms and tell him he got it formed in Gumby. His own childhood was just as nightmarish. Maybe even more so. Though their response to their tortured teenage years differed, Gumby knew what it was to hide as well. He'd hidden his sexuality his entire life. Fuck, he still hid as Screw did behind his gags.

Self-preservation was a powerful motivator.

"I get it. It makes a lot of sense, Screw. Why tell me now?"

"Copper made me enforcer." He ran a hand across his mouth. Gumby didn't mention how he noticed the quiver in those fingers. Screw's vulnerability was a gift he most likely didn't give to anyone, so Gumby would treat that gift with respect.

"He placed his trust in me to keep the club safe. It's more responsibility than I've ever had. More than I've ever wanted. A side effect of never taking anything seriously is that no one ever took *me* seriously. I've coasted through life fucking anything that walks and having a blast doing it."

Another piece of the puzzle fit into place. A large piece. Gumby would be lying if he said what he was learning didn't make him want Screw even more. "And now you have a very heavy weight on your shoulders." So much made sense now. Why he hid behind jokes and tricks. Why he always appeared to be playing.

"Yes," he said giving a solemn nod. "And for the first time, I want it. I want to prove to my president and my brothers that I'm worthy of their trust and their brotherhood."

"Screw…"

"But I'm scared as fuck."

Five little words was all it took for Gumby to forgive every sin the man had committed. He'd bet money on the fact the man had never admitted that to anyone, never opened himself up to another person. And Screw had chosen him.

Why?

They fell silent for a moment until Gumby reached out and threaded his fingers though Screw's. It was the first time he'd willingly touched the man outside of their sexual encounters and instead of bringing fear and panic, it felt…right to comfort the aching man. "What are you scared of, Luke?"

The anguish in Screw's eyes had him holding his breath. "Being nothing more than what everyone thinks I am. A fuckup.

A joke. Even though I made my own bed, I'm fucking terrified I'll be lying in it for the rest of my life."

Now it made sense, why he was willing to risk his president's wrath to get the inside scoop on the Chrome Disciples. The new enforcer had something to prove. Or at least he thought he did. Hopefully, Gumby could help him realize he didn't need to save his entire club by himself to be more than valuable to his brothers.

"I don't think you're a joke."

Screw snorted and rolled his eyes but didn't extradite his hand.

Gumby gave him a squeeze. "I'm serious. Last night…you were exactly what Jazz needed." Their gazes locked. "You were exactly what I needed."

Electricity crackled between them as Screw's gaze morphed from cold and aloof to heated desire. But this wasn't the time or the place, and Gumby had already leapt so far out of his comfort zone he feared he might never find his way back again. Another physical encounter would only fuck with his head further.

"You have good instincts, and I trust them. I wouldn't be here now if I didn't. You need to trust them too. But you also need to remember the title of Enforcer doesn't make you an island. You want to be worthy of the brotherhood you need to trust in the brotherhood as much as they trust in you."

The only response Gumby received was a silent nod before Screw faced front again, but he didn't sweat it. The other man clearly needed a few minutes to process. And he could have it.

After shifting the truck into drive, Gumby pulled out onto the single lane highway. Another mile into the trip, a quiet, "Thank you," came from Screw.

"I meant it. So…how we gonna play this? We'll be pulling up in under five."

"I filled you in on my encounter with the CDMC's prospect, Squirt, right?"

With a nod, Gumby navigated a particularly sharp mountain curve. "Yeah, you told him you live in Knoxville and have a cabin out here to escape the city sometimes. You're a bike freak but never been in an MC. You don't know shit about the Handlers beyond their reputation."

"Right. So we're playing it as two weekend warriors from Knoxville. Interested in club life but not quite built for it." He shrugged and scratched at his beard. "I thought about pushing it and seeing if I could prospect, but it's too fucking risky. Tonight's gonna be dicey enough. I'm just hoping to find some loose lipped idiot who'll blab something about their weapons trafficking or their plans for my club."

Pushing his glasses up his nose, Gumby said, "We sticking together or splitting up?"

"Might have better luck if we're not joined at the hip but try to remain within line of sight in case shit hits the fan."

"Don't fucking laugh, but we might want some kinda code word. You know, in case we're near each other and you hear something that makes us need to haul ass outta there. Can't just grab me and scream run. Little too obvious."

With a chuckle that had a nervous quiver to it, Screw rubbed his beard again. "Not used to this thing yet. It's itchy as fuck sometimes. All right, that sounds all Hollywood spy thriller, but not a bad thought. Any ideas?"

Well, besides a love of motorcycles and apparently each other's dicks, what the hell did they have in common?

"Jazz?" They both said at the same time.

With a snicker, Screw said, "Jazz it is."

After instructing them to make a left, the GPS announced they'd reached their destination. Gumby followed the vehicle in front of him, steering Screw's truck through an open gate in a high chain-link fence which surrounded the property. Coiled at the top, what he guessed to be razor-sharp, barbed wire ran the length of the fence. Aside from that, security appeared pretty lax.

No guard at the gate.

Minimal outdoor lighting.

Zippo as far as cameras, at least along the fencing.

Good for them, fucking sucked for women attending these parties. It was a fucking predator's dream.

"They got shit for security," Screw said, craning his neck as they drove through the gate. Another car followed directly behind them.

"Just thinking the same thing." Gumby turned right, then backed into a spot with easy access to the exit.

"Looks like a small warehouse, maybe what? Twenty years old?" Screw's gaze raked over the building that had become the CDMC's clubhouse.

"Yeah. Sounds about right. Look, there's one guy at the door there. Fucking behemoth."

Screw followed Gumby's gaze. "Shit yeah, he might even have LJ beat. Big motherfucker. But I don't see anyone else and who knows if he'll stay there all night. Bet he gets bored and comes in to party."

"You're probably right. They seem unconcerned with security." He pushed his glasses up his nose, catching Screw's grin from the corner of his eye. "What?"

"Nothing." Screw shrugged "The glasses are hot. Anyway, not sure if they're arrogant assholes, just haven't gotten to it yet, or if they're convinced my club won't come after them."

Gumby blinked at the offhand compliment before glancing out his window. "Probably a bit of all three. That can't be the only door. Priority one is to locate all the exits when we get in."

"Agreed. You ready?" Screw asked as he tied his loose hair in a knot at the base of his skull.

Gumby looked at the man sitting beside him. The brave man who cared so deeply about his club yet had no idea how to handle that, or most of his emotions. The urge to kiss him rose so quick and sharp in Gumby, he almost couldn't deny it, but the last thing they needed was to be seen making out in the parking lot. Not all clubs were as accepting of anything beyond heterosexuality as Screw's.

"Let's do it." Prior to leaving for this party, they'd hung at the Handlers' clubhouse until it was time to make their way here. Then, they'd begged off claiming hunger. Right now, Screw's entire club believed they were out grabbing a pizza. Not a soul knew they were walking into enemy territory, unarmed and unprotected. Yes, they had a few weapons in the truck, but if shit went south, they'd have to make it to the vehicle to have any chance of fighting their way out.

A few others made their way toward the warehouse turned clubhouse as well. Mostly women, teetering on stilts with skirts barely covering their asses and tit-revealing tops. They must be cold as fuck. Ahead of them, a guy wearing a CDMC cut was waved through the door with an obvious pistol resting at the small of this back. Right behind him, the women were patted down with heavy groping hands.

They giggled and shimmied under the touch, seeming unaffected by the 'accidental' grabs of their tits and asses.

"So that's how it's gonna be," Screw muttered under his breath as they waited for their turn to be frisked. "Bet every goddamned patched member in the place is armed."

"Pretty safe bet."

"The fuck are you?" The giant at the door asked, stepping in front of them so they had no chance of darting past him. Not that they wanted to start the night off on the wrong foot.

Patch on his chest read, Moose. Big as a house, the guy had a smooth head covered in tats, ear gauges, and a gold fucking tooth like some kind of B-movie mobster.

"Name's Luke," Screw said. "This is Will." He jerked his thumb over his shoulder at Gumby. "Met one of your prospects, Squirt, earlier this week." He shrugged as though he didn't give a fuck whether Moose let them in or not. "He told me to check this party out."

"Any weapons?"

"Nope. Feel free to check." Screw extended his arms and Gumby couldn't help but notice the way his sleeves clung to his thick arms. In the back, his shirt rode up an inch, giving Gumby a prime view of two dimples at the base of his spine. Fuck, he wanted to dip his tongue right in there.

What the fuck was happening to him? He'd been with men, but never had the overwhelming desire to run his tongue all over their bodies, and with Screw, it was almost a vital need. They'd have to fuck. He had to get the man out of his system. It was the only way he'd be able to move on and get control over himself once again.

"Hey! You fucking sleeping there or what?"

Shit.

"Sorry." Gumby stepped forward and extended his arms for the rough pat down.

Screw cocked his head and raised an eyebrow as if to say, "You cool?"

With a subtle nod, Gumby dropped his arms as Moose stepped back.

"Stay in the bar area. You wanna fuck, you leave, find a dark corner, or go at it right there. If you ain't patched in, you ain't allowed upstairs or behind any closed doors. Get it?" Moose's voice was surprisingly high-pitched for such a beast of a man.

"Got it." Screw said, all smiles as though totally pumped to be at the party. "Thanks, man." He held his fist out and Moose bumped it.

Gumby did the same, then followed Screw into the loud as fuck clubhouse. They'd clearly done a fair amount of work turning the warehouse into a livable space. The place maintained its industrial feel with exposed beams on the ceiling, and brick interior walls. A huge steel bar dominated the wide-open space they'd walked into. Off to the left, an open staircase led to the second floor which he assumed housed bedrooms. Aside from that, the place was plain. A few tables had been scattered throughout the room, but most of the space was jam-packed with bodies writhing to the music.

"Jesus," Gumby muttered as he walked past a man who had to be at least fifty with greasy gray hair, a beer belly protruding through the lapel of his cut, and a beard that touched said gut. The guy had his hand buried under some girl's skirt as she moaned and pumped her hips. A red cup full of God knew what nearly overflowed as she squeezed it. "She could be his daughter."

Screw laughed. "Fuckin' prude. This is my kinda playground." He shot Gumby a wink.

The words had something dark, ugly, and unfamiliar twisting inside of him. They made him speak without thinking. "You gonna fuck while we're here tonight?"

Christ, could he sound like more of a jealous boyfriend? What the hell was wrong with him. Screw could fuck whoever he wanted all day long if it made him happy.

"I woulda, even three weeks ago," Screw said, stopping dead in his tracks. "Then I got a taste of this woman I've been after, and haven't looked at another since."

"But—"

"But this woman's got a friend. Just as sexy as she is." He glanced around to make sure no eyes were on them before stepping close and whispering lower than the music. "He's got me just as fucking wrecked as she does. All I can think about is the two of them, lying in my big bed. He's hard and she's wet as fuck while they wait for me to make them both come."

"Christ." His dick responded just as the fucker must have planned.

"So no, *Will,* I'm not gonna find someone here to fuck because I can't get these other two outta my head."

Damn, that man was gonna be the death of him. "I need a fucking drink."

Screw smirked as his gaze drifted to Gumby's erection. "Gonna take more than one to deflate that bad boy."

A loud roar had them glancing to the right where a man was heading their way. "You fucking made it!"

"That's Squirt," Screw muttered.

Gumby didn't react beyond forcing himself to stay relaxed and chill.

"Hey, man," Squirt said, holding his fist out to Screw. "Who's your friend?"

"This is Will. He works for me."

Gumby nodded to Will.

"Well," the prospect said, lifting his hands. "What do you think?"

"I think it's…fucking crazy."

Squirt, whose pupils were pinpoints and who had a dusting of white power under one nostril laughed like Screw had told the funniest joke. "Who doesn't love fucking crazy?" He tipped back his head and let out a loud whoop. "Let's get you boys a fucking drink."

Screw met Gumby's gaze and a silent, "Game on," passed between them before he turned and started weaving his way to the bar behind Squirt.

Gumby's eyes fell to the plump, round ass guiding him. Screw had mentioned bottoming in passing at one point. Fuck how he'd like to get up in there. And, Christ, he wanted Jazz to be present and an active participant. Maybe getting fucked by Screw while Screw was getting fucked by Gumby.

Yeah, he was pretty sure there wasn't anything he wanted more.

"Lemme introduce you boys to my enforcer. He's one righteous motherfucker. His name's Crank."

Except maybe surviving this party.

Jackpot. Bring on the motherfucker.

Chapter Twenty-One

Why hadn't she canceled girl's night?

After the doorbell chimed for the second time, Jazz put down the bottle of wine she'd been about to break into and trudged toward the offending sound. It'd been foolish to think her friend wouldn't press that round button until the damn thing shorted out.

Ding-dong.

"Keep your apron on," she muttered as she reached the door.

Before she even had the door all the way open, a squealing Holly jumped into her arms.

"Hi, Jazzy!" Holly said as she squeezed the life out of Jazz. The high-pitched greeting had her wincing as the words scraped across her overworked brain.

Why didn't I cancel girl's night?

"Babe, girl's night is gonna suck if you have to drive Jazz to the hospital to have her ribs X-rayed." LJ stood in the doorway, a giant Tupperware in his hand, filling the whole damn space with his enormous form. Since he was such a sweet guy and amazing boyfriend to her best friend, Jazz sometimes forgot he could pulverize her, and most people, with one swipe of his pinkie.

"Oh, please," Holly said with a wave of her hand and a roll of her eyes. "Jazz knows I'd never smush her. I love her too much." She drew back and studied Jazz for a moment with shrewd eyes.

No doubt she noticed the bags under Jazz's eyes that two pounds of concealer did little to cover. A bottle of chemicals only went so far in disguising a night of shitty sleep followed by a day of extreme obsessing.

"I thought *I* needed to let loose tonight, but you look like you need it even more. Hmm." Without losing the bubbly smile, Holly spun to her man, grabbed his cheeks, planted a wet one on him, then whirled back to Jazz. "Get going, babe. Girl's night has officially started. Oh!" She turned again—Jazz was getting dizzy at this point—and grabbed the Tupperware with an air kiss. "Thanks!"

The snort LJ let out had both women snickering. "Love you too, sugar." After a quick slap to Holly's ass, he strode out of the house, chuckling.

"Reese's peanut butter cup brownies," Holly said, lifting the tub of sugary goodness. Her laughter faded once they were alone. "Something's up with you." She pointed an unpolished finger and narrowed her eyes.

Ugh, Jazz wasn't even close to prepared to divulge her inner turmoil right then. But she couldn't lie to her friend either. "I've just got some personal stuff going on." That sounded bitchy. She might as well have told Holly to mind her own damn business. "Sorry. I didn't mean—"

Holly held up a hand. "Do you want to talk about it?"

Jazz shook her head. "Not yet."

"Okay, then. You know I'm here whenever you are ready, so we won't harp on it." Holly linked her arm through Jazz's and tugged her toward her own kitchen. "Instead we'll get drunk and gorge on these sugar-free, fat-free, five calorie brownies."

And that's why she hadn't canceled girl's night. Not for the booze, though it was a definite bonus, but for the sisterhood. Her girlfriends rocked and could pull her out of her head like no other.

"Thanks, Hol."

Holly squeezed her arm. "So, what are we drinking tonight?" she asked as they reached the small kitchen.

The two bathrooms in her little rental house had probably been updated within the last five to ten years, but the kitchen, the kitchen hadn't seen so much as a coat of paint since the late eighties.

"Toni is bringing the booze. Something about Cosmopolitans and a Real Housewives marathon. But I have wine if we want to get a head start."

"I'm game. What's your house guest up to tonight?" Holly asked with a wag of her eyebrows. She set the brownies on the counter before pulling the lid off. The moment those babies were exposed to air, the intoxicating scent of chocolate and peanut butter wafted directly to Jazz's nose.

"Dayyyum those smell good. And, uh, I think he was gonna hang out with Screw," Jazz said as she got to work, opening a chilled bottle of Chardonnay. Thankfully, watching the corkscrew disappear into the cork gave her something to focus on besides any curiosity on Holly's face.

Too bad her friend wasn't unobservant.

"Whoa, whoa, whoa…slow down there, sister. My liver can wait a minute." She pulled Jazz away from the counter. "Let me get this straight. The guy who's spent the last eight months trying to get in your pants is hanging out with the guy who showed up from your past and who also happens to want to get in your pants. Those same two that caused you to blow your top at the party the other day? Is that what you're telling me?"

"Um, yes," Jazz squeaked out.

"Are they beating each other bloody? Do I need to find them and referee? Actually, you know what? Since Gumby showed up we haven't talked much. Are you guys…you know?" There went her hyperactive eyebrows again. "And does that mean you're totally done with Screw? How have I not asked you all this yet?"

"Um, you're busy with your own drama? It's not every day a man who was imprisoned for murdering someone you love but was actually innocent shows up on your doorstep. How are you handling all that?" Jazz went back to the task of opening the wine.

Holly wagged a pointer back and forth. "While that may be true, we're psychoanalyzing your life right now, not mine. So, nice try on the convo switch, but I'm not dumb enough to fall for it. Spill, sister."

I had a threesome with Screw and Gumby.

The words, though on the very tip of her tongue, just wouldn't fall out. "Remember when I said I wasn't ready to talk about it?"

Holly's eyes nearly bugged out of her head. "That's what you're not ready to talk about? Shit, girl, I didn't realize you meant man drama." Her sigh surpassed melodramatic after the first second. "Fine, leave me in the dark." Holly winked. "Just promise me you'll reach out if you need me."

"Promise. Here." Jazz held out a generously full stem glass.

"Just let me tinkle, then I'll take it."

Jazz laughed, probably for the first time all day, and a layer of tension melted away. "Tinkle? Really?"

With a shrug and a smirk, Holly disappeared down the hall toward the teeny-tiny half bathroom as Jazz sipped her wine.

Exhaustion settled heavy on her shoulders. Despite practically passing out after the powerful orgasm the men gave her, she'd spent much of the night tossing and turning.

They'd all woken around ten in the night, famished. She'd been too freaked out after waking with two men in her bed to allow them to stick around for a meal. In truth, it'd been the feelings of contentment that had really wigged her out. Screw at her back, Gumby at her front, both slumbering men with a hand resting on her still-naked body. She'd been warm, safe, and so damn comfortable, all she'd wanted to do was burrow in deeper and stay there forever.

That single thought had been enough to have her eyes flying open and her body jerking upright, which had woken both Gumby and Screw. They'd both seemed so…chill. As though what had happened between the three of them had been nothing more than sharing a soda. Meanwhile, she'd been screaming on the inside.

When Screw had stretched with a jaw-cracking yawn, triggering a monstrous rumble from his stomach, he'd suggested they order a pizza. Gumby had agreed without so much as a second of thought, and Jazz had been helpless to do much more than stare in confusion. When the hell had they become BFFs?

She'd been so thrown by the whole interaction, she'd ignored the clawing hunger in her own stomach in favor of telling them she was too tired to eat. When she hadn't moved to ask them to stay, Gumby went to his room and Screw took off for his own house. Of course, neither man left before kissing the ever-loving hell outta her.

God, just the memory of Gumby's lips on hers had her shivering. His kiss had been gentle yet insistent as he explored her mouth and awoke her arousal all over again. Then, with a wink and an offhand comment to Screw about them "hanging out" that night, he'd left her bedroom.

Since he'd fried her neural circuits, it'd taken a hot second for her brain to catch up to his words and just as she'd been about to ask Screw what the hell Gumby meant about them hanging out, the sexy jerk moved in and captured her mouth in his own kiss.

Two hot men, two sets of lips, two completely different experiences. Where Gumby had eased her into the lip-lock, Screw had pretty much devoured her. She'd barely remembered to breathe, let alone ask about Gumby's comment. After he'd released her, spun her, slapped her ass, and given her a gentle shove toward her bed, he'd gone on his merry way, whistling. Literally whistling like he was one of the seven fucking dwarfs.

It wasn't until a solid five minutes after he'd left, five minutes of sitting on the edge of her bed and staring at nothing as her lips tingled, she'd remembered what Gumby had said.

With a sigh, she'd flopped back onto her bed where she'd spent the next seven hours tossing and turning as her brain ran in wild circles. The hottest sexual encounter of her life had replayed countless times while she wondered what this meant for them all.

Now, more than half a day later, she still couldn't stop the whirring of her mind. Jazz was no stranger to threesomes. She may not have participated in one herself, but, come on, she'd spent many years around MCs. Threesomes were as common as leather with those guys. More than the number of participants, the *who* of the participants was fucking with her head. Screw and Gumby. Two men she'd though hated each other, then found out had an intense attraction to one another—and her apparently.

Top it all off with her blabbing the entire story of her scars.

Jesus what had she been thinking?

Of course, she'd been rewarded handsomely for the reveal. Soothed, comforted, made to feel safe, aroused, and given the orgasm to shame all other orgasms.

"Dayum, girl, only one thing puts that kind of smile on a gal's face. Care to share with the class?" Holly asked as she reappeared in the kitchen.

"Drink your wine." Jazz slid the glass toward her nosy friend just as the doorbell rang.

Thank God for small favors.

"I'll get it," Holly said as she took her glass and started for the door. "You finish that fantasy or…memory?"

With a snort, Jazz flipped her friend off causing a round of giggles to erupt from Holly. Within the next ten minutes her kitchen was full of all the women she considered sisters. Man, she'd have loved to have these women as blood, but they were all closer than some families, which filled a huge void.

And gave her enormous guilt for never sharing with her girls what she'd shared with Gumby and Screw last night.

"You know a lot of this is actually scripted, right?" Shell said about thirty minutes later as she munched on a Twizzler and sipped a ginger ale. At eleven weeks pregnant, she'd been craving the candy for the past few weeks. Jazz hadn't seen her without a bag of Twizzlers since before Christmas.

"Shut up! It's totally real." Izzy fired back as she threw a piece of popcorn at Shell. "You know you love it."

"What?" Shell laughed as she dodged the flying snack. "Of all of us, you're the one who I figured would hate this shit the most."

"Well, I do, but I'm here so I might as well watch it."

"Bullshit! You're a closet Housewives lover! Admit it!" Shell's eyes widened with so much glee, Jazz couldn't help but laugh along with the other girls.

If she were honest, which she tended not to be when it came to reality television, she'd admit she loved watching the ridiculous drama of these lady's lives unfold.

"You love it so much, I bet you dream of being on an episode of the Real Hells-wives of The MC. See what I did there?" Shell laughed as another puffed kernel flew past her head. "Someone help me! I'm under heavy fire here."

"All right, all right." Toni yanked the bowl of popcorn out of Izzy's reach. "Isabella, you're a mother now. You need to set a good example for your child."

With a snort, Izzy balled up her napkin and threw it at Toni. The crumpled paper bounced right off Toni's forehead making the whole group giggle. And they weren't even one full drink in. Well, Jazz was on her second, if that glass of wine she and Holly shared deserved to be counted.

She didn't think it did.

"Okay, we ready to do this?" Holly asked, grabbing the remote from the coffee table. "I've never seen it, so I might need one of you to fill me in."

"You've never seen it?" Izzy said, eyes bugging. "Are you from this planet?"

"Who knew she was such a reality TV psycho." Chloe leaned toward Jazz as she murmured the words.

Jazz chuckled. "Not me," she whispered back. Then louder, "Before you hit play, anyone need a refill?" Everyone but Stephanie raised their glass.

"I've pumped enough to enjoy tonight, so bring it!" Izzy's grin was slightly maniacal.

"Here, I'll help you." Toni stood and Jazz's stomach dropped. "We can just make a pitcher so we don't have to run back and forth all night." Her smile was sweet, but her eyes said, "You can't avoid me forever."

Jazz swallowed a lump but nodded at her friend and boss before walking to the kitchen. It'd been a miracle she'd managed to avoid her for the half hour or so they'd been in the same house. Time to stop being a chicken shit and apologize. And not for the sake of their working relationship, though that was important, but because she loved Toni like a sister and the guilt of going off on her had been eating at her all day. Right alongside her stress over two maddening bikers.

"Toni, I'm sorry," she said the moment they entered the quiet kitchen. "I was totally out of line yesterday. My inappropriate reaction to the tank top had nothing to do with you, the diner, or the shirt. It was some personal shit that came bubbling to the surface at the wrong time. Please forgive me. I can't stand having tension between us."

As though given permission to finally exhale, Toni let out a long breath that had her entire body sagging. "Oh, my God, Jazzy, you don't have to apologize. I'm the one who is sorry. I got so wrapped up in making all these decisions for the new logo, and changing the diner's name, I was just trying to get it done. I should never have pushed you so hard to try on the tank top. Were I a better friend, I'd have noticed the idea of wearing it made you genuinely uncomfortable."

They stayed quiet for a moment before bursting out laughing and moving in for a hug as though Jazz's at-work freak-out had never happened. When they broke apart from the embrace, Toni asked, "So we're good?"

"Yes, we're great."

"Good, I think I drove Zach totally bonkers today with how many times I told him you must hate me for being such a bitch." She poured a ton of vodka into the pitcher.

Jazz passed her the cranberry juice. "Toni, the last thing you are is a bitch."

In companionable silence, they finished making the cosmos. Out of her head, the room may have been quiet, but inside her brain a marching band of anxiety pounded. "I have scars," Jazz finally said, the words spoken so quickly, she had no idea if Toni had even heard them. Now that she'd said it once, now that she'd opened herself to the vulnerability, sharing with those she loved didn't frighten her quite as much as it had only days ago.

When her friend stopped mixing the drinks and turned her sympathetic gaze on Jazz, she knew she'd been heard.

"Something happened right before I moved from Arizona. Actually, it's why I moved away. It left me with significant scars I'm not comfortable showing to anyone. I don't really want to go deeper into it, but you deserve at least a little explanation for the way I reacted to the very reasonable request of trying on the tank top." She pressed her lips together, picking at her thumbnail while she stared at the ground.

Seeing the pity on her friend's face would be too much right then.

"Jazz," Toni said, grabbing her hand and giving a gentle squeeze. "I'm glad you feel safe enough to confide in me, but you don't owe me anything. Nothing at all. That being said, if you ever need to talk more, I'm here for you. My scars may not be visible under my clothes, but I promise you my insides are full of them. Painful ones I'm sure will never completely fade."

Jazz lifted her head and her gaze connected with Toni's. Instead of the pity and maybe doubt she'd expected, all she saw was understanding and compassion.

"Thanks, Toni," she said, returning the squeeze.

"Please," Toni replied as though her easy and unconditional acceptance was no big deal. "What are sisters for?"

Sisters. Not by blood, but definitely of an even stronger bond, love.

"Come on." Toni grabbed the pitcher. "Let's get in there before Izzy goes into Housewives mode."

Jazz's forehead wrinkled. "Housewives mode?"

"Mmm-hm, it's something to see. No one is allowed to speak without pausing the television. If you need to reach for a snack, you can't block her view, and if you need to pee you have to ask Izzy's permission. She'll determine how long you get in the bathroom."

Jazz's head fell back on her shoulders as she laughed. "What happens if you break her rules?"

With one eyebrow raised, Toni said, "You really want to know?"

"Nope."

Laughing, they reentered the den and sat down.

"Just in time," Izzy said as she held out her empty glass. "If you'd been any later, you'd have had to wait in the kitchen until I was willing to pause the show."

Jazz bit her lip to keep from laughing as she caught Toni's eye roll.

Four hours later the clock was closing in on midnight and just about all of the girl's eyes were drooping. Izzy had gone home about ninety minutes ago, needing to relieve Jig from baby duty, but everyone else had stuck around.

As usual, they'd had a fantastic time full of sugar, booze, and more laughing than should be legal. But the best thing about the evening was how it accomplished her number one goal: taking her mind off Screw and Gumby. And for a few blissful hours, she hadn't thought of either man. But now, as Holly clicked the TV off and the girls began to doze, the quiet brought a new round of spiraling.

She rested her head back on the couch, feet on the coffee table as she tried her damnedest to forget the way Screw's tongue felt against her clit. Or how Gumby's hands felt as he worked her breasts to aching points.

Just as Jazz let out a frustrated groan, a heavy pounding on the door had her jumping.

"Shit!" Toni yelled as she shot off the couch.

Shell grumbled. "Why the hell can't they knock like normal people? Sounds like the police are about to break the door down."

Another thump on the door. "It's open!" Jazz yelled.

Copper walked into the den followed by Rocket, Zach, and LJ. Man, they were an impressive group. Tall, muscled, tattooed. Don't-fuck-with-me vibes rolled off them in waves, but it faded away the second they all laid eyes on their women. She couldn't help but seek out both Gumby and Screw though she'd known they were hanging out by themselves. Nor could she help the foolish surge of disappointment at their absence.

"Ready, baby?" Copper asked as he bent down to kiss his pregnant and quite sleepy wife.

"Mmm," Shell responded, eyes closed. "You might need to carry me."

With a chuckle Copper said, "I can do that."

The rest of the men greeted their women in a similar manner. As Jazz watched, her mouth turned down in a frown. Usually, at this point, a shameful pang of jealousy tightened her gut. Never would she begrudge her friends their happy-ever-afters, in fact no one was happier that they'd all found their soul mates than she was, but knowing with her issues she'd be hard pressed to find such a relationship, well it stung to say the least.

Only tonight, that familiar sensation was absent. Instead, she imagined Screw and Gumby walking through the door hand in hand. They'd kiss her, one at a time, before sharing a lip-lock between themselves.

She snorted out loud.

Hello unreasonable fantasy. Even if both men wanted something with her, who the hell turned a threesome into a relationship? No one she knew.

"You all right there, Jazzy?" Zach asked.

"Right as rain," she said with a smile that felt forced.

Holly narrowed her eyes and stared as though seeing straight through Jazz's contented façade.

"All right, here we go," Copper said as he bent down to scoop Shell up. Before he had her in his arms, the blaring of multiple cell phones had them all jumping. Hell, it sounded like every phone in the house was ringing.

"The fuck?" Copper muttered as he shared a look with his men then pulled his phone from his back pocket. The rest of the guys did the same and within seconds a chorus of, "Fuck!" was shouted in Jazz's living room.

The thread of panic in each man's voice had all thoughts of sleep fleeing Jazz's head. She and her girlfriends all sat straight up with worried expressions.

"What's wrong?" Chloe was the first to ask.

"We gotta roll," Copper barked. "Now!"

Without so much as an air kiss or a word of explanation, the men sprinted out of the house.

What the fuck…

"Do not leave this house! You understand me?" Copper yelled from the open front door.

They all nodded in unison.

"I'm not fucking kidding. I find out any of you stepped one foot outside this house…"

"We won't, Copper. Promise." Though strong, Shell's voice held a note of tremor.

"Let's roll, Cop."

"Thunder's on his way in and Monty is already outside. They'll keep you safe." With a nod for his wife, Copper disappeared out the door leaving all five of them staring at each other with one question written all over their faces.

Safe from what?

Chapter Twenty-Two

The fantasy played out right before his eyes. In his head, it was so fucking easy. Reach out, wrap his fingers around Crank's throat and squeeze until the motherfucker's eyeballs popped from his sockets. His face would turn the most satisfying shade of purple as second by second, he ran out of oxygen.

Somehow, despite the way he could feel the man's pulse fluttering wildly beneath his fingertips, Screw managed to curl his hands in on themselves instead of killing Crank. But, oh, how he wanted to. He squeezed his fists so tight, his blunt nails dug into his palms no doubt leaving a host of crescent shaped indents.

"Yo, Crank, this here is the guy I was telling you about, Luke."

"Hey, man, welcome." Crank didn't bother extending his hand, but nothing in his face showed any signs of recognition, which was the most important point. "How do you like what we have to offer?" He asked, sweeping his hand toward a group of women dancing together. Their hands ran over each other's writhing bodies in a way that let every man in the room know they'd be down for pretty much anything.

For the first time since they'd pulled onto CDMC property, Screw took a full breath. Crank didn't know who he was. He and

Gumby wouldn't be shot on the spot or tossed in a dank basement to await certain torture.

He pasted a lecherous grin on his face. "Some sweet pickin's, man. Mmm. Seriously fucking sweet." He eyed the ladies, if they could be called by such a term, and for the first time in as long as he could remember didn't feel a flicker of arousal at the sight of the half-naked women rubbing up on each other. He sure as hell wanted Crank to think he was though. "Pretty sure I'll be leaving here with a smile on my face."

Beside him, Gumby tensed. Screw would kick his ass if he thought the words were legit.

"I got one every night, man," Crank said with a smirk. The man's slightly busted nose made the perfect target for Screw's fist.

"This is my buddy, Will."

Gumby nodded. "Hey."

Crank barely spared him a glance before he was focusing Screw's way again. "Squirt tells me you live in Knoxville."

"Yeah, I do. Got a cabin in Townsend though."

"Hmm." Crank pulled a dented pack of cigarettes from his back pocket. He stuck one between his lips then said around it, "You out this way often?"

Why the fuck did he care? Screw hadn't quite thought Crank would have given two shits about some random guy one of his prospects invited to their clubhouse. He risked a quick peek at Gumby, whose expression was unreadable. But the guy was smart; he had to be picking up on the odd vibe as well.

"Uh, yeah. Try to come out here every weekend when I'm free. Hate the fucking city, but you know, need my paycheck."

"What do you do?"

"I manage a furniture warehouse." He'd totally spit-balled the idea when Squirt had asked him earlier in the week.

"You ship out a lot?"

Oh, fuck. How to play this? If he kept his head out of his ass and dealt his cards right, this could be the in the Handlers needed. The CDMC shipped weapons. Did they want his trucks? He bit the inside of his cheek to keep a handle on his excitement. Then, with a nod, he said, "We do. All up and down the east coast."

"Huh." Crank shared a look with Squirt, then he was slapping Screw on the back. "You boys enjoy yourselves, huh? Drink, dance, fuck. I'll catch up with you later."

"Yeah, man. Thanks."

"All right," Squirt said. "What're you boys drinkin'?"

An hour and a half later, Screw stood with his back against the bar as he watched Gumby play pool with three club whores while also pretending to give a shit about whatever the fuck Squirt was rambling on about. The kid could talk, that was for fucking sure.

He'd learned a lot about Squirt, and the Disciples in that time, none of it useful for Copper and all of it nauseating.

Squirt was a racist, as were most of the other Disciples he'd met.

Squirt loved his coke.

Squirt was a raging homophobe. The amount of time he'd heard the words fag and queer thrown around in the most derogatory of ways had his ears ringing. And his senses on high alert. He and Gumby had been beyond careful to keep their attraction under wraps. In fact, they hadn't even spoken much. Gumby had been commandeered by the group of skanky bitches almost right away.

Watching them drape themselves all over Gumby had Screw's hackles rising. Sure, the man wasn't doing a damn thing to encourage them and wasn't reciprocating the attention or affection, but the girls weren't deterred. They giggled and thrust their overfilled tits his way every five seconds.

Screw ground his teeth as he chewed the fuck out of a cocktail straw and tried to burn the girls down with his eyes. Fuck, you'd think he was some jealous boyfriend or something.

"Your boy seems to be getting along real good," Squirt said with a laugh as one of the dumb bitches stroked the pool cue as though she were stroking a big dick.

Screw just grunted.

As though he heard the sound from twenty feet away over the pounding of the rock music, Gumby looked up. He mouthed something that looked like "Gotta take a leak."

Screw nodded once, then watched as Gumby headed toward what he assumed was the bathroom. One of the girls tried to follow, undoubtedly looking for a quick over the sink fuck, but whatever he said to her had her pouting and remaining at the pool table.

"So, hey, I wanted to give you a heads up about something, but you gotta keep your trap shut, hear me?" Squirt leaned in close as he spoke.

The hairs on the back of Screw's neck rose to attention. "Yeah, I hear ya."

Squirt glanced around then turned to face Screw. "Crank is gonna ask to chat with you later. He's got a proposition for you."

Here we go. A tingle of anticipation ran through him.

"A proposition?" Screw asked, going for chill and unconcerned. "What do you mean?"

"Well, we're looking for some help shipping some items up and down the east coast."

Ding, ding, ding. The fucking motherload. He wanted to jump up and down with fucking glee. Instead, he raised an eyebrow. "Oh, yeah? What kind of items?"

Guns, obviously.

With a shake of his head, Squirt said. "Can't tell you that yet, man. Club business. They'll have my ass for saying this much, but I wanted to let you know what a good fucking deal it is. You do not want to turn it down. The club will take good care of you if you know what I mean." He rubbed his thumb against his next two fingers in the universal sign for cash.

Screw scratched a hand through his beard. Itchy fucking thing. "Wow, I just thought I was coming here to get wasted, maybe find some easy pussy. Talk bikes a bit."

"Brother, you help us out and you'll be welcome here every damn time you're in town. You'll be drowning in pussy."

"So you guys need to start shipping some stuff?"

"Nah, not start. We're already up and running, but the prez ain't happy with how shit's going right now. Guys we're using are too slow. It's fucking with our bottom line."

"All right," Screw said as he pursed his lips as though giving it some serious thought. "We talking a big time commitment on my part? You need to move a lot of shit? This something that needs to be done on the down low? And who are you using now? There are some shitty companies out there which is why we do all our own shipments."

With a laugh, Squirt held up his hands. "Shit, simmer down. I'm glad you're taking this seriously, but I ain't supposed to be telling you anything. Can't give you much in the way of details."

He'd come on too strong. What he really wanted to do was shake Squirt until the information fell out. He lifted his hands. "Sorry, man. Didn't mean to put you in a bad position. Just think this could really be a good thing for me. I can use the extra cash for sure. Just want be prepared when Crank approaches me."

"Fuck." Squirt rubbed his hands together. "Okay, but I didn't tell you fuck all, got it? I ain't risking my patch to line your pockets."

"Of course not. I'll play dumb when I talk to Crank."

Squirt sniffed, wiped his nose, then nodded. "As of now, we're making runs to Knoxville twice a week, Monday and Thursday. We bring out shit to this mom and pop shipping company called Cranston."

Screw made a mental note of the name and dates. "Yeah, I heard of 'em."

Nodding, Squirt continued. "They were struggling and jumped at the chance when they saw the amount Crank was willing to pay them. Anyway, we bring stuff twice a week and they ship it out for us, split up over four trucks. Two go up to New York where they're picked up by our partners and two go down to Miami. You guys ship there?"

"All the fucking time."

"Good, that's reeeal good." Squirt said with a smile.

Screw could practically see the guy imagining himself strutting around with his CDMC bottom rocker. He didn't give a shit if the guy got patched in or not, but it wasn't going to happen here in Tennessee. That was for damn sure. Screw would do everything in his power to drive these guys out of town. No one fucked with his family.

"Yo, prospect, get the fuck over here," one of the patched members yelled from about fifteen feet away.

"I'm out. Go find yourself some pussy."

"Later, man." He slapped Squirt on the shoulder. "And thanks."

Squirt ran off to do his club's bidding, leaving Screw at the bar alone with a smirk on his face. Hadn't been too long ago that he'd been a prospect. Not long enough for the memories of being tortured by his now brothers to have faded. Thank God that phase of life had ended.

Gumby still hadn't returned to the pool table, so Screw took a second to finish his beer and assess his next move. He now had enough information to fuck with the CDMC's weapons shipment.

Mission accomplished. Risk well worth it. But it was time to get the fuck outta there before their luck ran out. He set his empty cup on the bar then started in the direction Gumby had gone. He took two steps then froze in his tracks.

Locked in a shock-filled stare from across the room, stood Jeremy, Jazmine's fuckwad of a neighbor. The same Jeremy who went to high school with Screw, dishing out homophobic slurs every chance he got. The same Jeremy who loved nothing more than to regale Screw with tales of his mother dancing on stage.

The same Jeremy who tried to prospect with the Handlers three times and had been denied based on Screw's word alone. To say they hated each other was like saying an orgasm felt *all right*.

Understatement of the century.

Jeremy caved first, his eyes shifting to where Crank stood across the room, laughing with a group of his brothers. The grin that curled Jeremy's smarmy fucking mouth was so goddamned sinister, nerves dove down Screw's spine.

The very second Jeremy twitched in Crank's direction, Screw sprang into action. He charged forward through the crowd, ramming unsuspecting partiers out of the way with his heavy shoulders as he ran. More than one drunkenly squealed curse followed him, and he was pretty sure he straight up knocked a club whore over. Maybe she'd get lucky and end up banging whatever guy caught her before she landed on her ass.

Jeremy was moving quick but not quick enough. "Hey, man!" he said in an excited tone as he slung his arm around the back of Jeremy's neck. Quick as lightning, he hooked his elbow and brought his forearm across the guy's throat cutting off his ability to shout for assistance. Thankfully, everyone was so damned wasted no one seemed to notice Screw dragging Jeremy to the side of the room.

Jeremy's weak struggles were no match for Screw's strength—*thank you, Zach for owning a gym*—and he easily muscled the gasping man away from the crowd and down a darkened hallway.

Closed doors lined the hall, at least three on each side.

One of those fuckers *needed* to be unlocked for this makeshift plan to work. Screw tried the first door cursing under his breath as the knob jiggled but didn't turn.

"Fuck you," Jeremy managed to rasp out when Screw's hold loosened for a fraction of a second. The man grew heavier in his arms as he no doubt tired from thrashing around. Adrenalin surged through Screw's blood, pumping in time with the rapid beat of the music.

He needed to get this show on the road, find Gumby, and get the fuck outta there.

No luck with the next door, either. Shit, time was running out.

Fuck it.

Screw towed a thrashing Jeremy to the end of the hallway. He'd hoped to find something to tie the man up with, but didn't have time to check all the doors. Tightening his chokehold on Jeremy's throat, he said, "You're the only one who knows I'm here. That means if the CDMC finds out, we'll know you ran your fat fucking mouth. And we'll come for you. Good thing I know where you live."

Jeremy thrashed and clawed at Screw's arm, scraping the top layer of skin in a move he didn't even feel. Adrenalin had taken over, driving him forward with the single need to get the fuck out of the clubhouse. All of a sudden, the grip on his forearm slackened and Jeremy went completely limp in his arms. Screw lowered him to the floor then booked it back into the bar.

This solution would buy a few minutes at best. If Jeremy were smart, he'd listen and keep his yapper shut, but they couldn't count on it. He and Gumby needed to act as though the entire club would be on their asses in a matter of seconds.

He spotted Gumby the second he entered the bar, back at the pool table with the skanks, but his gaze scanned the room, probably seeking out Screw.

Moving as fast as he dared without drawing unwanted attention, Screw zigzagged through the mess of gyrating bodies while AC/DC crooned about being shook all night long.

When he reached Gumby after what felt like hours, the perceptive guy immediately straightened.

"Hey," Screw said to one of the women.

"Well, hey there, sexy." She sauntered to him, hips and tits swaying to entice his focus, but his attention remained on

Gumby. "Nice dress," he said of the fire-engine-red scrap of material she wore. "Think my friend, *Jazz*, has the same one."

"Thank you, bab—Hey! Where're ya goin'?"

Gumby hadn't missed a beat. Without a word of goodbye, he turned and started for the exit at a rapid clip with Screw hot on his heels. "How much time we got?" he muttered.

"Sixty seconds, max." Screw glanced over his shoulder. So far so good. No horde of angry Disciples barreling down on them.

"Fuck."

"Yep."

They reached the exit in no time, rushing through the door despite Squirt spotting them and calling out. As predicted, Moose no longer served as bouncer.

"The fuck happened?" Gumby asked as they kicked up into a sprint.

"Jazz's fucking neighbor was there, sucking up to the club."

"Jeremy? The one who wants in her pants?"

"That's the one."

When they were a stone's throw from Screw's truck, the door to the clubhouse flew open so hard it slammed against the exterior wall making both men jump.

"There they are!" Crank shouted right before a bullet whizzed past Gumby's head.

"Shit! Go, go, go!" Screw shouted, as he jerked the truck door open. Gumby did the same, diving into the driver's seat. He had the engine fired and was peeling out of the spot before either door had been closed.

"They chasing?" Gumby asked as he jammed his foot on the gas and shot toward the gate.

Screw looked through his side mirror in time to see at least five Disciples running for vehicles. "Fuck. They are." Jeremy stood in the open door leading to the clubhouse, hands on his hips. He was a dead fucking man.

Just as Gumby began to turn onto the road, Squirt shoved past Jeremy, bursting outside. Crank, who still stood in the parking lot, drew his pistol and shot the prospect dead center between the eyes.

Just that fast, Squirt's life came to a violent end and the Handlers problems grew tenfold. If Crank was willing to murder his own prospect in such a way, what would he do to an enemy MC?

"Fuck!" Screw shouted as he slammed his fist on the dashboard.

"We're not gonna be able to outrun all of them, Screw. This truck is no match for their fucking sports cars."

Goddammit, this was exactly why Copper had told him to leave it the fuck alone. He was royally fucked. They'd tear the patch from his cut and skin his club tattoos with a rusty knife while dancing to his screams.

As Gumby navigated the curvy roads with skill, Screw pulled his phone out.

911. In my truck. CDMC in pursuit. Need diversion. Rudd Rd. 10 min out.

As soon as he saw the text, Copper would know Screw had blatantly ignored a direct order and gone to the party. He couldn't worry about that now though.

"I can't take these fucking turns fast in this goddammed truck," Gumby growled out as he was forced to slow and avoid careening off the edge of the mountainside.

The sound of shattering glass had both men cursing. "They hit the side mirror. I'm gonna return fire," Screw yelled as he pulled a gun from his glove box.

"Don't you dare get your ass shot, you hear me?"

He loaded the magazine then cocked the gun. "Not before you get a chance to ream it, you mean?"

When Gumby shot him an exasperated look, he winked before lowering his window and aiming back toward the truck.

"You're fucking crazy," Gumby mumbled.

For the next few minutes, Screw worked to hold off the fucking CDMC with one damn gun. He got in a few good shots, taking out a few headlights and even hitting a windshield which was probably the only reason their followers hadn't overtaken them and run them off the road.

Bullets pinged off his truck, making Swiss cheese out of the damn thing, but thankfully their aim sucked and he remained gunshot free.

"Where the fuck is our backup?" Gumby yelled above the sound of cracking glass as the rear windshield splintered. Cold air whooshed into the car through Screw's open window making both men shiver.

"Fuck if I know."

Though in his gut he knew it would never happen, part of him feared Copper had left him to dangle in the wind as payment for his disobedience.

The road changed, straightening out as they moved from the mountain to flatter terrain. Screw's truck whizzed past a crossroad and immediately, an eighteen-wheeler pulled out, blocking the entire road.

"Holy shit!"

An ear-piercing screech of brakes followed by the crunch of twisting metal rent the night air.

"Fuck yes!" Screw yelled, pumping a fist in the air as Gumby slowed to a complete stop a half mile down the road.

The smell of burning rubber filled the air, owning to the long skid marks left by whichever Disciple had tried and failed to stop before hitting the truck.

"The fuck?" Gumby swiveled in his seat. "That your club?"

"It's gotta be."

"Where'd they get the semi?"

"Who knows." Screw glanced around the quiet street. "We shouldn't stick around here. You good?"

"Yeah." Gumby hit the gas again, glancing in the rearview mirror as he drove. "I'm good, you?"

Screw ran a trembling hand through his hair. "I'm fine."

A mile down, three cars lined the side of the road. Still too fucking cold and icy for bikes.

"That's Copper's SUV. Pull over." His stomach bottomed out. Time to pay the piper.

"Hey," Gumby said after he braked behind Copper's vehicle.

"Yeah?"

Gumby reached out and grabbed his hand, out of sight of any of the Handlers. "Don't know if it'll make a lick of difference with your prez, but I've got your back." Then he linked their fingers and gave a squeeze.

Their gazes met and Screw would have loved to kiss him just then. Love to draw some calm and strength from the man, because his nerves had hit an all-time high. If there ever was a time to lay off the jokes, this was it. Copper needed to know how seriously Screw took his new position in the club, right before he ripped the enforcer patch right off Screw's cut.

"Makes a fuckton of difference to me," he said before opening the door, stepping out, and coming face to face with the angriest scowl he'd ever seen on his president.

Chapter Twenty-Three

The door flew open without warning, slamming hard against the wall as Copper stormed into Jazz's house followed by Zach, Rocket, LJ and finally a subdued Screw and Gumby.

Both she and Toni shrieked then sprung up from their spots on the couch. "Holy shit!" Toni yelled.

Shell rushed down the hallway from the bathroom. "What was that?"

The sight of both Screw and Gumby in her home, unharmed, had pounds of tension lifting from her shoulders. Jazz placed a hand over her chest as her heart beat out an erratic rhythm. "Jesus, guys, you scared the crap out of us. Maybe a little less storm-the-castle next time, huh?"

Then she took in the sight of Copper's face.

Yikes.

His green eyes had darkened to near black. Jazz tried to avoid his glare. Who knew what would happen if she got caught in his crosshairs? She might be burned to ash. Those mitt sized hands fisted and opened at his sides over and over. The veins in his arms bulged like the Hulk's did when he ripped off his shirt. He held his large body so stiff and rigid if he bumped his shoulder, an arm might fall off. And she wouldn't be surprised if he started beating someone with it.

Someone was in for it, in the worst way, and by the compressed set of Screw's mouth and the way he kept his gaze on the ground, Jazz had a sinking feeling he would be on the receiving end of Copper's wrath in about five seconds.

Her heart fluttered with anxiety as she tried to get either Screw's or Gumby's attention by sending telepathic messages. After a few seconds, Gumby gave her a small smile and mouthed, "we're okay." Looked like that was the best she was gonna get since Screw still appeared mesmerized by her worn, beige carpet.

"Copper what's wr—" Shell started.

"Kitchen, ladies," Copper barked.

Jazz flinched and began to move, as did Toni, but Shell stood her ground. "What's going on?" she asked, voice soft and soothing as though speaking to a wild animal.

"I said kitchen."

Shell raised an eyebrow and Jazz swallowed hard. She was a brave, brave woman taking on that scary man. Then again, she lived with him and it was well known she had the big, bad club president wrapped around her pinkie.

Copper blew out a breath then walked to his wife. "Sorry, babe," he whispered down to her before kissing her. "Can you guys give us a few minutes, please?"

"You know we can still hear you from the kitchen, right?" Jazz said.

Why had they come to Jazz's house instead of going to the clubhouse if they wanted privacy?

Just as she was about to voice the question, Copper ran a hand down his face as he glanced her way. "Fuck it," he said. "You got a right to know what's going on since you live here."

What the hell? Was she in danger? Was Paul—

No! That was her mind, running out of control. Paul was going to be locked up for a long time. This had nothing to do with him. She'd spent so much of her life worrying about where he was and when he'd return. Old habits were hard to break. She was safe from him. This was something club related.

The CDMC.

Shell turned her wide-eyed gaze on Jazz.

Her legs felt like lead, unable to move until Toni placed a hand on her shoulder. "Let's sit, hon."

Nodding, she dropped back down to the couch. Toni sat next to her, holding one of her hands while Shell also came to sit on the couch.

As though they actually had left the room, Copper turned his back on the couch and just…exploded.

"Give me one good reason why I shouldn't rip that cut off your back and burn the fuck out of it!" He screamed the words so loud, Jazz nearly jumped out of her skin. She'd thought they'd startled her when they burst through the door, but that was nothing compared to the fear Copper's tone elicited now.

Finally, Screw lifted his head, giving Copper the respect his president was due. Jazz had to hand it to him. She'd probably burst out crying and cower in the corner if someone screamed at her with such vehemence.

"Copper, I know you're pissed and that I deserve it. I ignored a direct order, but you need to hear—"

"Ignored a direct order?" He shouted. "That's what you think this is about? Goddammit."

"Do you understand what you've done here, Screw? Do you have any clue the danger your fucking screwball ways have put Jazmine in?"

Wait? What? *Screw* put her in danger?

"Who the fuck knows what Jeremy is going to do now? Who knows how deep he's in with the Chrome Disciples?"

Jeremy? The Chrome Disciples? What the hell was going on? What had Screw done?

It felt like she was at a tennis match with her gaze pinging between Copper and Screw. Screw appeared to be biting back some caustic words of his own as he stood there being chastised by his president.

"Do you give a shit about this club? Is this all just a big joke to you?"

Hey, now, Screw was many things. Yes, he was a jokester, a womanizer, a sex fiend, but Jazz had no doubt at all he loved his brothers and took his role in the club seriously. Showing it may not be his strength, but he felt it. Of that she was sure. Just as she was about to speak up, Toni's hand clamped down on her thigh and she bit back the words.

Shit, Toni was right. Copper wouldn't take kindly to her butting into club business, even if he was conducting it at her house, in front of her.

"No, prez. It's not a joke to me at all."

"You went to a party at the CDMC clubhouse without backup after I fucking forbade it."

What?

Her stomach soured as the magnitude of what could have happened to Screw hit her with the force of an avalanche. One look at Gumby's solemn face and she knew her friend had gone as well.

They'd lied to her.

"I think I'm gonna be sick," she muttered, pressing a hand to her stomach.

Toni rubbed her back in soothing circles.

"What the fuck am I supposed to think, huh, Screw? Explain it to me, because all I see is some fucking hotshot who thinks he can do whatever the fuck he wants!" He roared out a yell then slammed his fist into Jazz's wall leaving behind a giant hole.

"Hey!" She said then shrank back when Copper's furious gaze turned her way.

"He'll have it fixed," Toni whispered.

Jazz had been around the club for a while. She'd seen the guys and their women go through some serious shit. An FBI raid, Izzy being beat up, Chloe attacked, betrayal from Holly's father, the list went on. Through all of that, she'd never seen Copper lose his cool like this.

Her hands began to tremble, so she tucked them under her legs. The Jeremy link still made no sense, but all she could think of was the danger the two men who'd given her so much had put themselves in.

They went to a party at the CDMC clubhouse without telling anyone. Were they insane?

"Copper—" Screw began.

Gumby stepped forward. "I know it's hard to see beyond the way this ended and how he went behind your back, but Screw has some information for you that could give your club a huge edge over the Disciples." He spoke in the calm, rational way she'd come to expect from him.

"How about you keep the fuck out of my club's business?" Copper advanced on Gumby and Jazz couldn't keep her mouth shut any longer.

"Stop!" She yelled.

Copper whipped his head in her direction, no less furious than when he'd started yelling.

Now that his attention had shifted to her, whatever she'd been about to say died in her throat. "I...uh..." God, he was a scary man sometimes.

"Your club may not be my business, but Jazz is." Gumby spoke with such strong conviction, his words chased away some of her chill. "Jeremy is the reason we had to get the fuck outta there. He recognized us and ratted us out to Crank. Otherwise, we'd have been home free. Now, is he just some hang-around the club doesn't give a shit about, or is he on his way in? Who the fuck knows, but he lives next door to Jazmine and if she's in danger, it is my business."

Everything began to click into place. Of course, Jeremy had been at the party. The guy was starved to be part of an MC and after being rejected by the Handlers more than once, he probably saw the CDMC as his second chance. His way of finally having the life he coveted.

Did he know what assholes made up that club? Was he so desperate to fit in, he didn't care what they got up to?

Screw stepped forward, placing a hand on Gumby's shoulder. A silent thanks-but-I-got-this-now.

"Copper I'm under no illusion that I don't deserve your anger. I even expect you to take away my position as enforcer. I broke your trust and I get that. But I didn't do it lightly. And I didn't do it because I don't care about the club. I did it because I needed to. I needed to take this risk and do something to give us a leg up on those fuckers. They came too close, Cop. Too close to hurting Toni. Too close to hurting *your* woman."

The set of Copper's shoulders eased somewhat as he finally listened to Screw.

"And you know what, Copper?" He pounded his fist into his palm. "It worked. It fucking worked and I have an idea of how we can hit them and hit them hard without them knowing it was us."

"For real?"

Copper's eyes shifted between Screw and Gumby, who nodded. The only indication his need for verification from Gumby hurt Screw was the subtle ticking of Screw's jaw.

With a deep sigh, Copper rubbed his beard. "All right. Fuck. Church tomorrow. I want every fucking detail from the second you pulled into that clubhouse until I rescued your stupid ass."

Screw nodded. "Of course, Copper." He stuck out his hand.

Copper glanced at it then began to move.

Her heart sank down through the couch. But then Copper grabbed Screw in a huge bear hug, slapping him hard on the back, and relief hit Jazz so fast, it was dizzying.

"Glad you're okay, brother."

Screw nodded without saying anything and if Jazz didn't know better, she'd have thought he was too choked up to respond. But Screw didn't do choked up. He did laughs, and jokes, and deflection.

None of that came from him now.

"Thanks for having his back," Copper said to Gumby, extending his hand.

Gumby grasped it, giving Copper a solid shake. "Anytime."

A look passed between Gumby and Screw she couldn't decipher. Something more than just the hot lust they had for each other.

Did they feel something for each other?

Her gut twisted as an image of the two of them waking alone together in the morning popped into her head.

Jesus, was that jealousy?

Her head began to pound. God, they all needed to talk. To figure out what the hell was going on between the three of them. Not to mention she needed to give them a piece of her mind for lying about their plans for the evening.

But one look at the stress lines scrunching Screw's forehead, and all she wanted to do was comfort him in any way possible.

"Jazz, I'll send LJ out to take care of that tomorrow," Copper said.

"Huh?" She blinked as he pulled her from her head. Oh, the wall. With a wave of her hand, she shook her head. "Whenever."

After hugging her girls, they took off with their respective men, leaving her alone with Gumby and Screw. Suddenly, the air thickened and she couldn't think of a single thing to say. Part of her wanted to rail at them as Copper had for putting themselves in danger. The other part wanted to squeeze the hell out of them while sending up a prayer of thanks that they hadn't been hurt. And yet another part, the part she didn't fully understand yet, wanted something darker and more pleasurable from both of them.

"I need a fucking drink," Screw announced. "You got anything stronger than wine?"

Jazz shared a look with Gumby then said, "Uh, yeah, there's some Jack Daniels in the cabinet above my refrigerator."

"Great." Screw headed into the kitchen.

She followed him with her eyes. "Do you think he's okay?"

Gumby pulled his glasses off, giving his eyes a good rub. "I'm not sure. What I've learned of that man is he feels a lot, and all of it much deeper than he ever wants anyone to know."

"Hmm." She'd wondered that about Screw. If his joking and bullshitting was a front. "You like him."

"I…" He shrugged. "I'm sorry I never told you."

"Told me what?"

"You know that I'm—that I like—" He cleared his throat.

"Oh, that you're bisexual? Why would you be sorry about that? It's your private business. You didn't owe that to me, or anyone for that matter. Whatever you're comfortable with."

He grunted.

Ahhh, so that's how it was. He wasn't comfortable with it. At all. In fact, as he'd just demonstrated, he couldn't even say the words out loud.

As if things weren't complicated enough. Now she not only had something weird and messy going on with two men, but one of them was closeted.

She couldn't just do things the easy way, could she?

"Should we check on him?"

"Yeah, go on in. I'm just gonna hang up my jacket."

"All right." As she began to walk away, Gumby grabbed her wrist and tugged her to him. He crashed his mouth to hers in a kiss full of more hunger and need than he'd given her yet. The lingering flavor of whiskey hit her senses, combining with his taste and stealing her breath.

God, he made her weak in the knees.

"We're gonna figure out all this shit, okay, baby?"

Did he mean with the club or with her and Screw? With her head buzzing more from that one kiss than the wine she'd drank, she nodded.

"And don't worry about your neighbor, either."

Jeremy, right. What a disaster.

"Go check on him." He gave her ass a light swat, shot her a wink, then headed down to the guest room.

She basically floated into her kitchen, coming to a stop right in the doorway. Slumped in a chair that had been turned away from the table, sat Screw, the uncapped bottle of whiskey on the table next to him. Since she'd never opened the bottle, the level of liquid let her know he'd already taken a few healthy swallows.

His legs were spread wide in that way men so often sat, with his hands resting on his flat stomach. His head tipped back against the top of the chair and his eyes were closed. Someone who didn't know him, might find him at peace, maybe even sleeping, but not Jazz. She noticed the frown, the tension in his jaw, and the lines running across his forehead.

The need to reassure him, to take away whatever pain he tried so hard to hide, grew impossible to ignore. Without thinking, without allowing herself to analyze or question her motives, she walked into the kitchen with a single-minded purpose.

When she reached him, she immediately lowered onto his lap, straddling him. He jolted and his eyes flew wide. She took full advantage of the moment his mouth dropped open, capturing his face between her hands and kissing the ever-loving hell out of him.

He hardened in an instant. The impressive erection pressed into the V of her thighs. Jazz moaned into his mouth and ground her pelvis against his.

"Jazz," he rasped as he tore his mouth from hers. "Be sure. Christ, Jazzy, be sure because I've wanted this. Wanted you for so fucking long, I'm not sure I'll be able to stop once I get you under me."

She didn't believe that for a second but knowing how much he wanted her had wetness soaking her panties. "Yes," she said on a moan as he licked the side of her neck. "I'm sure, Screw."

A noise from the entrance to the kitchen had both their heads swiveling to find Gumby leaning against the door frame, an obvious tent in his jeans.

Jazz looked back to Screw who raised an eyebrow. "I'm sure," she said, breathless. Then she held her hand out to Gumby. "Be with us tonight, Gumby. We'll figure out the rest tomorrow. But tonight, be with us."

Chapter Twenty-Four

Gumby had a few short seconds to make a choice. A choice with the power to alter his entire life.

No.

He wouldn't let one decision, one night define his existence.

Yes, this would be more than a quick blowjob to fulfill a physical need he ignored most of the time. Those nights, even the one with Screw, he could rationalize away as quick stress relief. No big deal.

Even their threesome last night, he'd been able to play off as doing what needed to be done for her. For Jazmine. Not because his dick throbbed, and his balls ached with the need to unload every time he came within touching distance of her or Screw.

Though he may have these errant attractions to men, he didn't plan to live his life dating men or choosing one to build a relationship with. He liked women as well and that's where the focus would be.

But he didn't live here. His club wasn't here. His family wasn't here. And anyone who knew him and would be shocked to find him with Screw's dick in his mouth was more than a thousand miles away.

And fuck, did he want Screw's dick in his mouth. He'd been salivating for it as much as he wanted a taste of Jazz's pussy.

Only he wasn't sure he was strong enough to give into that particular desire.

He walked forward and slid his palm along Jazz's, curling his fingers around her soft hand. Looked like he'd made his choice. One he'd have to make sure she kept under wraps once he got back to real life. This whole thing would be written off as a wild few weeks of chaos and out of character choices.

Happened to everyone at some point.

Screw stood, hands full of Jazz's tight ass as he lifted her. She squeaked drawing a grin from Screw. The sight of them together…Jesus, Gumby could come just from watching them. He let out a growl he hadn't realized formed in his chest.

"That sound is hot as fuck," Screw said, eyes blazing with lust. "Get in the fucking bedroom."

Jazz shivered in his arms as Screw attacked her neck. When she whimpered, Gumby's dick twitched and he could no longer merely stand by, watching and not participating.

With another rumble, he slid his hands through Jazz's dark hair, gripping the short strands. He used the leverage to tip her head back, exposing more of her neck for Screw's feasting. The other man wasted no time diving in. Gumby turned her head, finding her mouth, delving his tongue between her parted lips.

As he drank in her moans, he ran a hand down Screw's back to the man's firm, rounded ass. When he gave a solid squeeze, Screw lifted his head and speared him with a molten glare

As if drawn by some invisible force, Gumby moved his mouth from Jazz's to Screw's. The man tasted of the whiskey he'd downed in the few minutes he'd had alone. His kiss was rougher than Jazz's, darker, promising pleasure just as powerful yet so different than he experienced with a woman. And to know he was about to get both at the same time?

He shivered.

Mind blowing.

"Oh, my God," Jazz whispered, drawing both their attention. Her soft smile seemed almost awestruck as she reached out and caressed both their faces. "Do it again. You're so beautiful together. So sexy."

Screw smirked. "Far be it for me to deny a lady's request. Suppose I can suffer through another one of those for Jazz."

Gumby snorted then grabbed the back of Screw's head and yanked the man in for kiss. Screw would never be the overly serious type. It just wasn't in his nature. Even in times of stress, despair, and apparently intense arousal, his larger than life personality shone through with the goal of making others laugh.

And, look at that, Gumby realized he wouldn't want the man any other way. His ability to make shit laughable was so interwoven with his charm, he wouldn't be the charismatic man everyone loved and wanted if that part of his personality changed.

The kiss was rough, hungry, and Screw's scruff rubbed against Gumby's face leaving no doubt that it was a man he kissed. Neither Jazz nor Screw were aware that until last night, he'd never tasted another man's lips.

Had his dick sucked? Yes.

Fucked some nameless, faceless guy in the bathroom of a club? Yes.

But never allowed the intimacy of kissing. It was too much. Too real.

When Screw growled into his mouth, Gumby tightened his hold on the other man even more. Soft fingers sifted through his hair, so in contrast with the rawness of the kiss, holding his mouth against Screw's.

When his lungs screamed with the need to suck in air, Gumby finally released Screw's lips. A smirk and a wink were what greeted him on Screw's face. That and swollen lips, fiery eyes, and flushed skin.

"God," Jazz whispered. She leaned in, licking Screw's bottom lip before she treated Gumby to the same act.

He hadn't thought it possible for his cock to get harder, but knowing Jazz had both his and Screw's flavor on her tongue had his dick swelling to the point of painful.

"I don't know what any of this means," she said in a near whisper. "Screw, I fought you for so long, and Gumby we came so close to having a chance but were robbed. Everything is such a mess right now, and so confusing. My head is a jumble of insane thoughts, but there's one thing I know for certain."

"What, Jazzy?" Gumby asked.

"I've never felt before like I did last night. Yes, physically it was incredible. But even more than that, I felt so…safe with you two and free to let go. Right here, and right now, I want you both more than I want to breathe."

"You have us," Screw said with a wink.

"Bedroom?" Gumby's throat had dried to the point the words sounded more like a croak.

"Your show, Jazzy. You want us in your bed?"

"Yes," she said, a gorgeous smile expanding across her face. "That's exactly where I want you, boys. My bed."

"Well then give this pony a slap and let's giddy-up on in there." In a feat of strength that had Jazz yelping, Screw shifted her from the front of his body to the back. Her yip of surprise turned into laughter when Screw neighed like a horse and did a little gallop.

"You're crazy," she said on a laugh. Then she reached down and gave him a sharp slap on his ass. "Let's go, boy."

With another ridiculous neigh, Screw galloped down the hallway, giving Jazz a piggyback ride to her room.

Gumby couldn't help but chuckle as the sound of Jazz's joyful laughter filled the house. It was the perfect break in a moment growing a bit too intense. A bit too real-life. This was about sex. Exploring a kink all three of them got off on.

Screw *couldn't* handle more than a few romps. Gumby *wouldn't* form a relationship with a man. And Jazz? Well she might be willing to engage in this threesome behind closed doors, but she'd never want or expect to go public.

Gumby reached the room just in time to see Screw toss a giggling Jazmine on the bed.

"Well, sweetheart," Screw said, "How do you want us?"

With her cheeks flushed and her eyes glassy, Jazz looked downright edible. "Clothes off," she said.

"Don't have to ask me twice." Screw reached for the hem of his shirt.

"Nuh-uh." Jazz shook her head, lower lip between her teeth. God, why did she have to be so damn tempting? "Undress each other."

Fuck. Part of him had been hoping they'd focus solely on Jazz. Figures she'd want to see him and Screw together as well.

"Even better," Screw said. He moved in front of Gumby, smirk in place. Cocking his head to the side, he waited for permission to proceed. Though Gumby was under no illusion this was the man's way of asking for consent. It was a challenge. Throwing down the gauntlet to see if Gumby was man enough to accept.

And, fuck, how he wanted it. Wanted it so bad his hands shook. Wanted to feel Screw's hands all over his body as he removed every stitch of clothing Gumby wore while Jazz watched. Then he wanted to return the favor, revealing Screw's body inch by inch.

This meant nothing. Experimentation. Exploring. None of this defined him in any way.

A single nod was all he gave Screw before the man's hands landed on his chest.

"He may not have my bulk, but he's certainly no slouch in the muscle department, Jazz," Screw said as those hands drifted down the fabric covering his abs. Leaving one hand on Gumby's stomach, Screw circled around to his back. He brushed his nose against Gumby's neck, inhaling a long breath. "Damn, he smells good. All man."

A hand gripped his T-shirt on either side of his waist.

With her rapt attention on him, Jazz's chest began to rise and fall in a rapid clip as though the anticipation of seeing him without his clothes was foreplay in itself.

"Arms up, handsome," Screw whispered in his ear.

That deep voice skirted right down Gumby's spine, settling in his full balls and making the need to come surge. He lifted his arms and his shirt was gone before he even had the chance to fully straighten them.

"Fuuuck," Screw said. "Long lean muscles everywhere. May I touch him?"

Biting her lip through a mischievous smirk, Jazz shook her head. "Not yet."

Jazzy wanted to play.

"You're killing me, baby," Screw said with a groan.

"You'll be rewarded."

Screw's eyes darkened. "Yeah?"

Jazz spread her legs, running one finger along the seam of her yoga pants. The one that ran directly over her pussy and damn if the spot didn't look a little darker than the rest of the material.

Gumby locked his knees to keep from pouncing on her while Screw muttered, "Fuck me."

"Keep going."

Screw dropped to his knees at Gumby's feet, the move so reminiscent of when he'd sucked him last week, memories of the intense pleasure swamped him. The man went to work on his boots, unlacing and removing them one at a time. Next were the socks.

The only sound audible in the room was the huffs and puffs of their combined inhales and exhales.

Once the footwear had been removed, Screw's eager hands moved to the button of Gumby's jeans. He rose to a tall knee, once again giving Gumby the chance to refuse.

"Do it."

Another smirk and then Screw popped the button and lowered the zipper one tooth at a time. Once the zipper reached its endpoint, Screw dove his hands down the back of Gumby's pants, giving his ass a firm squeeze.

"Fuck," Gumby yelled as his dick twitched. Damn, that strong hand clenching his ass made him want to howl at the moon.

"That's the way, baby," Screw said with a snicker as he shoved the jeans down Gumby's legs. "You haven't had the pleasure yet, Jazzy. His arms and legs aren't the only long appendages our man's got."

Our man.

Jesus, those words shouldn't turn him on as much as Screw's touch. In fact, Screw's touch shouldn't turn him on like it did.

And yet...he nearly shot his load in his boxer briefs the moment those skillful fingers cupped his length. God, why did it have to feel so fucking good?

"Please," Jazz whispered, no longer lounging back. She now sat, perched on the edge of the bed, her gaze fixed to where Screw's hand was driving him crazy. "I want to see him."

"Yes, ma'am," Screw said before slowly peeling the maroon boxer briefs down his body. His cock sprung out, bobbing up and down before settling out long and proud.

With a small whimper, Jazz slid off the bed and came to her knees in front of him. Gumby blew out a shaky breath. Both on their knees in front of him. He had to be dreaming.

"You want it?" Screw asked her. "Wanna suck him? Promise he tastes incredible. Almost as good as you," he winked.

"Yes," Jazz said as she licked her lips. She wasted no time, palming his sack with one hand and stroking his cock with the other. "You're so hard," Jazz whispered before licking a drop of precum from the tip of his dick.

Gumby hissed as a lightning strike of pleasure shot up his spine and nearly exploded his brain. Jesus these two were going to send him to an early grave.

"You're right. He is tasty," she said before sucking him into her mouth with a little hum of enjoyment.

Gumby fought the natural reaction of his eyes rolling back in his head because he wasn't going to miss this visual for the fucking world. Jazz's head bobbed up and down on his dick while Screw stroked a hand over her round ass.

When she moaned, the vibrations transferred to his cock and he cried out, losing the battle to keep his eyes open. But then, in the next second, he felt both suction on the tip and a greedy tongue on his shaft.

His eyes flew open once again to find Jazz sucking the head of his dick and Screw coasting his tongue up and down the length. Jesus, had there ever been a hotter sight?

When Screw's tongue met Jazz's lips, she pulled off his dick to engage in a hot as fuck kiss with the man. Their tongues battled in a sloppy, needy kiss full of more passion than skill.

Gumby grabbed his wet dick and pumped as he watched them make out.

Jazz pulled back, panting. "You're still dressed," she said to Screw.

"So I am." He cocked an eyebrow. "What are you gonna do about that, big guy? Think you got what it takes to wrestle me out of my duds?"

He had what it took to shove his dick in Screw's mouth to keep more snark from pouring out. But it was time to stop fucking around and get to the straight up fucking. He yanked Screw to his feet by the front of his Henley.

The guy's eyes widened. Having the upper hand over the quick and witty Screw felt damn good. With quick movements, he ripped the shirt over Screw's head then went to work on his jeans. He had the button and zipper released in no time.

Figures Screw would be wearing tight-assed jet-black briefs that hugged an impressive bulge.

Screw cleared his throat, drawing Gumby's attention from his dick to his face. "Forgetting something?" he asked with a smirk.

Gumby glanced down to see him wiggling a still-booted foot. "Shit."

"I'll help you," Jazz said from where she knelt on the carpet. "You work on getting that monster out."

She divested him of his shoes while Gumby set about driving Screw out of his mind. He ran his fingertips over the fabric covered erection, smiling when Screw tensed, and his nostrils flared. Finally, Screw had no clever quip or teasing remark. He'd become just as swept up by this storm as they all were.

Their gazes locked as Gumby hooked his thumbs in the sides of Screw's briefs. "No going back," Screw whispered, once again issuing a challenge.

Without responding, Gumby pushed the underwear over Screw's firm as fuck ass, giving his own squeeze to the thick globes.

Screw grunted.

God, the hours that man spent in the gym were well worth every drop of sweat.

Both naked now, they shared an unspoken idea, turning to Jazz.

"Your turn, baby," Screw said with a grin.

Jazz rose to stand, the long line of her smooth throat shifting with the force of her swallow. Trepidation flickered through her gaze while she let out a shaky laugh. "I feel like you two are about to ruin me for any future sex."

Gumby nearly frowned at the thought of someone else getting their hands on her down the road.

"That's exactly what we plan to do, gorgeous," Screw said with a wink. "But I'm thinking you won't be the only one ruined tonight."

And that's exactly what terrified Gumby.

Chapter Twenty-Five

Jazz's legs trembled as she stood under the lustful gazes—yes gazes, plural—of the two men watching her as though they would ravage her any second. Her insides quivered even more than her limbs and a small part of her worried she'd chicken out.

Not because there were two men, though the experience certainly wasn't anywhere near her comfort zone, but because the vibe in the room felt heavier than mere sex.

And that kind of thinking was...dangerous. Screw had an aversion to all things relationship, and Gumby lived in Arizona. More than lived there, he was in an MC there which meant he wouldn't be willing to leave. Jazz didn't think she could live there again, no matter how much she'd loved her friends. The traumatic memories were too deeply embedded in the desert sand. So the one man who might be willing to invest time and energy into her beyond fucking wouldn't work either.

Fine. She could keep this physical. No problem.

"Hey," Gumby said, narrowing his eyes. "You still with us?"

"Yes. Of course."

"Because if you change—"

Jazz whipped her shirt over her head, leaving her in a blood red push-up bra that actually made her look like she had tits.

"She's with us." Screw said, chuckling. He advanced on her and the predatory look in his eye had her stepping back. When her legs hit the bed, he said, "Where you gonna go now?"

"Maybe here?" she reached out and wrapped a hand around his erection, giving a firm squeeze followed by a stroke. He must not have expected the move because his entire body bucked and he cursed out loud.

Behind him, Gumby laughed then stepped forward as well. He kissed the side of Screw's neck once, then again as Screw let his head fall to the side exposing his powerful throat. The man was a delicious mountain of muscles, all earned since he'd prospected with the club.

Jazz continued to stroke him, loving the way he shamelessly moaned and thrust into her hand, until Screw gave her a little shove and sent her tumbling to the bed.

He crawled up onto the bed over her body, to give her a shiver-inducing kiss. As she and Screw tangled tongues, Gumby peeled her yoga pants down. "Jesus," he said once the red thong which perfectly matched her bra came into view.

"Fuck!" Screw suddenly yelled, ripping his mouth from her.

Jazz peaked over his shoulder to see Gumby stroking a finger up and down the crease between Screw's ass cheeks.

"You want up in there?" he asked, breathless.

"Yes," Gumby answered. "Sometime soon. But tonight, my dick's in the mood for pussy."

Something passed between the two men. A look of understanding she didn't quite grasp. As though they had some inside experience, she hadn't been privy to. Had her brain been functioning at full capacity she'd have made a mental note to ask later.

"Come here and look at her," Gumby ordered in a no-nonsense voice.

"What?" Somehow, she'd imagined they avoided looking too closely at her body. Being naked was one thing, being scrutinized was another. "No."

"Hey." Screw barked out the word with enough strength she immediately sought his gaze. He captured her face between two strong palms. "You're fucking gorgeous, scars and all. I'm gonna look at you, Jazzy. *We're* gonna look at this beautiful body, so get used to it." He tempered his severe words with a wink.

Her heart melted. Shit. How was she supposed to keep this physical when they knew exactly how to get under her skin?

"Besides," Screw said. "I'm pretty damn sure I left a few marks of my own last night and I'd like to see my handiwork. Sit up a bit."

Heat rushed to her face, same as it had when she'd forced herself to look in the mirror that morning. There'd been no less than five hickeys overtop of the largest of her scars.

When she lifted to her elbows, he reached under her. One flick of the wrist and he had her bra open like some kind of underwear magician. Screw then pushed off her, taking the satin bra with him before moving to stand by Gumby at the foot of her bed. "Damn, baby, those are some sexy panties you got on there."

Lying there, with her feet on the floor, legs slightly spread under the perusal of two of the most attractive men she'd ever met took all her courage. Her hands itched to move to her breasts. To cover the scarred mounds and misshapen nipples. Though as she'd learned last night, those nipples were anything but insensate and man she'd like to feel one of their lips on them again.

"Jazmine, you see how hard we are, right? You see how much we both want you? How sexy we think that body is?"

"Hey!" Screw said in an overly affronted tone. He wrapped a hand around Gumby's cock. "I'd like to think this bad boy isn't *all* for her."

How had she never realized how hot it would be to watch two men together? But then, maybe it wasn't all men she liked to watch getting each other off. Maybe it was just these two. Whatever it was, she hoped one time she could simply sit back and watch them pleasure themselves. Tonight, she was feeling selfish and too needy to simply observe.

"Screw," Gumby said, voice ragged. "Be a good boy and go suck Jazzy's tits while I see how ready she is to fuck us."

Oh. My. God. Where had that commanding tone come from? She'd expected it from Screw, but to see Gumby turn all alpha dog was hot as could be.

With a sexy growl, Screw gave Gumby one last squeeze, kissed him square on the mouth then came around to the side of the bed. He dropped down to his knees, resting his elbows on the bed.

He reached out, cupping one breast and thumbing her nipple. She shifted as the sensation zinged straight to her pussy.

"So responsive," he rumbled.

Gumby lowered to his knees as well, pushing her legs apart as he sank. "So wet as well. Goddamn, Jazzy this thong is fucking soaked."

"I was thinking about Henry Cavill while you guys were undressing."

Screw tweaked her nipple. "Watch it, sassy."

Jazz laughed until Screw's mouth closed over her nipple making her back arch and dragging a moan from deep within. God, the hot, wet, tug of the suction made the emptiness between her legs feel so weighted. She was seconds away from begging Gumby to fuck her when his fingers rubbed over her wet thong.

When her hips wiggled, seeking more contact, he chuckled. "Impatient?"

"Yes! Oh, fuck," she cried out as Screw switched breasts, sucking hard. She fisted his long hair, holding him against her as his soft beard tickled her skin.

With one finger, Gumby hooked her thong and dragged it away from her pussy before taking a long lick of her juices.

She gasped, arching her back and pushing her breast farther into Screw's mouth. Before she even had time to process the amazing feelings flooding through her, Gumby slid a long finger into her channel and sucked her clit at the same time.

So many—almost too many—sensations bombarded. Two mouths, two sets of hands, two men. "Please," she said on a moan.

Screw looked her in the eye. "Please what, baby."

"Please tell him to fuck me. I need it now."

He kissed her, pulling and tugging her nipples which did nothing to ease the intensity of the moment. "You heard the woman," he said.

When Gumby's finger and mouth left her, she almost cried out in protest but managed to hold it in since what was coming promised to be even better.

"Condom?"

Shit. She was so far gone she'd never have thought of it on her own.

"Got a few in my jeans." Screw kissed her again. "Never leave home without 'em." He winked and it was just so typical Screw she couldn't help but laugh.

Gumby was only gone about twenty seconds, but far be it for Screw to waste those precious ticks of the clock. He glided his hand down her body, straight between her legs. Gumby returned just as Screw shoved two thick fingers inside her.

She fought the heaviness in her eyelids as Gumby positioned himself between her legs. Jesus, watching him roll the condom down his healthy length while Screw fingered her was like being privy to her own live sex show. Or being a part of one.

When the latex was in place, Gumby scooped her legs up and knelt between her spread thighs. Screw withdrew his fingers, holding them to Gumby's lips. As Gumby licked Screw's fingers clean, all Jazz could do was watch and whimper.

Had she ever seen anything sexier? How would she ever go back to *regular* sex after spending time with these two in her bed?

"Ready, baby?" Gumby asked and the endearment had funny things happening in her chest. From Screw, it was just a turn of phrase. Something he called any and every woman he met, but Gumby had never used the term on her before and it made her feel…special.

She was fucked.

But she nodded because she was also a masochist, apparently.

"Do your worst."

Screw whistled while Gumby's mouth turned up in a half smirk. He grabbed his cock, arranging it at her entrance before locking eyes with her and pushing into her body.

It'd been so long, way too long since she'd taken a man, and the burn associated with the stretch only amplified the pleasure.

"Fuck, Screw, she's so goddammed tight." He groaned once he bottomed out inside her.

Jazz shuddered around his length. Thinking grew near impossible as the endorphins made her brain feel nothing but ecstasy.

"You're gonna lose your mind, Luke."

Luke.

She gasped, eyes locking with Screw. Gumby called him Luke? When had that started? "Use my name, Jazzy. Here, when it's the three of us. Or when it's you and I. Use my name." One of his hands stroked over her upper body, breasts, sternum, arms, shoulders, paying extra care to her scars. The other, he had wrapped around his own erection, stroking slowly. His gaze shifted from her face to where Gumby had begun to slowly pump into her. "Shit, that's the hottest thing I've ever seen. That long cock disappearing into your body again and again. You take him so well, baby." He smoothed his thumb across her bottom lip, and she sucked it into her mouth, nipping at the tip.

When both his eyes and nostrils flared, she had the vision of a powerful bull being taunted to the point of charging. Suddenly, the need to be connected to both of them surged within and she rose up on her elbows.

"Wanna taste you, Luke," she said to Screw then cried out as Gumby's thrusts grew in intensity. "God, that feels so good."

Screw scrambled off the bed then angled his cock toward her mouth. She licked around the head in a circle, gathering the salty essence that had leaked as he'd watched Gumby fuck her. Then she sucked him into her mouth, as far back as she could. The position, with her head turned made it difficult to deep throat him but Screw sure as hell didn't seem to mind.

He shouted, his head falling back as she sucked hard. "Fuck, that mouth is incredible, Jazzy." His hips thrust, but not with much force, just enough to add a little extra friction. "Shit, yes, baby, just like that."

Jazz felt euphoric; if she hadn't know better, she'd have sworn she'd taken some kind of psychedelic drug. Being able to reduce a man like Screw, a man who'd had more sex than Casanova, to a babbling mess was a drug in itself.

Then there was Gumby, grunting and groaning as he powered into her again and again. His constant praise of her body made her feel like a queen. Once she started blowing Screw, he'd backed off on the strength of his thrusts, probably so she wouldn't gag.

Considerate and a sex god.

Lethal combination.

The three of them went on like that for a while, Gumby fucking her with not gentle but not full-on powerful pumps of his hips while she devoured Screw's length. When her arms began to tremble from holding herself up for long minutes, Screw gently pulled his wet cock from her mouth.

With a look she must have misinterpreted as tender, he wiped saliva from her lower lip. Her arms gave out then. The very second, her back hit the bed, Gumby began fucking her like a man possessed.

She shouted as he slammed into her again and again. Above her, Screw resumed his exploration of her upper body, paying extra attention to the tight points of her nipples. Gumby shifted, hiking her legs up even farther and hitting a spot in her that made her pussy clench—hard.

"Fuck, that's the spot isn't it, baby?"

"Yes!" she shouted. "Yes. More."

With a snarl, Gumby hammered into her again, hitting the sweet spot at the same time Screw pinched her nipples.

Jazz's back arched off the bed as light danced behind her eyes. She shook and quivered, the pleasure so great, everything faded around her. It took a few seconds for her to register the harsh grunt and shout of Gumby as he came in the condom, his powerful tremors shaking her body as well.

"Jesus, you killed me, beautiful."

She smiled, limp and sated with her eyes resting shut as a pair of lips met hers.

The respite didn't last long.

Jazz opened her eyes as the bed shifted, to find Screw standing between her legs where Gumby had been, a feral look in his eyes. His condom covered cock, thicker than Gumby's, jutted out, ruddy and near pissed off looking.

He wanted his turn.

"Can you take more?"

It'd been so long for her, she'd be sore tomorrow for sure, but she'd take soreness over missing this opportunity any day. And the fact that he'd checked in with her?

Hello warm fuzzies. She'd kinda expected Screw to just dive in and fuck without foreplay or care.

How wrong she'd been.

"How do you want me?" she said with a sassy grin.

"Oh, baby, I want you in every way possible. But for tonight..."

He grabbed her hips and flipped her so fast she couldn't do anything but shriek and laugh. As she scrambled to all fours, Screw wasted no time sliding his cock right into her. Wet and soft from the orgasm, her body provided no resistance, but the sensitivity of her pussy had her crying out as the intense sensations bombarded her.

With a grunt, Screw fucked her like this was his one shot at having her. And who knew, maybe it was. Shaking off that gloomy thought, she met him thrust for thrust. If this was gonna be it, she sure as hell planned to milk every second of pleasure out of it.

"Christ, you were right, G. She's tight as a damn fist. So goddammed good, Jazzy."

"Hmm." Gumby lounged on the bed, watching them with sleepy, sated eyes.

Screw curled his body around her as he fucked her. Mouth drifted to her ear. "Look at him," he said and though she couldn't see his face, she imagined his gaze trained on Gumby.

"He's so fucking satisfied. Look at that spent cock lying soft across his thigh. You did that, baby. With this beautiful body."

His words made her quiver.

"W-we did that."

He chuckled, low and deep, running his hands over her body. "Yeah. We did."

She turned her head, needing to deepen the connection to him, however foolish for her heart.

Screw eagerly met her mouth, kissing her with the same intensity he fucked her. The man did nothing in half measure. One hand stroked over her ass then around her body, finding her clit as though he had a road map to it.

She jolted at the first touch as electricity skittered across her nerve endings.

"Give me another one, baby. Give it to me so I can come."

Jazz moaned which only made him gently capture her clit between his thumb and forefinger. "Screw!" she shouted against his mouth, her body beginning to make the climb once again.

He stopped moving.

"No!"

"What'd I tell you to call me? Only you two. Only like this."

Oh, my God, he was going to make her fall for him, the bastard. But there was no way she could deny the request. "L-Luke."

"Yes!" He rose up, gripping her hips and jackhammering into her like he'd lost control of himself.

Her arms and legs trembled and before she knew it, she was tumbling to the mattress. A hand stroked over her head. "You're so beautiful, Jazz. So perfect. You took us both so perfectly."

The softly spoken words caused a ripple deep in her core.

"Oh, fuck!" Screw shouted. "Whatever the fuck you just did, G, do it again. She squeezed me like a vise."

"Just told our girl how goddammed perfect she was taking our cocks."

This time the ripple lasted longer.

"Fuck yeah she is. Jesus."

"Come, baby. Come for him and let him feel that pussy lose control."

"Oh, God." Gumby's words were magic. Jazmine screamed into the mattress, fisting the sheets as a powerful orgasm crashed into her. It didn't roll through as they sometimes did. No this one hit like a powerful knockout punch.

"Fuck!" Screw shouted, his body going rigid above her. Sweat dripped onto her back. He held her hips so hard, she'd have bruises to add to her collection of love bites tomorrow.

And she'd never felt better in her life.

Boneless, she lay sprawled on her stomach atop the mattress. Screw pressed a kiss to her shoulder, then her cheek before getting up, presumably to dispose to the condom. Once his weight lifted off her back, Gumby grabbed her and pulled her over his body like a human blanket.

"Mmm. If you're not careful, I'll fall asleep like this." Her tongue felt thick making her sound slurred, drunk.

"That's what I'm counting on, Jazzy," he said, running his hand up and down the length of her spine.

He'd started calling her Jazzy like most of the Handlers did, and she loved it. His use of the nickname made her feel he accepted and wanted to be a part of the life she'd made for herself in Tennessee.

The bed dipped, causing her to open her eyes in time to see Screw slip under the covers.

He was staying. Again. At least for a little while.

Screw rolled to his side and scooted close until he was flush against them. Then he threw his arm and leg over top Jazz's body, effectively locking the three of them in one tight embrace. It was lights out for both men in a matter of seconds,

Jazz, however, took much longer to fall asleep. Her brain ran wild while her body absorbed the feeling of warmth and safety that came from being tucked between two strong men.

For the first time in a long time Jazz felt insulated from the potential horrors of the outside world. With two sets of arms holding her, it seemed as though nothing evil could ever get to her.

Not the Chrome Disciples.

Not Paul.

Not even her own negativity.

But as extraordinary as it felt, she couldn't allow herself to slide too deeply into that feeling of security.

There's no way it would last. Gumby would return to Arizona. Screw would return to…screwing around.

And she'd be right back where she started.

Alone.

Chapter Twenty-Six

"I'm back from my honeymoon for less than two hours when I get a text about an emergency exec board meeting." Maverick chuckled and kicked his boots up onto the table.

Screw rolled his eyes. Only reason Mav was able to get away with that shit was because Copper hadn't left his office yet.

"I hear you're the fucker who screwed the pooch, pardon the pun." Mav smirked and interlaced his fingers behind his head.

Screw flipped him off. Smug asshole.

"You know this kept me from fucking my wife after I got off the plane, right?"

Screw was pretty sure Mav spent the entire past seven days buried balls deep in his new wife, and they were supposed to feel sorry the guy had to delay one romp?

He snorted. "Sure she's sick of your inked dick by now anyway. I'll swing by on my way outta here. Take care of her for ya." He shot Mav a snarky wink.

"Ha, as though that cocktail weenie you're sportin' could satisfy anybody."

Mav raised his pierced eyebrow as though to say, "You're up."

Never one to be outwitted in the trash-talking arena, Screw snickered as he vaulted to his feet. Before any of the guys had time to realize his intentions, he had his jeans unzipped and shoved down to his knees.

He'd gone commando that day.

"Oh, Jesus, fuck, man. Cover that thing up." Zach held one hand in front of his eyes and the other straight out to ward off the sight of Screw's uncovered cock, as did most of the other guys.

"Huh, pretty big dick you got there, Screwball," LJ said as he also rose to his feet. "Can't say it's the biggest in the room though." He began unbuckling his belt, a conceited fucking grin on his face.

Motherfucker. It was well known throughout the club thanks to one mouthy Honey that LJ's snake was of the anaconda variety.

"Fuck, LJ, I don't wanna see that thing," Jigsaw said as he smacked LJ's hands, disrupting his task. "Before we know it, you're gonna be jerking each other off."

"Nah," LJ said as he sat back down. "Holly took good care of me this morning. Sorry you had to crash on Jazz's lonely couch last night, Screw."

If they only knew.

He laughed as he tucked himself back in his jeans and sat.

Mav leaned back, haughty satisfaction in his gaze. Asshole probably loved the fact he started this shit show.

"All right." Copper strode into the room, immediately shoving Maverick's boots off the table. "You know the rules, fucker."

Screw laughed and Mav flipped him off.

"Welcome back, by the way." Copper took his spot at the head of the table. "Guessing you enjoyed yourself."

"Well, let's see, there was sun, warmth, good fucking food, shit ton of booze, and my sexy as fuck wife who was naked for about ninety-six percent of the week, so yeah, it didn't suck." The haughty fucker practically glowed.

"Well, sorry to call you in the second your ass hit American soil." He shot a scowl Screw's way. "Couldn't be helped."

A smartass comment about hittin' Mav's ass tingled the tip of Screw's tongue, but he scraped it across the back of his teeth instead of letting it fly free. He'd gotten himself in enough hot water. Copper's disappointment in him felt like a noose around his neck, tightening with each passing minute. Normally, his go-to method for dealing with such emotions was to shit all over them with humor and snark.

That morning, he'd dropped Jazz at the diner before heading to his own house for a shower and change of clothes. Sweetheart that she was, Jazzy hooked him up with a steaming cup of coffee and a muffin the size of his head. Since they were the only ones in the diner besides Thunder, who'd been taking a piss, Screw had paid for breakfast with a toe-curling kiss.

Just before he walked away, she'd whispered six words in his ear. Six words that had been ping-ponging around his head ever since she'd uttered them.

Your brothers trust you. Trust yourself.

Trusting himself meant no jokes, no quips, no bullshit. He made his decision and had to own it as well as deal with the consequences.

He had to be a fucking adult.

And he could do that. He could be what his brothers needed in an enforcer, and he could make Jazzy proud.

Wait...what? Make Jazz proud?

What the hell did that matter?

But it did. It mattered a lot for some insane reason. He wanted the next time he saw her to be with a smile on her face because he'd done well. He'd done what was right. He didn't have much experience making people proud and fuck if he didn't want Jazz to be pleased with him even when he had his clothes on.

Fuck, what the hell was going on with him?

"Screw you think you could actually pay attention since you're the reason we're all fucking here?" Copper said.

"Yeah, of course. Sorry, just running through things in my head."

Copper blew out a long slow breath, and Screw's nerves flared. Same damn feeling he'd had each and every time his mother had been called in for a meeting with his principal. Jesus, he was a twenty-six-year-old man feeling like the fourteen-year-old chump who'd pantsed his gym teacher.

"All right," Copper said. "Everyone here knows we got an SOS call from Screw last night. He was at a CDMC party with Gumby, who is Jazz's friend from an MC in Arizona." He looked at Mav as he said that last part. Catching the guy up.

"Well, fuck me," Mav said, eyes on Screw. "You're a ballsy motherfucker, ain't ya?"

"Ballsy or stupid," Jig added. "I mean what the fuck did you think was gonna happen besides getting your ass shot or fucking tortured?"

His heart sank. He'd been hoping some of his brothers would have had his back without question. Looked like he'd be digging out of a hole for all of them.

Copper lifted a hand. "Trust me, I've already ripped him a new one. Let's hear him out because I was told he has some promising information for us."

"Come on, guys," LJ said. "This is our brother. Give him the fucking benefit of the doubt. Screw may fuck around a lot, but he always acts in the club's best interest."

Thank you. He and LJ had prospected together. The guy knew him better than anyone.

"Except that time he fucked that girl who slashed my tires instead of his," Mav said with a chuckle.

The other guys laughed and much of the tension in the room dissolved, taking with it the brick in Screw's gut.

"Start talking then," Copper said as he leaned back in his seat.

"'Bout a week ago, I met Squirt, a CDMC prospect at the gas station where Jazzy ran into a bunch of their club members. I wasn't in my cut and we started shooting the shit about bikes and his club. Told him I lived in Knoxville but came out here on weekends to get away from the grind. He invited me to their party."

"You met him on purpose," Mav said.

Screw nodded. "I needed to do something proactive. We can't just sit around and wait for them to make the next move. You all know one is coming. After all they went through making Lindsey trick Shell and Toni, they're not gonna fucking forget us." The CDMC had used the thirteen-year-old girl to lure Toni and Shell into a trap that nearly got all three of them killed. Lindsey hadn't wanted any part in it but had no choice in the matter. Thankfully, everyone survived with only minor injuries, but the incident had lasting negative effects on the girl.

"Well, he's right about that," Zach said. "They want us out." As he spoke, he rotated his shoulder. Was he even aware of the move? By now, it was mostly healed, but Zach had told him it ached like a motherfucker pretty frequently.

"So, even though you told me not to go to the party, I'd planned to go." Screw held up a hand. "I knew it could have been a trap. There was a chance Squirt knew exactly who I was and planned to fuck me up. It's why I took Gumby. Backup they for sure wouldn't recognize. We needed eyes inside there, Cop. We needed to see their dynamic. How they operate. Who's at the top of their food chain. Hell, even what their whores are like. Any information could be useful because we had nothing."

"Bet you focused on the whores, huh?" Mav asked with a snort.

Enough of this shit. He was being serious and they needed to see it that way. "No, Mav, I fucking didn't. But I did learn how they're shipping weapons, and I got invited to join their operation. I know exactly how and when they're getting their guns out of here. And I have an idea of how we can fuck with their business. Make them lose tens of thousands. Maybe if we can make this area seem like a money suck, they'll leave without fucking killing any of us."

The chapel fell silent as the gazes on him shifted from tolerant to respectful. Copper rubbed his beard. "Tell me." His voice held a grudging admiration.

"They work with a shipping company called Cranston based in Knoxville. Mondays and Thursdays, they take a supply of weapons to Knoxville where they're all divided up between a number of trucks making deliveries up and down the east coast. They're looking for a new shipping company. Squirt said this one has been unreliable and they're losing money."

"He say where they get the guns?" Zach asked.

Screw shook his head. "No. But if I had to make a guess, I'd say they're pretty well stocked right now. I'm betting that they brought a shit ton of weapons back with them while they were gone those few weeks. Now they have product to unload and need to move it."

Jigsaw leaned forward, resting on his elbows, fully engaged. "So what're you thinking? Intercept them on the way to Knoxville?"

"We could, but then they'd know it was us, or at least highly suspect it. I'm thinking we fuck with the trucking company. Here me out." He shifted forward as well, tapping a finger on the table as he spoke. "Weapons get loaded onto the trucks Monday and Thursday nights. They go out Tuesday and Friday mornings. We get our asses in there after the trucks are loaded. Steal the guns, maybe some other shit too so it doesn't look so deliberate. It's fucking Knoxville. A city. I doubt they'll connect it back to us here in Townsend."

"Could work," LJ piped up. "We fuck up their transport enough times, they'll lose a shit ton of cash. Could crumble the club or drive 'em away."

"It'll be hard to do more than once. They'll beef up security after one hit." Mav owned a PI company and was somewhat of a security expert. "I'm sure we'll have to get around cameras, maybe a guard, or some fucking dogs."

"What if we get someone on the inside? Someone hired as a driver. They could discreetly fuck up some trucks. Another way to delay or miss a shipment." Screw bounced his leg under the table.

Jig pointed at him. "That could work. Tex grew up on a dairy farm. I know for a fact he's got a commercial driver's license. We could get him in there. He's fucking foaming at the mouth to make up for his mistake."

Tex, a newer prospect, had been on protection detail for Toni and Shell a few weeks ago. He'd fucked up royally and dropped the ball the day they were kidnapped. Toni took the blame, swearing she'd been the one to convince him to hang out in the kitchen of the diner for a while, which allowed her and Shell to slip out unseen. Her story was the only reason the guy hadn't had his cut shredded. He had something to prove and would love the chance to do it.

"All right. Jig you move on getting him hired and working as soon as fucking possible. I want every single detail he could possibly provide us about the company. Set up, schedules, security, types of trucks, no detail is too small."

"Got it, boss."

"It's a solid plan." Finally, Rocket spoke up, drawing the attention of all the guys. He'd been a black ops asset for years. Having his approval would go a long fucking way with Copper. Add in the fact he didn't voice his opinions often, and Screw felt validated.

"We might want to bring Jazzy's friend, Gumby in on this too," Rocket added.

Sounded like a good idea to him, but would the rest of the guys agree to let an outsider so deep into the fold?

"What the fuck?" Zach asked.

"The guy's a mechanic. Might prove useful if we're disabling trucks."

Rocket had a point. A good one. Most of the guys in the club knew their way around a bike, but most didn't have the skill or knowledge to pull off this job properly. Gumby would be an asset on this job and after last night, Screw wanted to spend as much time with the guy as possible. While he wasn't ready to admit that out loud or analyze the whys of it, he just knew he wanted Gumby at his back yet again.

"Shit, we could use one of those in the club," Copper said. "Someone get him in here later. I'll talk to him. See where he's at."

"He'll do it," Screw said. "If it helps protect Jazz, he'll do it."

"I see one major flaw in this plan," LJ said as he shot an apologetic look across the table.

"What's that?"

Damn. Screw had known this was too smooth to work.

"One of the Disciples told you all this shit, right?"

With a nod Screw said, "Yeah, Squirt, the guy who gave me the invite."

"Okay, so I'm sure by now he's told Blade or Crank all about what he squealed to you. Hell, they'll probably be ready and waiting for an attack by us."

A heaviness settled on Screw's shoulders. Logically, Squirt's death wasn't his fault. The guy chose to get mixed up in a vicious club. He also chose to run his mouth against Crank's wishes. Still, the kid would still be alive had Screw not gone against his president's wishes and gone to the party. Playing a role in the kid's death went down like jagged shards of glass.

"Um." He cleared his throat and looked up at the ceiling. "He wasn't supposed to tell me anything he did. Crank wanted to meet with me later in the night to test the waters. It's possible Squirt fessed up to what he'd told me, but everything happened pretty damn fast after that and as Gumby drove away from their clubhouse, I saw Crank shoot Squirt in the head."

"Fuck," Zach said as the full magnitude of what the club was capable of sank in. If Crank could shoot one of his own without blinking an eye, he wouldn't hesitate to take out any of the Handlers.

Or even their women.

"How did you guys get busted?" Mav asked. "Sounds like you were home free."

"Jazz's neighbor was there partying. He recognized me."

"Jeremy?" Mav asked and when Screw nodded, he added, "Man, I hate that fuckwad."

"Tell me about it," Screw muttered. He'd known Jeremy since middle school. He'd been one of the kids who frequently snuck into the strip club where Screw's mother worked, and the asshole took unending pleasure in tormenting Screw with lurid details. Hell, he was pretty sure the guy had fucked his mom at some point.

And Jeremy wondered why he wasn't voted to prospect with the club. Now the guy had his eye on Jazz? Wasn't happening. Last thing she needed was a slimy weasel like Jeremy. She'd been through enough in her life.

And great, now he was thinking about Paul. At some point he needed to have a chat with Gumby about locating and ending that asshole.

"We need to keep an eye on his movements," Copper said.

"On it. I have a prospect tailing him today."

"Good. Thanks for being proactive about that." Copper nodded his approval which made Screw's chest puff. Finally, he'd done something right in his president's eyes. "All right. Let's get moving on this right away. Church tonight at six. We'll fill in the rest of the club. Screw, stick around a minute."

Oh, fuck. Here's where Copper said something along the lines of, "Thanks, but you're still out as enforcer."

Well, it'd been fun—and stressful as fuck—while it lasted.

As the room cleared, each and every one of his brothers slapped him on the back or squeezed his shoulder. Ugh, even they knew he was on the chopping block.

Copper sat in his chair, rubbing his chin in what they'd all come to know as his thinking mode. None of them knew if he was even aware of it, but it was the guy's biggest tell. So, Screw sat without speaking and waited for his president to formulate his thoughts.

After a minute or so, Copper folded his giant hands on the table. His silver wedding ring still made Screw chuckle. It'd been no surprise to anyone that he'd locked down Shell fast once he'd finally pulled his head out of his ass and got with her.

"I've worked with Zach as my enforcer for more than five years. His instincts were rock solid, and I trusted him to make most decisions without even running them by me."

Screw nodded. None of this was new information. Working under Zach, he'd seen the way the president valued him.

"I should have trusted you more. Zach vouched for you and I agreed to make you enforcer, but I didn't put my full trust in you. This won't work if I don't give you that."

"I get it Copper." His shoulders sagged. "Now you feel like you can't trust me. I'm sorry I didn't do the position justice."

His prez held up a hand stopping him from offering the enforcer patch back before he had to hear the man actually ask for it. "No, Screw, I'm saying I do trust you and I should have at the very least entertained the idea of someone attending the party when you came to me. Your instinct was dead on, and you brought us remarkably valuable intel we never would have gotten any other way."

"I—uh, shit, thanks, Copper." His face heated. Fuck, praise wasn't something he had much experience with. Maybe it was his own fault for always giving people a reason to roll their eyes at him instead of praise him. Regardless, felt damn good to be appreciated and valued by his president.

The president apologized.

Wait until he told Jazz and Gumby.

Or not…because, why would he?

"The club will pay to have your truck repaired too. If I'd entertained the idea, you'd have had back up and gotten out of there quicker. Hopefully with fewer bullet holes in your truck."

"Appreciate it, Cop."

"All right, get your ass outta here. I promised my woman I'd stop by the diner for breakfast."

With a lightness he hadn't expected to experience today, Screw stood and extended his hand. "Copper, I love the fuck outta this club."

"I know you do, Screw."

With that, Copper shook his hand and Screw was on his way with only one thought on his mind.

Heading to the diner to have a meal with Gumby while they watched Jazz work. He'd have much preferred for the three of them to lounge around in bed all morning, exploring each other. The hard-on he'd woken with nearly had him begging for relief, but Jazz had to be at work damn early and he'd had church. So he'd been forced to put his lust on the back burner. From the tent in Gumby's boxer briefs, he hadn't fared much better.

Good thing they had all the time in the world later.

Chapter Twenty-Seven

"Well, hey there, sir, would you like to see a menu?" Jazz said as she greeted Gumby at the diner's entrance. She flashed him a flirty grin. Damn, she looked cute in her short denim skirt, combat boots, and her diner T-shirt. Of course, she had a cardigan covering her arms, but hopefully, one day she'd feel confident enough to bare some of her scarred skin.

Back in Arizona, she'd been different. Freer. While, she'd never been promiscuous or dressed in the slutty way many of the women involved with the club did, she'd had no problem showing some skin. Skimpy tank tops, short shorts, bikinis, sexy dresses. He'd been treated to the sight of her in all of them. Her hair, still in the pixie cut, had been streaked with colors she loved to change up. She'd been gorgeous and attracted scores of male attention like any beautiful woman did. Fuck, it used to drive him crazy to walk into the lobby of the autobody shop only to find some meathead slobbering all over her. And it happened plenty of times.

But that was all before. Before her body had been scarred.

Now, she dressed with the sole purpose of evading male attention.

"I'll take one," he said, tagging her around the waist and yanking her flush against him. "But I'm pretty sure I already know what I want to eat." God, those glossy lips just begged to be kissed. But this was her place of business, and he respected her enough to honor that. The lip-lock would have to wait.

She shivered in his arms before glancing around. "Jesus, Gumby, way to get me all hot and bothered at work."

He snickered, snatched the menu out of her hands, and followed her to a booth.

Across the room, Shell stood with an overflowing tray balanced on her hand and her jaw on the floor.

Whoops. Guess that was one closet he no longer had the comfort of hiding in. He'd have to make sure Screw kept his role in all this on the down low. It wouldn't do to have anyone calling Jazz a slut for sleeping around. And the last fucking thing on earth he wanted anyone finding out was the fact that the three of them were fucking around together.

No matter how hot it was.

"Sit. I'll grab you some coffee while you decide what you want."

After slipping into the booth, he held the menu back out to her. "Surprise me. You know what I like."

Jazz paused before taking the menu and sauntering off.

It was an intimate request, having her chose his meal. He shouldn't be doing shit like that. With each day that passed, he observed just how well she'd settled into a life here in Tennessee. She loved her job, her friends, the MC. Even dropping hints to her about moving back to Arizona seemed like a wholly selfish move. He'd have to leave her here when his time was up. Leave her to Screw who they both knew would never claim her. Never claim anyone.

He'd go back to fucking everything on two legs. Gumby would go back to the desert where he'd bury himself in the closet and go back to nameless, faceless fucks in the dark.

And Jazz would be left cleaning up the mess of their short-lived kinky affair, wondering if they'd lied about how little her scars affected her beauty.

Their futures were the picture of depressing. It's not like he could stay…

What? *Stay?*

Shit, that was crazy thinking. Of course, he couldn't stay. His life was in Arizona. His job. His club. His family. A man didn't just leave an MC and move across the country for a woman. And he didn't want to uproot. He loved his life in Arizona.

After Jazz returned with his coffee, his phone buzzed against the table.

The sight of the caller ID had his eyes widening. "Hello?"

"Well, well, well, fucker. You *are* alive. Striker had me convinced you'd tumbled down the side of a goddammed mountain."

Shit, had the man known where Gumby's disloyal thoughts had drifted? He pulled the cell from his ear and stared at it before returning to the conversation. "I'm sorry? I think you have the wrong number. Who are you looking for?"

"Fuck you."

Gumby laughed. Damn, it was good to hear his brother's voice. "Jester, how's it going, man?"

A grunt came through the phone. "Huh, I'm surprised you remember my name."

Gumby dropped his head, pinching the bridge of his nose above his glasses. "All right. Message received. I've been shit at keeping in touch."

"Fuck, brother, you've all but up and disappeared." Jester's voice turned playful. "Guessing you found Jazmine and shit's going *real* well. You gonna be able to convince that little pixie to get her sweet ass back here over the next week?"

A week? Not likely. Ever? Well, that wasn't looking good either.

"That when Striker wants me back? A week?"

"Yep. I've been officially assigned the task of telling you you've got seven days to wrap your shit up and get the fuck back to Arizona."

Fuck. "Look, Jest, there's some shit going on here with the MC she's hooked up with."

"She's attached to a club? What the hell? She someone's ol' lady?"

"No, no, nothing like that. She's just gotten tight with a bunch of the ol' ladies here. Manages a diner owned by one of 'em. She's squarely under their protection."

"Huh. And they got trouble?"

"Yeah, some shit with a rival club." For a shameful second he almost entertained the thought of being grateful for the club drama. Gave him an excuse to stick around besides not being ready to stop fucking her.

And Screw.

"And you want to stick around until it's cleared up?" Jester asked.

"Um, yeah I think it's for the best." He stirred the coffee, watching the liquid swirl around the mug.

"You don't trust this club she's hooked up with? Don't think they can keep her safe?"

"What? Nah, that's not it. I've been helping a bit. Running protection on Jazzy so they don't have to. Helping with some car shit."

With a chuckle Jester said, "Jazzy? The fuck?"

"Oh, uh, shit. Sorry. Someone started calling her that here and apparently it stuck. Guess it's rubbed off on me."

"Yeah, something's rubbing on something, I'm sure. Or someone. You better not be getting too cozy out there in Tennessee, you hear me, fucker?"

Gumby stared at the table for a moment. Had he heard Jester right? Jesus the man really had been inside his head. Guilt slammed into him. "Fuck, no, brother. Don't be fucking insane."

Too cozy in Tennessee. With Jazz. And Screw.

He needed to shove those thoughts away. Now.

Yet… Jazz hovered behind the counter, laughing with a couple eating at the counter. Her smile lit her face, infectious and so gorgeous he found his mind drifting toward thoughts of seeing that smile more often. As in every day.

No. He shook his head, and if he'd been alone, he'd have given himself a sharp slap to the cheek. Damn Jester for watering the seeds of lunacy in his mind.

"Hey, you fucking listening?" Jester practically yelled into the phone.

"What? Yeah, sorry, I'm in a diner. Got loud for a second. Say it again," he said without taking his attention off Jazz. She caught him staring and winked before disappearing into the kitchen.

Damn, she belonged right here.

"Said I'll run it up the chain. Let you know what Shiv thinks about you kicking it out east a little longer."

"Thanks, brother. Owe you one."

"Ha, pretty sure you'll be owing me quite a few before this shit is all said and done."

The comment made no sense, but he had an odd feeling Jester wanted it that way. "Hey, before you go. How's Em and that sweet kiddo she made?"

"Hey, I made half that kid!"

With a snort Gumby said, "That remains to be seen."

Jester laughed. "They're great, fuck you very much. Em is hot as ever and—"

Whatever else he said got lost in a buzzing in Gumby's ears. A ripple of awareness coursed through him as though he'd picked up on some primal shift in the room's energy field. Just as he was about to look over his shoulder, Screw slid into the booth opposite him.

Jesus, was he that in tune to the other man? So much that he walked into the diner and Gumby grew aware of it?

"Uh, yeah, brother, let me know what Shiv says and kiss your fam for me."

He didn't bother to wait for Jester to respond before hanging up. It would have been something about not kissing his woman for anyone but himself.

"Hey," Screw said, lacing his fingers behind his head. "Club checking in?"

God, he looked so…fuckable. That scruffy beard, the ponytail, the freaking T-shirt that barely contained his biceps. Biceps which were prominently on display due to the position of his arms.

"Give me your phone. I'll snap a selfie. This way you'll have it whenever you need to unload your balls and I'm not around." Screw smirked in that self-satisfied way that made Gumby want to punch him and fuck him at the same time.

"Christ!" he said, glancing around. "Keep your fucking mouth down, huh?"

"Oh, please." Screw waved a hand. "No one's listening. And even if they were, I'd say that to any of my brothers." Then he leaned forward and dropped his tone. "Any of my brothers looking at me like they wanted to know what my cock tastes like."

Oh, fuck, he wanted that. He'd never. Never crossed the line from receiving to giving, but with Screw he found himself wanting everything he'd be fighting an internal battle against for the past twenty years.

"Hey, Screw." Jazzy appeared at the side of her table.

When Gumby straightened and cleared his throat, she frowned, her head bouncing between the two of them. "Everything okay?"

"Yep," Screw said, popping the *p* as he lifted his mug. "Please, may I have some coffee, pretty lady?" His pout had Gumby rolling his eyes. For someone so sexual, he could play the adorable little boy damn well.

With a snort, Jazz filled his cup. "I saw you come in and added your usual to the table's order. Gumby, if you don't mind waiting an extra minute, I'll have it brought out at the same time."

Screw waggled his eyebrows. "What do you say man? Will you wait for me to eat? I'll let you have a taste of my sausage?"

"Oh, my God, are you thirteen?" Jazz asked with a laugh.

He winked. "Pretty sure you're both well aware nothing about me resembles a thirteen-year-old. If you need a refresher…" His hands dropped beneath the table.

Jazz flushed before rolling her eyes and turning her back on them. Her face remained the cutest damn shade of pink as she checked in on a few other tables.

"You gotta knock that shit off," Gumby said.

Screw's hands went back behind his head as though he was lounging on a poolside chaise instead of waiting for an early lunch in a diner. "What shit?"

"You know what shit. The implying things." Gumby leaned in. "Between me and you, me and Jazz, you and Jazz. Someone's gonna overhear and I don't want anyone calling Jazz a slut."

Screw let out a loud snort that turned into genuine laughter. "What the fuck kinda prude club do you belong to? Pretty sure most of us know what a slut is. Jazz could fuck five of my brothers at once and not a single person I know would think that of her."

"Doesn't mean you have to broadcast it where she works."

With a scoff, Screw dropped his hands to the table, leaning in. "First of all, I didn't broadcast shit. No one knows a fucking thing beyond this booth. I wouldn't disrespect Jazz that way. Or you for fuck's sake, but I'm glad to know you think I'm that much of an asshole." He shoved to his feet then dug in his back pocket before tossing some bills on the table. "Jazzy," he called to her. "I'm gonna need mine to go." Then he turned back to Gumby. "Pretty sure you need to get shit right in your head. Because there's only one person here who's ashamed of what's going on. And it ain't me or Jazz, or anyone in my club."

"Screw—"

He held up a hand. "Copper's gonna be calling you to ask for your help with something. I was gonna fill you in, but I'm not in the mood." He covered his hand with his mouth. "Ooops, I said 'in the mood.' Bet everyone in here heard that and now thinks we're fucking."

With that, he stormed over to the counter where Lindsey was boxing up his order. When she handed it to him, he flashed her his most charming grin, leaving the thirteen-year-old with pink cheeks and a smile. But his walk from the counter to the exit was more of a stomp and the smile had morphed into an angry scowl.

That did not go well.

Gumby's left hand throbbed, a stark reminder of why he hid.

"What was that?" Jazz asked as she appeared with his food. After placing the plate in front of him, she took the seat Screw had vacated.

"Thanks, hon." He sighed. "That was me pissing him off."

She frowned as she watched Screw drive off through the front window of the diner. "What happened?"

"Nothing for you to worry about." His phone rang just as he took a bite of the perfectly seasoned hash browns. "Shit. That'll be Copper. I gotta take this."

If it was even possible, her frown deepened, and a V formed between her eyes. "Copper? Why is he calling you?"

"Fill you in later." He lifted the phone to his ear. "Hey, Copper, Screw told me to expect your call."

Jazz narrowed her eyes in that way women had of letting a man know he wasn't even close to being off the hook.

Now he owed an apology to Screw and an explanation to Jazz.

Fuck my life.

He chatted with Copper for a moment before agreeing to head over to the clubhouse once he'd finished his meal. After uncovering the mystery of what Copper needed, he'd find out where Screw lived and pay him a visit.

An apology visit.

Which would maybe lead to a round of make-up sex.

Really? That's where his mind decided to go? He shifted on the booth. His mind and his dick apparently.

Seriously, fuck my life.

Chapter Twenty-Eight

Jazz watched from behind the counter as Gumby spoke with Copper on his cell. Every sixth sense, red-flag-o-meter, and inner sage she possessed had gone on full alert the moment he'd taken that call.

Copper would call Gumby for one reason and one reason only. Something was going down with the club and they needed his assistance. But why? What could Gumby offer as a club outsider that the MC itself couldn't provide?

As the handsome man nodded his head then pushed his glasses up his nose, she smiled. The move had always endeared her to him. Truth be told, Gumby was the least biker looking biker she knew. Sure, he wore leather, boots, a cut, plenty of metal and carried himself with the confidence of the bikers she knew, but strip it all away and he could easily play a handsome businessman or even a geeky gamer.

Gumby kept his hair short, neat, and well styled. Only a few tattoos decorated his skin. As far as she'd seen he'd never even let his face get scruffy, and for a mechanic, his fingernails seemed to have much fewer permanent grease stains than all the other No Prisoners who worked in the garage. Even Acer, who'd been raised in a high society family, had more of a badass look to him. Gumby seriously gave off an extra-tall Clark Kent vibe, and she dug it. It ticked all her boxes. While he may not look the rugged, alpha biker, appearances could be deceiving, and Gumby could throw down with the best of them.

He hung up, dropped his head, and his shoulders rose and fell before he quickly downed his meal. The urge to go to him and demand answers rode her hard, but the bell jangled, indicating a customer had arrived. When she saw it was Mama V and Viper, she darted over to greet the beloved couple.

"Cassie," she said, wrapping her arms around the thin woman. "I can't believe you're here!"

"Hello, my girl," Mama V said, patting Jazz on the back.

"Viper." Jazz kissed the older man on his furry cheek. "I can't tell you how thrilled I am to see you two in here. Come sit." She guided them to a booth, slipping in next to Mama V. "You must be feeling a little better if you're out and about."

She'd been diagnosed with lymphoma not too long ago and was well into an intensive course of chemotherapy. One that had wrecked her more than the disease. Or at least that's how it seemed, watching her get sick after each treatment.

"She woke up from a nap hungry as a horse," Viper said, giving his wife of thirty some years a smile.

Cassie captured Jazz's hand in hers. "I'm feeling well today, yes. And tomorrow I have chemo which means a few days of misery, so I figured I'd take advantage of this good day and fill my belly with delicious food. Plus, I wanted to see my girls."

Jazz couldn't keep the smile off her face. She'd been so worried for Cassie. "Can I come visit in a day or two? Give Viper a break from nurse duty?"

"I'd love that, honey. Yes."

"How are the treatments going?"

"Doc says she's a dream patient," Viper said with a proud smile. "They couldn't be happier with the way it's going. We are well on the way to remission." He shot his ol' lady a wink.

Sweeter words had never been spoken. "Oh, that's amazing."

Mama V's eyes grew misty. "I'm a little afraid to be relieved, but yes, my oncologist says things couldn't be progressing better than they are."

Jazz's own eyes prickled. "God, that's so good to hear. I don't know what I would do without you two." She gave Cassie a hug then shook her head to clear the tears. "That's enough with the heavy stuff. What can I get you to eat?"

After taking their order, she returned to fill their coffee cups. Halfway back to the kitchen, Gumby intercepted her.

"Hey," she said. "You on your way out?"

"Yeah. You got a prospect here, right?"

"Yep." She nodded toward the end of the row of booths. "Monty is my babysitter extraordinaire. What did Copper want?"

Way to play it cool, Jazmine. She could have kicked herself for blurting that out, but she had to try. Wondering what the club had gotten Gumby into would eat at her all day.

He tilted his head, giving her a knowing look. "You know the game, Jazzy. It's club—"

Oh, hell no.

"If you tell me it's club business, I'm gonna lose my shit. This isn't your club, buddy. I'm already worried about Screw because he's the fu—" She glanced around at the curious eyes of a few customers on her and dropped her voice as she dragged Gumby to the side. "He's the friggin' enforcer and gonna be smack in the middle of this CDMC war. Now I've gotta worry about you, too? I'm gonna lose my fu-friggin' mind over here. You gotta give me something if you expect me to be able to sleep at night."

"Hey, hey...shh." Gumby guided her to her office, calling out to Lindsey to cover her tables as they walked. He shut the door behind him before drawing her into his arms. "I had no idea you were this worried."

Neither did she, to be honest. Not until she opened her mouth and her fears tumbled out in a nervous bout of verbal diarrhea.

Christ, they were supposed to be fucking around and now she sounded like an anxious girlfriend.

With two boyfriends.

God…

Bottom line, as much as it would freak out both men, she cared about them. Cared about these two men who not only gave her more physical pleasure than she'd ever experienced, but who showed her such compassion and tenderness she'd been able to divulge her deepest darkest secret.

Yeah, she cared about them and liked them. A lot. Too much. If something were to happen to either one of them…well, she'd be destroyed.

"Sorry," she said against Gumby's firm chest. "It's just…after the close call the other night, I know something's coming. Something big that will put Screw in danger. And now you might be in danger too…"

She focused on the large hand stroking up and down her back in a pattern meant to be soothing. And it was, but it also reminded her of how his hands felt on her skin under her clothes, making her grow damp between her thighs.

"I don't know what Copper wants from me. Yeah, I'm guessing it has something to do with whatever the Handlers have planned for the Disciples, but I'm as clueless as you are right now. That's why I'm going to meet with him."

"Hmm." She inhaled the fresh scent of whatever shower soap he'd used. The one her guest bathroom always seemed to smell like now. "Will you help them?"

His hand trekked lower, cupping her ass before journeying up her spine again. "Of course."

"No matter what he asks of you?"

"Yes, Jazzy, I'll do whatever is needed of me."

"Why? They aren't your club. You barely know them." She tipped her head back, gazing into his dark eyes framed by those sexy glasses.

"Pretty sure you know why," he said, both hands now holding her bottom.

"Because of me?" She held her breath, afraid to hope he might feel a fraction of what she was coming to feel for him.

"Yeah, baby, because of you. You're attached to them. You mean something to that club, and they mean something to you. I'd do anything to make sure you were safe and happy."

"And Screw?" she whispered as she stared at his face, trying to decipher any reaction he might have. She shouldn't push. It didn't even matter. Gumby's life was in Arizona no matter what answer he gave in that moment.

His lips pressed together before he nodded. "Sure, he's becoming a good friend. If I can help make his job easier, I will. I'd do it for any friend."

What a pat, PC answer. "He's more than a regular friend, Gumby. It's okay to admit that. No one outside the three of us knows what's going on and no one has to. Screw and I understand you aren't comfortable being out yet. We'd never betray your trust."

He stiffened before reaching back and pulling her hands apart. With a gentle push, he stepped away from her. A mask of indifference had fallen over his face, but the rigidity in his shoulders and the cold look in his eyes let her know how her words affected him. Whatever his reasons for denying who he truly was, they ran deep.

Was it his club? She'd known the No Prisoners for years and couldn't imagine them shunning him for being bisexual. Something or someone in his life had made him afraid to show the world who he truly was. Come to think of it, she knew little to nothing about Gumby's background and childhood. Maybe his reluctance to come out stemmed from his upbringing. Had his parents been rigid? Overly religious? Unaccepting?

"I'm sorry if this makes you uncomfortable, Gumby, but I think it's something we need to talk about. It's okay to want Screw. It's okay to want him to want you. And it's okay for the three of us to fuck like we've been doing. And anyone who says differently doesn't matt—oof."

Her back met the door as Gumby descended on her. His mouth took hers, cutting off any additional words and scrambling her brain until she couldn't even remember what they'd been talking about.

The lingering flavor of coffee tickled her senses and had an odd sense of pride surging alongside the lust. Something about being the one to feed him, take care of him got her going even more.

"Gumby," she said on a gasp as his sinful mouth began a trail of hot kisses down her neck. "I'm at work."

"Don't give a fuck." His mouth latched on to her collar bone sending a shiver down her spine. "Just don't scream when you come."

Oh, shit. "That's gonna be hard."

"I'm fucking hard."

The growled response had her giggling.

As his mouth returned to hers, his hands hiked the short denim skirt up and over her ass. The cold wood of the door met her skin at the same time he slid a long finger into her and she couldn't stem the sharp cry from flying out here mouth.

"Shh," he crooned as his other hand covered her mouth. "Wouldn't want me to have to stop because someone knocked on that door, would we?"

She shook her head behind his hand. Another finger joined the first, stroking her inner walls and weakening her knees. In the back of her mind, she knew this might all be a ploy to stop talking about his sexual orientation, but it felt so goddammed good she'd die if she didn't get the chance to come soon.

She rocked her hips, riding his hand as he fingered her closer and closer to an explosive climax.

"That's it, baby. Take what you want."

Her eyes fell closed, head hitting the door with a loud clunk.

Gumby chuckled. "If no one comes to check after hearing that, we might need to worry about what your coworkers think of you."

She could barely process his words, just moaned in response because though he spoke with a calm, almost unaffected tone, his fingers were working fucking magic inside her.

He hit a particularly sensitive spot, making her eyes fly open and her hands reach for his. As she held him in place, he cocked his head. "Feel good?"

"Mmm-hmm."

God, how she wanted to scream out her pleasure, but his palm prevented it. As he watched her climb higher, his grin grew predatory. There was something so erotic and slightly forbidden about him holding her captive against the door with his hand covering her mouth.

Just as she was reaching the pinnacle, as her pussy began to pulse around his skillful fingers, he pulled them from her sex.

Her muffled, "Nooo," was met with a dark, almost desperate chuckle.

"Need to fucking taste you," he said seconds before he dropped to his knees and buried his face against her pussy.

Thank God that he was tall enough to keep muzzling her, because the second his tongue hit her clit, she screamed into his palm. God, the man was a fucking pussy maestro, licking and sucking until her legs trembled with astonishing force.

She gripped his hair, unsure if she wanted to hold him close or shove him away as the sensations grew almost too intense. He took the decision away from her when he gripped her ass with both hands, holding her firmly against his hungry mouth as his tongue lashed her clit.

Jazz bit her lower lip, needing something to smother her cries now that her mouth was free.

The moment he glided those fingers back inside her, she knew it was only a matter of seconds. Then when his lips wrapped around her clit, giving a hard suck, Jazz erupted. She brought her hand up to her mouth, biting the fleshy pad of her thumb as a powerful climax stole through her. Her pussy clamped on his fingers, holding him right where she wanted him. She gripped his hair so hard, she'd owe him an apology later, but all her muscles had locked up in the throes of orgasm and she couldn't have controlled them if she tried.

"Holy shit," she whispered as the mighty contractions slowed to trembling ripples.

"Fuck, you taste good." Gumby said. He stood, wiping the back of his hand across his mouth as she righted her skirt.

"I need to sit." She stumbled her way to her desk chair as he chuckled behind her.

When she flopped onto the soft leather, he gave her a smirk. "Gotta go, beautiful. Copper's waiting."

Guess she wouldn't be returning that particular favor right now. With a wink, he left her sprawled in her chair feeling like a pile of goo.

Well, today's shift hadn't exactly gone as expected.

After a few moments of staring into space, Jazz's head began to get back in the program. It was then she realized how effectively Gumby had avoided talking about his sexual orientation. Not that she was complaining about his methods, but…sneaky man.

At some point, they'd have to discuss it. Screw didn't live his life that way. Hell, he'd probably never spent a day in the closet. How was he going to handle a relationship with a man who couldn't admit his own sexuality out loud?

A relationship?

"Jesus," she whispered. "Do you hear yourself? Get that nonsense out of your head before you end up with an annihilated heart."

But even as she said the words, she couldn't help but wonder if it was too late. If she'd already fallen in too deep with these men to walk away unscathed.

With a sigh, Jazz forced her wobbly limbs to carry her back out into the dining area. She finished her shift with a smile. Thankfully, the rest of the employees seemed oblivious to the fact she'd had a major orgasm in her office. After she closed down the diner, Monty followed her home where she spent an hour stewing in her own frustration.

She wanted to see her men. Wanted to talk to them, touch them. Hell, she just wanted to be in their presence.

"Screw it," she said, rolling her eyes at the unintended pun.

After bundling back up in her winter gear, she strode outside to where Monty sat in his idling truck. He rolled down the passenger window after she tapped against it. "I'm heading to Screw's house. He needed me to help him with something."

"You got it, Jazzy. I'll follow you there. If you're gonna be there a while I might take off."

With a nod she said, "Yeah it'll be a bit. I'm sure he'll be fine with you taking a break."

Monty's jaw hardened and he reached for the handle of his truck with a muttered, "Fuck."

"What?" She glanced over her shoulder to find Jeremy emerging from his house. She turned back to Monty who no longer sat in the truck. "Wait, wait, wait," she said as she ran around the front of his truck. "Hold up." She placed her hands on Monty's chest, holding him back from charging.

"That's the fucker who nearly got Screw killed."

"Yes. He is. And I want to speak to him. Alone."

Monty scoffed and looked at her like she'd been speaking in some alien tongue.

"I'm serious. I want two minutes. Just give me that." The MC world may be filled with alpha boys, but two of those boys were hers—if only for a hot minute—and Jeremy had nearly gotten them killed. Fuck standing on the sidelines.

"I don't know, Jazz. Screw will have my nuts if he touches you. Tex is already on thin ice because of you fuckin' ol' ladies. I don't need to be there too."

"Okay, first off, I'm not anyone's ol' lady. And second, if he so much as lays a finger on me, you can have at him, okay?" She held her hands up as she took a few steps backward.

Monty rolled his eyes as he folded his thick arms across his chest affecting a decidedly aggressive posture. "Fine but I'm not sitting in the fucking truck."

"Thank you." With a nod of appreciation, Jazz strode toward Jeremy, shoulders back, head high. They met on the narrow strip of grass separating their house.

He wore a leather jacket, much as he always did, but this time, a very obvious CDMC prospect patch seemed to stare right at her.

Shit.

"What the fuck, Jeremy?" Not the most diplomatic way to begin the conversation, but she wasn't feeling too friendly at the moment. In fact, she was edging toward downright murderous.

Apparently, Jeremy wanted to engage as much as she did. He walked straight up to her, invading her personal space with his bigger body until she had to tip her head back to see his face.

"Hey, fucker," Monty called. "Back the fuck up." The sound of his boots drawing closer had Jazz extending a hand. "Jazmine," he growled.

"Why?" she asked. "What the fuck did you have to gain by ratting my friends out?"

"Shit's changing, babe," he said with a newfound arrogance. Little boy thinking he could roll with the big boys now that he had a few new friends. "Ain't gonna be good for your guys. Might wanna switch your allegiance."

Switch her allegiance? Was he out of his mind? "Jeremy, the Handlers are good guys. I know things didn't work out with them for you, but—"

"They're fucking assholes, Jazz, and they're gonna be driven out of town. Now's your chance. I can protect you when it all goes down, but you gotta get on board now." He could protect her? How, by knocking people out with that onion breath?

"For fuck's sake," Monty said with a booming laugh. "We're not going any-fucking-where. Stop trying to play in the big kid's league."

"Jeremy, I'm not going to walk away from people I care about." She kept her tone level and unaggressive. Last thing she wanted was a fight between Jeremy and Monty on her front lawn.

He leaned in, whispering in her ear. "People like that fag Screw and the tall guy. What's his name? Gumby? He a fag too? You watch while they fuck each other?"

I wish.

"Be careful, Jazz. I gave you a chance. If you turn it down, I won't be able to protect you. They may end up watching you get fucked at some point."

A shiver ran down her spine as his tone grew as ugly as his words. That's it, Monty could have him. She stepped back, yelping as she collided with Monty.

"Get in my fucking truck," he said.

As though on auto pilot, she did as he asked, watching out the window as Monty slammed Jeremy's back against the hood of the truck. Monty leaned in, face contorted with rage as he barked a warning to her neighbor.

She didn't recognize the man Jeremy had become. This cold, threatening biker who was clearly more dangerous than she ever gave him credit for. She placed her hand over her left shoulder where the scar from Paul's very first cut tingled. Not realizing the depths of what a man was capable of could be one of the most dangerous mistakes in life.

She knew that from first-hand experience. So much had been taken from her due to her inability to see the truth about a person until it was too late. And it was happening again. How had she ever thought Jeremy harmless?

The encounter only served to rachet up her worry for Screw and Gumby. Unease had her stomach churning.

A storm was brewing. A cyclone she hoped wouldn't scar her insides to match her outside.

Chapter Twenty-Nine

Screw clicked the television off, tossed the remote on the couch, and drained the last of his beer. Waste of his fucking time. Why the hell did the ol' ladies watch this Housewives shit? Catty Barbie dolls who caused more drama in one episode than he'd be willing to put up with in a fucking lifetime. Yeah, that's right, he'd been watching reality television. Only because he wanted to see what Jazz did with her girls.

Relationships. Who fucking needed them? Certainly not him. People just used each other until they got what they wanted and left or until they'd torn each other to bits. How many times had he seen it with his mother?

Countless.

And if he'd ever needed the swift kick-to-the-nuts reminder of that, he'd gotten it today. What the fuck kinda man couldn't even admit who he wanted to bone?

Fucking was fucking. If it felt good, do it. Who gave a fuck if you wanted your mouth on pussy, dick or a little of both? And if someone wanted to take it up the ass? More power to 'em. That shit felt amazing.

A heavy knock on the door had him peeling himself off the couch. Better not be any kids selling shit he didn't want. "Ain't interested," Screw called as he yanked the door open. "Huh," he said, grabbing the top of the door frame.

He didn't miss the way Gumby's gaze fell to the strip of stomach now on display from his shirt riding up. Guy was the king of mixed signals. Turning his back on Screw one minute then staring at him with starving eyes the next. And did he have to look so fucking sexy with those glasses and his solemn expression?

Despite his anger, he wanted Gumby. Wanted him with an explosive force.

"Turns out I am interested." Screw said, his gaze perusing the other man in a way that would leave no doubt to erotic intention. "Too bad you can't say the same. Guess it's a good thing I've got a phone full of men ready to fall on my dick at any time. Or who'd like me to fall on theirs." He winked. "I'm easy."

Gumby didn't react in the least. He just stood on the stoop, hands in the pockets of his leather jacket, charcoal beanie keeping his head warm. Those goddamned glasses made him look like blonde fucking Superman in disguise and made Screw's dick hard every time he saw them.

Now being no exception.

"You just here to decorate my doorstep?"

"When I was fifteen years old," Gumby began, "my old man caught me with my neighbor's dick in my hand. He was a year older, openly gay, and more than willing to teach me my way around an ass. We had fun for a few weeks, sneaking off whenever my old man was at work. He blew me a few times. I didn't do much beyond jerk him off or finger fuck him. I was too nervous. It was all too new. Since I was attracted to girls too, I was...confused."

He looked off to the side with a sigh and Screw's anger melted away. He'd been lucky in some respects. With a stripper as a mother, talk of sex in all its forms was more common than getting help with his homework. His mother's friends were all in the industry and often took pay for sex as a way to make an extra few bucks. Screw grew up not having a single bit of shame where his own sexuality was concerned. Of course, on the flip side, he had to live with the humiliation of his mother being the town slut…

But he knew it wasn't the same for many. Hell, for most. Maybe he should have been more sensitive to Gumby's issues.

"So what happened?"

"Huh?" Gumby turned back to him.

"What happened when you got caught."

"Oh. My dad broke my hand with a hammer. Said I couldn't hold a dick if my fingers were busted."

Shit. The way Gumby said it, with this detached voice as though reading from a dictionary made Screw's heart clench. He wanted to reach out for the other man but didn't know how his touch would be received. He was so far out of his element, he found himself terrified of doing the wrong thing.

"Then he beat the shit out of me so bad I couldn't go to school the next day. Shit started happening to the neighbor's family too. Bad shit. The kid was jumped and beaten nearly as bad as I was. A fire destroyed his father's office. Their car was tampered with. No one was ever caught, but I knew who it was."

"Christ, Gumby, that shit's fucked up."

"My dad took the hammer he'd broken my fingers with and hung it from a hook on the wall right next to my bedroom," he went on as though Screw hadn't spoken. "Told me if he caught me so much as looking at another guy, he'd shove the handle up my ass until I was *cured*." The word fell from his tongue as though a vile expletive.

Screw stayed quiet this time, letting him purge the toxins. Finally, he began to understand what made Gumby tick. Not only did he understand it, he'd lived it in another form. No one knew better than Screw how parents could fuck up their kids, giving them lifelong issues.

"He'd always been on me, calling me a fag and a fairy. I think he could sense my interest in guys." Gumby let out a harsh, ugly bark of laughter. "But after that day, it became relentless."

He fell quiet and just when Screw thought Gumby was done talking, he continued.

"Pretty sure there wasn't a time he was in my presence from that day forward that he didn't remind me of what he thought of men who wanted other men. It was drilled into my head every single day for years. And it was beaten into my body at least two dozen times from that day forward. Until I was eighteen and slammed the fucking door on that phase of my life."

Slammed the door but didn't shake the demons.

They stared at each other, white puffs flowing from their mouths as they breathed the cold air. The frigid breeze stung Screw's skin but he barely felt it.

"Did he ever…" Christ, did he really want to know?

"No. He never sodomized me with the hammer. He didn't need to. All the broken bones throughout the years and the daily reminders of how disgusting I was did the trick."

"So…am I…"

Gumby tilted his head and a small smile finally graced his lips. "Are you the first guy since then?"

Screw just nodded, unable to even suck in a breath. The weight of that responsibility settled heavy on his shoulders.

"No. You're not. I've been sucked off a number of times, and I've fucked a few guys. But I always waited until the need became too strong to ignore. Then I'd drive to a city two hours away. Find the seediest gay bar I could and fuck some nameless, faceless dude with my eyes closed, my stomach revolting, and my disgust in my heart."

Screw nodded. So much made sense now. But it hurt. *Disgust.*

"Did—" Christ, was he really going to ask this? This man was turning him into a fucking pussy. "Did you feel that way with me?"

Gumby's eyes widened. "No. And that's why I freaked the fuck out. I can't say it out loud yet, Screw. I'm working on it, but I just can't put a voice to my needs or desires. Maybe someday. I'm just not there yet. But I can tell you this, I won't deny you like I did today. When it's just us and Jazz, and we're joking around, or…whatever. I won't run from it. I'm all in for however long this lasts."

It was his turn for a bit of internal panic. His natural inclination to balk at the idea of relationships tried to rush to the surface, but Screw shoved it back down. Gumby had just made himself vulnerable in a way he didn't seem to have done before. Rejection would sever their shaky connection. Screw stepped aside. "Come on in before you freeze your nuts off. They'll be of no use to me all cold and shriveled."

With a chuckle, Gumby walked into the warm house. "One track mind."

And just like that, they were back on even ground. Screw couldn't believe the relief he felt at having mended that rift. He winked. "You know it." As Gumby strode past him, Screw grabbed his arm. "Thank you," he said.

Gumby nodded.

"I won't push. Promise. Take the time you need." Screw swallowed the terror his next words evoked. "I'm not going anywhere."

For a second, Gumby hesitated, then he cupped Screw's jaw in his large hand and kissed him. It was a tender meeting of lips, perhaps the softest kiss he'd ever received. Their tongues tangled for a few moments before Gumby pressed one last chaste kiss to lips then whispered, "For the record, you're only the second man who's had his lips on mine."

The first obviously being the kid Gumby experimented with.

And damn if that didn't do something warm and unsettling to Screw's insides. Something that hit on his hot button. Something he couldn't yet talk about. So instead, he said, "Want a beer?"

As Gumby shrugged out of his jacket, he said, "Yeah, that sounds perfect right about now. Thanks."

Gumby looked so right, standing in Screw's house. Like he belonged there. Now they just needed Jazz to walk in the door and his little fantasy would be complete. But that was a fool's wish, especially since Gumby had just come from a meeting with Copper where he was asked to aide in fucking over an enemy club.

And on that note…

"You met with Copper?" Screw called from the kitchen as he grabbed them each a winter ale. He returned to the den to find Gumby placing his jacket over the back of the couch.

"I did, yeah."

"And? You in?"

Gumby nodded. "I'm in. I'll be at church with you guys to plan."

Screw held out the bottle. "Good. Thanks." God, this was awkward as fuck. Maybe they should talk more about the club and the CDMC, but Screw just wanted to enjoy Gumby's company for a bit. They needed to just…hang. So instead of continuing that discussion, he said, "You wanna watch a movie or something?"

Gumby walked toward him, a smile on his handsome face. He reached out and rubbed his palm on Screw's beard. Screw wanted to lean into the touch like a contented cat. So he did. Then he captured Gumby's hand in his own, drawing it away from his face. This must be the one that had been broken. How had he not noticed the slightly crooked pinky and how his middle finger didn't fully straighten? Though he hadn't planned on making the mood heavy again, Screw lifted Gumby's hand and placed a kiss on his knuckles. He wished he could do more to heal the man, but how could he right a youth filled with abuse and hatred? "Does it hurt at all, Will?"

Gumby shrugged. "Once in a while. If I over do it. This cold weather sure doesn't help. I'm all right, Luke. Promise."

They stared at each other for a heated moment before Gumby tilted his head and gave Screw a half smile. "You on the other hand are not." This time he tugged on Screw's beard. "This is getting a little out of control there, man."

With a laugh, Screw scratched his chin. The itch had mostly gone away, but Gumby was right. It was looking messy as hell. "First time I've let it get longer than scruff. I'm liking the beard, but I don't really know what the hell I'm doing with it. Which is why it's looking all raggedy."

"I can help you trim it up if you want?"

Screw raised an eyebrow as he took a sip of his beer. "Sure this isn't just a ploy to get close to my jugular with a pair of scissors?"

Gumby threw back his head and let out a laugh. Finally, any lingering tension dissolved and all that remained was two guys enjoying each other's company.

"Leave it to you to think along those lines."

"I had to check," he said with a wink.

Bumping his shoulder, Gumby said, "Come on, where's your bathroom."

Screw lead him through the house into the master bathroom.

"Nice place," Gumby said.

He wasn't much for decorating, but at least his place wasn't a filthy shithole of a bachelor pad. For some odd reason, Gumby's opinion of his home mattered. "Thanks. Could use a woman's touch. Maybe Jazz would be willing to spruce it up a bit."

"Bet she'd love that."

"Right through there." Screw gestured for Gumby to head into the master bathroom. Once they were both inside the master bath, he fished out his supplies and handed them over.

"What are you thinking?" Gumby asked.

"Just neaten it up. I think I'll keep it cut pretty close. Whatever you think looks good. I trust you."

The air thickened as their gazes caught. Screw propped his ass against the vanity, waiting for Gumby to get to it. Watching the other man lay out the clippers, scissors, and beard oil proved to be a treat. His long, deft fingers gave a man all sorts of naughty ideas. Especially someone like Screw, who pretty much had dirty thoughts all day long.

And the way he smelled? In the confines of the small room, Gumby's natural aroma of soap, motor oil, and something unique to him overwhelmed Screw's senses.

"Ready?" Gumby picked up the clippers and started them up. An incessant buzzing filled the room.

"Do your worst."

"I'm just gonna do your neck and even up the sides first." Gumby got to work, trimming the sides of his beard with slow, gentle strokes of the clippers. Every touch of his hands, though not intended to arouse, drove Screw crazy with need.

Screw couldn't get enough of watching him. The way his lower lip tucked between his teeth as he concentrated. The way Gumby's glasses slipped down his nose, just a millimeter, but enough to have him shoving them back up with a tiny grunt of irritation. The way his eyes narrowed as he focused on the task.

It was taking everything in Screw to keep from ripping the clippers from Gumby's hands, dropping to his knees, and sucking him until he collapsed.

Once he was satisfied with the job, Gumby grabbed the scissors and trimmed the longest of the hairs, the stragglers. Then he returned to the clippers and gave the overall beard a good trim. Screw practically purred like a cat being petted by its favorite owner.

Both of them were fully dressed. Hell, they weren't even skin on skin in any way and Screw's cock was so hard, it was becoming near impossible to ignore. Especially for someone not used to denying that particular part of his body. Gumby either didn't notice or had a kink Screw hadn't known about that involved torturing his lovers with severe blue balls.

"Okay," Gumby said, oblivious to Screw's pain. He grabbed Screw's shoulders and leaned back, eyes darting back and forth from left to right. "Looks pretty damn even. Not too bad if I do say so myself. Take a look."

Screw turned, assessing himself in the mirror. "Shit, G, this auto mechanic thing doesn't work out you have a career as a barber. I'm looking fly." He rubbed his cheeks and chin, turning his head as he admired himself.

"Turn back, let me oil you up."

Yes please, oil every inch of me while you're at it.

"Sure." Screw turned in time to see Gumby drop a few beads of beard oil onto his callused hands. The scent of sandalwood filled the room adding another layer to the sex factor.

Hovering only a few inches above him, Gumby used his long fingers to massage the oil into Screw's beard. As he stroked in a circular motion with gentle pressure, Screw's eyes nearly rolled back in his head at the simple pleasure of it all. The moment felt heavy, intimate, perhaps one of the most intimate he'd ever experienced with another man…hell, with anyone.

When Gumby slid his fingers into Screw's hair, massaging his scalp as he'd stroked his face, Screw lost the battle to remain stoic. He moaned and gripped the other man's hips, pulling him in until their groins met. When he realized Gumby was as hard as he was, he groaned. "You're fucking killing me. Need you so bad."

Gumby's answering groan might as well have been his hand fisting Screw's cock with the way it made him jerk. The taller man leaned in close, brushing his smooth cheek against Screw's neat beard.

"Feels so good," Gumby whispered. "The hair on your face." He pried Screw's fingers from his hips and interlaced them with his, keeping their pelvises joined. "The roughness of your hands."

Screw bit his lip and rocked his hips forward. His cock needed friction like his brain needed oxygen. Neither was getting enough of what it craved at that moment. He wanted more, but apparently, Gumby wasn't done torturing him with his words in a way Screw had never experienced.

"The way you're so hard," he went on as though Screw wasn't seconds from combusting. Gumby grabbed Screw's cock through his clothes, giving a none-too-gentle squeeze. "Not just here, but all over." Screw nearly came in his pants when his cock got another squeeze at the same time Gumby grasped his bicep. "So fucking hard. And then when Jazz is with us? Balancing it all out with her softness, her sweetness, her wet pussy…fuck, Luke, it's goddammed heaven."

"Will," he managed to say, voice deep and ragged in a way he'd never heard from his own throat. "I can't take much more." In seconds, he'd be begging, completely shameless in his need to feel relief. Something he'd never had to do. He'd always dove in, took when he needed, then jetted. No one had ever played with him, made him wait, made him crave.

Gumby gave him a quick, bruising kiss, swiping his tongue against Screw's for just long enough to be another tease.

As his flavor hit, Screw froze. Was that… "Do you taste like Jazz?"

"Sure do," he said with a wink and the thought of Gumby eating Jazz out before he came to him was unreal. "I want to suck you," Gumby whispered by his ear.

"Jesus Christ." Screw gripped the countertop behind him. God, he wanted that. Wanted it with a force that nearly had him shoving the man to his knees. But rationality somehow prevailed. "Gumby…"

A finger landed across his lips. "Don't tell me I don't have to. I know that. I may be a little rough around the edges since you're my first, but I fucking want it, Luke." Gumby's dark eyes practically smoldered as he ground his erection against Screw's.

Gumby was a big boy. If he said he wanted to suck Screw, who was he to deny the man?

"Yeah," Screw said, rolling his hips against that tempting erection. "You do want it, don't you? Want a mouth full of my big cock."

When Gumby growled and practically ripped Screw's sweatpants down, he knew there was a fucking God. No other explanation for this prayer being answered.

As Gumby slowly sank to his knees, letting his hands stroke down Screw's thighs, he took the sweats with him. Screw peeled his T-shirt over his head. The only thing he wanted to feel on his skin was Gumby. Not the fabric of his clothes. Hell, not even the air in the room.

Just Gumby.

His dick stretched toward the man on his knees as though it knew what was coming and couldn't fucking wait another second. A flash of hesitation crossed Gumby's face and as much as Screw would give in that moment to have the man's lips surround him, he wouldn't sacrifice Gumby's psyche. Now that he knew what made the man tick, what shaped his view of himself and the world, he wanted to protect not only Gumby's body, but his heart and mind.

God, what a head fuck.

"Will…"

"Shut the fuck up, Screwball. I'm blowing you whether you want it or not."

Screw laughed. "Pretty sure the house could burn down around us and I'd still want it. Just don't want you to feel pressured."

Their gazes met and he saw the gratitude in Gumby's right before the man opened his mouth and sucked the tip of Screw's cock into his mouth.

"Jesus, fuck," Screw said as heat and suction made his head fall back on his shoulders.

With a curiosity he wouldn't have expected, Gumby played with his dick, learning how to pleasure him with licks, sucks, and even the occasional hum.

For his part, Screw let Gumby know exactly what he liked. Not that it was a chore. He whimpered every time the man licked right under the head of his dick, a particular favorite of his. After a few moments, Gumby grew bolder, taking Screw deeper and deeper into his mouth. When he finally hit the back of Gumby's throat, the man gagged, making Screw yank back.

"I'm good," Gumby said with a smile. "Gotta figure this shit out."

Screw snickered but it was as strained as the rest of his muscles from holding back. Gumby dove down his dick again, this time relaxing his throat and managing to avoid triggering his gag reflex. Then he did it again. And again.

"Fuck, baby," Screw said. "God, you're getting it. You're sucking me like a fucking master now."

"Mmm."

His hands fell to Gumby's head, gripping the short strands. "Tell me if it's too much. I just need… Oh, fuck."

The suction increased with a sharp spike as though the prick of pain in Gumby's scalp did it for him.

Screw's balls were full and ached with the need to unload down this man's throat. As though he sensed Screw's thoughts, Gumby cupped his sac giving it a light tug.

"Fuuuck me," Screw said on a groan as his orgasm drew closer.

Just as his eyelids fell closed and he completely lost himself to the pleasure, a soft gasp had both men freezing.

Screw's eyes popped open and his jaw hinged wide. Slack-jawed in the entrance to his bathroom stood Jazz, looking cute as fuck in black leggings and a V-neck sweater. Might not seem like much, but that small show of skin was more than she'd bared since he'd known her. A few thin scars were plainly visible where the sweater dipped, and pride swelled in Screw. She was so strong.

"Jazzy," he said, making Gumby pop off his dick with an indrawn breath. He rocked back on his knees, turning to stare at her.

The three of them stayed that way for a moment, staring without words. Then Screw began to notice a few things, like the flush to Jazz's face. And the way her chest rose and fell. The twin points of her nipples poking through the fabric of her sweater.

She wasn't shocked by what she witnessed; she was turned the fuck on.

"Jazzy," he said again and this time the sound of her name seemed to snap her from the trance.

"Don't stop," she whispered. "God, don't stop. It's hot, so freakin' hot, but it's also beautiful." Her gaze shifted to Gumby whose tense body seemed ready to bolt at any second. "You two are so gorgeous together." Then she chuckled. "Maybe that's not what you want to hear, but God, it's incredible."

Slowly, as though he wasn't certain she spoke the truth, Gumby began to relax. Jazz walked toward them and once she was close enough, she ran her fingers through Gumby's soft hair.

She tilted her head as if to ask, "Okay?" and when Gumby nodded once, she guided him back to Screw's hard-on which hadn't waned one bit with the pause in action.

"Open," she said. Gumby immediately obeyed, and when she bent down to his ear, whispering, "Suck him hard," both men groaned.

The smile playing across her lips was positively devious.

"Take your top off," Screw rasped as Gumby licked his length. "Let me see those tits while his mouth is on me."

Her eyes flared at the same time Gumby followed her directions to a T. He sucked like he was trying to get straight to the center of his favorite Tootsie Pop. "Fuck, that mouth…God damn."

Jazz stripped out of her top then did him one better by shedding the leggings as well. She stood before them, hot pink lace cupping her tits. With a sassy smile, she spun, giving him an unobstructed view of the pink string disappearing between her smooth ass cheeks.

If he could have spoken, he'd have complimented her, but his throat dried up as Gumby sucked him to the root.

Electricity raced down his spine, landing in his balls and making his whole body jolt. Two more seconds of suction and he'd unload down Gumby's throat. While that had seemed like the perfect ending a few moments ago, he now had other ideas.

"Enough," he barked, gently pulling from Gumby's mouth.

The man at his knees and Jazz stared at him like he'd lost his mind.

And maybe he fucking had, because in that moment all he could think about was being connected to these two people in the most primal of ways.

"I want to fuck you," he said to Jazz. "I want us both to fuck you. Both inside you."

When she gasped and said, "At…um…at…"

He nodded. "At the same time."

Chapter Thirty

Jazz's heart stuttered then took off like a sports car going zero to sixty in one point two seconds. Sure, she'd thought about this moment. About the possibility of making this a true threesome, but that was before she *felt*. Before she worried about every move these men made. Before she stressed about Gumby returning to Arizona and Screw growing bored. Before she feared for their lives against the CDMC.

If she did this, it'd be more than three people fucking to get off. Maybe not to them, but it was time for her to be honest with herself and admit what she felt for these men. What exactly that was, she hadn't had the courage to dig into. Because she knew deep down in a place that terrified her, it was something close to a four-letter word.

The four-letter word that had the power to create unbreakable bonds. Yet that same word could tear down empires, ruin lives, and destroy hearts.

But as she gazed upon the two men in the bathroom, one naked and staring at her as though he could eat her up, the other on his knees with much the same need in his eyes, she could no sooner deny them than she could live without water.

"I want that," she said, realizing as she spoke how true the words were. Her body readied itself instantly, growing wet as could be between her legs.

She hadn't been certain what she'd walk into after the way the men left things at the diner. When no one had answered the ringing doorbell, she'd feared walking in on them icing split lips and blackened eyes.

They'd been going at it all right, just not in the way she'd expected. And fuck, if it hadn't been the most erotic sight she could have imagined. Porn directors would salivate over the opportunity to film these two together.

Screw stalked toward her as Gumby rose to his feet, ripping his own shirt over his head.

"You're fucking gorgeous," Screw said, hands going to her ass. He yanked her flush against him, pressing a quick, brutal kiss to her lips.

One of his hands trailed up her leg and under the string of her thong, tracing it up and down the cleft between her cheeks. "Have you ever—"

"Yes," she said, shuddering as his touch brought goose bumps to the surface of her skin.

"Hmm, naughty, Miss Jazmine." He smirked, making her roll her eyes.

Like he had the market on raunchy sex.

"And?"

Her face heated. "And…it's been a while, but I liked it. A lot."

"Well, well, well, I must say I didn't expect this."

"I wasn't always afraid to let people see my body," she said with a shrug. "Back in the day I had an active and varied se—"

"Shh," Screw placed a finger over her lips. "I'm finding thoughts of you with anyone but me or Gumby make me murderous."

What? Her eyes nearly fell out of her head. He had to be kidding, right? Mr. Fuck anything and everything was…what? Jealous?

No freaking way.

"Yes fucking, way," he said with a chuckle, making her realize she'd blurted the thought aloud. "I'm feeling mighty possessive at the moment so let's skip the walk down memory lane."

"You started it," she said with a wink.

A chuckle drew their attention to where Gumby stood shirtless, leaning against the counter.

"You got something to say, G?"

He smiled. "Nah, just watching my naked man and my nearly naked woman chat about the past while they should be getting on with the fucking."

Hearing them referred to by the word "my" had Jazz's insides melting. First Screw acting like he couldn't stand the thought of her being with another man, and now Gumby calling them his. And they were standing around teasing, enjoying each other's presence as much more than just sex buddies.

God, she was in way too deep. The kind of deep that might drown her.

But heaven help her, she wasn't sure she ever wanted to surface.

Gumby pushed off the counter and pressed himself along Screw's back. When he nipped a sharp bite into the curve of Screw's neck, Screw hissed and shivered against her. "How about we take this party to your bed, huh?"

"Fuck yes," Screw said.

In a move she never saw coming, he dropped to a squat, pressed his shoulder to her stomach and hoisted her over his shoulder. Jazz squealed as the world flipped upside down. She never had time to get accustomed to the position change because before she knew it, the world was shifting again. She landed on the bed with a soft bounce.

"This is a big bed," she said moving her arms as though making a snow angel on top of the king-sized mattress.

"Perfect for three," Screw said with a wink.

He crawled up the mattress, past her head, until he reached the headboard. Then he sat with his back to it, scooped her up under her arms, and dragged her flush against him, seated between his legs.

"You know, I can move myself," she said, eyes on Gumby as he stood at the foot of the bed, shucking his jeans.

"Where's the fun in that?" Screw answered her. "Damn, Gumby, your cock is busting out of those boxer briefs. Lose 'em."

Jazz licked her lips as Gumby drew the royal blue fabric down, revealing his erection inch by inch.

"You look hungry, Jazzy," Gumby said with a wink.

"I am." God how she was hungry for him. For them.

Screw's hands slipped under her arms and around to her breasts where he plucked her nipples through the lacy bra. The added texture from the lace abrading her sensitive flesh made her tremble within seconds.

"Guess I should feed you then." Gumby crawled onto the bed then knee walked until he was able to stroke his cock against her lips. As he did just that, she let her tongue peek out and have a small lick. He jolted as though she'd shocked him then cursed when she opened wide and took him deep, mimicking what she'd seen in the bathroom moments ago.

"Baby," he said, hands sliding into her hair. "I could spend my life being sucked by you."

Did he realize he just implied something long term between them? Of course not. It was just words uttered in the throes of passion. But it made her want exactly what he'd proposed. Spending their lives pleasuring each other.

God, she was a fool…

Screw chose that moment to abandon her nipples, reach under her thighs and pull her legs up. She positioned her feet near her ass as she sucked on Gumby's length.

Her thong had gone from damp to soaked long ago, and when Screw brushed his fingers across her saturated panties, she released Gumby's cock with a sharp cry.

"Jesus, she's wet, G. Drenched. So ready for you to fuck her." As he spoke, Screw stroked a fingertip up and down the wet strip hiding her pussy. She squirmed against the too light touch, needing more. Needing one of them inside her.

Jazz opened her mouth to swallow Gumby down again, but he backed off.

"I need to see." His voice sounded like ground glass, strained, rough, ready to fuck. "I'm too on the edge for you to suck me. Let me see, Luke."

Screw let out a small grunt then pulled her legs back even farther, fully exposing her to Gumby's ravenous gaze.

"Fuck, you're right. So wet. Probably soft and hot too, huh?"

Jazz just stared, her legs quivering and pussy clenching with need under Gumby's stare. To go from no male attention for so long to being the heated focus of two very intense men was as thrilling as it was overwhelming. She'd hidden her body for so long and now wanted nothing more than to be naked with these men as often and as long as possible.

"Swear to God, Luke, every time you run you finger across her she gets even wetter. Our girl wants us to fuck her."

Screw kissed her neck. "Do you, baby? You need us in you?"

"Y-yes. Please."

Gumby leaned in, pressing a kiss to the damp thong.

"Please," she said again as the need to be filled grew to near unbearable. "Please, Gumby, I need you." Maybe later, she'd be embarrassed by the shameless begging, but now the need overrode any embarrassment.

Screw released her thighs, allowing Gumby to peel her thong down her legs. Once he'd rid her of the soggy fabric, he brought it to his nose, taking a long, slow inhale. Behind her back, Screw's dick twitched. But when Gumby tossed him the thong and Screw repeated the move, his cock grew significantly harder against her.

Gumby flopped down on his back next to her and Screw. "Want you to ride me." In a move that had her yelping, he grabbed her hips, spun her, and settled her across his lap.

"Shit," she said as she planted her hands on his chest to keep from collapsing. "When'd you get so strong?" The thought of riding him sent a thrill through here. Especially if Screw planned to…

He reached into his nightstand, pulled out two condoms and a bottle of lube. After tossing one of the condoms to Gumby, he dropped the other next to the lube on the bed and for the first time since they started this, a ripple of nerves shot up Jazz's spine.

Screw must have sensed it because he moved in behind her, soothing her with a shoulder massage. "Beautiful," he whispered as they watched Gumby roll the condom down his length. His massage moved lower, until his hands were full of her ass, squeezing and rubbing her cheeks. "You gonna let me in here, gorgeous? You gonna let us take you at the same time?"

God help her but yes, yes she was. Despite the nerves, despite the inevitable heartbreak, she was going to let these two men own her body in a way no one had before.

"Climb on his cock, baby. He's ready for you. Waiting. Look at how he's sweating, holding back the need to flip you over and pound into you."

"Fuck, Luke," Gumby said as his dick jumped.

She locked eyes with him as he gripped her hips. With one hand, she circled his dick, giving it a solid tug before lining him up with her dripping pussy. Once she had him exactly where she wanted him, she descended, slow as could be.

As she took him into her body, she forced her eyes to stay open. Forced herself to watch the clenching of his jaw. The way his fingers curled into her hips. The subtle arch to his back as pleasure worked its way up his spine.

"You feel so good around him, baby," Screw whispered, his hands roaming all over her body.

"He feels so good inside me."

"Tell me. Tell us what he's doing to that pussy."

Their pelvises met. Jazz rolled her hips, moaning as his cock stroked inside her. Gumby's nostril's flared. It was clear he was trying to control himself. Trying to hold off the actual fucking until Screw had also worked his way inside her.

"He's stretching it. Stretching me. It's so good. I love it." Jazz began a slow, gentle ride. God, she wished she could spend her life right here, soaking up every sensual experience these two had to offer.

The snick of a cap had her jumping and peeking over her shoulder. Screw squeezed lube on to two of his fingers. "You okay, baby? Just gonna get you good and ready for me."

She nodded, unable to speak as nerves and excitement collided inside her.

"Come here," Gumby said, drawing her mouth to him. They kissed, a hot desperate tangle of tongues.

The position left her ass perfectly open and available to Screw. With a gentle touch she wouldn't have expected from him weeks ago but had come to treasure, he stroked a finger over her rear entrance.

She flinched but he soothed her with nonsense words and soft touches while Gumby lightly thrust inside her and devoured her mouth. Sensations bombarded her from every angle, making it difficult to focus on just one, which was how Screw worked a finger inside without her fully realizing what was happening.

"You okay?" Gumby asked against her lips. He must have sensed a tautness in her posture.

She nodded. "It's intense." And it was. The pressure, the vulnerability, the trust she'd put in these men.

Screw's lips landed on the middle of her spine. He kissed his way up as he gently fucked her ass with his finger. "Can you take more?" he whispered against her ear.

She moaned and dropped her head before nodding.

He worked another finger in and spent a few minutes preparing her for his cock. When he finally pulled his digits out, she moaned at the loss of fullness.

"Don't worry, Jazzy. I'm coming back." The snick of the cap on the lube bottle helped ease some of her nerves. Screw was taking good care of her.

Pressure at her anus had her tensing. The heat from his skin combined with the coolness of the lube, making her shiver. Though his fingers were thick, his cock was thicker. Sweat dotted her brow. Hopefully she could take him. Could give her men this. Could give all of them this.

"You're so perfect, Jazmine," Gumby whispered from below her. He'd stopped moving, holding still deep within her. "Relax for him. Let him in and I promise he'll make you feel better than you've ever imagined."

She blew out a breath, focusing on the swirling depth of Gumby's brown eyes. He stroked his hand over her sides, not paying any attention to her scars. If she hadn't known better, she'd have thought he wasn't even aware they existed.

As he pushed forward, Screw held her hips, but didn't yank her onto his cock. He took his time, working his way into her body as she panted through the sharp increase in pressure and unavoidable bite of pain. Once he pushed past that tight outer ring of muscle, she sighed in relief and he moved with increasing ease.

Inch by inch he entered her until her arms and legs trembled and the ultimate feeling of fullness overrode every other sensation.

"Screw," she whimpered. "Do you feel it?"

"Yeah, baby. I feel it."

"Gumby?" She didn't know why it was so important. Why she needed the verbal confirmation, but it became imperative the words fell from each man's lips. It felt like she'd wanted them forever and now she had them. All together. As one.

"Fuck, I feel it."

They were all connected inside her body just as she'd foolishly allowed them to join together in her heart.

Chapter Thirty-One

Gumby's whole world shrank down to the people and acts occurring in Screw's bed. Buried balls deep inside the woman he couldn't get enough of, his cock practically begged him to move. To take. To fuck.

But then, Screw slowly filled her ass and Gumby nearly lost his mind. With every millimeter Screw wedged into Jazz's tightest channel, Gumby experienced the drag along his cock.

Jazz wanted to know if he felt it?

Jesus, did he feel it. He felt Jazz, hot and tight all around him. He felt Screw's length all along his. He felt Jazz's fingernails biting into his pecs. He felt Screw's powerful thighs bracketing his and Jazz's sweat-soaked bodies. He felt the rise and fall of his own chest as he fought to calm his racing heart. And he felt this odd sensation under his ribcage. A twist directly in his heart. A sense of rightness so terrifying, he shoved it away and focused instead on holding back his orgasm.

"God, Jazzy, please tell me you're okay, cuz I gotta move," Screw said as he curled his body over her back. "It's just too damn good."

"Yes," she said. "Please. Just…go easy."

Screw pressed a kiss to her shoulder then her cheek before his gaze locked with Gumby's.

His palms itched to touch the other man, so Gumby ran his hand up Screw's arms and over his shoulders. Perspiration coated the other man's body, a testament to how hard he worked to restrain himself.

When he gave Screw's shoulders a sensual squeeze, the other man pressed a kiss to Gumby's forearm. This whole scene was so sensual, so intimate, so…loving.

Finally, Screw moved his hips, drawing slowly out of Jazz. She moaned, a long, low sound as her nails dug even deeper into Gumby's chest.

When just the tip of Screw remained, Gumby flexed his hips slightly, nudging farther into Jazz. As Screw thrust back in, Gumby withdrew. They moved in tandem, working up to a steady rhythm that had both men grunting with every pump.

"Fuuuck," Screw said. How he was able to speak, Gumby would never know. "You're so perfect, Jazz," he said as he thrust into her with more force than before, making Gumby groan as their dicks rippled across each other. "You're taking us so good. Every time I move, Gumby's cock strokes mine inside you. And when you clench around us—"

"Like this," Jazz said, breathless as she squeezed her internal muscles.

"Oh, shit," Gumby said, arching his back. His brain began to cloud as pleasure and the need to come took over. His hips moved in a frenzy, out of his control. Nothing had ever felt this incredible.

Screw increased his pace as well, fucking into Jazz's ass. For her part, she tried to add to the thrusts, rocking her pelvis in time with them, but when they moved with frantic, unsophisticated strokes, all she could do was claw at his chest and whimper.

Screw held her hips, grunting each time he bottomed out inside her. Gumby kept a hold on Screw's thighs, the damn hairs tickling his palms.

His dick had never been squeezed like this before. Never been in such a tight cavern and fuck if he didn't think he could give this up. Heat shot down his spine straight to his balls, which ached with the need for release.

Above him, Jazz's small tits bounced so temptingly. He arched up as best he could, capturing one nipple between his teeth and giving a sharp nip. Jazz's whole body jolted like she'd been electrocuted.

"I'm gonna come," she shouted. "Oh, my God, I'm gonna come."

"Fuck yes, baby. Give it to us." Screw pounded her like a man possessed from behind as Gumby did the same from below. Suddenly Jazz's back bowed, and she wailed out a powerful climax, her body quaking and bucking. "Don't you fucking come until she gives us another," Screw ordered in a harsh tone that had Gumby clenching his teeth.

"Fuck you. I need to fucking come." The intense rhythmic pulsing of Jazz's pussy had him right there, ready to go over, but at Screw's words, he did his best to mentally name all the tools in his shop.

Screw half chuckled half rumbled. "Not fucking yet. Come on, baby, one more for us."

Jazz moaned. "I can't."

"You can. Come on, beautiful. G, work her clit."

"Oh, God," she whispered the moment his thumb stroked over the swollen bud of her clit.

He worked it with gentle circles as they both continued to fuck her. Sweat rolled down Screw's face and Gumby swore he'd die if he didn't come in the next few seconds. He'd never worked so hard in his life as he did to stave off his orgasm right then. The pleasure was a high he'd chase for the rest of his life, and when he did finally let himself come, he'd probably pass out for a week.

Barely a minute later, Jazz's pussy began to flutter around him.

"Fuck, she's close again. Her ass is strangling me."

"Yes," she said. "Yes, my God, I'm close. Oh, fuck…yes!" This orgasm had to be just as powerful as the last because she screamed and then her arms gave the fuck out. Jazz collapsed hard against his chest, her body twitching, breath sawing in and out.

Gumby's eyes crossed as he wrapped his arms around her, holding her close while he unloaded into the condom deep inside her. Screw arched back with a primal roar, planted himself deep inside her ass and came. The muscles in his neck, shoulders, and biceps strained as shudders racked his body. The prominent veins running up and down his tattooed limbs popped even more than usual.

All he needed to do was pound his chest to complete the savage image.

"JESUS, FUCK," SCREW said as he fell forward, allowing weight to settle on Jazz's back. Everyone was well aware he'd done more than his fair share of fucking, which meant he'd had a lot of orgasms. Some good, some okay, some fucking out of this world. But never, ever had he had an orgasm like this one where for a split second, he actually wondered if it would kill him.

And he hadn't given one single shit. If that was the way he was gonna leave this earth, he'd go with a big fucking smile on his face and jizz erupting from his cock.

After lying in a sated heap of limbs and sweat for who knew how long Screw slowly came back down to earth. He gripped the edge of the condom around his dick and withdrew his softened cock from Jazz.

She moaned as he left her body.

Once he'd hopped up and disposed of the condom, he returned to his two lovers still in the exact same position with Jazz sprawled out on top of Gumby. Gumby's dick had slipped out of her, so Screw gently rolled her off the other man and onto her back.

"You alive, Jazzy?" he asked as he came down next to her.

What he saw on her face had him freezing, the need to beat himself bloody rising sharp and fast.

Tears dampened her cheeks, still leaking from her eyes.

"Jazz?" Gumby said, his voice heavy with concern as he rolled to his side. He reached out and squeezed Screw's arm. Their gazes met and he didn't see any recrimination in Gumby's stare, but that didn't alleviate the sick feeling in his stomach in the least.

Fuck. He'd been too rough. Too eager. Too fucking lost in how out of this world it felt to be in her ass while Gumby took her pussy. He'd completely lost his mind and fucked her like some kind of animal. In the ass.

What the hell was wrong with him? He deserved to be horsewhipped.

He shook his head when Gumby reached for him, beginning to draw back. Jazz opened her eyes, took one look at him and frowned.

Jesus, she couldn't even stand the sight of him.

"No!" she said, reaching out.

"Oh, fuck, Jazzy, I'm sorry."

"No!" she said again, sitting straight up. She grabbed his arms, staring him straight in the eye. He had no choice but to gaze on her tears while she tore him a new one. "I'm not hurt, Screw. Not at all. Not one bit." Her voice dropped and she stared at the bed. Gumby's hand stroked up and down her back, his eyes a deep pool of worry. "It was just...powerful. I'm sorry. I didn't mean to freak you out. Just...all three of us were so together. So in sync. It felt so good, I got a little emotional."

It was a little too soon to allow relief in. "I didn't hurt you?"

"No."

"But I was…at the end there I was…"

"Perfect. You were both perfect."

Oh, thank Christ.

Her gaze shifted between the two of them. She grabbed both of their hands, bringing their joined hands to her heart. "I can easily say I've never come like that before, but it was more than that. I just felt so…"

"Cherished," Gumby interjected.

Screw's heart stuttered to a stop. They were treading on dangerous ground. Feelings, emotions, relationship ground. Things that made his skin itch and his feet eager to run. But the way Jazz's face lit at Gumby's simple word had him rooted to his spot on the bed.

"Yeah," she whispered. "I felt cherished." Her cheeks flushed and she shrugged. "Sorry," she said with a wave of her hand. "I'm just being silly."

"You are," Screw blurted.

"What?"

"You are. Uh, cherished that is. Not being silly." Christ, he was like a fifteen-year-old goober who didn't know how to talk to a woman. And maybe he was, when it came to real, heavy conversation. He'd certainly avoided it his whole life and sure as fuck hadn't had deep heart to hearts with his mother. Their talks consisted of him being told what a disappointment he was, and her asking him to get lost so she could bring over the latest man.

Still beaming, Jazz leaned forward and pressed a soft kiss to his lips right before treating Gumby to the same sweet taste of her. This would normally be where he'd take his leave. They'd all come spectacularly, so it was time to jet. He'd already spent the night in bed with them on more than one occasion which went against everything he believed in.

But as he sat there in his bed with drying sweat, cum, and heavy emotions surrounding them, he found the last thing he wanted was to be without these two. Not only did he want to extend their company this afternoon, he wanted them in his bed tonight. Yes, for a repeat, but also to sleep entwined with one another.

So instead of ushering them from his room and out the door, he kissed Jazz again then said, "How about I order a pizza? Pretty sure we deserve a few carbs and calories after that workout."

"Ooh, yes!" Jazz said. "I'm starved. And disgusting." She glanced down at herself. Mind if I shower while we wait for it?"

"Long as you don't mind company." He arched an eyebrow at Gumby. "What do you say, big guy? Up for a little slippery fun followed by some grease and cheese?"

"Hell yeah. Not sure which sounds better." Gumby winked at Jazz.

He was sure. Screw knew exactly which of those activities he was most looking forward to. "Let's do it." Before he thought better of it, he captured Gumby's chin between his thumb and forefinger, holding the man close for a kiss. It was supposed to be a quickie, but when Gumby licked across his lower lip, Screw prolonged the kiss. It stayed light and dare he admit, sweet, but lingered for long seconds.

Jazz's happy sigh had him smiling and finally leaving Gumby's lips. She tilted her head. "I could seriously watch you guys do that all day long. Okay, maybe that's a lie. I might need to see you fuck at some point before the day was up."

And damn if the thought of her watching Gumby fuck him or vice versa didn't have his dick twitching. "Jesus, woman," he said as he swelled to half chub. "You two milked every last drop of cum from my balls. I shouldn't be able to get it up for a week, but one mention of those eyes watching Luke have a go at me and I'm hard all over again." He pointed to Jazz. "You're a fucking sex witch."

She laughed hard and when Gumby joined in, Screw's heart swelled more than his cock. Maybe there was some truth to it because witchcraft had to be the only explanation for his out of character behavior.

After a warm, sudsy, and handsy shower complete with a few more orgasms, the three of them piled back into Screw's bed where they devoured an extra-large pizza in record time. He and Gumby wore only their underwear while Jazz borrowed one of his shirts, and damn if it didn't do something to see her in his bed wearing his shirt. Smelling of him. Once their bellies were full, they lounged around talking, petting, and learning more about each other.

Gumby told Jazz the disturbing details of his childhood, giving her the same insight into his sexuality issues he'd given Screw.

Hell, he'd even opened up, sharing the challenges of growing up with a mother half the town had seen naked. Jazz had teared up over both their stories, hugging them close and murmuring all the right words of comfort.

Eventually, the conversation worked its way around to Jazmine.

"Can I ask you something?" he asked Jazz. He and Gumby lay side by side in the bed. Jazz was sideways, with her head on Gumby's stomach and her legs draped across Screw's abs.

"Sure."

"Where is Paul now?"

Some of the light dimmed in her eyes. "He's, uh, locked up in a psychiatric prison in Illinois."

Screw shifted his gaze to Gumby. "Did you know this?"

With a nod, Gumby said, "Yeah. He attacked a woman in Chicago. It'll be years before he's out."

"Good. Okay, that's good." Though it destroyed his ability to fuck the guy up. And he wasn't sure how he felt about that yet. "So he has no contact with you."

Jazz looked away which made Gumby straighten. "He doesn't contact you, right Jazz?"

"Jazz?" Screw asked. "What the fuck? Is he in touch with you?"

Shaking her head, she said, "No." Then she ran a hand through her hair which was a mess from the afternoon's activities. "Not directly, anyway. I have a virtual PO Box where my parents can send me letters or forward my mail. It's received by a company who sends the mail to me here. Anyway, a few times Paul has sent a letter to the house for me and my step-dad forwarded them to me."

"What the actual fuck?" If he hadn't been pinned under her silky-smooth legs, Screw would have jumped off the bed to prowl the room. "What the hell is wrong with that man?"

The pizza in her stomach began to feel like a rock. "I don't know. I've stopped asking that question where his son is concerned. Anyway. I read the first letter then haven't opened any of the others. It's not worth the stress and mental anguish it causes me. I save them in case…I don't know. I just save them."

In case he ever found her. She didn't need to say the words out loud to have a shiver of dread racing down Screw's spine.

Gumby grabbed one of her hands and kissed her palm. "That's smart, Jazz. And I'm glad you don't read them."

"Can we talk about something else? I don't want to bring down this afternoon. It's been perfect."

"Sure, babe," Screw said, but his gaze met Gumby's. They didn't need words to be on the same page about this. As soon as this business with the CDMC was taken care of, they'd be moving on to Paul.

They shifted to easier topics, growing more playful by the minute. By the time their arousal grew, and they turned to each other once again, his head was full of thoughts he'd never experienced. Things like waking in the morning to hot kisses, blowjobs, breakfast in bed. Watching Jazz dress for work while he lounged a few extra minutes. Coming home to her or Gumby's hungry kisses and searching hands. Watching them brush their teeth in his bathroom before falling into bed and losing themselves in each other.

Crazy thoughts.

After watching his lovers come for the third—or was it fourth—time that day, Screw lay on one side of Jazz with Gumby on the other. She passed out almost immediately, tucked warm and safe between them.

Gumby on the other hand, lay on his side, his curious and unapologetic gaze on him. He knew the other man had just as many rampant thoughts running through his head as Screw did.

Thoughts like how today might possibly have been the best day of his life.

And what the fuck was he supposed to about that?

Chapter Thirty-Two

The next two days passed in a haze of what could only be described as bliss. Jazz spent every spare hour with Gumby and Screw. Sure, reality existed in the form of work for her and Screw, church for the guys, and Gumby spending time at the clubhouse tinkering with whoever's car needed work. But both before and after those tasks, the time was theirs to do with as they pleased, and they spent it talking, touching, kissing… fucking.

And laughing.

Jazz hadn't laughed so much in her whole life as she had the past two days. Their playful dynamic developed to its fullest the more time the three of them spent together.

Turned out Screw really enjoyed being naked, or nearly so. Around the house, be it hers or his, he was barely ever seen in anything more than boxer briefs. Gumby followed his example after the first day and before she knew it, Jazz was treated to a visual feast every time her eyes were open.

They cooked together. They ate together. They showered together. They played together. They relaxed together. They argued over television shows, debated politics, and discussed their favorite pastimes and hobbies.

All in all, the past three days had been perfect—or nearly so. There were two topics they hadn't broached. Two major subjects she'd compartmentalized into neat boxes in her mind. Now, on day four, when she had a weekday off from work and the guys were at the clubhouse, reality on a deeper level began to intrude. No longer could she deny her feelings. No longer could she ignore the fact they didn't once speak of the future or the fact they were acting as though they were in some sort of committed triad relationship.

No longer could she lie to herself about how deep she'd fallen for both men. Never in her wildest dreams had she pictured herself falling in love with Screw. He was supposed to be the easy one. The one she had this crazy physical chemistry with, but nothing more. Their connection should have been shallow, surface level. But for some reason he'd let her in as he'd let Gumby in and now she saw the man beneath the witty quips, innuendos, and whoring around. She saw the wounded little boy who grew into a man that protected his heart with an iron coat of armor. But once it was pierced, what lie beneath was a supportive, caring, compassionate man who actually felt the deepest of emotions.

Then there was Gumby. The man she'd wanted fiercely back in Arizona. The man she'd fantasized about a future with late at night alone in her bed. Their future had been violently torn away before it had an opportunity to flourish. Hell, before it even had a chance to begin. Turned out, Gumby's waters ran just as deep as Screw's. He was a man struggling to accept himself and his place in the world. Working so hard to feel comfortable in a skin he'd so often been led to believe was wrong, unacceptable, dirty.

Watching him gain confidence in himself these past few days had been nothing short of a beautiful experience. With Screw's—and she hoped her own—acceptance and desire for him and who he was, he'd seemed to realize there wasn't a goddammed thing wrong with him.

But how could it last? Hell, maybe she was the only one who wanted it to last. She had no idea, because she'd been far too chicken to ask and neither of them seemed to want to rock the boat either.

Adding to all the personal drama was the ever-looming Chrome Disciples Motorcycle Club. The other undiscussed issue. Sure, Jazz knew something was going down. She still had a babysitter at work or whenever she was without Screw or Gumby. And the men, Gumby included, had daily meetings at the clubhouse where something was being planned, but she hadn't wanted their bubble of happiness to pop so she'd pretended that problem didn't exist.

Now, for the first time in the past few days, she had prolonged alone time. Hours to sit around and obsess. So many minutes crawling by at a snail's pace where her mind drove her insane with what-ifs and worry.

After ninety minutes, she'd grown disgusted with herself and sick of the freaked-out voices in her head. Those ninety minutes had been spent stress-cleaning her already spic-n-span kitchen. Finally, revulsion with her own company drove her to leave the house in search of an understanding and non-judgmental sounding board.

And that's how she landed on Cassie's doorstep, uninvited and unannounced.

She pushed the bell as she cursed herself for not calling ahead. How selfish could she be? Here she was ready to unload relationship drama on a woman fighting for her life. Maybe she should just leave. Cassie could be sleeping for all she knew.

As she contemplated leaving, she glanced over her shoulder where Monty, who'd driven her over, was chatting with Thunder. They'd been assigned to watch over both women while the men were in church. The door opened, making Jazz's head whip back around.

There stood Cassie, Mamma V, wearing sweatpants and a fuzzy red robe. Both hung on her tiny frame made smaller by months of battling cancer.

"Jazmine!" she said, eyes lighting. "Come in. Come in. It's freezing out there." With a wave for the guys at the curb, she pulled Jazz in by her puffy jacket. "You're just in time. I brewed a fresh pot of coffee. It's decaf, but it's hot and if you want it bad enough, you can almost feel a caffeine buzz."

Jazz chuckled. "Thank you. I'm so sorry I didn't call first. After I rang the doorbell, I wanted to kick myself." She shrugged out of her jacket and pulled her woolly hat off, smoothing down her wild hair.

"Please, honey, you are always welcome anytime and without notice. Plus, you caught me on good day, so you won't be subject to me vomiting. Lucky you."

How she could stay in such high spirits despite all she'd been through over the past few months would always remain a mystery to Jazz.

"Just drape your jacket over the chair there, honey, and come get some coffee."

Cassie padded into the kitchen as Jazz did what she'd requested. She entered the kitchen to find Cassie doctoring up two steaming mugs of coffee.

"So," Cassie said as she turned from the task. "Want to tell me why your eyes are sad and you're at an old lady's house when you should be out enjoying your day off?"

Tears immediately prickled the corners of Jazz's eyes and clogged her throat. "Can't a girl just visit her surrogate mom because she loves her?" Oh, God, even to her own ears she sounded choked up.

"Yes," Cassie said with a patient smile. "She sure can. And she has, many times. But today, she's here because she needs a little mothering, am I right?"

That was all it took for the floodgates to open. A few kind words from someone who'd never judge her. Water erupted from her eyes, falling down her face in big, fat ugly tears. Jazz's shoulders shook as the first wrenching sobs tore from deep in her gut.

Cassie immediately embraced her, wrapping her thin arms around Jazz's shoulders and rocking her side to side. "Oh, honey," she said, in the most soothing tone. "Promise you, whatever it is, it can't be as bad as you fear."

Jazz hiccupped out a laugh. "It's w-worse."

With a soft chuckle, Cassie rubbed her back then guided her into a chair. "Here, sweetie." She handed Jazz a tissue she seemed to pull from thin air.

"T-thank you." As Jazz dabbed her eyes and nose, Cassie set the coffee mugs on the table.

"Okay, sweetie. Spill it. What's going on?" She sat, scooting her chair so their knees were pressed up against each other, then she reached out and captured one of Jazz's hands in her soft ones. They were much gaunter than they used to be but still so loving and exactly what Jazz had been looking for that morning.

A new round of waterworks kicked up. She covered her eyes with her free hand as she said, "I think I'm in love with two men."

Cassie's eyes widened and her mouth fell open before she shut it again, but those were the only indications of shock she'd given. Of course, the news came as a shock. Jazz had kept her… thing with Screw and Gumby completely quiet from everyone she knew.

"Oh, honey." She stroked her thumb over the back of Jazz's hand. "I'm so sorry. I can't imagine what kind of pressure you must be under trying to make a choice like that."

"Oh, God." Jazz sniffed. She stared at their joined hands, face hot as she said, "That's not even the issue."

"What do you mean?" Though her tone was full of compassion and acceptance, Jazz couldn't lift her eyes and meet Cassie's gaze. She'd die if she saw disapproval in Mama V's eyes when she admitted the truth.

"It's not a love triangle. It's more of a love…circle."

Silence fell, and finally the curiosity got the best of her. She lifted her head, staring straight at Cassie.

"Do you mean the three of you are in a relationship?" her friend asked carefully.

With a hiccup and a nod, Jazz whispered, "Yes. Though I think I may be the only one who considers it an actual relationship." She looked down again. "This is so embarrassing."

"Honey," Cassie said, voice firm. "Look at me."

Jazz glanced up, feeling like her face might melt right off.

"I've spent more than thirty years around motorcycle clubs. Child, I've seen and heard everything. And I mean *everything*. There's nothing you can shock me with. You think you're the first woman to be in a triad?"

Jazz blinked. Huh? "You don't think it's weird?"

"Honey, if cancer has taught me anything, it's that life is so very short. I am not going to spend my precious minutes judging anyone else's life. I have much better things to do with my gift of time." Her smile was full of acceptance and love.

Jazz sighed out a small laugh. "Mama V, you are truly my favorite person in the whole world."

"Of course I am, dear," Cassie said as she patted Jazz's hand. "Now drink your coffee and tell me all about it. Leave no details out." She winked.

Jazz could only hope to be half as amazing as Cassie when she grew up. As instructed, she sipped from the Harley Davidson mug. As the warm liquid slid down to her stomach, it heated her from the inside out, chasing away the chill of fear she'd been combating all morning.

"Ooh, can I guess who it is?" Cassie asked, eyes sparkling. She waggled her eyebrows.

Damn it was good to see her zest for life returning.

"Seriously? I come to you in crisis and you're gonna sit there and get all hot and bothered." As the heavy weight lifted from her shoulders, Jazz grinned.

"I sure am. I need to live vicariously through your spicy young life." She winked.

"Please, I'm sure Viper still gives it to you pretty damn good, Mama V."

"That he does, my dear. That he does." Another wink. This one followed by Cassie fanning her face.

Jazz laughed and a lightness entered her heart. "You old dog, you."

With a girlish giggle, Cassie actually blushed. "Enough about me. It's that young man who came to visit you, right?"

"That's one of 'em." Her comment elicited another round of giggles. Damn, it was nice to talk to someone about this. Keeping secrets may have been a prime contributor to all the stress. She had a close relationship with her girlfriends. The women of the MC were more of a sisterhood who typically told each other everything. Hiding her activities from them felt deceitful and left her without a cathartic outlet.

"Screw. He's the other, right?" Cassie clapped her hands. "That boy has had his eye on you for quite some time."

"Pretty sure it wasn't his eyes that wanted me," Jazz muttered before taking a long sip of coffee.

"Who's the dog now?" Cassie asked as she raised a gray eyebrow.

They looked at each other for a quiet moment then blurted, "Screw!" at the same time before cracking up.

"Oh, God, thank you, Cassie," Jazz said, wiping tears for an entirely different reason. "This is exactly what I needed."

"I take it none of your girls know anything about this."

"They do not."

"So you're in love with Screw and Gumby. Both of them." Cassie wrapped her hands around the mug, probably trying to absorb the warmth into her thin digits.

Not a question.

Jazz sighed. "It didn't start that way. I had…difficulty dealing with some things from my past. They were around to witness my meltdown. Both men said all the right things after I poured out this long, sordid story I've never shared with anyone. One thing led to another and the next thing I knew…" She sipped her coffee with a shrug.

"Jazz sandwich?"

As she laughed, coffee slipped down her windpipe. Jazz coughed while Cassie just sat there with her mischievous twinkling eyes. Finally, after a good thirty second coughing fit, she could speak again. "Seriously? You trying to kill me?"

"Sorry," Cassie said, not looking an ounce repentant. "Couldn't help myself."

"Well, since you're right, I'll let it slide. Anyway, it's continued, and we've all grown…close."

With her mug held between her two hands, Cassie said, "I'm guessing you don't mean only in a physical sense."

Jazz propped an elbow on the table, letting her head fall onto her hand. "No. In every sense. Whatever it is we're doing has become so much more than I think any of us anticipated or even wanted, to be honest. We've bonded, connected. We've made love," she whispered. "I sound like I belong in a cheesy rom com, but it's true. When we're together, it's…it's deep."

A smile broke out on Cassie's face. "Not cheesy at all, sweetie. I completely understand."

"What do I do, Mama V? Pretty sure a day hasn't gone by where Screw didn't let the entire world know what he thinks of relationships and Gumby not only lives in Arizona, he can't even admit out loud he's bisexual. I don't think he could even entertain the idea of a relationship that involves a girl and another dude. Christ, how did I let this happen?" She lightly banged her head on the table.

Cassie caught her head on another downward trip. "First thing, a brain injury will not help you at all, so either grab Viper's helmet or strop trying to break your skull."

She straightened up. "What do I do?"

"You know what to do, honey. There's only one answer here and you know what it is. You don't like it, which is why you came here. So, I could be the one to say it for you. But I'm not going to do that."

Jazz groaned. "Now you're really acting like you're my mom. Can we go back to the sex talk?"

There went another of those patient smiles. "Sure. After you say it."

"Damnit." She was right. Cassie was dead right. Jazz knew exactly what had to be done, but the thought alone had her insides twisted in knots. Her shoulders drooped. "I have to talk to them."

"Yes, ma'am," Cassie said before crossing her legs. "Jazzy, you need to be honest with them. Their reactions might surprise you."

With a snort, she said, "Screaming and running from me as fast as they can? Nah, I'm pretty sure that won't be a shocker."

Cassie stayed silent, watching with sympathetic eyes.

"Ugh!" She threw her arms up. "I know you're right." Then she shook her head as her stomach rejected the idea. "I know you're right," she said softly. "I'm just afraid I'll lose it all and have less than I do now. I'm afraid they'll both walk away."

"Honey," Cassie said, leaning forward. "Any man who walks away from you is an utter fool. If that happens, you send them my way and I'll deal with them for you. But I really think they might surprise you."

Once again, she was near tears. "Thank you."

At the sound of the front door opening, Cassie straightened.

"Cas?" Viper's voice sounded from the front of the house. "Got a few men here with me claiming they're supposed to have a late lunch with Jazmine."

"We're in the kitchen," she called out before dropping her voice. "All right, girl, fix your face, straighten your wig, and hike up your tits."

The moment her men entered the kitchen, Jazz's stomach flipped, and her heart fluttered as though it'd been months instead of hours since she'd seem them. Each sought her out immediately. Screw's eyes zeroed in on her face and with a frown, he tilted his head as though to ask, "You okay?"

She nodded at him with a smile.

They stayed for a few moments chatting with Viper and Cassie before heading back to Screw's house.

As soon as the three of them were alone in the privacy of Screw's kitchen, he said, "Jazzy, we need to talk to you about something."

Shit. This was it. Her stomach lurched and she nearly had to dash for the sink to lose her coffee. "Uh, about what?"

About what?

Way to take Cassie's advice. At no point did she recommend playing dumb.

Gumby walked up behind her, slid an arm around her waist, and drew her against him. He dropped a kiss on her cheek as though the sweet gesture was the most natural thing in the universe.

Screw sighed as he leaned against the counter with folded arms. "We haven't talked about the CDMC since the disastrous night of the party, but they're still out there and they won't go away unless we take action. We can't just sit around hoping they'll disappear or waiting for them to make a move against us."

Wait...they didn't want to talk about their relationship?

Maybe later, she'd feel ashamed of the staggering relief that coursed through her, but at that moment, she embraced the ability to keep her head in the sand a bit longer. Not that the CDMC was a more welcome topic of conversation.

"Uh," she cleared her throat, finally finding her voice. "Yeah, I know you guys have been working on something. Guess I was just kinda hoping it'd all vanish. Stupid, right?"

Gumby tightened his arms. "Not stupid. Think we'd all love that."

"You ain't kiddin'," Screw said. He walked over to them, ran his hand through Gumby's hair, then kissed her.

God how she wanted this every day of her life.

"We've got something going down tonight. I can't give you details. If I could, I would."

Stomach twisting with newfound worry, she held up a hand. "I know, Screw. Don't worry about that. I know how the club works."

He tilted his head, giving her a half-hearted smile. "You're too good to be true, Jazzy."

"She sure is," Gumby added before saying, "We'll be gone most of the night."

Screw nodded with his mouth set in a serious line. Oh, God, he was worried. Very worried. And that only served to terrify Jazz. "Um, okay," she said. "What's the plan for me? Tex gonna hang at my house or something?"

"Girls are gathering at Copper and Shell's. Slumber party style from what I hear," Gumby said. "We'll come get you when it's all over."

"Sounds like a plan." Could they hear the false bravado in her tone? The feigned confidence?

Screw cupped her face between his strong palms. "Baby, it's okay to not be happy about this."

Apparently, they could sense it.

"Yeah," Gumby said in her ear. "No one expects you to be strong for us and hide your fear."

"Tell me, baby," Screw said. Then he kissed her again, softly and with so much care she wanted to cry. Did they really not see it? Not see how wonderful they worked as a three-lover team?

She almost laughed. A three-lover team. Was that even sustainable in the real world where people knew about them?

"I'm scared," she whispered putting a voice to so much more than just the club's activities.

"We'll be all right. This isn't as dangerous as you're thinking." Screw looked straight into her eyes as he spoke.

"But it is dangerous?"

"Fuck, Screw," Gumby said. "Not helpful."

"I'm not gonna lie to her," he said with a scowl for Gumby as he released her face.

"No," Jazz cut in, patting Gumby's hands where they rested against her stomach. "It's okay. I don't want to be coddled. I'm strong enough to handle it."

"Yeah, you are," Screw said. He kissed her again. As she sank into the pleasure of his mouth melding with hers, Gumby's lips landed on her cheek. Then Screw's. Then hers again. Before she knew it, they were engaged in a three-way kiss.

They held each other tight as their lips and tongues performed an unsophisticated and somewhat sloppy yet utterly perfect dance.

Jazz's clenched her eyes shut as she absorbed the fulfilling sensation she only felt when the three of them connected in this way. When they said with their bodies what they couldn't voice.

When she could pretend this would last forever instead of leaving her with a shattered heart when it ended.

Chapter Thirty-Three

"LJ's gonna cut the security cameras in forty-five seconds. They will be out for exactly five minutes. Not a second more." If the security officer didn't check in with the alarm company within five minutes of losing camera footage, the authorities were automatically notified. Screw spoke into the comm unit Rocket had seemed to procure from thin air. Rocket, the man with black ops history who should probably be the one running this mission.

But that job fell to him. The fucking enforcer.

"10-4," Mav replied followed with confirmation from the other two-man teams.

Since the day after the CDMC, they'd had eyes on the trucking company the CDMC used to transport weapons. Not only did Rocket commandeer comm units, he'd also procured a high-tech drone complete with hi-res imaging capabilities. And Christ if that didn't make surveillance a fucking breeze.

In fact, this entire operation had gone smoothly thus far. Starting with LJ getting hired as a security guard. The initial plan had been to have someone apply for a driver position. They'd gone so far as to have Tex take an interview. During a tour of the yard, the manager mentioned how they were in desperate need of a nighttime security guard. Theirs had up and quit right before Christmas, forcing them to hire a contract security company which cost a shit load of cash. After learning that, Copper sent LJ in. He was hired on the spot. No background check, no references, not a goddammed thing. They put him on shift that night probably based on his size alone.

Mistake for them. Big fucking win for Screw and his brothers.

Now, not only did they have daytime footage from the drone, they had a fucking security guard inside. After days of surveillance, they basically knew every detail of how this company ran their trucks, exactly which ones the guns would be on, and—thanks to Gumby—the fastest and most effective way to disable them.

"Cameras out in five…four…three…two…one. Move," Screw said, as he darted across the yard to the truck he and Gumby had been assigned to. Plan was to sabotage the trucks making it impossible for the weapons to be delivered on time. Gun running wasn't the kind of business where deliveries could be rescheduled, or second chances were given. Whoever waited on the other end would be fucking furious and drop the CDMC no questions asked.

As much as Screw wanted to swipe the actual weapons, they couldn't take that risk. First place Crank and his fuckhead club would look was the Handlers. Here, the blame could lie squarely on the trucking company who'd had a break in one night.

When Screw reached the truck he and Gumby had been assigned to, he planted his hand on the side of the trailer and tried to control his breathing.

Though this operation was relatively low risk, his heart pounded with the force of a stampede, making him lightheaded and queasy. Jesus, he'd never had a panic attack in his fucking life, yet he felt seconds from completely flipping the fuck out.

"Hey," Gumby appeared next to him looking calm, collected, and sexy as fuck in all black with a dark cap, comm unit, and his glasses in place. He reached out and muted Screw's comm before doing the same to his own. "Breathe. This is a cake walk. We planned the fuck out of it and have about eighteen contingency plans for everything from a hurricane to a terrorist attack. We fucking got this."

"That's not even...Oh, fuck." He sucked in a breath that sounded strangely like a whistle being blown.

"Shit," Gumby glanced left then right before capturing Screw's face between his hands. "You got this Luke. You're a fucking badass enforcer. Your prez trusts you, your brothers trust you, I fucking trust you. You. Have. Got. This." Then he kissed him hard and fast before picking up the gas can and getting to work.

Christ that was exactly what he'd needed to hear. They'd planned well and each man there tonight knew their role. He trusted those men with his life. What he didn't trust was himself. The weight of responsibility nearly ground him to dust.

Letting down his club was not an option. But his club wasn't the only concern here. Gumby could be hurt. Jazz could be hurt. No, he would not allow this operation to fail.

"Hey, you gonna make me do all the work, slacker?" Gumby winked and the small gesture was the final kick he'd needed to get his ass in gear.

"Fuck you," Screw said without any heat.

Gumby chuckled before laying on his back and worming his way under the truck. As he'd made the club practice at least fifteen times, he followed the gas line until he reached the anti-siphoning device. "Got it," he called after disabling the device.

As Gumby worked his way back out from under the truck, Screw got the tubing set up and began siphoning the diesel. They didn't need to get it all, just enough to allow them to dump gasoline in the tank. It was the perfect solution. Ten miles out, the trucks would fail. The weapons wouldn't reach their destination and by the time the company realized they'd been sabotaged, the CDMC's deliveries would be fucked.

"That's good. Good, good, good. Come on," Gumby said beckoning Screw with his hand.

Screw tossed him the tubing which Gumby stowed in a black duffel then he grabbed the canister full of gasoline.

"Jesus, motherfucking Christ," Screw said as sweat ran down his face and into his eyes. "My hands are fucking shaking."

"Here, I got you. Done this a hundred times." Gumby took over, inserting the canister into the gas tank.

"Seriously? Hundreds of times."

With a laugh, Gumby looked over at him and winked. "What the fuck else do you do when you're sixteen, bitter, and live in a sandy town that doesn't even have a McDonalds?"

"Apparently, you vandalize cars."

Gumby winked. "You got it, babe. Done." He pulled the can out, kissed Screw then flipped both their comms back on. "Team one objective complete."

Screw stared after the confident man as he strode away, ass looking like every porn star's goal. They made a good team. Gumby the ever-calm presence and Screw, his hyper self.

"Team three objective complete." The words spoken in his ear were followed almost immediately by team two.

"Team four, check in," Screw said.

"Getting there. Having trouble with the fucking anti-siphon piece of shit," Mav said. It was followed by some grumbling. "Fuck. Something ain't right here."

Screw checked his watch. They had exactly ninety seconds until the alarm company would alert the cops. "Gumby," he said into his comm device so Mav could hear.

"On it." As he watched Gumby jog over to where Mav was, his heart rate kicked up again.

Thirty seconds passed.

Forty-five.

"Fuck, they fucking jerry-rigged his motherfucker. Any chance you can buy me an extra minute?" Gumby's frustration bled through the ear piece.

"No," Screw answered honestly though it killed him to be unable to offer help. "Look if we have to abandon it, we still got three—"

"No." Gumby's voice came through the comm. "Fuck that. I'm getting this bitch done."

It was on the tip of his tongue to say, "I'm telling Jazz you said that," but he bit back his natural instinct to break the tension with humor. This wasn't the fucking time. And high tension would keep Gumby working as fast as fucking possible.

"Fuck." LJ stuck his head out of the guard booth. "We got a problem. Alarm company called one minute early. Cops are on the way. Two minutes out."

"Shit. Fuck," Screw bit out. "Let's roll. Everyone out?"

"Mav, Gumby, get the fuck out of there," he called as he started for the exit. They had a truck idling down the street. If they sprinted like Olympic runners, they'd make it.

"Right behind you," Mav said in his ear.

"Me too."

Screw breathed a huge fucking sigh of relief as Gumby's voice crackled in his ear. He ran, legs pumping as fast as they could down the street to the waiting van. Rocket hung out the back with his hand on the open door. As the sound of a siren wailing registered, he yelled, "Like the ground's on fucking fire, boys."

Screw picked up his pace. The sound of pounding feet behind him had him confident Mav and Gumby were only steps behind. He jumped into the back of the van and spun just in time to see Mav do the same. As Rocket went to pull the door closed, Screw shouted, "Wait! Where the fuck is Gumby?"

Rocket's eyes widened in shock as he seemed to do a mental tally of who was in the van. "Shit! The crazy fucker stayed."

"Gumby?" Screw said into his comm. He was the only one still wearing the headset. "Motherfucker you better be running out of there right fucking now. Lights are coming down the street."

He held his breath until he heard, "Screw, I got it! Two seconds and I'll have the gas in the truck."

"You don't have two fucking seconds." He spun away from his brothers and lowered his voice. "Please, get the fuck out of there." Jesus Christ. What the hell was he going to tell Jazmine? That Gumby was arrested because of him? And what would he tell Copper? The CDMC would know what they'd done in mere hours. Retaliation would be swift and brutal.

"Gumby?" he said with no response just as four police cars came screaming down the street, skidding to a stop in front of the truck yard.

"Oh, fuck." Screw collapsed forward with his hands on his knees trying to stave the nausea.

"We can't stay," Rocket said as he pulled the door closed. "Drive, Jig." A hand landed on Screw's shoulder. "We won't go far, and we'll come back for him."

"He'll be in fucking jail."

Christ, he'd just sent his man to jail. He was going to puke. What would he tell Jazz? How would he get through the day knowing Gumby was behind bars and possibly suffering? He and Jazz were the best parts of Screw's day.

Fuck, the best parts of his life.

THE SIRENS GREW in intensity until it became obvious they were right outside the trucking yard, then they cut off.

In his peripheral vision, Gumby could see flashing red and blue.

He was pretty much fucked. If by some miracle the cops didn't get him, Screw would have his ass for sure. And not in the way he'd promised would blow his mind, and his load.

Jesus, he was spending too much time with Screw and his raunchy mind.

"Come on, come on," he whispered as the last of the gasoline poured into the tank.

Yanking the canister out, he made to run…somewhere, when a hand grabbed the back of his shirt. "Get in the cab," LJ whispered as he unlocked the door and practically tossed Gumby in. "Fold your big fucking body up and stay outta sight until I come get you." He ripped the comm unit out of Gumby's ear and stashed it in his pocket.

LJ shut the door as soundlessly as possible while Gumby wedged his six-foot-four frame under the steering wheel. He might never be able to unwind, but if it kept him off the cops' radar he'd happily live as a bent and crooked man.

"Good evening, officers." LJ's booming voice sounded through the quiet yard. "I'm working security tonight."

"We got an emergency call from the alarm company. Cameras cut out. We're gonna need you to let us search the premises, sir. And we'll need to see your clearance paperwork."

"Sure, yes, of course," LJ said as he used a jangling keychain to unlock the chain-link gate. Gumby could barely hear it rolling open on the squeaky tract over the blood rushing in his ears.

"Here you go." LJ said. "My company ID. Feel free to look around, but…uh…this was totally my fault. It's only my third night and I fucked up with the cameras. Thought I had the hang of it, but…"

The guy deserved an Oscar for the way he made himself sound so sheepish and embarrassed, Gumby could picture the mountain of a man rubbing the back of his neck as he stared at the ground in defeat.

Silence fell. Gumby held his breath as he waited to hear whether the cop bought LJ's act. His knees and ankles began to ache from the kinked-up way he'd wedged himself beneath the steering wheel. Hopefully nothing a little Motrin and a hot shower couldn't fix later on.

Of course, if he ended up spending the night in a jail cell…

"Look, buddy, we're gonna scope the place out because we have to. Part of the protocol when the alarm company contacts us. If you fuck up again, just give them a call. They'll either talk you through the problem or fix it from their end. Save us all a whole lot of trouble, yeah?"

"Yes, sir. I'm so sorry for the inconvenience. I didn't want my boss to think I couldn't handle the job."

"Sure, whatever. We'll look around then be out of your hair."

"Okay, thank you. Let me know if you need anything from me."

Footsteps sounded, but they were too light to be LJ's. The big guy most likely stayed in the yard to see if his lies held up.

"That guy's a fucking idiot," one of the cops mumbled way too close to Gumby for comfort.

"Tell me about it. Fucking up our night cuz he's too prideful to call the alarm company and ask for help. Let's get this shit over with," a deeper voice, the one who'd been talking to LJ said.

"What do you want us to do? Look in all the trucks?"

Sweat trickled down Gumby's spine, causing a maddening itch. He bit his lower lip—hard. Maybe the pain would override the compelling urge to rub the irritation off his back. They'd discover him for sure and he'd be up shit's creek.

"Fuck, no. I ain't wasting any more time on this nonsense than absolutely necessary. Check around and under the trucks. That's it. Then we get the hell outta here."

"Got it, boss."

Gumby's eyes fell closed and he concentrated on slow, even, quiet breathing. Ignoring the discomfort in his joints grew harder by the second as the annoying ache progressed to an extreme burning sensation.

He needed a distraction and he needed one fast, or he'd be thrashing around to scratch his back and stretch his long limbs. As he endured time crawling by slower than the drip of molasses, he pulled up his favorite go-to memory from the past week. The one where he'd walked into Jazz's kitchen to find her bent over as she pulled something heavy from the oven. She'd been wearing nothing but his T-shirt and a skimpy pair of panties. Before he'd had a chance to move in for the kill, Screw had sidled up next to him and with a low wolf whistle, alerted Jazz to their presence. What had followed was hours of sensual play he'd forever use as go-to spank-bank fodder.

Tonight, however hot the memories, he was safe from growing hard. Not only was he so scrunched up, there wasn't any goddammed room for an erection to expand, his joints throbbed so bad, his lovers could be naked in the truck with him and he probably wouldn't be able to get it up.

Screw had to be losing his mind. Even if he hadn't left his phone in the truck, he couldn't risk making a sound to text and put Screw's mind at ease.

Finally, after what felt like hours of torture, the deeper voice rang out again. "All clear in here, buddy. You have yourself a good night and remember what I said about communicating with the alarm company."

Gumby blew out a silent breath as relief flowed through him. He fought his body's need to unwind. Until LJ opened that door and set him free, they weren't out of the woods. Sweat poured down his face as the seconds ticked by.

Christ, what the hell was taking so long?

It had to have been a solid ten minutes since the cops said they were leaving. Had it been some kind of trick? Had LJ been apprehended and taken in? Fuck. How the hell long was he supposed to wait there before he went to assess the situation?

Another few minutes passed with an agonizing slowness. "Fuck it," Gumby mouthed into the dark and empty truck cab.

Just as he was about to maneuver out from under the steering wheel, the door opened, and fresh air flooded the car.

"Fuck, sorry, man. They were fucking chatting more than the ol' ladies when they get together. Couldn't get rid of the fuckers. You all right?"

With a snort, Gumby said, "Might need a wheelchair to get me out of here."

"Sure hope not. I ain't pushing your ass around, lazy fucker."

They laughed then Gumby began the painstaking process of getting free from the truck. "Oh, fuck," he said when his boots finally hit the ground. After a few minutes of tentative flexing and extending, his legs were ready to move. "I gotta get word to Screw."

LJ nodded. "Already did. He knows you're okay."

Gumby held out a fist. "Thanks, brother. Owe you a big fucking one."

"Fuck that," LJ said as he bumped Gumby's fist. "Pretty sure we still all owe you one. You didn't have to risk yourself that way. We aren't even your club."

After shrugging, Gumby lifted the hem of his shirt, using it to wipe the sweat from his face. "Did what had to be done. What's the plan now?"

"Now, we're outta here. Soon as all the trucks start craping out tomorrow, they'll know I was either involved or a piece of shit guard, so there's no point in me sticking around. I made sure the security cameras never caught my face. Just gonna grab my file, even though it's fake info, and we'll be outta here."

"Are you in their computer system?"

"My picture is for my badge. They hadn't gotten around to entering me into payroll yet. I already deleted any files associated with me including my badge image."

"All right." Gumby rolled his neck back and forth. He'd be sore as shit later. Worth it, but still no fucking fun.

Together, they entered the office where LJ rummaged through the file cabinets until he found his name. "Ready?" LJ asked.

"Ready to have Screw tear me a new one?" Gumby chuckled. "Not sure."

LJ winked. "I've heard the guy knows his way around an ass. Maybe it won't be as bad as you think."

He coughed, saliva abrading his windpipe as he tripped and nearly face planted. Did LJ know? Did he sense something.

Fuck.

"Jesus, man I was just kidding. Screw is bisexual, but don't worry, he's got plenty of fish to choose from. He's got no interest in turning you." Then he laughed and walked off toward his parked truck, oblivious to Gumby's internal freak-out. "Let's roll," he called over his shoulder. "Have a feeling there's a little pixie who will be very glad to see you."

Great, so they were on to him where Jazz was concerned, but oblivious to his involvement with Screw. Strangely enough, he had to bite his tongue to keep his involvement with Screw from blurting out. The man had done something great for his club tonight. Who wouldn't be proud to be with Screw?

Thoughts of his two lovers had the need to see them, to touch them making him jog to LJ's car. He couldn't wait to be with them, yet the thought of LJ knowing sent him into a tailspin.

I'm a hypocritical asshole.

Chapter Thirty-Four

Typically, girls' night consisted of booze, gossip, sex stories, sugar, and raucous laughter. Tonight, none of that happened. Not so much as a giggle, or hell, barely even a smile from any of the tough-as-nails sisterhood.

They'd all tried, showing up in cutsie pajamas with these phony smiles plastered on their faces, and their bottles of wine. Hell, Holly even brought six types of cookies. Nervous baking as she'd confessed as soon as the men had left. She'd been on her own for the past few nights while LJ did...whatever it was the club had asked of him.

Turns out, they'd all had the same plan: play along for the sake of the guys. Last thing they needed while doing whatever super-secret shit they were doing was to worry about their ol' ladies. The moment all the men left, each woman began their own stress induced rituals. Shell had been pacing in front of her television on and off for the last few hours. Some sitcom played in the background with the volume so low, no one even seemed to realize the TV was on. Toni sat with a notebook, supposedly brainstorming new menu items for the diner. In reality she alternated between chewing the end of the pen and tapping it on her leg while the page remained blank. Chloe was knitting or trying to learn to knit. She had a blob of yarn growing unevenly as she cursed at it. Stephanie surfed her phone, the quietest of the group which was unusual for her. Holly tried to get everyone to eat, but they all must have had the same stomachache Jazz did, because no one took so much as a bite. The only one in any state of relaxation was Izzy who'd passed out an hour ago after putting baby Joy to sleep in a pack-n-play in Shell's spare room. The poor new mom was so exhausted, she'd probably be asleep if the zombie apocalypse was occurring outside.

Jazz spent most of the time watching her friends. Her mind ran in too many circles to concentrate on one task or even play around on her phone. A huge part of her was tempted to blurt out her arrangement with Screw and Gumby just so they would know she deserved to share in their worries.

"Enough is enough," Shell blurted, sometime near midnight.

Though her eyes felt heavy and her body fatigued, Jazz was pretty sure she wouldn't get a wink of sleep all night. Instead, with the amount of adrenalin pumping through her system, she could probably go out and run five miles without breaking a sweat.

"We need to do something to take our minds off this. We're driving ourselves freaking nuts here. Gimme a damn cookie." She held her hand out to Holly who was lying with her legs hanging over the armrest of the couch. Shell's flannel pjs with pink hearts made her look about seventeen.

"Oh, uh," Holly scrambled to a seated position. She had flannel pjs as well, hers with various emojis. "Which one do you want?"

"Surprise me." Shell tapped her foot and wiggled her fingers as she waited. Though her man was at the clubhouse and not with the rest of the guys, she was just as worried for her family as each of the ol' ladies.

"Here." Holly placed a giant chocolate cookie in her hand then sat back with an expectant look on her face.

"Thanks." Without even looking to see what flavor she'd been gifted, Shell took a huge bite. A moan left her lips and she stared at the ceiling as though seeing God. "Oh. My. God. These are so freaking good, Hol."

"They must be," Stephanie said with a snort. "That one clearly gave you an orgasm." Steph wore a Hell's Handlers T-shirt with black sweats.

All the ladies cracked up and it was exactly what they needed to cut through the thick tension.

"You're right, Shell," Toni said, playing with a button on her buffalo plaid pajamas. "We need to try to be normal if only to pass time faster."

Jazz sat forward. "Okay, I could use a cookiegasm. Give me one of those babies."

The next hour passed quicker. They chatted, ate cookies, and only checked their phones once every five minutes instead of every sixty seconds as they'd been doing earlier in the evening.

"Guys," Jazz said, picking up a cookie with white chocolate chunks and some kind of nut. "This is my last one. You hear me? She turned to Chloe who sat next to her on the couch. "If you see me reach for another one, you smack my hand. Hard."

"Huh, I can do that," Chloe said with a grin just as the front door flew open.

As though all controlled by one button, all the women—save for Izzy—jumped to their feet.

One by one, the men strode into the house, much more subdued than she'd been hoping for. In her mind, they'd burst into Shell's house whooping and hollering over their success with…whatever.

Instead, each man walked to his woman, gathered her up in his arms and held her. When Screw walked into the house, the air crackled with agitation. Though frowning with tense muscles and clenched fists, he was in one piece with no visible blood, so she counted that a major win.

As much as she wanted to leap into his arms, they didn't do that outside the privacy of their homes. Instead, she gave him a pleased smile before glancing over his shoulder in time to see Rocket close the door behind him.

Wait…

"Gumby in the car?" she asked Screw. When the only answer she received was shared looks between the men, her stomach bottomed out. "Screw? Where's Gumby? Oh, my God, is this why none of you are smiling? Did something happen to him? Where is he?"

She grabbed Screw's jacket, shaking as hard as she could which barely moved the muscle-bound man.

"He's still in Knoxville," Screw said as though telling her, "It's raining today."

"What?" She dropped the fabric and pressed a hand to her stomach. "Oh, shit, I'm gonna be sick. What happened?"

"Jesus, Screw," Maverick said. He whispered something to Stephanie, who nodded, then he came over to Jazz.

"Tell me," she said, transferring her attention to Mav. "Is he hurt? Was he arrested?" She grabbed onto the edges of his cut now.

"He's fine." Mav said, wrapping his arms around her. He held her tight. "We had a little trouble and he stayed behind to get the job done despite Screw telling him to get the fuck outta there."

Jazz moaned and her knees weakened. All of a sudden, she was bombarded with the million possibilities of what could happen to Gumby. Her skin felt too tight for her body and she wanted to scream as she clawed it off.

"Shhh, honey, he's okay. It was a close call, but he is fine. He's with LJ about an hour behind us. Okay?"

She planted her forehead against Maverick's chest. "Thank you."

"Hey," he whispered in her ear. "Screw's taking this hard. Personally. Feels like he should have planned better. We had a few hiccups, but it was an overall success. Mission accomplished. He's not seeing it that way. He's gonna drive you home. Go easy on him, okay?"

Jazz nodded against his chest. "Thanks, Mav."

"No problem, baby cakes."

She huffed out a small laugh before stepping out of Mav's embrace.

"Let me just grab my bag," she said turning toward Screw and —whoa the man was glaring freakin' flaming daggers at Mav.

What the hell?

A glance over her shoulder showed Mav staring right back at Screw with a shit-eating grin while Steph rolled her eyes and tried to tug her man away.

"I'll be in the car," Screw said.

"Sure. What the hell was that, Mav?" she asked once Screw walked outside.

"Don't worry about it, hon, just giving the man a wakeup call."

Whatever. She didn't have the mental capacity to deal with male politics right now. After hugging her girls goodbye and finding her purse, she made her way to Screw's idling truck.

A few failed attempts at small talk had her enduring the ten-minute ride in silence. At his house, Screw hopped out, came around and opened her door for her. She followed him up the short walk to his home.

Without a word, she walked directly into Screw's kitchen. Over the past week, she'd spent enough time there to have learned her way around. As she poured them both a healthy few swallows of whiskey, the energy in the room shifted. A glance over her shoulder revealed the agitated man had followed her, though his attention was fixated elsewhere.

He'd shed the dark jacket, leaving him in some kind of black cargo pants with a short sleeved black T-shirt. Clothing worn for stealth. As he paced the length of his kitchen, his fists curled at his sides and his back bunched with tension. In that moment he reminded her of a jet-black panther, captured, caged, and dying to be let loose. At some point in the near future, the pressure in his body would expand enough to cause an explosion. Call her a masochist, but she wanted to be the one to throw herself on that grenade.

"Here," she said, holding the glass out to him. He took it without looking at her and tossed the liquid back with two long swallows.

It wasn't the time, but damn if she didn't want to lick his throat as he gulped the whiskey down.

She stood there, sipping her own drink and bouncing her leg as he continued the restless prowling. After a few moments, she couldn't take it any longer. "Luke," she said stepping into his path.

He tried to sidestep her, but she put her hands on his chest, rubbing up and down. Like the wild animal he portrayed, her touch seemed to ground him a tiny bit.

"Hey," she said, grabbing his face and forcing him to look directly at her. "He is okay. He was not hurt, he was not arrested. Gumby is okay and will be here in a little bit."

He grunted, circling her wrists with his strong hands. But instead of the tight hold prying her away, he just held her palms against his bearded cheeks.

"He is okay, but if he wasn't, it wouldn't be on you, Screw. You did what your club needed. He is a grown man who made a choice to stay behind. That is not your fault. You did not fail him. You did not fail your club. You did not fail me. And you sure as hell did not fail yourself."

He cocked an eyebrow and opened his mouth.

"No!" she said, placing her palm over his lips. "No jokes. I want the real Screw."

He moved so fast, all she could do was gasp as her back hit the wall. The near violence of the move had heat flushing through her. He'd never hurt her, not in a million years. There wasn't a single part of her that feared his agitated mood. But he might take his aggression out on her in another way and that knowledge awoke a primal need deep within her.

Screw's hands slapped the wall on either side of her head. He pressed his lower body into her, erection nestled against her stomach. His chest rose and fell with heavy breaths. "You say you want me to be real?"

"Yes," she said on an exhale, unable to resist the urge to arch her body into his erection.

"You say it, but I don't know if you mean it. I don't know if you can handle it." He tapped the side of his head. "It can be a dark place. A fucking disaster *I* can barely deal with."

"I want it," she said, voice steady as she looked into his eyes swirling with hesitant need. "I want the gritty, raw, emotional mess who feels totally out of control right now. Give him to me." As he frowned down at her, she gripped the hem of her fleecy pajama top and pulled it over her head, bearing her scars to him. She'd forgone the bra, so every deformity, every mark was plainly on display. With a trembling hand, she pulled his off the wall and placed it over her breast, the disfigured nipple stabbing into the center of his palm. "I gave it all to you. Every painful part. I won't hurt you, Luke. Give me everyt—"

He crushed his mouth to her in a kiss that shot her into orbit. It was frantic, dirty, bordering on sloppy as they attacked each other without finesse. His hand curled around her breast, molding the flesh while she shivered beneath him. It was as though they were trying to consume one another. Trying to absorb the other's pain and replace it with erotic pleasure.

"Luke," she said on a gasp as he licked his way to her neck. When he sucked hard on her pulse point, she gripped his hair and held him against her, wanting nothing more than to bear evidence of their desire tomorrow.

Screw wasted no time divesting her of the rest of her clothing. He shoved her pajama pants and panties down, kicking them across the kitchen when they hit the floor. His thick fingers found her entrance as though they were connected by some magnetic force.

"Oh, fuck, you're wet. You want me, Jazzy? Want me in this pretty pussy?"

"Yes."

"Want all of me?"

"Yes."

"Want me even though I'm fucked in the head right now? Want it hard and rough and fast?"

More wetness slid from her body, coating his hand where he played with her. A smirk curled his lips like he didn't need her to answer because her body had done it for her.

Still....

"Yes, Luke. I want you exactly like that. Fuck yes." He was alive, safe, and with her, and now she needed her body and heart to understand that as her mind did.

As he fumbled to open his belt and pants, he cursed then said, "Only goddammed time I don't have a fucking condom on me."

No doubt, he had plenty in the house, but damn if either of them wanted to take the time to locate one.

Jazz grabbed his arms. "I'm religious about my birth control pill. You and Gumby are the only ones I've been with since I've been tested."

He growled and pulled himself out, fisting his cock and giving a few rough tugs. "Got tested before Christmas. Haven't been with anyone but you two either."

Her eyes nearly fell out of her head. "Christmas was *weeks* ago."

"Fuckin' know it, baby."

Holy shit. For most, weeks without sex might not be a newsworthy event, but for Screw...

"Why?" She asked even though her body was screaming at her to shut up so he could fuck her. But she had to know. Because for him to act so out of character had to mean something, right?

He grabbed her ass, hiking her up into his arms with jerky movements. The head of his cock nudged her opening, making her moan and try to thrust her hips forward. But he held her captive. "You know why," he said in a harsh whisper against her ear as he powered into her.

Jazz cried out at the sudden intrusion. Even as wet as she was, his girth made her need a second to adjust, but he didn't give it to her.

Instead, he did exactly as she'd asked. He poured every ounce of stress, worry, pain, guilt, and agitation into fucking her.

He pumped hard, thrusting with abandon over and over. He buried his face into her neck, small grunts getting lost in her skin with each animalistic jerk of his hips. For her part, Jazz held him tight, absorbing his aggression. Her back ground into the wall so hard, there'd be bruises on her spine and shoulder blades tomorrow for sure, but damn if it wasn't worth it, because the pleasure he was wringing from her overrode any and all discomfort.

"Yes, Luke," she shouted as he tightened his grip on her ass.

She was completely naked while he remained fully dressed. Something about the feel of his pants scratching her thighs made her pussy clench. Maybe it was knowing he wanted her so bad, he couldn't even get his clothes off.

The room blurred and her mind numbed to everything but the incredible feelings of Screw unleashing his emotion powered lust on her. Somewhere in the back of her mind, she registered a sound, but not enough to give it even a second of her brain power. There were far too many pleasurable sensations to focus on.

"Fuck, baby, you meant it, didn't you?"

Meant she wanted all of him?

"Yes, yes, yes."

She wouldn't have thought it possible, but his strokes increased in strength, hitting something inside her that had her shouting his name.

And then it was…gone.

Every single sensation disappeared.

Jazz's feet hit the ground with a thud. Her legs buckled, forcing her to reach for Screw.

But he was gone.

Slamming her knees back to keep from falling, she gained control of her legs. "Wha—"

Oh, shit.

Across the kitchen, Screw had Gumby jammed up against the wall, his forearm crushing their lover's windpipe. His dick was still out, wet from their fucking and semi hard, but he seemed to have lost all desire for sex as he growled.

"What the fuck were you thinking?"

Naked and with arousal coating her thighs, Jazz slowly walked over to the two men she was head over heels in love with. "Screw. It's too much. You're hurting him."

Gumby's face turned a light shade of purple, but he didn't struggle. Instead, he held Screw's gaze, calm as could be.

Her words must have gotten through at least a little because he let up enough for Gumby to breathe and begin to speak. But his words were immediately cut off by another growl from Screw.

"What the fuck were you thinking?"

Chapter Thirty-Five

He must be one sick puppy because neither the pissed off man, lack of oxygen, nor pain across his neck did anything to deflate the hard-on Gumby had gotten at the sight of Screw and Jazz's animalistic fucking.

"Screw," Jazz said for the second time. She lifted her hands, placing them on the man's arm where it crushed across his throat.

Finally, the pressure evaporated. Gumby sucked in a giant gulp of air but didn't move or try to shove Screw away. Instead, he stayed, flattened against the wall, his dick now a spike in his pants.

"Why?" Screw asked in a voice laden with agony and torment.

"Because I had to." His voice sounded scratchy from the choking, but there was no pain. The truth of his simple statement seemed to be good enough to have Screw backing off. More words would probably help, but they'd probably send the other man running. Hell, they'd probably send Gumby running. Yet they hovered there on the tip of his tongue.

You've changed me.

I've never felt like this.

I had to make sure the mission succeeded.

I'd do anything to help you and your club.

I couldn't lose either of you.

I love you…

Both of you.

"I'm sorry," Screw said with a shake of his head. "I was just so fucking…" Another head shake. Another man who couldn't put voice to his feelings.

Gumby nodded. The apology wasn't necessary. He'd flip his shit if either of them purposefully put themselves in danger as well. He got it. He took one step from the wall, then kissed Screw. It was a soft meeting of lips, so contrary to the volcanic emotions swirling just beneath the surface of his skin.

Screw kissed him back for long seconds. Until Jazz's hands threaded through both their hair, giving a light tug. Then he turned toward her. "I'm sorry," he whispered, pressing his forehead to hers.

Her hands came up to frame Screw's face. "Lucky for you, watching you two kiss gets me wet. Pretty sure we can pick up right where we left off."

Screw growled and grabbed Jazz by her ass, hoisting her up into his arms. Walking with sure steps, he took them over to his kitchen island. The island that seemed perfect fucking height.

When her ass hit the cool granite, Jazz let out a small yelp that Screw cut off with his mouth. If he thought he was hard a few moments ago, the sight of Jazz's bare legs wrapped around Screw's clothed body as he kissed her senseless proved him wrong.

Now he was fucking hard.

Damn, they were a sight to behold.

Gumby stripped out of his shirt, then lost his boots and pants as well. Once he was as naked as Jazz, he gripped his cock and stroked to the gorgeous visual of his two lovers going at it.

After one more quick, hard kiss to Jazz's swollen lips, Screw turned his heated gaze on him. "Did you notice I was in her bare?"

Gumby froze. Had he noticed? No, he had not, but the thought of it had precum dripping from the head of his dick.

Gaze on his cock, Screw chuckled. "I see you like the idea. You clean?"

He squeezed the head of his dick to keep from coming right then and there. "Yeah. Swear it."

"Us too."

He held Screw's gaze until the other man said. "Want you in my ass."

Jazz gasped and Gumby groaned. Fuck, how he wanted that too. So bad his balls had drawn up tight and ached like a motherfucker.

"Want you in there while I'm fucking her." Screw's voice promised a long night of sexual fulfillment.

"Jesus, Screw," Jazz said.

Gumby reached down and fished the packet of lube out of his pocket. He'd stuck it there earlier that evening. Wishful thinking for a heated night following a successful operation.

Though they'd encountered a few craters in the road, it looked like he'd be getting his wish.

Naked as Jazz, he stalked across the room feeling like a jungle cat preparing to pounce.

Screw and Jazz had gone back to making out, so he fitted himself to Screw's back and kissed the side of his neck. As he nibbled and sucked across the soft flesh, Gumby worked Screw's loose pants down his legs. They pooled at his feel and if he'd had patience, he'd have gone to his knees to remove the man's boots, but that would waste precious seconds. When he'd finished with that task, he gripped Screw by his long hair, pulling him away from Jazz's hungry mouth.

Both of them groaned in protest, making Gumby chuckle. "Patience, lovers." When he had Screw upright, he pulled the man's shirt over his head, tossing it somewhere behind them. Over Screw's shoulder, Gumby watched Jazz lick her lips as all those tattooed muscles became available to her.

She reached up, tracing the ridges of Screw's abdomen, and Gumby swore he could feel the touch as though it was his own skin she caressed. "You're so beautiful," she whispered, awe in her voice.

"View's not too bad from this side either," he said as he ran his hands down Screw's back to his ass where he cupped the firm cheeks with a hard squeeze.

Screw groaned, grinding himself back. As Screw's ass brushed his dick, Gumby spread the man's cheeks and rubbed his dick over the tight hole. "This ass is gonna fucking strangle me, isn't it."

With a dark chuckle, Screw said, "You have no fucking idea."

"What are you waiting for, big guy?" Gumby whispered in Screw's ear. "Fuck her."

Jazz gave them a sly smile as she eased down onto the counter. Widening her silky legs, she planted her heels at the edge of the granite.

He'd probably spontaneously orgasm while eating breakfast tomorrow from the memories of what was about to happen in this kitchen.

"You heard the man, Jazzy." Screw's anger seemed to have dissipated, leaving the fun and playful man they'd come to expect. "You ready?"

She winked. "I'm pretty much always ready for you two."

Damn, if that didn't hit him square in the chest.

As Gumby continued peering over Screw's shoulder, his guy gripped his cock and positioned it right at Jazz's opening, but didn't push in. She squirmed, clearly needing more.

"Screw," she whined which only made the devious man chuckle.

"What's wrong, babe?" He slid his dick through her wetness as her eyes narrowed in warning.

Two could play this game.

As Screw continued to torture Jazz, Gumby slid his finger into his mouth, coating it in spit. Then without warning he dove it between Screw's ass cheeks until he found that puckered hole. One firm tap was all it took to have Screw shouting and jamming his hips forward, right into Jazz's waiting pussy.

"Yes!" she shouted at the same time Screw yelled, "Fuck."

"That's some dirty pool, William." Screw said with a growl. "You're lucky it feels so damn good that I want more."

"More like this?" He slowly increased the pressure on Screw's hole until the man released a breath and relaxed, letting him in. "That's it," Gumby whispered as his long finger sunk deep into Screw's ass. "Christ, this is a tight asshole."

Screw grunted. He'd buried himself balls deep in Jazz but didn't move beyond that as he adjusted to the invasion. Beneath him, Jazz stroked everywhere she could reach, murmuring how hot Screw was, how good he felt, how well Gumby was gonna fuck him.

Screw shuddered, his head dropping forward as Gumby began to fuck him with his finger. After a few seconds of listening to the man pant and curse, he pulled his finger out. This time, he spit onto his fingers, coating two of them even further before returning his hand to Screw's ass.

As he slid two fingers in deep, Screw said, "Fuuuck."

"You okay?"

"Yes. Very fucking okay."

"Mmm," Gumby said. "Not sure I'm gonna survive being in this ass."

"You better," Jazz said. "I've got plans for you."

Jesus, these two had him by the balls.

And the heart.

As Gumby prepared Screw for his cock by fucking and scissoring him with his fingers, Screw began to tilt his hips, thrusting into Jazz with small strokes. The muscles in his back bunched and flexed as he moved. Then there was his ass, contracting around his fingers with every thrust. Jazz sighed in pleasure as she continued her exploration of Screw's muscles. Gumby increased the pressure, searching around for—

"Oh, fuck!" Screw shouted as his hips jammed forward with force.

Jazz cried out as well. "What was that?"

Gumby did it again, and Screw slapped the table while groaning.

"I believe I just nailed our man's prostate."

"Fuck yeah, you did. Do it again." No one could ever accuse Screw of being shy about asking for what he wanted.

"Yeah, do it again," Jazz echoed.

So he did. A few times, loving the way it made Screw fuck hard into Jazz. Sweat beaded up along Screw's spine. Gumby couldn't resist taking a lick of the salty fluid.

The ache in his cock could no longer be ignored. "I need to be in this ass, now," Gumby said.

"I ain't stopping you." Screw panted as Gumby's fingers left his body.

After taking a quick nip of Screw's shoulder, Gumby grabbed the packet of lube from the table. He ripped it open with his teeth and drizzled a generous amount on his cock. The tip was already wet with precum, in fact, a line of sticky fluid stretched from Screw's thigh to the tip of Gumby's dick.

Once lubed up, he fitted the head of his cock to Screw's hole. Just that, just the pressure of it fluttering around the head of his dick had fire racing up Gumby's spine. "Ready?"

"You're sweet and all to check in, but get that fucking thing in me already," Screw said with a near snarl.

As he began to drive forward, Gumby bit his lower lip. Screw was clearly no stranger to being fucked because he blew out a breath and bore down, allowing Gumby entry with minimal effort. The second he slipped past the tight ring of muscle, both of them sighed.

He'd never been in anyone bare and the heat and clasp of Screw's tight ass was like nothing he'd ever felt before. In seconds, he'd worked his entire length into the man, breathing like he'd run laps around the house.

Screw still had his head bent forward which allowed Gumby to lock eyes with Jazz. Heat and desire stared back at him along with something else. Something so damn intimate it took all he had not to run from it by closing his own eyes.

Last time they'd been together this way, all three of them as one, he'd written the feelings off as the anomaly of his first threesome. Now he knew better because there it was again. The rightness. The closeness. The absolute perfection of the moment.

The feeling that he was exactly where was meant to be with who he was meant to find.

SCREW CONCENTRATED ON not blowing his load inside Jazz before Gumby got to actually fucking him. He'd had plenty of threesomes, but always as the outer cookie, never the creamy center. And now he fully understood why everyone went nuts for that cream.

Without the barrier of a condom, Jazz's tight, wet heat nearly seared him. Her hands roaming all over his skin ignited millions of nerve ends making his entire body tingle and fizz. Behind him, Gumby licked up his spine. Gumby's end of the day stubble abraded his skin and added to the sensory overload.

Then there was his cock. That long shaft, buried to the nuts in Screw's ass. He was so fucking full and stretched he felt he could split in two. Despite it all, he wanted more. So much more.

He wanted it all.

But he'd have nothing if he shot off like a freshman getting his first up close and personal with a tit.

As slowly as he slid in, Gumby drew back but not fully out. Then he pushed forward again. With intent this time.

"Fuck," Screw whispered as the force of Gumby's stroke powered him into Jazz. She moaned, curling her fists into his sides.

As Gumby picked up the rhythm, Screw kept himself braced on his arms. He'd planted one hand flat on the table on either side of Jazz's head.

"Oh, God," Jazz said, gripping him so hard, her nails pricked his skin. "Every time he fucks into you…"

Hell, yes. "I fuck into you."

"Yes," she said, meeting the next thrust with a pump of her hips.

"Shit, that's hot," Gumby said as he thrust.

"More." Screw barked. "Fuck me harder, Will. Fuck us both harder."

With a feral growl, Gumby hammered into Screw's ass. He barely needed to move his own hips because the man behind him and the woman beneath him were fucking themselves on his body with such vigorous enthusiasm.

"Your ass feels so fucking incredible."

"Yeah, well your dick's fucking talented," he said just as Gumby reamed his prostate making him slam into Jazz. She seemed to love that, crying out each time Gumby nailed the gland as though she felt it too.

"I believe that's my line," Jazz said then gasped when Screw bent forward and nipped at the side of her breast.

"Fuck, right there, G. Right fucking there." The talented fucker shifted, hitting Screw's prostate on every stroke. His head was gonna blow straight off his body.

Talking stopped after that. Maybe it was the ability to talk that flew out the window.

Screw gave himself over to the care of his two lovers. His pleas for more seemed to have unleashed something in Gumby as the other man's thrusts became near frantic. He managed to keep his eyes open and locked on Jazz as together, he and Gumby drove her toward the finish line.

Three more hits to his prostate and Screw knew he'd about reached the end of his ability to hold on.

"Baby," he ground out. "You need to come. Now."

Jazz just moaned in response, her eyelids falling shut. "So c-close."

Screw shoved one hand between their sweat-slicked bodies—thank God for many, many hours of upper body exercises—balancing on one hand above Jazz.

The very second he found her clit, she stiffened beneath him then let out a cry of satisfaction that no man could resist.

The spasms of her pussy around his cock pulled his orgasm straight from his balls deep into her. "Shit," he shouted, slapping his palm on the table once again. The orgasm consumed him. White flashed through his vision. Every cell in his being sang with pleasure as spurt after spurt of hot come ejected from his dick.

Just as his ass rippled around Gumby, the man also stiffened, then jerked and grunted as he blew his hot load into Screw's ass.

Jazz sagged, her arms falling from his sides to hang limply off the edges of the table. Screw bowed his head as the events leading to this volatile encounter came back to him.

He'd been stressed out of his fucking mind. The highs and lows of the night had taken his mind and battered it beyond recognition. It was the only excuse he could muster for attacking Gumby when he'd walked through the door.

Gumby pressed a line of kisses across Screw's shoulders as his softened cock slipped from his ass. Screw followed, leaving the warm wet cavern of Jazz's body. When she let out a tiny whimper of protest, he couldn't help the small chuckle.

Gumby's cum dripped from his ass, probably making a mess on his floor. Hell, his cum was probably trickling out of Jazz as well. They could clean it later. Or not at all. There was something so filthy and erotic about their mingled sex juices staining his house.

He spun, taking Gumby's face in his hands and giving the man a hot and heavy kiss. Jazz sat up, wrapping her arms around his waist and her legs around both of them as best she could. Her heels most likely dug into Gumby's ass to keep them all joined in the tight hug.

"I'm sorry," he whispered against Gumby's lips. Jazz had asked him to be real, so real she'd get. And if Gumby couldn't handle it…fuck him. "I was so goddammed scared when I realized you weren't behind me. If you'd been ar—"

"Shh," Gumby said, kissing him.

Jazz's soft lips landed on his back again and again.

"I know. I'd have reacted the same way. But I had to finish what we started. For you. For Jazz. And you know you would have done the same damn thing."

Fuck yeah, he would have. If it had been him who knew how to solve the problem with the truck, he'd have stayed behind to fix it as well. They were alike in their deep-seated loyalty to brotherhood.

And to Jazmine.

And as it turned out…each other.

Chapter Thirty-Six

Jazz stood in front of the bathroom mirror wearing nothing but a light blue bra as she blew her hair dry. Progress. Sure, she'd had to force herself, but spending a fantastic afternoon/night with two men who made her feel like the most beautiful woman in the world had given her the courage to take the next step. And the next step was becoming comfortable in her skin again.

It would take some work as the sight of the scars not only brought back horrific memories but made her cringe with a bite of disgust. Hopefully both reactions would fade with time and practice. Lucky for her, she had plenty to think about besides what happened to her.

Like the hours and hours of pleasure Gumby and Screw had given her last night. She visibly shivered in the mirror. Damn, it'd been incredible. And way more than just physical. The three of them connected on a deeper level with their bodies but also their stories.

Jazz set her hairdryer down and cocked her head. The trill of her cell phone rang from her bedroom. "Thought I heard you," she mumbled as she jogged across her room to where her cell lay on her bed.

Wasn't often her phone began ringing before work since she arrived at the diner at six thirty in the morning, but if it did, it typically meant someone was calling out sick.

She didn't recognize the number but answered it anyway since she didn't have every employee programmed into her phone. "Hello?" As she spoke, she moved to her dresser to find some socks.

"Jazmine? This is Lynn Sampson."

"Oh, Mrs. Sampson, hello. How are you?" she asked of her elderly landlord.

"I'm well, dear. I'm sorry for calling at this time, but I know you go to work early."

"It's no problem at all," she said slipping her foot into her favorite socks. They were covered in dogs. As soon as life settled a bit, she planned to get a dog. Or a few. "Is there something wrong with my rent check?"

"Oh, heavens no. It's nothing like that at all. I have been looking all over my house for a sewing machine that used to be my grandmothers." She chuckled. "I thought I was losing my mind and then I remembered I boxed it up and put it in the shed over there. Would you mind fetching it so my son can come pick it up?"

Would she mind going out to the shed where she'd last seen a snake?

Uh, yeah, she minded. She minded a whole lot.

"No, Mrs. Collier, I don't mind at all." She'd have one of the guys do it for her later today. "When is he thinking of coming by?"

"Probably around nine this morning. If you don't mind just leaving it on the porch before you go to work, he won't need to get in your hair at all."

Well crap. Gumby had left with Screw just five minutes ago. He planned to work out while Screw opened Zach's gym. It was on the tip of her tongue to ask Mrs. Sampson if her son could just go into the shed and retrieve it himself. But she bit the words back. She was an adult for crying out loud. So she saw a small snake once. Didn't mean the place was infested. It was winter anyway. Didn't that mean the snakes had migrated somewhere warm?

Like the inside of the shed.

Even as she shuddered in revulsion, she forced the words, "Sure, I'll run out there right now," past her lips.

"Thank you, honey. You're such a sweetheart. You have a good day."

"You too, Mrs. Sampson." Jazz groaned the second she hit the end button.

It was then she remembered Thunder had pulled up right before the guys left. He'd get it for her. He'd also tease her until her dying day.

No, it was time to pull up her big girl panties and go out to the shed. Grumbling, Jazz slipped into her heavy winter coat and stuffed her feet into her unlaced boots. As though walking to her doom, she trudged across the backyard to the large light blue shed in the back-left corner.

She stared at the farmhouse style door for a good thirty seconds before rolling her eyes. "You big baby," she muttered before yanking the door open. It opened easier than she remembered the last time she'd been brave enough to venture out there, but then, it'd been well over a year so who knew if her memory was accurate.

"Okay," she murmured as she reached out to pull the string attached to a single light bulb. "If I were a sewing machine, I'd b —oh, fuck."

Jazz stopped dead in her tracks as she gazed around the contents of the shed. Not snakes. God, how she wished it'd been full of snakes.

Never had she thought she'd be wishing for the slithering reptiles but even a shed full of the most venomous of serpents was preferable to what she found in her shed.

Hundreds of big angry assault rifles.

* * *

SCREW LET OUT a low whistle as he watched Gumby work the speed bag. "Looking good there, baby," he said as he propped his shoulder against the wall with his arms folded across his chest. "Sexy as fuck. Who knew you were so good with little hanging sacks?"

Even as he snorted out a laugh, Gumby scanned their surrounding as though worried someone would overhear their flirty banter. He chose to ignore the pang of discomfort at the thought the man might never be able to own his sexuality and claim Screw in public because, well, he didn't want Gumby to claim him in public.

He didn't want anyone to claim him in public.

How the hell would he get new tits and ass if people thought he was locked down?

Not that he had even a passing interest in anyone but Jazz and Gumby these days…

After the epic night the three of them spent together, his heart and body were on Team Relationship while his head remained stubbornly on Team Never Gonna Happen. He'd never felt closer to two people, and it freaked him the fuck out. He didn't want closeness or emotion, or that goddammed *R* word. He also chose to ignore the inner voice telling him he was full of shit.

As soon as Gumby saw they were alone he said, "Zach didn't have any shirts in your size?"

Screw barked out a laugh. "He did, but this one draws in more customers." He winked as he flexed. Sure enough the tight polo stretched across his chest and nearly popped at the sleeves. Truth be told, he hated the damn thing. Way too uncomfortable, but as Z said, it did draw lots of stares.

Gumby's included. "Mm-hmm," he said as he faltered and missed the bag.

Screw snickered. "Careful there. Don't wanna drop your guard and have someone mess up that pretty face. Your girlfriend might protest." His phone rang. "Speaking of," he said, as Jazz's name flashed across the screen. "Hey, sexy lady, I was just talking about y—

"Screw, I'm out in the shed in my backyard and it's full of guns."

He blinked. "What?"

"Big nasty action movie type of guns. Assault rifles or whatever they are called."

He shoved his hand into his hair, gripping the strands hard. "You're fucking kidding me. Please tell me this is your idea of a bad fucking joke."

Gumby went on alert, dropping his arms and stepping closer.

"No. Not a joke at all. I don't know what to do. What do I do? I'm totally freaking out over here." Her voice bordered on hysterical.

"Okay, babe, calm down. Breathe, you hear me?"

He listened as she sucked in a few deep breaths then released them. "Y-yeah. Okay. I'm okay."

"Listen to me, Jazz. Gumby and I are on our way. I want you to go back in the house. I'm going to call Thunder and have him go in to sit with you until we arrive. Do not go back outside for any reason. Do you understand?"

"Um, yeah. Okay."

In the background, he heard the sounds of her closing the shed and hopefully returning to the relative safety of her house.

Without even knowing what the issue was, Gumby had ditched his hand wraps and began stowing his gear in his duffle. At this hour, only a few members were working out, but it wasn't as though Screw could leave them in the gym unsupervised.

Gumby pulled out his phone. "I'm calling Zach," he said as though reading Screw's mind. He'd exchanged numbers with most of the club before their raid on the trucking company.

Screw nodded to the other man. Damn, not only was Gumby an eager and skilled lover, he was a loyal team player who'd shown Screw without words how much he trusted him over these past few days. His blind acceptance of a problem and action to solve it proved that.

"I'm inside," Jazz said through the phone.

Screw kept his gaze on Gumby who paced away while updating Zach.

"Lock the door. Did you see Jeremy at all while you were out there? Do you know if he's home?"

"Jeremy? Why—oh, my God. Do you think this was him?"

Who else would it be? Had to be fucking Jeremy. As a prospect for the CDMC with easy access to Jazz's backyard, and a strong aversion to all things Hell's Handlers, he was the prime and only suspect. But to what end? To set Jazzy up? Maybe to set the MC up? Or was it legitimate storage of his club's weapons in a place no one would ever think to look?

Everyone knew Jazz was too skittish of snakes to venture out to the shed a second time. Hell, it'd been a running joke at the clubhouse. It wasn't out of the realm of possibility to think she mentioned—

"Oh, shit," she said as though talking to herself. "A few weeks ago, I told him about my snake encounter. Oh, I'm so stupid."

He heard a slap as though she'd palmed her own forehead.

"I told him I'd rather die than go in that shed again. Why did I do that?" she said with a groan.

Gumby hustled over. "Zach will be here in five," he mouthed holding up five fingers. He stayed close, but didn't touch Screw at all, as if he needed the nearness but couldn't allow himself that last final link. At least not in public.

It sucked, but there were more pressing matters at hand. "Jazzy, baby, stop. Why on earth would you have thought twice about telling him? At the time, he was just your helpful neighbor." A neighbor who wanted in her pants, but it probably wasn't the time to mention that particular detail. "Sit tight. Gumby and I are leaving as soon as Zach gets here. Five minutes tops. I'll call Thunder as soon as I hang up."

"Okay. Careful driving over here. Precious cargo in that truck."

Despite the thrum of anger and fear pumping through his veins, he smiled. "Will do." Jazz cared and she'd worked her way into his heart, bringing life to the organ in a way no one else had been able to.

Well, maybe one other. Shit, he couldn't stop from wanting both Jazz and Gumby even at the worst times.

"Zach just parked," Gumby announced as Screw hung up.

"Okay, let's roll," he said before bringing the phone back to his ear, this time with Thunder's cell ringing on the other end.

"Hey, Screwball, what's up?"

"Need you to get in Jazzy's house ASAP. She found weapons in her shed."

"Fuck," Thunder murmured. The sound of his car door slamming alerted Screw to how serious the prospect took this task. He'd make a great brother and sooner rather than later. "The fucking prick next door?"

"It's gotta be." He held the door for Gumby, who jogged through then out to the driver's side of the truck. Screw tossed him the keys and slipped in the passenger seat while Gumby fired up the truck.

They worked well together. In sync almost as if with one mind.

"I haven't seen him at all the past few days. If he's coming and going, he's doing it when Jazzy isn't home."

"Yeah." Fucking asshole.

Another door slammed in the background. "I'm inside with her."

"Thanks, Thunder. Gumby and I are on our way. Zach probably called Copper so others may show up before us."

"No worries, man. You and Gumby are all good, I'll take good care of your girl," he said in a knowing tone. As though the three of them weren't fooling anyone. Guess if someone was gonna figure it out, it'd be Thunder. Not only was the guy more open minded than anyone Screw knew when it came to sex—probably from his years-long career as a go-go dancer—he'd been tailing Jazzy more often than not over the past few weeks.

"All right. See you in a few."

He hung up but didn't stow his phone, instead, tapped it against his thigh in a nervous rhythm. The idea of Jazz being so close to this, being caught between two warring MCs was the perfect kindling for a raging wildfire.

"Hey."

Screw startled at Gumby's voice, not that he'd forgotten the other man was there, but he'd started getting sucked into the quicksand of anxiety. This wasn't him. This stressed out, angry, fucking emo…mess. He was the guy who laughed shit off, cracked others up, and walked through life with a who-gives-a-fuck attitude.

And now? Now he was wishing more than anything that the man next to him would what…comfort him as he worried over the woman who had come to mean just as much to him as this man?

Enough of all this. Time to straighten out his shit and get back to who *he* was before he lost himself.

"Screw? You coming?"

He blinked. Shit, when had they pulled into Jazz's driveway? Another example of how he was unraveling. He turned to see Gumby still in the driver's seat, door open. His concerned gaze fell on Screw.

"Coming?" Screw grunted. "Fuck, not yet, but if you wanna suck me off before we go in there, I'm down. Or…we could up our game. Ask Thunder to join us." He winked. "There's not much that guy hasn't seen and done." God, the thought of Thunder so much as touching either Jazz or Gumby had Screw wanting to crawl out of his own skin.

Gumby didn't react. Not a laugh, not a disgusted eye roll, which was the reaction Screw deserved. Nope, he just reached out and interlaced their fingers. The simple gesture was exactly what he'd been both hoping for and dreading like he dreaded fucking gonorrhea.

He closed his eyes and took a breath. "I'm sorry. I'm an assh —"

Gumby's lips landed on his in a soft kiss. "I get it, Luke. I. Get. It."

Screw opened his eyes and what he saw had him swallowing a lump in his throat. Gumby did get it. The reason behind the jokes, the confusion, the unfamiliar emotions. He got it all and that settled Screw more than anything could have. He wasn't alone. Not in dealing with the CDMC. Not in keeping Jazz safe.

Not in the complex but real relationship they had fallen into.

"Come on," Gumby said. "Let's go help our girl."

Yeah, that's exactly what they'd do. And afterward? The three of them would cocoon themselves away from the rest of the world for the night as they'd done every night recently.

And he secretly hoped they'd do for many nights to come.

Maybe even…forever.

Chapter Thirty-Seven

Half an hour later, Jazz's house was abuzz with at least seven Hell's Handlers all voicing loud views on the motivation for Jeremy stashing the guns in her shed and what should be done with them.

Gumby's head had been throbbing for the past twenty minutes, he could only imagine what Jazz was feeling as her home was invaded by loud-mouthed, opinionated bikers.

She sat on her couch, where she'd parked after getting everyone coffee and answering at least a hundred questions.

Once it appeared he could sneak away, Gumby lowered onto the couch next to Jazz. "How you holding up, Jazzy?"

She tipped to the side until her head rested against his arm, which he then slipped around her, pulling her into his side.

"I feel so stupid and guilty. Like I did something wrong. Something I need to apologize for even though the logical part of my brain knows I didn't." As she spoke, she picked at a small fray in the knee of his jeans. "I mean how the hell was I supposed to know Jeremy would prospect with the CDMC? And how would I know he'd use my yard to hide his…contraband."

His lips quirked. "Contraband?"

"I don't want to say guns. I'm sick of saying guns. It's making me sick to think one of those things could be used in a school shooting or something equally horrifying."

"I know, baby." He dropped a kiss on the top of her head. "You stole my speech though."

She shifted, gazing up at him. "Your speech."

"Yup," he answered with a nod. "I was all prepared to give you the there's-no-way-you-could-have-known-what-he-was-planning speech, but you gave it to yourself."

With a huff she resumed toying with his pants. "I've given it to myself at least fifty times."

"There's a joke in there somewhere. If I were Screw, I'd be on top of it."

Jazzy chuckled. "There's one in your statement too. He must be rubbing off on us."

Their gazes met, then they burst out laughing.

"Thank you," Jazzy said, snuggling closer. "You knew just what to do to make me feel better."

Her arm banded across his waist and he gave her a squeeze. The way she fit there, so snug and warm in his arms was just... well it was perfect.

From across the room, Screw caught his eye. The other man paused mid-conversation and sent Gumby a tentative smile. Screw struggled so much to recognize his worth. To accept his ability not only to be just what his club needed, but also what Jazz and Gumby needed.

It was a goddammed shame, and something Gumby vowed to make right. Before he left, he'd make sure Screw knew just how incredible he was.

Before he left...

Suddenly Gumby had a flash of the future. Of sitting there, just as he was with Jazz nestled into his arms. She'd always do that, reach to him for comfort in times of need, but also for celebration in times of joy.

As would Screw. It might take the man some time to get on board, but he was in the vision too. A strong force, making every day sunnier and bright. Making sure they enjoyed their lives to the fullest.

The fantasy was, well, just that. A fantasy. Something to think about and mourn once he was back in Arizona with his own club.

Screw wandered over as his brothers began to file out. Some went to the back yard, while others through the front. "Okay," he said, running a hand across his mouth. He stood, feet apart, hands braced on his hips. "Mav scouted around outside Jeremy's house. No cameras there. None in or around your shed. He's a stupid fuck, but that's good news for us. Means it may take him a while to figure out we moved his shit."

"You're getting rid of them?" Jazz asked, straightening.

Screw nodded. "Yeah, there are risks seeing as how the CDMC will know it was us, but we can't leave them. If their plan is to frame you or one of us, Jeremy could call the cops to come raid you here at any point in time. Even if you swear up down and back that you didn't know the weapons were there, the cops will make your life a fucking nightmare until you can prove it."

Gumby agreed wholeheartedly. The cops finding out had disaster written all over it.

"LJ is backing the club's van up to your fence right now. We'll load the guns up and get out of here without you neighbors being aware of what we removed. Tell 'em it was lawn equipment if they ask."

Jazz shuddered. "Good. I'll tell them anything you want, I just want those guns out of here."

Screw sat on the other side of Jazz, pulling her in for a kiss on her temple. His mouth was set in an uncharacteristic hard line and his eyes held what looked like regret.

Something else was coming, something she wouldn't like.

He gave her a somber look. "You can't stay here, Jazzy. Not until we're sure they won't retaliate against you."

There it was.

She let out a defeated sigh as she sagged against Gumby. "I figured." She glanced over her shoulder at him then looked up at Screw again. "You got room for two strays?"

"I sure do," Screw said, pinching Jazz's chin between his thumb and forefinger. He tipped her head up and whispered, "We need to get outside and help. You're handling this like a rock star," before kissing her.

Jazz reached her hand out for him, so Gumby scooted close. He draped his arm across the back of the couch, hand landing on Screw's shoulder. When Screw ended his kiss with Jazz, he leaned in a little.

Gumby swallowed. Outside, Screw's club brothers milled around moving a shed full of weapons. Sure, they were alone in the house, but would someone walk in?

He's eyes met Screw's. When he saw the patience there, the understanding, he knew it was safe to…take a leap. As his lips met Screws, and Jazzy let out a blissful sigh, a zing of happiness shot through him.

A loud bang followed by, "Hey, bitches, I have arrived," in a booming voice he'd know anywhere had him jerking violently away from his lovers and scooting all the way to the opposite end of the couch.

"Guys in cuts out front told me to walk right in. What the fuck?" the big man, the No Prisoners Sergeant at Arms said in his booming, bullhorn voice.

Gumby couldn't move. It felt like his limbs had frozen solid.

No. No. No.

The word repeated in his mind again and again until he opened his mouth, emitting a squeak that was drowned out by Jazzy's squealed, "Jester!"

She launched herself off the couch and straight into the arms of the mountainous man.

This couldn't be happening. The room spun and for a second, Gumby worried he'd pass out.

"Who the fuck is this?" Screw growled as he began to rise.

"SAE of my club," Gumby managed, voice ragged as though someone had rubbed his vocal cords with sandpaper. He needed to get up. To greet his No Prisoners family, but he couldn't fucking move. Jester had seen. He'd walked in the very moment Screw's lips touched his.

Not once had he ever given his club any clue he was attracted to men. None of the men were openly gay or bisexual. Sure, they were cool guys, but Crystal Rock, Arizona wasn't exactly a Mecca of homosexual activity. Actually, the tiny town was pretty much the opposite, full of more bigoted assholes than anything else.

Men like his father. Just the thought of his old man had Gumby's insides firing up with the need to protect himself. To run. To hide.

To deny.

"Well, fuck me. The guy's as big as LJ," Screw said with a laugh as he rose.

"His personality is bigger," Jazz said as Jester lifted her off her feet.

Shit. They were all there. His friend. His club. His brothers. There to witness his relationship with a woman and a man. The ache in Gumby's left hand roared to life as memories of his father's fists flew at him.

"Damn, girl, you're looking fierce," Jester said as his huge arms swallowed Jazz whole. Her feet dangled a good twelve inches off the floor.

She squealed again. "Oh, my God! Striker! Hook!"

Jester released her and she treated the other two to the same enthusiastic greeting. "I can't believe you guys are here." He could hear the tears thickening her voice as she reunited with his club brothers.

"Hey, man, I'm Screw." He extended his hand to Jester who wrapped his big mitt around Screw's hand and pumped vigorously. He cast a glance in Gumby's direction as though assessing how he'd handle the situation. And, Christ, was that disappointment in his eyes?

Gumby watched the entire scene as though sitting through a horror film. Jester smiled at Jazz, hugging her again. Screw shook each man's hand making them laugh as was his specialty. Only Striker kept his focus on Gumby, one eyebrow arched in question. Would he react like Gumby's father? Would he lose his shit? Kick him out of the club? Take his cut? The urge to cover his eyes, to bury his head between the couch cushions surged in him yet he couldn't tear his gaze away from the bloody scene.

And then the murderer went for the fucking kill.

"Yo, VP, you won't believe the shit I walked in on. G, here had his lips on this Screw dude, and Jazzy was all happily sandwiched between them." Jester waggled his eyebrows and grinned a smirk that would make the devil run and hide. "Whatcha got going on here, Gumby? One woman ain't enough for you anymore? Gotta add a little dick to the mix?"

Even from ten feet away, he felt Screw stiffen. Jazz did the same, pulling away from Hook and stepping up next to Jester who still wore the shit-eating grin.

"Um, Jester," she said, glancing between Gumby and Screw.

Deny. Deny. Deny.

Gumby stood. "The fuck you been smoking, Jester?" He laughed as he pulled his brother into a hug. "Think you need glasses, old man. What's the matter? Married life getting so boring you need to invent exciting sexual scenarios?"

Christ, he'd taking the front page of Screw's book, shitty jokes to avoid real issues. And was anyone buying it? As the words tumbled off his tongue, Gumby knew he was being a colossal asshole. He didn't need the stony mask of Screw's face or the way Jazz's smile fell straight to the floor to clue him in. But he couldn't stop it. The instinct for self-preservation had been so deeply ingrained into him, so painfully beaten in, the denial came naturally.

"But..." Jester glanced between the three of them, his brow furrowed.

Jazz stood beside him, wringing her hands, face devoid of color and lips pressed together.

"Sorry, brother. I thought..." Jester cleared his throat. "My bad. Maybe you're right and these old peepers are going."

"That or your mind. Hallucinating and shit." God, why couldn't he just shut up?

Striker stepped forward, clapping Jester on the back. "Hey, brother, why don't we give these three a second. We can go out and let our ladies know we arrived, huh?"

Hook had already slipped out the door.

"Yeah, sure," Jester said before casting an odd look Gumby's way. He took the path Hook did, preceding Striker out the door.

Just before stepping outside, Striker paused with a hand on the door frame. He peered over his shoulder at the three of them who were just standing like statues staring at each other. "I can see we fucked up," he said, regret in his voice. "I'm sorry we just popped in unannounced. We've just been worried about you, G." With that, he tapped his fist on the doorframe and walked outside, pulling the door closed behind him.

"Gumby..." Jazz strode toward him, wrapping her arms around him.

He couldn't return the embrace, feeling like a wooden statue.

"It's nothing," he said as she stepped back with a frown. "I'm glad they're here. It's getting to be time for me to head back to Arizona anyway. Don't want them to think I've abandoned my club."

"But...I...we..." Jazz looked between him and Screw.

If she expected the other man to jump in and help, she was in for disappointment. From his rigid posture to crossed arms, Screw's body language screamed fuck off.

"What was that?" Screw asked. "Said you need to get back to get some head in Arizona?" He laughed and the bitter sound pierced Gumby straight in the heart.

God, what this must be doing to Jazz. He risked a glance at her. Her forehead had scrunched, and her eyes had narrowed. She shook her head as though needing to shake the words around here brain to get them to make sense. "No, wha—"

"Sounds good, man. It's been fun. Need to get back in the game as well. Those Honeys ain't gonna suck or fuck themselves, right?"

"What?" Jazz whispered as her hands fell limp at her sides. "You can't mean that."

Screw laughed again. The sound was so ugly, Gumby flinched. "Of course, I mean it, Jazzy. You know who I am. What I do. Don't tell me you thought this was different? Special?" As he spoke, he indicated the three of them in a triangular motion with his finger.

Jazz's eyes fell shut. "You need to go, now," she said in a calm, though trembling voice that must have been a shit load of work to maintain.

Each word hit him like a bullet, tearing through his skin and wounding his organs. He'd done this. He'd caused Screw to fall back on old habits and Jazz to push him away. He'd hurt the two people who'd given him so much. The two people he wanted above all. He'd destroyed them.

"See you 'round the clubhouse, Jazzy. Have a good trip back, Gumby." He lifted his hand in a wave as he walked out the door, swagger in high.

Jazz turned her bleak eyes on him. She swallowed as a tear slipped from the corner of her eye and tracked down her cheek. "I—" She sucked in a breath that made her whole body shudder. "I'd like you to pack your things and stay at a hotel, p-please."

Her subdued demeanor terrified him. She was shutting down before his eyes. As she spoke, she tugged on the sleeves of her work shirt. Did she regret sharing her secrets? Is that what she was thinking about? How she poured the most painful part of her soul out only to be denied and rejected as if he were ashamed of her? Ashamed of them?

Fuck, this was all his fault. Yet he just couldn't summon the words to fix it all. He couldn't run after Screw because the thought of his club disapproving of him or casting him aside scared him above all. Yet as he watched Jazz turn her back on him, he wondered if the pain in his chest might be far worse than what he'd experience if his club shunned him.

Chapter Thirty-Eight

Screw stormed into the clubhouse and straight over to the bar. He dropped onto a barstool with a heavy plop. When no one showed up five seconds later, he called out, "Hey, can I get a fucking drink," to the empty room.

Of course, the goddammed place was empty. It was fucking nine thirty in the morning and everyone was dealing with the huge haul of weapons LJ just arrived with from Jazz's house.

What a clusterfuck. Goddammed Gumby and his fucking inability to admit he liked cock. Screw blew out a breath. Gumby's words had incensed him so fast and so fiercely he'd jetted without even making sure Jazz had protection and a place to stay. Of course, he'd remedied that by making sure Thunder stayed behind to help her pack and asking LJ if she could crash with him and Holly.

When they both looked at him with questions in their eyes, he'd fucking bitten their heads off with harsh words and stormed to his truck. Gumby could find his own fucking ride with his own fucking brothers who watched Screw with wary gazes as he left smoke in his wake.

"Fuck."

Just as he was about to get up and grab a bottle, morning be damned, the click-clack of a women's high heels reverberated behind him. Screw glanced over his hunched shoulder to find five-feet-nine inches of va-va-voom walking his way.

Giant tits, swaying hips, miles of skin on display, all topped off with some serious fuck-me heels and about a yard of platinum hair. She wore a seductive, red-lipped smile as she sauntered her way over to him. She was one of the newer Honeys, whose name failed him now. One he'd nearly slept with the fated night he watched Gumby and Jazz leave the clubhouse together, walking away from him.

The same night he'd first tasted Gumby.

Something he would *not* think of now.

"Well, hey there, handsome. Haven't seen you as much around here lately." The honey-thick voice of—*what the hell is her name?*—floated through the room.

Yeah, she hadn't seen him because he'd been too busy being a stupid fucking cliché and getting his heart stomped on. Never again. A hot and easy fuck was exactly what he needed. So what if he'd need to get wasted on a Wednesday morning to make that happen?

"Well I'm here now, and trust me," he said with a wink. "There's a lot of me to see."

She giggled, the sound raking across his eardrums like nails on a chalk board. He barely managed to contain a wince. Yeah, alcohol would be needed in fucking spades.

"Whiskey?" she asked as she made her way behind the bar. "Noticed it seems to be your drink of choice." She batted her thick eyelashes his way. "I've noticed a lot about you, Screw, and that includes that there is a lot of you to notice."

A generous glass of whiskey landed in front of him. He reached for it, but she didn't release it, keeping her red tipped fingers firmly around the glass. "You gonna pay the toll?" she asked, lips which matched those nails pouting.

Kill me now.

No he fucking wasn't paying any goddammed tolls. Especially not with a kiss. He wouldn't be kissing for a long damn time. He'd drink this booze. Then have another. Maybe another one or two after that while flirting with this Honey. Hopefully his banter and sexy talk would get her wet and he could just take her up to his room, bend her over, fuck Jazz and Gumby out of his system then send whatever the hell her name was on her way. Then he'd drink more and pass out, hopefully to wake up forgetting the fact he'd let himself fall in love with two people.

There it was.

The two-ton elephant, not in the room, no this one was sitting squarely on his chest, crushing the fucking life out of him.

"Hey? Not much of a kisser? No problem. I'm more than happy to save these lips for your cock." She released the glass, then straightened with a smirk as she watched him down it in two large gulps. When he set it down, it was full again in under five seconds.

What service.

And why the hell wasn't his cock reacting to the thought of bimbo here sucking him off? He always got hard at the offer of a blowjob. Hell, he'd probably get hard if fucking Copper offered to blow him.

But not this chick, apparently.

Maybe he needed more whiskey. Two more swallows and the next glass was gone.

"Thirsty, huh?" she asked with another of those annoying giggles.

Who cared if her giggle bothered him? Soon her mouth would be too full to giggle anyway.

"So, looks like you got shot off that skinny bitch with the butch haircut, huh?" she asked as she rested her elbows on the table, giving him prime view of two ginormous tits.

Tits he'd have loved just weeks ago before Jazz and her natural, reactive, sexy as fuck body got her hooks into him. And then there was Gumby…

Wait…what the hell did she just say? His blood ran cold and a pit of ice formed in his stomach.

"I heard she was frigid as fuck," the Honey went on with a conspiratorial whisper as she leaned even closer. "Heard she tried to take on two of you. *I* can take two. I looove taking two so feel free to bring your friend."

Over his dead body. No way in hell would this alley cat get her claws anywhere near his man. And this shit about trash-talking Jazz ended now. As she began to straighten, he shot his hand out and grabbed her wrist. The bimbo misunderstood his intentions and moaned as though the none-too-gentle touch got her all fired up. "Who the fuck is running their trap about Jazz that way?" he asked giving her arm a shake.

"What? Ow, Screw, that's too hard."

He slackened his grip but didn't release her. If these bitches were gossiping behind Jazz's back he'd have each and every one of them banned from the clubhouse, permanently. "Tell me who?"

"Uh, no one," she said, all flouncy bravado gone. "It's just silly girl talk."

He raised an eyebrow and stared her down. She seemed to wilt before his eyes.

"I-I mean, look at her. She's skinny and barely has tits. Her hair is short and she's always wearing those long-sleeved shirts like a nun or something." She shrugged a bare shoulder. "I guess we just can't understand why you're playing with that lately when you could have all this." She indicated her own scantily clad body. "Hell, you could have a few of us." Some of her confidence returned as she no doubt thought he'd never be able to resist her.

Christ, how had he gone for this type of woman for so many years? She reminded him of all the skanks he grew up with in his life. Friends of his mother who gave it away like candy on Halloween and didn't give a shit whose dick they rode. He'd admittedly been that way too, until he met two people who changed his whole fucking outlook on life. Now, thoughts of anyone but Jazz and Gumby paled in comparison to what he'd been getting. Amazing sex along with closeness and connection. He'd fought it for so long, but now that he'd had it, he wasn't sure he could live without it.

"Fuck that," he said as he stood and snatched the bottle. He yanked her forward until their faces were inches apart. Her eyes widened. "I hear the name Jazz from your lips or any of the Honeys' lips, you'll be out on your fake ass before you have the chance to reapply your lipstick. Jazz is more woman than the lot of you combined will ever be."

He released her and stomped away from the bar to an enraged shout of, "Fuck you, Screw!"

Yeah, fuck him. He was pretty sure no one but his right hand would be doing that for a long time because, who the fuck was he kidding? The thought of getting it on with anyone beside Jazz or Gumby held no fucking interest anymore.

They'd gone and ruined his cock.

And his fucking heart.

BAM BAM BAM.

At the pounding on his motel room door, Gumby dragged himself away from the very riveting activity of staring at the ceiling and mentally kicking his own ass. Striker stood on the other side, hands in his pockets and a cigarette dangling between his lips.

"Pretty sure Lila would kick your ass until you were bloody if she saw that," Gumby said as he moved out of the way to allow his VP into the room with its lumpy bed, sad, snot green curtains, and barebones carpet.

"We've got a deal. When I'm out of town I'm allowed to smoke as much as I want. Gives me my occasional fix and keeps her from riding my ass."

Gumby snorted. "You'd probably like it if she rode your ass."

Striker strode into the bathroom and put the cigarette out in the sink. "You may be right. I'd let that woman do just about any damn thing to me she wanted. Now sit the fuck down and start talking. I know we surprised you by showing up uninvited, but fuck, brother, we had no idea we'd be walking into such a shitstorm. What the fuck is going on?"

With a heavy sigh, Gumby sat on the edge of the bed while Striker took the lone chair in the dimly lit room. He filled his vice president in on everything that had gone down between the Handlers and the CDMC.

As was his custom, Striker listened with full attention, but once Gumby finished, he sat back and propped one ankle on this thigh. After fishing another cigarette out of his pocket, he stuck the thing between his lips but didn't light it.

"Look, Gumby, this is all shit I need to know and should have been told already, but it's not what I was asking and I'm pretty sure you know it. Jester is pretty damn sure he saw you kiss that guy, what was his name, Screw?"

Gumby stared at his VP waiting for the rush of panic he'd experienced earlier when Jester busted in on them. It never came. His insides were too heavy to allow the jitters of anxiety. He'd fucked up in a way he'd never done before and as he'd packed his bags and left Jazz's house and as he'd stared at the peeling paint on the motel ceiling, he'd come to the stark realization that he didn't want to hide any more.

If the price for remaining in the closet was this gaping hole in his heart, he wanted no part of it. He wanted to be comfortable in his own skin. He wanted to be good with who he was. And who he was, was a man in love with a woman and another man. The way he'd hurt those two people…Christ that could never happen again. It nearly killed him as much as it must have hurt them. Jazz especially, since they'd both lobbed their shit her way.

So it was time for him to grow some balls, get the fuck over his shitty childhood, and deal with the fear that came with coming out.

He took a deep breath. "I'm bisexual," he said. "I've been seeing Jazz and Screw together and I'm pretty sure I'm in love with both of them."

He waited for the nausea. For the heart-pounding, sweat-inducing anxiety. He waited for mockery, revulsion, and castigation from Striker. Hell, he waited for his VP's fist to fly across the room and crash into his jaw.

He got none of that.

Instead his insides…lightened. An airy feeling of being free engulfed him.

Striker frowned and raised an eyebrow. The cigarette drooped to his chin. "That it?"

It was Gumby's turn to frown. "What do you mean?

"What do you mean what do I mean? I said what I meant. That it? That's the fucking crisis that has you moping like an emo teenager? I'm assuming you didn't just come to this conclusion yesterday." He spoke around the dangling cigarette.

"Striker, we've known each other for over thirty years. I just told you I like cock."

"Yeah, brother. Heard that part." Striker shrugged then plucked the cigarette from his lips. "I like pussy, which it seems you do as well." He lifted the white stick. "I like cigarettes too. So the fuck what?"

"You're not…I mean, you don't care? You're not freaked out? Or disgusted?"

Striker's face scrunched in confusion before his eyes widened. "Oh, fuck you, G." He stood and paced the length of the room. "If you tell me you've kept this shit to yourself for all these years because you were worried about *my* reaction, I'll kick your ass back to fucking Arizona." He whirled, charging forward.

Gumby jumped up, meeting him head on.

Striker's eyes had darkened to near black and his jaw ticked like he was biting back some seriously caustic shit. His VP was not pleased.

"Fuck you for that shit," Striker said with a snarl, face contorted in fury. "You say we've known each other since we were kids. Then I think you fucking know I don't give two fucks if you like pussy, cock, some combination of the two or alien fucking probing." He was screaming now, red-faced and practically vibrating as he let loose.

Shit, his VP was pissed like Gumby hadn't seen in years.

Shame washed over him as the words sank in. Striker was right. He knew his friend, his brother, better than that. Hell, he knew every man in his club better. All of a sudden, it hit him. Striker wasn't pissed. He was hurt, maybe even feeling betrayed one of his closest friends kept such a monumental secret. He'd worried so much about what would happen if his club found out his secret, he'd never considered the fallout from keeping such a large part of himself locked away from the people he loved.

A knock on the door followed by Jester's tentative, "Uh, Striker? You guys good in there?"

Striker stomped over the door, yanked it open so hard it practically ripped from the hinges, then admitted Jester with a swoop of his arm.

The big guy took one look at the two of them and grimaced. "Okay, so, not good?"

"Guess what, Jest? Gumby likes cock as well as pussy."

With his gaze bouncing between the two of them, Jester answered with a slow "Uhh, yeah. I kinda got that when I saw that dude's tongue down his throat a few hours ago. Which did happen by the way." He pointed at Gumby. "Don't try to tell me it fucking didn't, asshole. My eyes work damn well. Emily makes me eat carrots," he muttered under his breath.

"And do you give a shit that he likes cock?" Striker stuck the cigarette back between his lips, but at some point, he'd crushed the thing so with a scowl for Gumby, he tossed it on the table.

"Huh?" said Jester. "What? No. Why're you asking me that shit? How long have you known me, Striker? I don't give a shit how people fuck as long as they're fucking. Everyone should be fucking as often as possible. Now, it might make him a greedy fucker that he's claiming two for himself, but I'm down with greedy." He shot Gumby a mischievous grin.

"Why? G? Why the fuck did you think we'd flip out on you?" Striker ran a hand through his brown hair.

"His old man," Jester said with the confidence of someone who knew what the hell they were talking about.

Gumby's jaw dropped. "What? How did you—"

"Come on, G. He's legendary around town for being a colossal douche bag. Stories I heard about that fucker made me wish I could raise him from the dead just so I could kill him. Pretty sure there ain't a person in the world who got misty when he finally kicked it. It's not a stretch to think he fucked with your head about liking cock."

"Shit," Striker said as he plopped back down in the chair. "That's it, isn't it?"

With a nod, Gumby said, "Lost count of the number of 'reminder' beatings he gave me. Just to make sure I wasn't slipping. Don't want to tell you what he did to a guy he found me making out with when I was fifteen."

Striker took out another cigarette. "I can guess. Look, brother, none of us give a fuck who you want to fuck. And if someone does, I'll take care of it. Gonna break my heart to lose you, you know."

His spine shot straight. "Huh? What? I'm not going anywhere."

Striker and Jester exchanged a glance then started laughing and Gumby had the feeling he was the butt of a joke he didn't quite understand yet.

What he did understand was that he not only had some soul searching to do, but some serious groveling.

Chapter Thirty-Nine

Jazz was tempted to lock her phone in her office just so she wouldn't check the time again. She loved her job. Really loved her job, and, normally, the hours spent in Toni's Diner flew by, but today a slug would have passed the clock.

She'd done what she needed to make it through the day. Plastered on a cheery grin she didn't feel, made small talk she didn't have the energy for, and ignored the heavy pit in her stomach as best she could. Though the effort wasn't overly successful. She'd slogged through the morning in a fog of heartbreak and despair fighting tears every few moments.

And when the door jangled, alerting a new customer? Well she'd been convinced one or both of the men would come to their senses and seek her out.

She'd been wrong.

Dead wrong.

Had it all been in her head? The deep connection that seemed to extend beyond physical, reach into her soul, and soak into every cell of her body. If it was, she needed therapy because she'd done a bang-up job of misreading the situation.

All right, one more peek. She checked her phone and breathed out a sigh of relief. Fifteen minutes until closing. Another hour of clean-up and she'd be out of there.

A knock on her office door had her glancing up at Ernesto, their head chef. "Hey, Jazz, sorry to bother you. I made way too much of that chicken tortilla soup. You want to take some home?"

Ugh, the thought of eating did not appeal to her at the moment. "Um, you know what? Pack it up to go and I'll give it to Thunder."

Ernesto flashed her the sexy Latin smile he swore drew ladies like flies even though he was in his early fifties. "Sure thing, boss. The dining room is nearly empty, and I've already started cleaning in the kitchen. We should be able to get outta here in thirty."

Finally, some good news. "Thanks. I'll come in and help in a minute."

With a wink and a nod, he left her office.

Two minutes later, Thunder popped his head in the open door. "Hey, babe, Viper is planning to swing by in about forty-five minutes. He's got something Copper wants him to hand off to me. We still gonna be here?" He smiled as he spoke. The man had a smile that made women forget their names. He knew it, too, and worked it to his advantage.

"Yeah, sure. That's no problem," she replied, unable to keep from grinning back at him. "Ernesto is packing up some left-over soup for you. Make sure you grab it before we head out of here."

"Thanks, babe." After tapping his knuckles on the door frame, he winked and left.

Well, that'd keep her there an extra fifteen minutes, but to help the club, she didn't mind hanging around a little longer. Not like she had any plans beyond going back to Holly's where she got to watch the happy couple ooze sweetness all over each other.

Ugh. She'd officially hit pathetic. The night before she'd laid awake staring at the ceiling of Holly's guest room for hours, reliving every moment since the night she confessed her most painful secrets to the two men she'd fallen in love with. After hours of obsessing, once the initial sting—okay stab—of Gumby and Screw's rejection wore off, she saw the scenario with a bit more clarity.

Gumby had panicked, which set off Screw's anxiety, which caused them both to run. She understood, even empathized with them, but now, more than twenty-four hours later, neither had sought her out. So maybe it really was over. Maybe they'd used the time apart to realize a three-person relationship wasn't what they wanted while she came to the firm conclusion it most certainly was what she wanted. Or maybe they just plain didn't feel the same way about her as she did them.

The one good thing was that she hadn't humiliated herself by professing her love to two men who didn't want her.

With a heavy sigh and an even weightier heart, Jazz dragged herself from her office. After forcing more smiles and chit-chat, she helped clean up then waved the last of Toni's employees off.

"See you tomorrow, Jazz," Ernesto said as he walked toward the rear exit. "You sure you don't want me to stick around until you guys leave?"

"Nah, get on home. I'm sure you have a date to get ready for tonight. Besides, Thunder is out there in full bodyguard mode. I'm good."

"All right." As he walked by, he pressed a kiss to her cheek. "See you in the a.m."

"Enjoy the rest of your day."

A wave of his hand and he was off.

Jazz made her way back out to the dining area in time to catch Thunder walking in.

"You almost ready to go, Jazzy Jazz?" He was so good looking. And the guy could mooove. A few weeks ago, he'd given them all an impromptu twerking lesson that still made Jazz laugh to recall. "Viper will be here in a few, then we can bust outta here."

"Sounds good," he said as he slipped onto a stool at the counter.

"You hungry?"

"Nah, Jazzy, I'm good. Shell brought me some food on her way out earlier. Besides, I'll grab that soup to eat later."

Oh, right. Shit, how had she forgotten that already? "Sorry, my brain is a little fuzzy today. Slept like shit last night."

With a nod of that handsome head he said, "Finding a buttload of heavy artillery in your yard will do that to you."

"Huh? Oh, yeah." Ha, she'd nearly forgotten all about that.

Losing two men would do it even more.

Thunder cocked his head. "Somehow, I don't think it's the guns that had you flipping off the sandman last night. Hard enough trying to make it work with one person. Can't imagine with two. And two bikers? Shit, girl, you don't do things the easy way, do you?"

Her jaw dropped as she blinked at him. "Wha—how?"

He winked. "I'm that good, baby. I'm that good."

As she was about to put him in his place, the bell over the door rang and in walked Viper.

"Hey, V!" Thunder said as he got up to greet his former vice president. "How's Cassie?"

"She's well." Viper practically beamed. "Really well."

"Fuck, that's good to hear. Give her my love, okay?" That was Thunder. Charming as fuck, and truly a nice guy.

"I got those tools loaded in the back of your truck." Viper said as he opened his arms to Jazz. "Copper will grab them from you at the clubhouse."

"Got it, man."

Jazz scurried around the counter into Viper's wide embrace.

"Hey, kiddo," he said into the top of her head. "You smell like cinnamon."

She laughed. "No surprise there. I think it's permanently embedded into my skin." She drew back looking at the smile on his face. A smile that had been absent since his wife was diagnosed with cancer, but seemed to be back now that the prognosis was extremely positive. "Thunder, let me grab your food from the walk-in."

"You guys hang there. I'll grab it," Thunder said as he jogged into the kitchen. He'd been guarding her so much lately she and Toni gave him free rein of the place.

"So, how are you holding up after yesterday?" Viper asked, as he gave her a very stern, fatherly stare.

How the hell did he know? First Thunder, now Viper? Was everyone aware of what happened between her and her men—oh, wait...

"I'm doing all right. The guys got rid of the guns," she said with a shudder, "I'm just hoping I can go back home soon."

Viper nodded. "Yeah, we just gotta make sure the CDMC isn't going to retal—"

A high-pitched sound of shattering glass had Jazz jumping and Viper shoving her behind him.

"What happened?" she yelled, heart rate triple what it'd been five seconds ago. Peeking over Viper's shoulder, she saw the obliterated front window of the diner and thousands of glass shards scattered across the tables and floor. A brick lay among the glass in the middle of the floor. "Holy shit!"

"What the fuck was that?" Thunder came flying from the kitchen only to skid to an abrupt stop as something else flew through the window. "Fuck!" he screamed. "Grenade."

Jazz's breathing completely ceased, and her body froze in place. Did he say *grenade*?

So much happened in the next few seconds, Jazz knew it'd be days before she sorted it all in her mind.

"Get down!" Viper screamed, shoving her to the ground as Thunder shouted. "I see him! It's that fucker, Jeremy. I can fucking catch him."

She hit the unforgiving linoleum floor with a bone-rattling crash.

"Go get him!" Viper called. "I got Jazz."

Out of the corner of her eye, Thunder's form streaked through the dining room. He leapt onto a booth bench then hurdled through the fragmented window.

At the same time, Viper rushed toward the grenade instead of away. In a split second, Jazz came to the sickening realization he was going to try to toss it back out the window before it blew to save the diner.

Who cared about the fucking diner? He'd never make it in time.

"Viper, no!" she screamed, launching off the ground as she fisted handfuls of his shirt and yanked with every ounce of strength she possessed.

The scene played out in slow motion even though in reality, it happened over mere seconds. The noise came first, a deafening boom that made her ears instantly ring with a shrill hum. Then a blinding flash blurred the entire diner. The next thing she knew, she was crashing to the ground again, this time with Viper's body shielding hers.

Tables and chairs hurtled across the dining room as ragged shards of glass, plaster, and wood exploded through the air. Viper curled around her protectively, only clinging tighter as she tried to escape.

No, no, no. He can't do this!

He couldn't protect her at his own expense. Beneath him, she began to shake with startling force. Tears careened down her face. Viper grunted more than once as flying debris pelted his body. But it was when he went limp, his full weight slumping onto her that she lost it.

"Viper!" she screamed.

He didn't answer. Didn't flinch. Just lay on top of her completely slack and lifeless.

The sound of hissing water hit her ears seconds before they were doused in wetness as the sprinkler system came to life. Smoke filled the air and small fires burned in multiple spots around the diner. Grimy water rained down as it mixed with the smoke and settling fragments.

"Viper!" she yelled again, using all her strength to shove his shoulders down her body and wriggle out from beneath him.

Her head ached, and blood ran down her face, but she ignored her own needs. After struggling free, she rose to her knees beside his prone shape. "Oh, God, Viper!" Blood poured from a giant horizontal wound across the back of his head and a triangular wedge of metal stuck out from the center of his back.

"No!" she shouted. "Viper, wake up!" As gently as possible, she nudged him even knowing deep in her heart he wouldn't respond.

He'd saved her life. And died for it.

Pain crushed her chest with so much force she grew dizzy.

"Wake up!" she screamed again and again, until her voice became ragged and her throat raw. "Why the hell did you do that!" She bent over his still body, trembling and moaning in despair.

All of a sudden, strong hands scooped under her arms, dragging her away from Viper. "Oh, thank you!" she said, shivering. The wetness combined with the frigid air flowing into the wrecked restaurant chilled her to the bone. "He needs help. Help him please. Wait!"

The person hauled her backward, away from the disaster of the diner.

"No! I'm fine. Help him! Call nine-one-one. Please! Help him!" Her hoarse shouts were completely ignored as the person tugged her out the shattered front door. Sharp shards cut into her calves as she was heaved across the glass-ridden floor. She refused to take her attention off Viper, staring at him for any signs of life.

As though her body remembered it could move, Jazz began to struggle. "No! Stop." She kicked and bucked but couldn't break the hold. "Forget about me. I can walk. Help Viper!"

"I need to save you. I'm getting you out. Saving your life."

Oh, my God.

Her stomach heaved, bile rising to her mouth.

"No," she whispered as she finally looked up at who she'd thought was her savior. "Please."

This couldn't be happening.

"I told you, Jazmine. I knew it would catch up to you one day. The devil is inside of you. This is proof. You should have let me finish."

She lost it then, screaming and flailing as she fought with all her might to get away. But as in the past, she was no match for the strength born of paranoid delusions. She wrestled for long minutes, until her filthy, aching body sagged in complete and utter fatigue. Cold seeped into her bones. Her fingers burned and tingled as her wet clothing seemed to freeze around her skin, making every move painful and sluggish. Unable to exert any additional escape effort, she sobbed as Paul drew her farther and farther across the parking lot.

Maybe it was true. Maybe she did have some evil force working inside of her.

Gumby and Screw had rejected her.

The diner was destroyed.

Viper was…God, she couldn't even think the word.

And she was back in the clutches of the one man who made her wish she'd died alongside Viper.

"That's better," Paul whispered in her ear as he pulled open a car door. "Don't fight it. I'll take care of you, Jazz. Don't worry. I'll get him out." He shoved her into the rear seat. After he slammed the door and circled to the driver's side. She tried to open the latch with fumbling, useless fingers. As they slipped off the handle, she realized her hands were covered in slippery red blood.

Hers? Viper's?

Didn't matter, it had to come off. She began to rub her hands on her wet jeans so hard, her skin was raw and freezing in seconds.

One last time, she tried the door.

Paul sat in the driver's seat with a chuckle. "Child lock, Jazz. You're not going anywhere. I'd turn the heat on, but we both know the devil thrives on heat, so I'm sorry, but you'll have to be cold a little while longer. Trust me, this will just make it easier to save you."

Trust him? If she'd been able, she'd have laughed.

"H-how did you find me?"

"God was on my side. I wrote you a letter ten days ago. Dad told me he forwarded it to you. It went to your neighbor's house instead."

"J-Jeremy?" she said, unable to keep the shock out of her voice. Jeremy told Paul how to find her? The man was pure evil. She'd lived next door to him for over a year. How had she missed it? How had she been charmed by his willingness to help her out and his supposed crush on her?

"He called me. Told me all about you. Where you work. The disgusting things you've been up to with two men. Did you know he watched you through your window one night? He made it possible for me to get to you before the devil destroys you. See? It's meant to be. I've been chosen to save you." He smiled as he spoke. The insane words made perfect sense in his mind.

"B-but how d-did y-you escape?" Her teeth chattered so loud she could barely hear her own words over the clacking.

"Oh, Jazzy. God works in mysterious ways."

That was all she was going to get from him. Her eyes fell closed as hot tears poured down her cheeks. No one knew where she was. No one would find her. Would this be the time Paul drew enough blood to end her life?

If so, the two men she loved would never see her again.

They'd never know she forgave them.

They'd never know she loved them.

Chapter Forty

Gumby strode through the clubhouse, fully aware of all the curious gazes tracking him.

After his chat with Striker and Jester, the three of them grabbed Hook, got some pizza, and then he drank himself into a stupor. Part of him had wanted to go to Jazz and Screw that night, but his brothers convinced him to give them time to… breathe.

He just hoped Screw hadn't breathed too much. As in breathed in someone else's air while sucking their face…or other parts of their body.

"Hi," he said to a tall blonde bombshell behind the bar. "I'm looking for Screw."

She rolled her eyes. "What do you want with that fucker?"

"Hey!" Jigsaw said from a few stools over. "Pretty sure that ain't your business, hon." He turned to Gumby. "No one's seen him since he grabbed a bottle and disappeared in his room yesterday."

Shit, he'd be feeling even worse than Gumby today.

"Top of the stairs, make a right. Third door on the right."

"Thanks."

"Mmhm." Jig lifted a hand as he returned to whatever paperwork had him captivated.

Gumby jogged up the stairs and made his way to the door Jig had directed him to. Just twenty minutes ago, he'd stood outside Screw's house with the same pit of nervousness in his stomach. When that knock hadn't been answered, he came to the clubhouse.

He almost went to Jazz first, but making up with Screw would go a long way toward fixing what he'd broken with Jazz. If they came to her as one, begging for forgiveness, she'd have to grant it, right?

Gumby blew out a breath and knocked lightly on the door. A groan came from the other side. "Go away," Screw's sleep-roughened voice called.

Instead of following the command, Gumby opened the door and slipped into the room. Music played from an Echo on his nightstand. Screw lay face down on his bed naked except for a pair of black boxer briefs. His eyes were closed, but he said. "Told you it wasn't fucking happening. Get the fuck out."

So, someone had tried to get with him. No surprise there. But he'd resisted. Gumby smiled as he silently toed his boots off. He shut the door, which hopefully Screw interpreted as his departure. Then stripped out of his jacket and Henley before losing his jeans.

After tiptoeing to the bed, he crawled up and onto the mattress, laying himself directly on top of Screw.

"What the hell?" Screw jolted and tried to roll out from under Gumby, but he linked their fingers, pressing Screw's palms into the mattress and scraped his teeth along the back of his biker's neck.

"Gumby?" Screw said in a half question, half plea.

His name spoken in that gravelly, sleep-heavy voice had Gumby's dick hardening against Screw's ass which drew a groan from the man.

"What the fuck are you—"

"I'm sorry," he whispered against the shell of Screw's ear. "So fucking sorry. I fucked up huge and ruined it all. I don't want to be like this, Screw. I don't want to fear being…out. I swear I'm fucking trying, and I'm sorry I failed. I told my brothers all about us."

Screw remained silent as he ground his ass against Gumby's rock-hard erection. But then he said, "Let me turn over."

Releasing his hands, Gumby pushed up to a plank position allowing Screw to roll to his back. When he settled down once again, their dicks slid against one another and both men hissed. Thank fuck Screw was as hard as him. Screw still wanted him. At least he had that going for him.

"You're not the only one who fucked up. I did a pretty stellar job of that myself." Screw reached up and removed Gumby's glasses, setting them on the pillow beside his head. "I've got something to say and then I think it's time we go get Jazzy back."

Gumby closed his eyes as he let Screw's words wash over him. Sure didn't sound like the other man was done with him. Done with them. "What do you want to say?"

"First of all, yesterday is forgiven."

"Same."

Screw smiled. He smoothed his palms up and down Gumby's back in a hypnotic rhythm that made him want to purr. That was until Screw closed his hands over Gumby's ass and squeezed Then he wanted to howl. "I love you, Gumby. I don't care if I can't ever announce it to the fucking world. I love you and I love Jazz. I think you're loyal, and smart, and the perfect amount of calm to my insanity. I think you're the sexiest man I've ever met. You're a man I'm proud of and proud to be with. I can't lose you and if that means waiting until you're more comforta—umph."

Gumby crashed his mouth down on Screw's. It only took his lover a second to get with the program before he was attacking Gumby back. They kissed as they rutted against each other.

"I love you, too, Luke. Jazmine just as much. You might not believe me, but I promise I'll prove it to you." He pulled back, breathless as he stared at his man. "You care so much, so deeply and I'm so fucking proud of how you're learning to accept that about yourself. You're perfect for me. Perfect for us. I'm gonna love you so good, you'll wonder why you ever feared relationships."

This time Screw cut him off with a sharp nip to his lower lip before he bucked his hips and flipped them over.

"Never fucking thought I'd want to hear those words," Screw said, grinding their hips together. "But they're incredible."

Gumby arched his neck as sharp need nearly had him begging for more. He held Screw's arms so tight, his nails scored the skin around those sexy fucking biceps. The pain only made Screw thrust harder against him. God, he loved this. The way he could be as rough as he wanted. The way they could take their near violent urges out on each other. Screw would never balk at harsh treatment and neither would Gumby.

No, he'd fucking demand it.

"I've avoided it my whole fucking life," he continued his hot mouth doing sinful things to Gumby's chest and nipples. "Say it again."

"I love you." Gumby grunted when his proclamation was rewarded with a sharp bite to his pec.

"Again."

"I fucking love you." Another bite. "Aw, fuck, more."

"I love you too." Screw bit him again and Gumby swore he'd come in his underwear if something didn't give.

Bam. Bam. Bam.

They stilled. Screw dropped his head to Gumby's chest. "Fuck. This better be fucking important."

"Y-you need to get downstairs. Um, now." LJ spoke through the closed door.

Screw lifted his head, his confused gaze meeting Gumby's. "He sounds freaked."

With a nod, Screw called. "On my way."

"No, uh, both of you. And hurry." The sound of LJ's retreating footsteps echoed through the room like sonic booms.

"Shit," Gumby said as they both scrambled off the bed. "Think something happened with the CDMC? Retaliation? Why do I feel like the rug is about to be yanked out from under us?" He located his jeans and shoved into them the same time Screw found his.

"Because it fucking is." Screw lifted his shirt off the foot of the bed, sniffed it, then shrugged. "Let's go," he said, working it over his muscular shoulders as they left the room. Normally, Gumby would hang back a second to appreciate the sight of Screw's ass as he jogged down the hallway, but today he kept pace though each step brought with it an increasing sense of doom.

Part of him wanted to keep running straight out the door but he stopped with Screw at the bottom of the steps. There stood a handful of Screw's brothers, each with wild-eyed gazes on him and Screw.

Copper and Zach stood side by side each yelling into separate phone calls, but it was the devastation scrawled across Maverick's face that had Gumby grabbing Screw's hand, onlookers be damned.

"What the fuck's going on?" Screw asked the crowd at large.

An eerie hush of silence descended on the room. Copper ended his call then walked to where he and Screw stood, hands still linked. With each step that drew Copper closer, Screw squeezed Gumby's hand tighter.

Once he stood directly in front of them, his expression one of solemn despair, Copper said, "Thunder called. There was an explosion at the diner. Jeremy threw a brick and a grenade through the window. Thunder chased him down and caught him, but Jazz and Viper were inside."

Screw's knees buckled. Copper reached out and caught him while Gumby staggered backward, shaking his head.

No.

Oh, fuck.

No.

His heels hit the bottom step, causing him to lose his balance. He went down hard, his ass landing on the fourth step up. God, he couldn't think. He could barely breathe. "Is—is she—Oh, fuck." He dropped his head into his hands as the room flip-flopped.

"We have to go," Screw said, attempting to push past his president. His voice rose, thready and panicked. "We have to go."

Copper held him back.

"Copper let me fucking go to her."

"Wait!" Copper yelled. He shoved Screw so he was on the steps next to Gumby.

"She's alive, Screw. She's fucking alive."

"Oh, thank Christ," Gumby said, the words hitting him square in the gut. Beside him, Screw sagged.

Copper got right in Screw's face. "Listen for one fucking second. She's alive, but someone dragged her off."

"What?" both he and Screw shouted as they shot off the steps as one.

Copper held his hands up. "As Thunder was dragging Jeremy back, he saw some guy shove Jazz in a car. He couldn't catch them, but he did get Jeremy and he'll be here any second with that mother fucker."

Wait…so that meant? "Where the fuck is she?" Gumby felt the overwhelming urge to shake Copper until the words he wanted to hear fell from his mouth.

"We don't know."

Not those words. Ice slithered through Gumby's veins as the stark reality of that statement set in. Jazz survived an explosion only to be hauled off. Was she hurt? She had to be fucking terrified.

"CDMC?" Screw croaked.

With a shake of his head, Copper said. "Don't know."

Gumby shot to his feet. "I wanna see him."

"Let us have five fucking minutes with him and we'll know what the fuck is going on." Screw got in Copper's face. "Fuck!" He shoved past Copper, kicking a chair halfway across the room with the force of his anger.

"They're less than a minute out."

Screw turned. "Did you ask Viper if he got a look at the guy?"

"Viper didn't make it." Copper's voice broke. "We think he died protecting Jazmine."

A sound of pure torture ripped from deep within Screw as he doubled over.

Gumby barely knew Viper. Only on a few occasions had he met the former Hell's Handlers VP, but it'd been enough to see how the loss of his life would ravage the club. Screw's gaze met his and when he saw tears shimmering from his lover's eyes, Gumby couldn't possibly hold back. Even if this hadn't been a prime opportunity to prove just how much he really did love Screw by claiming the man in public, Gumby would have gone to him. How could he stand by and watch the man he loved suffer such deep agony?

He moved with purpose, grabbing Screw and hauling the man into his crushing embrace. "Fuck, I'm sorry," he said, even as the club watched, agog. "I know this is killing you, Luke," he whispered, "but you gotta stay strong. I need you to be strong. Jazz needs you to be strong. We're gonna find the fucker who took her, get her back, and make sure she knows how much we fucking love her. You hear me?"

Screw nodded his head into the crook of Gumby's neck.

He dropped his voice. "And we'll make that motherfucker beg for death." Jeremy, or whoever took Jazz, didn't really matter which asshole he'd been referring to. Anyone involved would pray for death by the time he and Screw were done with them.

Rocket popped his head in the building. "They're here."

Screw ripped out of Gumby's hold and charged toward the exit.

"Fuck!" Copper yelled. "Screw, wait!"

At that moment, Gumby didn't give a shit what the president or anyone else wanted. There were two people he cared about in the world right them. One was missing and one was gutted. He rushed after Screw, bursting out into the parking lot in time to see Screw yank Jeremy from Thunder's truck and slam him against the side of the vehicle.

"Where the fuck is she?" Screw screamed, spittle flying in Jeremy's face.

"Jesus, Screw. Not fucking here. We're in broad daylight," Copper said, glancing around as though cops were gonna pop outta the bushes.

The asshole must have been stupider than Gumby realized because instead of cowering in fear, he fucking smirked.

"Something fucking funny?" Gumby asked, coming up next to Screw.

"Lose someone?" he asked.

Before Jeremy's lips had the chance to quirk up again, Screw's fist slammed into the bastard's face with a satisfying crunch.

A rush of elation surged through Gumby as blood poured from Jeremy's nose and mouth. He smiled again. He wasn't gonna tell them shit.

Time to mix shit up. He shoved aside his fear for Jazz, concern for Screw, and anxiety over this entire clusterfuck and focused on making Jeremy mad enough to fuck up.

"You know," Gumby said, winking at Screw before he brought his focus back to Jeremy. "I thought you had a hard-on for Jazz. But you don't, do you? Fuck, maybe you do, but you want him too, huh?" He inclined his head in Screw's direction.

"Oh, shit!" Screw said, smart enough to get on board immediately. "That true, Jeremy? That why you fucked with me all through school? Did you have a little crush you were afraid someone would find out about?" He held Jeremy against the truck with a strong forearm across his chest.

Jeremy spat on the ground. The blood tinged wad landed inches from Gumby's boot. "Fuck you. Don't want no fucking dick. I ain't a fucking queer."

Gumby hummed. "Oh, but I think you are. I think you want him. Think you've wanted him a long time. Was he why you tried so hard to prospect with the Handlers? So you could be close to him? Shit, I bet it killed you to know he voted against you every time. Oh…shit, did you not know that?" he asked with mock innocence.

Jeremy's face grew redder with each word from Gumby's lips until it was near purple. "Fuck. You."

"Nah, you ain't my type. Apparently, we have the same type." He winked and Jeremy lunged uselessly.

Screw knocked him back against the truck without breaking a sweat. "Where the fuck you think you're going?"

Jeremy seethed, breathing through clenched teeth. Drops of blood and spit sprayed from his mouth with every exhale. His body vibrated with bubbling rage.

And then he snapped, struggling against Screw's unbreakable hold. "I hope he destroys her," he screamed at Gumby. "Hope he fucking kills her for being a dirty fucking slut. She's disgusting. I hope he carves her up until there's nothing left this time."

Gumby froze until Screw whispered, "Paul." He shook Jeremy —hard. The man's head banged against the truck with enough force to have him groaning. "Is it fucking Paul?"

The twitch of Jeremy's lips was all the confirmation they needed.

"Jesus fucking Christ," Screw whispered. "You're a goddammed monster." He yanked Paul from the truck and passed him off to Jigsaw. "Put him in the box. I'll deal with him later."

Gumby was already pulling up a number on his contacts when Screw faced him. "How the fuck do we find him? He's got way too much of a lead on us." Screw asked running his hand through his hair.

Gumby grabbed Screw's fingers and pried them away from the strands before he balded himself. "I'm on it. I've got a guy back home." He pressed a kiss to Screw's knuckles as he lifted the phone to his ear.

"Hey, G! Hear you've been a busy man," Acer said in greeting.

"I need your help. Right fucking now," he barked into the phone, aware of the near hysterical thread to his voice.

Acer's voice lost all its teasing. "Anything. I'm at my computer now."

"Jazz's brother Paul somehow got out of lock up and he came here. He's got Jazz. I need everything you can find, Acer. Hotel room, rental car, credit cards if he has 'em. I need to know everywhere he's taken a shit over the last week."

"On it. I'll be in touch as soon as I can."

"You need his last name?" Gumby asked.

"Nah, I got it."

They hung up without any other words. Now that there wasn't anything to do but wait, all the emotions he'd been squashing over the past ten minutes came rushing to the surface.

"Fuck," Gumby whispered as he and Screw walked back into the clubhouse. A heaviness born of intense grief had settled over the men. No one spoke. Most sat staring at nothing with hard eyes and clenched fists while they waited for some word on Jazz. Waited to take action. Waited for blood.

"I'm gonna skin him alive." The croaked vow was spoken with deadly assurance as Screw began to transform his pain and fear into fury.

"And I'll hand you the fucking knife." That was if Gumby could keep himself from using it first.

Screw drifted closer, just a fraction of an inch, but the intent was clear. Gumby didn't think twice about wrapping his arms around his man and kissing him right in front of his entire fucking club. So much had fallen into perspective over the past day. What mattered and what didn't.

Screw mattered.

Jazz mattered.

Family mattered, but if they couldn't get on board, then they weren't real family. This group accepted him with open arms, and he'd be damned if he was going to lose another member of his newfound family.

They'd get Jazz back or he'd fucking die trying.

Chapter Forty-One

Jazz couldn't stop the shivering. Her muscles trembled and her body shook with an out of control fury. She'd bitten her tongue twice with the force of her chattering teeth. Blood had been pouring in rivers down her face since the explosion in the diner. A clumsy touch with her frozen hands revealed a gash along her hairline. She must have gotten hit in the blast. The volume of blood coating her face, clothes, and arms seemed tremendous.

Breathe, you know head wounds bleed a lot.

After driving into the mountains for fifteen minutes with the windows down, Paul threw her over his shoulder and carried her into a house.

She'd fought, best she could, but her limbs had grown clumsy and inefficient. Struggling wasted what little energy she'd mustered. Still, the feeling of skin gathering under her fingernails as she'd raked them across his flesh had been satisfying.

He'd sat her on a couch before opening all the windows in what was actually an adorable house. Quaint, with a modern farmhouse feel, the home could have come straight off Joanna Gaine's TV show.

At first, she'd attempted talking to Paul. Tried begging, pleading, rationalizing, promising him the world. Anything that could possibly trigger sanity and get him to release her. But as she'd known from the other times he'd gotten his hands on her, conversation was another useless endeavor.

All he'd done in response was mumble some sort of prayer of defense against evil spirits.

So now she sat in someone's house, shaking on the outside and screaming on the inside.

Viper was dead.

He'd died protecting her.

Viper was dead because of her. She could barely muster fear for the pain Paul would inflict because the agony of Viper's death exceeded anything her stepbrother could do to her.

"I know it's cold. It has to be that way."

"F-fuck y-you," she said, teeth clanking.

Paul moved faster than she'd have thought possible considering how he'd been gasping for breath after hauling her into the house. He was pale, sweating, jittery, clearly not in good health. Maybe even coming down from his latest high.

He yanked her up from the couch. "Your words can't hurt me, devil," he said as he grabbed her shoulders and shook her, hard.

"Paul! Stop!" The room spun as her brain rattled around in her head.

He released her and took a step back. "This is the last time, you hear me?" He spoke as though truly communicating with a demon spirit present in her body.

Jazz took a step back, but he'd fucked up her equilibrium. Her vision flipped upside down as she tumbled to the floor with a cry.

Paul came at her, knife in hand. The familiar scene caused terror to rip through her.

"N-no." She shook her head, scrambling backward on numb hands and feet. "No, P-Paul. P-please."

As she clambered, crab-walking away, he kept coming.

"S-stop!" she cried as her bloody hand slipped. Paul came closer. "P-please." She scooted her ass along the floor, pushing with aching thighs. Terror overrode the cold but her limbs still moved with a slow inefficiency.

Her back hit the wall. God, she was trapped.

Nowhere to go.

No one to save her.

Helpless to stop him.

Her heart pounded, increasing the gush of blood from her scalp.

Paul bent over her and grabbed the front of her shirt. She tried slapping his hands away, but only managed to nick her forearms on the sharp blade. With her hand and arms numb, she barely felt the knife slice her skin. But more blood ran from her body.

As she struggled and whimpered, Paul slipped the knife under her shirt, sawing through the fabric. Once he'd gotten halfway up her torso, he gripped the fabric and tore it straight in half.

"It'll be better soon, Jazz. It'll be all over soon."

He grabbed her flailing arms and lifted them above her head. One hand held her wrists anchored to the wall while the other brandished the knife.

"N-no." She tried to yell but it came out as a whimpered plea. Cold sweat broke out all over her body. "P-please, d-don't do this."

He pressed the knife to her sternum. Right between her breasts. He stared straight at her, a maniacal grin matching the bloodlust in his gaze.

She flattened her back against the wall. Anything to get even a millimeter of space between them.

The tip of the blade bit into her skin. Paul slowly dragged his arm downward.

Jazz screamed as the hot slice of burning pain made her vision blur.

"It's working Jazz! It's going to work this time," Paul shouted with a wide grin and gleeful tone. "Can you feel it?"

He dug the knife into her side. Not deep enough to sink beneath her skin. But enough to have her screaming again.

There was only one devil in the room, and it wasn't inside of her.

MOST OF THE patched members of the MC waited with him and Gumby in the clubhouse in various stages of grief. Some railed at the universe and promised violent retribution against any and every member of the CDMC. Some sat in silence, lost in their anguish. Others moved about, pacing with a restless agitation. Copper sat in his office, no doubt mentally beating the fuck outta himself.

Shell could have been in that diner just as easily as Jazz. And to top it off, Copper had lost one of his closest friends today. And they'd all lost a brother. Screw rubbed a hand over the ache in his chest. It wouldn't be going away anytime soon.

Gumby checked his phone every two minutes or so even though the volume was cranked as high as it would go. Every few moments, he'd run a hand up Screw's thigh, giving a little squeeze before settling but not severing the connection. That touch, the tiny link to Gumby was the only thing keeping him from flying into a million pieces.

After what was only an hour but felt like an eternity, Gumby's phone buzzed.

Screw's heart rate skyrocketed as he watched his lover flick the screen open. "Jesus, he's fucking good," Gumby whispered before jumping to his feet.

He shot up as well, grabbing Gumby's shoulders. "What? What the fuck did he find?"

Gumby lifted his head, meeting Screw's gaze, and the deadly grin he wore had Screw's veins icing over. His lover was out for blood.

"Paul is at an Air BNB about ten miles from here. He's driving a rental car. I got the address and the plates."

"Holy shit," Screw said on an exhale. "How the fuck did he get that so fast?" He'd have kissed the computer genius if he was there.

"Does it fucking matter?"

"No." Screw kissed Gumby hard on the mouth. "Good fucking work. Come on, let's go get our girl." And they would. And she'd be whole.

He refused to allow his mind to entertain any other possibility.

His stomach on the other hand, churned with the knowledge they might be too late.

After arming themselves in record time, Screw, Gumby, Rocket, LJ, Maverick, Jigsaw, and a few others busted ass to get to the Air BNB while Copper and Zach led a group to the diner.

In order to function, to keep his head clear and sharp instead of spiraling down in a pit of despair, Screw had no choice but to force thoughts of Viper from his mind. He couldn't let the immense loss or the worry over how this would destroy Cassie worm their way in. If he did, he'd crumble and right then he needed to be strong as fuck to get his woman back.

"What's the plan?" he asked Rocket.

Yes, he was the enforcer, but this kind of operation needed to be run by someone who wasn't in love with the hostage.

"This guy's an amateur," Rocket said as he navigated around a slow-moving vehicle on the one lane mountain road. He didn't slow as he took a sharp curve, causing Screw to scramble for the oh-shit handle. A glance over his shoulder showed Gumby did the same. With his jaw tight, and eyes focused on Rocket, Gumby seemed as eager for blood as he felt.

"Paul rented the car under his own name and did the same with the Air BNB. That indicates one of two things. Either he's arrogant as fuck and can't fathom anyone will figure this shit out. Or he didn't think this shit through. He acted on impulse without a well-conceived plan."

"Second option gets my vote," Gumby said from the back.

As Screw nodded, Rocket said, "Me too. So we're going in hot. Busting in the doors from the front and the back. Hopefully a loud, startling show of force will knock him off his game and we can easily get Jazz. Those kinda guys tend to break when a bigger, stronger presence is shown."

"And if he's armed to the teeth?" Gumby asked.

The same question Screw had been wondering but he'd been terrified to ask.

"It's a risk." Rocket sailed around another bend in the road and Screw swore two of the Land Rovers wheels lifted off the ground. "But a calculated one. If he's not thinking rationally, taking it slow and trying to talk him down probably won't work."

Fuck. Rocket had a point.

"All right. You taking point, Rocket?"

"You good with that?"

Screw glanced at his brother. Rocket was focused, calm, cold. Functioning without the riot of emotions Screw was struggling to disguise. Though it pained him to admit, he couldn't lead this charge. He couldn't be trusted to make an objective smart decision if shit went bad. Jazz and Gumby were his priorities and he'd make sure they got out alive.

Whatever it took.

Admittedly he'd put their lives above everyone else, his own included. So no, he couldn't take the lead here.

"Yeah. You need to."

Rocket nodded once, game-face on. "Three of us are taking front door. LJ and Jig have the back. Mav will position others around the house in case the fucker goes out a window. We care about taking him alive?"

"No," both he and Gumby answered at the same time without any hesitation.

"Will Jazz feel the same?"

Screw ran a hand through his hair. "I don't know. He *is* her stepbrother. And he's sick. But, Rocket, he's fixated on her for years. Violently. He's hurt her fucking bad and we can't risk it happening again."

A grunt from Rocket. He'd have no problem taking Paul out.

A hand squeezed his shoulder and he turned to see Gumby's fear-filled eyes. "Don't go in planning to kill, but don't hesitate if it becomes remotely necessary."

Okay, Screw could get behind that plan. He'd be down with beating the fuck outta the guy before sending him back to a prison psych ward. This time one he couldn't break out of.

And then they could move on to Jeremy, who he had every intention of killing.

Christ, how could Viper be dead? How would the club move on from that?

Killing Jeremy would be the first step.

"We're close," Rocket announced. "Thirty seconds out."

Screw checked his weapon. Clicks from the back indicated Gumby had done the same. His heart rate doubled as the house came into view. As Rocket had informed them, the place was isolated, partway up the mountain without neighbors.

Maybe Paul had put some thought into this. Didn't fucking matter. Going in full force was the only option. No way could he stand by while Rocket tried to convince Paul to let Jazz go.

The rental car sat in the driveway. The passenger side door hung open. One of Jazz's Converse sneakers lie on the ground midway to the front door.

She was inside.

Thank fuck.

Part of Screw, a part he forced himself to ignore had feared Paul would take her elsewhere.

Rocket coasted to a stop about a hundred feet from the house. Without a sound, the three men slipped from the SUV, leaving the doors open to avoid noise.

Jig's truck was right behind, and Mav's behind him. Men jumped out the doors quiet as fucking death, and ready to kill.

Some had shotguns, a few carried pistols, but most wore an AK47 strapped slung over their shoulder.

They were fucking ready.

Screw's heart kicked into overdrive as Rocket and LJ exchanged hand signals. With a nod, LJ gestured to Jig and the two of them took off for the back of the house.

"Too fucking quiet," Gumby whispered against his ear. "Fucking creepy."

"Yeah. You good?"

"As I can be," Gumby said, pushing his glasses up his nose. "You?"

"Same." Which pretty much meant, "Hell no, I'm not good but I'm ready."

"Let's move," Rocket whispered.

They took off after him, jogging with light, near silent steps across the wide front lawn of the Air BNB. Mav waved his arms, alerting men to their positions while Screw and Gumby shadowed Rocket up the three concrete steps to the rust brown door.

A trail of splattered blood marked the steps. Screw clenched his teeth as he peered over his shoulder. Sure enough, the stains seemed to originate from the car.

"Christ," Gumby said, voice pure tortured anguish.

Screw's nostrils flared.

Once in place, Rocket held up a hand. The universal sign for *hold up*. Screw wasn't sure he could. His heart pounded out of control. Sweat coated his palms making the weapon slippery in his grasp. He bounced slightly on the balls of his feet, unable to stand completely still with the amount of adrenalin firing through his veins.

In. Out. In. Out.

The measured mantra kept his breathing from running out of control.

Seconds ticked by like hours.

Drops of perspiration rolled down his face despite the forty-degree temperature. The heat of Gumby at his back was the only thing keeping him from splintering into a thousand pieces. If Rocket didn't move soon, he was going to fly apart.

And then, none of it mattered.

A high-pitched scream of suffering pierced the wooded quiet and all three of them reacted. Quick as a ninja, Rocket lifted his heavy boot and rammed it next to the doorknob.

Thank God for rentals whose owners didn't give a shit about security. The door flew open and Screw charged forward, ignoring the bite of pain as a wood shard scraped his cheek. He shoved past Rocket, Gumby hot on his heels, coming to a dead stop at the sight before him.

Jazz, bloody, crying, cowered in a corner, protectively hugging her drawn up knees. And Paul, standing over her with a wicked looking knife.

A bloody knife.

Wild sunken eyes stared at them, not sane or even afraid. Paul's complexion was pale and waxy with dark rings under those eyes. "Don't move!" he screamed. "It's not safe. I have to finish. I have to save her from him."

Jesus.

The guy didn't give a shit they'd just barged in, guns blazing. The demons in his brain had him so single mindedly obsessed with Jazmine, he couldn't recognize true danger.

"I have to finish!" he yelled again. "She's possessed. The devil lives in her. I can get him out." He spoke so fast, the words ran together, difficult to understand. He also used his hands, waving the knife about with clumsy, reckless movements.

Jazz stayed silent, her body visibly trembling in the corner. Her face was covered in blood that ran from a wound near her hairline. Any other injuries were impossible to catalogue.

Paul turned toward Jazz, leading with the knife. "Just a few more," he muttered.

Screw didn't think, he just reacted, sprinting forward with one goal in mind.

Killing Paul.

Paul spun back around with a spine-chilling war-cry. He lifted his knife wielding arm, poised to throw, but it didn't slow Screw. He barreled onward with a loud battle cry of his own.

The sound of his name being screamed registered somewhere in the back of his mind, but the thunder of blood in his ears and rage in his heart dulled it to a muffled roar. Paul's arm advanced forward, the knife a fraction of a second from soaring through the air.

The loud crack of a gun reverberated through the room. One beat later, the knife tumbled from Paul's hand. Jazz screamed. The knife landed on the laminate floor with a clatter. Screw skidded to a stop in time to see the man's eyes dim as he crashed down beside his knife.

Screw whirled around.

Gumby stood off to the side, chest heaving as he lowered his gun. For one flash, his eyes appeared as feral as Paul's, but then he focused on Jazz and sanity returned.

Screw collapsed to his knees beside her. "Jazzy?" They needed to assess her physical injuries, but she threw herself into his arms with a choked cry. Her naked skin was so cold, it made him jump.

Gumby knelt beside them, wrapping his long arms around the two of them.

Jazz sobbed loudly.

"We got you, baby. You're safe. We got you," Screw whispered in her ear though the words were as much for him and Gumby as for Jazz.

Gumby kissed the top of Jazz's head, then Screw's, lingering for long seconds as he held them.

Jazz struggled to sit back. Fuck, she was covered in blood, and now Screw was too. "V-viper," she said, body shivering violently.

Screw exchanged a look with Gumby. They needed to get her to a hospital. "I know, baby. I know."

"He c-covered me," she sobbed, tears mixing with the blood and causing trails of pink to run down her cheeks. "He held me under him. I tried so hard to get out. I didn't want him to do that. Why did he do that?" She grabbed the front of Screw's shirt, giving a him a weak shake. She barely seemed to realize she was topless, freezing, and a bloody mess.

"Oh, baby," Screw said as his throat thickened. "He did it because he loved you. So much. And he knew we needed you. Gumby and I."

"We do, Jazz," Gumby said. "We need you so much. He saved you for us."

Her bloodshot eyes widened, and she choked out another sob as her body hitched. "You do?"

"Christ, yes, Jazz," Gumby said.

Screw wanted to interrupt. To tell her how much he loved her, but he gave Gumby this first moment to confess his feelings for her. For them.

"It's so much more than need, Jazzy." He cupped her face, blood be damned. "I love you. So goddamned much. I love you and I love Screw. When we thought we lost you today…"

She gasped, tears still falling. "God, Gumby, I love you too."

Her gaze shifted to Screw, wary and unsure and that nearly killed him. He'd spend every day for the rest of his life making sure these two people had full faith in his love for them. They'd never doubt it, never doubt him again. He wouldn't give them cause.

He winked. "You don't think I'd let you two be in love without me, did you? Come on, the bed would be way too empty." He pulled Jazz onto his lap. "I love you," he whispered in her ear. Then his gaze met Gumby's. "I love that man over there too. No way in hell are either of you getting rid of me now."

Jazz let out a half laugh half sob. "I love you, Luke."

He smiled. "Of course, you do. Who wouldn't?" He kissed the top of her head. "Now can we please get you some medical attention." He shrugged out of his jacket, wrapping it around Jazz's uncovered shoulders.

"Yes," Jazz said. "Just, can you two please stay with me? I was terrified I'd never see you again and I'm not ready to be out of your sight."

"Just watch them try to make us leave," Gumby said with a small smile.

Screw let Gumby gather Jazz in his arms and carry her out of the house. His brothers had left the house, giving the three of them a few moments. None of them were overly worried about cops showing up. The house sat far up the mountain and hunting in the area was typical. A single crack of a gun wouldn't be questioned.

He rose to his feet then turned. Paul's corpse lay crumpled in a heap on the ground. Rocket and LJ reentered the house.

"You okay, brother?" LJ asked.

He took one more look at the body of the man who'd terrorized his woman for so long.

One animal down. One more to go.

Fuck yeah. "I'm good."

Chapter Forty-Two

Jazz's hand trembled as she knocked on Cassie's door for the second time that week.

This time, however, everything had changed.

Life no longer made sense.

On the one hand, she had everything she wanted. Everything she'd thought she'd lost. Gumby and Screw loved her. Their future, though they still had some challenges to overcome, looked bright and shiny. Full of love, pleasure, and opportunity. A huge part of her heart felt full to bursting.

But then there was this hole. This gaping emptiness created by the loss of Viper's life.

And the guilt. God, the guilt nearly crushed her with its immense weight. The man had thrown his body on top of her, shielding her from the worst of the blast, and lost his life for it. How could she not feel responsible?

"Jazz!" Shell opened the door and immediately pulled her into a gentle hug. "God, honey, I'm so glad to see you. Come in, come in." Shell ushered her through the door. Her eyes were bloodshot and there was a sluggishness to her movements, as though she hadn't slept well because she'd spent the night crying.

Jazz fully understood.

"Cassie is letting Beth help pick out her clothes. Who knows what she'll come out wearing." She chuckled, but it was forced, like she felt obligated to be a light presence in the house.

Moving a bit like a robot, Jazz followed Shell into Cassie's living room. They sat next to each other on the beige microfiber couch.

Jazz blew out a breath. Viper's presence was everywhere in the house. From the Harley prints on the wall, to the shelf full of model motorcycles he'd assembled through the years. Then there was the framed photo, taken a good few years ago, of Viper, Copper, Zach, and Jigsaw. Each man had a more youthful appearance. Especially Viper. But what made her heart weep were the smiles. The happiness and ignorance to what would befall the beloved vice president.

God, she couldn't do this. Couldn't face Cassie. What if the woman hated her? What if she ordered Jazz out of her house? It might very well happen.

"How are you feeling, sweetie?" Shell asked in a soft tone.

"What?" Jazz pulled her focus from the photo. "Oh, I'm fine."

Shell gave her a sweet, empathetic smile. "Not so sure I'd say you're fine just yet." She ran a light finger over the bandage on Jazz's head.

The six-inch gash she'd received at some point during the explosion had required thirty-seven stitches to close. Another twenty closed up the sternum wound. Then there was the warming blankets and heated saline for mild hypothermia. And a visit from a psychologist. The bumps, bruises, and smaller cuts were fixed with a few butterfly bandages and round the clock Motrin. She'd spent seven hours in the hospital before the doctors released her to Screw and Gumby's care.

They had been beyond amazing, staying by her side the entire time, holding her when she cried, letting her squeeze the hell out of their hands when the doctors stuck a needle directly in the gash on her head, and whispering words of love when she seemed close to shattering.

Then they'd taken her home and held her as she sobbed over Viper's death. Eventually, she'd cried herself to sleep. Even then, her men held her tight all through the night. And when she'd woken soaked in sweat with a screaming nightmare? They kissed her, rubbed her back, whispered words of love, and soothed her back to unconsciousness.

She didn't want to talk about herself or her injuries. They were nothing compared to Viper's death and focusing on them only compounded the guilt.

"So, uh, what's the plan for the diner? Have you talked to Toni?" She couldn't continue to talk about Cassie right then.

Shell pursed her lips, hesitating as though she wasn't going to allow Jazz to change the subject. But then she tucked a loose curl behind her ear, and said, "Well, the dining area is completely destroyed, but the kitchen was surprisingly spared. Very minimal damage. Rocket's crew is going to get started on renovations early in the week, once their supplies come in. He's estimating a few weeks of work. So, we'll be closed down for about a month."

They all fell quiet, each lost in their heads until Cassie emerged from the hallway hand in hand with Beth.

"Jazmine," she said with a hitch in her voice.

Shooting to her feet, Jazz wanted nothing more than to run into the woman's arms, but her feet remained rooted to the spot. She'd gotten Cassie's husband killed. The only reason she was standing there was because Cassie's husband was dead.

God, she shouldn't have come.

"We'll give you a few minutes alone," Shell said as she stood and made her way to her daughter. "Come on, Beth. Let's get started on those cookies we were going to make."

"Okay," Beth answered, all smiles.

"We haven't told her anything yet," Shell whispered as she passed Jazz.

All Jazz could do was nod as she stared into the red rimmed eyes of Cassie. Clearly the woman had spent much of the last day crying.

"I want to hug you, but I'm afraid to hurt you," Cassie said as she approached Jazz slowly, as one might approach a wounded animal. She wore a simple pair of light blue pajamas and her long gray hair hung past her shoulders. "Sweetheart," she said on an exhale, "God, I'm so glad you are alive and well enough to visit me today."

"What?" Jazz said, the choked sound coming out as more of a sob than a word. "H-how can you stand the sight of me?"

Shit, she'd promised herself she wouldn't lose it. Vowed she'd stay strong for Cassie's sake, but one sentence and she was seconds from coming undone.

"Oh, sweetie." Cassie gathered Jazz in a gentle hug, her thin arms holding tight but not squeezing.

The tender embrace broke the dam and Jazz's emotions sprung from her eyes in a torrent of scalding hot tears. "I'm sorry," she said as she wept against Cassie's shoulder. "He shouldn't have done it. Why did he do it, Cassie. Why?" Her body quaked with the force of her hysteria, making Cassie shake as well.

"Shhh," Cassie said, rocking her back and forth. "Sit, honey, before you fall down."

The woman's husband had just died in a horrific manor and there Cassie was comforting Jazz. "I'm sorry. I'm being so selfish," she said as she lowered to the couch.

"You're being no such thing." Cassie also had tears rolling down her face, but she gave Jazz a tight smile. "I'm going to tell you a few things and I want you to really listen and hear me. Okay?"

Jazz sniffed and wiped her nose with the back of her hand as she nodded. She looked straight into Cassie's somber eyes.

"He did it because that's who he was, Jazmine. It's just that simple. The man has always been a goddammed hero." She let out a watery chuckle. "He was mine. And now he's yours too. And he'll always be remembered as a hero. He loved you. He loved his club. And he protected what he loved at all costs." Her voice hitched, but she seemed to be holding it together better than Jazz was.

"He loved you most of all," Jazz said as her heart ached.

"Oh, sweetheart, I know." This time, Cassie's smile held a bit of happiness. "There isn't a doubt in my mind how he felt about me. I had many, many wonderful years with that man and not a single day went by where I wondered if his love for me had faded."

Of course Cassie was grieving, devastated, but seeing that she hadn't been destroyed helped bolster Jazz. Part of her had worried she'd walk in the house to find Cassie near comatose in bed. "You're so strong," she whispered.

"As are you."

Jazz shook her head. "I'm not. Maybe if I had been, I could have done something.
Gotten away from Paul and saved Viper somehow. I might have been able to do…something. I should have seen the evil in Jeremy earlier. Or if I hadn't found those damn guns…" She shrugged helplessly.

"Okay, honey, this stops right here and right now." Cassie's tears slowed as her face hardened. "You are not responsible for a single thing that happened yesterday. It was a product of a complex hatred between two clubs. Honey, you can't take it on. You need to let it go. For me. For Viper. Do not waste the life he saved by feeling guilt, regret, and punishing yourself, you hear me?"

Every word squeezed her bruised heart tighter. "Damn, Cassie, you fight dirty," she said around a sniff. "But I hear you. And I promise you I will live every day of my life to the fullest. Viper's sacrifice will not be in vain."

"Oh, honey, I know that. And so did he. You know, after I started chemotherapy and was feeling so awful, we had many long, deep conversations about our lives, our wishes, our hopes, and our plans should one of us end up alone. Every time he left the house for the past three weeks, he hugged me, kissed the hell out of me, and said, 'I loved you yesterday, I love you today, and I'll love you tomorrow whether you're here with me or waiting on me among the stars.'" She winked. "Bet you didn't know he was such a romantic at heart."

"God, Cassie..." Jazz had cried so many tears over the last day, there shouldn't have been any left, but still, they poured down her face unchecked. "That is incredible."

Cassie ran a trembling hand through her silvery hair. "I repeated the words back to him. We, more than most, were aware that life is fragile and can end at any moment. We've lived in this world a long time and we knew it often comes with loss."

Jazz squeezed Cassie's hand as she nodded. The lump in her throat made it impossible to speak.

"I don't blame you. I don't blame the club. I don't blame anyone but the man who threw that bomb. I had so many wonderful years with Viper. So many moments and memories I will cherish for the rest of my days."

Jazz leaned in and hugged Cassie. "I love you, Mama V."

"Oh, sweetie, I love you too. You're one of my chicks." She sniffed and kissed Jazz's temple. "It will take some time," Cassie whispered. "But I will be okay. I've lost Viper, but his love is still here with me and that I cannot lose."

Jazz tightened her arms. Pain shot through the wound in her chest, but she ignored it.

"Live your life honey. Love those two men. Make every day count."

"I will. I'll make you proud. I'll make Viper proud."

Cassie huffed next to her ear. "Oh, sweetie, you already have."

She stayed a bit longer, reminiscing with Cassie and Shell. They shared stories of Viper. He'd been like a father to Shell, so she felt the loss with an extra sharp pang. But like Cassie, she was a strong woman, and she'd come out on the other side even stronger.

Eventually it was time to leave. Monty drove her to the clubhouse where she'd wait for her men to finish their task. The club had Jeremy down in the box. He wouldn't be walking out, and while Jazz would never consider herself a violent or vengeful person, she couldn't find it in her to care. After what he did, Jeremy deserved what was coming to him.

As vicious as it was bound to be.

"I CAN DO this all day," Screw said before slamming his fist into Jeremy's jaw.

Again.

The beaten man's head whipped to the side on impact, blood spraying from his mouth.

"Did the Chrome Disciples authorize the attack on the diner that nearly killed my woman and did kill a member of my family?"

Jeremy groaned, his head falling forward. A line of blood tinged drool hung from his lower lip. Screw grabbed a handful of his hair, jerking his head up. "Hey," he said giving a couple of firm taps to Jeremy's cheek with his palm. "It's not fucking nap time."

Jeremy spoke, the words slurred and unintelligible from his swollen mouth.

"What was that? Speak up, don't think the kids at the back of the class heard you." He turned Jeremy's head so the bastard had Copper and Zach in his line of sight. Though he might not be seeing too well with those puffed up eyes.

Copper and Zach stood side by side, their backs resting against the wall and arms crossed in almost a twin stance. Only difference was Zach's smirk was visible while Copper's hid beneath his beard.

"No one was supposed to be there," Jeremy said. "It was after closing."

"Ohhhhh," Screw said. He dropped Jeremy's head and paced away, throwing his arms up in the air. "Well, shit, guys. He didn't think anyone was there. He never planned to murder Viper and injure Jazz. He just wanted to destroy our fucking property. Well, this changes everything."

From the wall opposite Copper and Zach, Gumby snickered. Screw shot him a wink. He'd been floored when Copper invited his lover into the box. Had Gumby been Jazz's boyfriend and not his, Copper never would have allowed it. He'd done it as a favor to Screw. One which he was extremely grateful for. Not only because Gumby deserved this justice too, but his presence settled Screw.

How in such a short time, he'd come to require not one but two people's presence in his life, he'd never know, but he was done questioning it. Done trying to return the gift life had given him.

"She's hurt?" Jeremy asked.

Screw laughed as disbelief washed through him. Was the fucker for real? "Seriously? You're worried about her now? You stashed weapons at her house, you ratted out her friends at a CDMC party, and you blew up her fucking place of business. Yesterday you told me you hoped her psycho stepbrother cut her to bits. But you're worried she got hur—oh, wait a minute." Screw snapped his fingers as the light bulb went off.

"You really did want in her panties, didn't you? I guess Gumby was wrong. Gotta admit, he was convincing. I started to wonder if you'd been after me. But you wanted the girl after all. That why you were always doing shit like shoveling her driveway?" He laughed again. "Cute, Jeremy, really cute." He circled behind the chair they'd positioned the bastard in, bent down, and spoke at the man's ear while keeping his gaze on Gumby. "The thing is, asshole, you never stood a chance of getting with Jazz. She doesn't want a pathetic little boy. She wants a man. Which is what she has." He fisted Jeremy's hair again, this time turning him to face Gumby. "You've met,

Gumby. The sexy fucker over there with the glasses. Well, when we're done here, he and I are gonna take Jazz home. To *my* house. And we're gonna fuck her. And we're gonna fuck each other. Then the three of us? Well, we're gonna live happily fucking ever after. And you? Well, you're gonna die, Jeremy."

Dropping Jeremy's head, he circled around front again, gripping the arms of the chair. He shook the thing, making Jeremy groan as his battered body jostled and banged against the chair's metal frame.

"There's just one thing left to decide, Jer. Hey, look at me." He smacked Jeremy's face again with a sharp open-palmed slap. The wannabe's head rolled across his shoulders, but he managed to keep his bruised eyes open. "You wanna go out quick, or slow with a ton of fucking pain? Now, personally I'd like to be the one to decide, but I'm actually in a pretty good mood. Probably because of all that fucking I told you I was gonna get to later. So I'll let you pick. Quick and painless—relatively speaking, or slow, sweet, torture?"

Jeremy mumbled, "Quick."

"Well that's no fun for me, but all right." He blew out an exaggerated sigh. Chances were, he was getting too much enjoyment out of torturing the guy. It couldn't be healthy, but that was the beauty of the box. Down here, Screw and his club could exact revenge, rid the world of filth, and watch the evidence slide down the large drain in the center of the room. Then he could walk up the stairs and emerge into the light, leaving the darkness where it belonged. In a ten by ten room under the ground.

"Now that we got that out of the way, I'll ask you one more time. Did the Chrome Disciples sanction the hit on the diner?" He asked the question slowly as though speaking to a child.

"No."

"Huh? What was that?"

"No," Jeremy muttered.

"Gonna need you to expand on that answer, Jer."

"Water?"

"What'd you say? You need some water? Sure, that's no problem."

Screw motioned to Gumby who picked up on his intention immediately. At first, it freaked him out how in tune they were, but now their near ability to read each other's minds was a comfort. Gumby walked over, handing Screw the end of the hose. Then he returned to his spot near the wall and cranked the spigot all the way.

With a grin that probably made him look like a madman, Screw pressed down on the stream with his thumb. He aimed it at Jeremy, hitting the guy in the face at full blast with the icy spray.

Jeremy sputtered and flopped around in the chair like a fish on land. When he nearly fell on the ground, choking and coughing, Screw nodded to Gumby who cut the water.

"Better?"

Jeremy didn't answer, he was too busy spitting bloody water from his lungs.

Finally, he said, "The club lost a shitload of money this week. Their gun shipment was fucked and never got delivered. Blade is freaking the fuck out. They got all these guns and no one to move 'em. So I offered to store a bunch in Jazz's shed." He groaned through a mirthless laugh. "She's lived there almost a year and a half. Been out to that damn shed one time." He closed his eyes and shifted; face contorted in misery.

"Keep talking."

Jeremy spit a bloody wad of phlegm on the ground. "When the guns disappeared, Crank kicked my ass out and set my fucking cut on fire." Jeremy lifted his head and even through the mess of his face, his absolute hatred of anything Hell's Handlers came blazing through.

"So you decided to hurt us."

"Fuck, yes." It was then Jeremy seemed to realize he'd never leave that room. His last moments would be spent with four men he despised. He grinned, cracked and swollen lips curling in a grotesque sneer. Hell, even his teeth were caked in red. "I really thought the place was empty. Didn't mean to kill anyone. But when I heard Viper died?"

Jeremy's grin spread and Screw reacted before he even realized what he was doing. He sped forward, jammed the gun against the left side of Jeremy's chest and turned until he found Gumby's gaze.

"I was so fucking ha—"

BOOM.

Screw never once looked away from Gumby. After he fired the weapon, Gumby stepped forward and held out a hand. He let the gun fall to the ground, confident his prez and VP would take care of the clean-up. He had one goal in mind as he took Gumby's hand.

"Let's get our girl and take her home," Gumby said, right before kissing him.

He sank into the kiss, pouring all his grief, rage and now, relief into the man he loved.

"You did good," Gumby eventually whispered against his lips.

Screw pressed his forehead to Gumby's as he nodded.

Hand in hand, they walked up the stairs and out into the light of day, leaving the horror and gore behind.

After a quick change of clothes and a wash-up, they found Jazz upstairs in Screw's room, dozing on his bed. Fuck, she looked so small and fragile there with bulky bandages reminding him of how close he'd come to losing her.

How close they'd come.

Gumby squeezed his hand as though reading his mind once again.

Jazz's eyes fluttered open and a smile appeared but fell a second later. "Is it done?"

They hadn't spoken with Jazz about what would be happening today, but she was nobody's fool.

"It's done."

Her eyes fell shut and she breathed out. "Good." With no more than a slight wince—though it was still too much for Screw—she hoisted herself to the edge of the bed then walked to them. "Take me home," she said, tilting her face up.

They both obliged her, Gumby kissing her first, then Screw.

"Love you guys," she whispered, wrapping her thin arms around them as best she could.

"Love you, Jazzy," Gumby said.

"What he said." Screw tilted his head in Gumby's direction, making Jazz beam with happiness.

Their lives were far from perfect. In fact, they were pretty fucking messy right then. Gumby lived and worked across the country, Jazz's place of business was in ruins, the club had a formidable enemy still on the hook, and one of their own had just been lost.

If ever there was a time to fall apart, this was it. But there, with the three of them wrapped up in each other, Screw was happy.

He felt excited. Ready to take on the future.

He felt home.

He felt loved.

EPILOGUE

Three months later

Screw watched the tall man walking toward him with so much anticipation, he could barely keep from dashing forward and tackling him right there. Instead, he leaned a hip against his truck and gave Gumby his best come hither look.

Damn, his man looked good. Tall with jeans not too tight not too loose. They probably made his ass look spectacular. In fact…

"Hey, you!" Screw shouted. "Tall guy with the sexy glasses."

Gumby smirked, then stopped walking. "Me?" he asked, holding a hand to his chest as he looked around. "You talking to me?"

Ohh, this is fun.

Gumby was still a good thirty feet from him. "Yeah, you. Could you maybe turn around, bend over a bit?"

A woman walking by gasped, muttered, "Pervert."

Hell yeah, he was a pervert. For fuck's sake, he hadn't touched his boyfriend in forty-five days. He was about to spend the next forty-eight hours being a pervert. He was gonna pervert the fuck outta Gumby. Jazz too.

Speaking of, Gumby didn't bend over, but he stalked forward, eyes hot and needy. Screw had spent more time with his hand and FaceTime than he'd thought possible over the past month and a half. Though there'd been plenty, and he meant plenty of times where he'd gotten to fuck Jazz stupid while video chattin' with Gumby. Their lover sure loved to watch them while he got off. Those were some damn good memories, but nothing beat the three of them touching, tasting, all being together.

Gumby stopped just out of reach and crooked a finger. "Come here."

"You want me to come right here? Really?" Screw shrugged and reached for his belt. "Figured you'd want Jazz here too for the first time, but, you know me, I'm always game."

With a laugh and a roll of his eyes, Gumby closed the distance and yanked Screw against him. "Fuck, I missed that smartassed mouth. And now I get it back. Whenever I want. Forever." He grabbed the back of Screw's head and crashed their mouths together in a kiss that curled his toes and weakened his knees.

Oh, fuck, he was hard as a rock in the airport arrivals lane while his boyfriend rubbed all over him with an equally hard cock.

"Jesus Christ," Screw said as he gulped in air and tried to ignore the ache in his balls. "Get in the fucking truck, G. We need our girl with us."

Gumby winked, kissed him once more, then went to stow his suitcase in the back.

Damn, he was glad that man was home.

DAMN, IT WAS good to be back in Tennessee. It'd taken longer to sell his house and share of the business than expected, thus the thirty-day trip turned into forty-five. If he'd had doubts about his triad relationship before leaving—which he hadn't, but if he had—they'd have flown out the window within the first twenty-four hours.

Being without Screw and Jazz sucked.

"So how'd it go last night?" Screw asked as he watched Gumby buckle his belt.

"It was rough, to be honest. Good, but a little rough." His club had thrown a huge blowout sendoff party for him the night before. Though it wasn't customary, or even technically allowed, the club had been beyond cool about him handing over his colors to go live in Townsend.

Next obstacle would be a vote to see if the Handlers would let him in without prospecting. He'd do what he had to, but fuck he wasn't looking forward to another tortuous prospecting year.

"You having second thoughts?" Though he stared out the windshield and sounded unaffected, Gumby knew Screw's insecurities well by now.

"Second thoughts? No. Fuck no. Just hard to say goodbye to people I've known my entire life. I grew up with a lot of my club brothers."

Screw glanced his way then reached out a hand which Gumby gladly took. After weeks of not being able to touch, he planned to spend the next few days connected to his lovers in every way.

In a rare display of utter seriousness and sincerity, Screw said, "I hope you know Jazz and I realize the sacrifice you're making to be with us, and we will not take it for granted."

He lifted Screw's hand and kissed the knuckles. "Not a sacrifice." A tiny whimper from the back seat had Gumby glancing over his shoulder. "Uh, Screw? What the hell is that? Or should I say, what they hell are they?"

With a toothy grin, Screw said, "They are our new guard dogs."

Gumby laughed as he reached in the back and pulled the box containing two fuzz balls onto his lap. "Guard dogs. Seriously?" He stroked a finger over the soft and tiny head of one puppy then the other.

"We'll they aren't guard dogs today, but they'll grow." Screw shrugged. "I don't like it when Jazzy is home alone. Two pit bulls might have prevented Jeremy from breaking into the yard."

He had a point there.

The three of them had been staying at Screw's until Gumby left. Now that he'd returned, they planned to look for a bigger house to buy. It'd be nice to know Jazz wasn't alone in the house on late nights.

"They boys or girls?" One of the puppies was a light gray with a few irregularly shaped white patches, including one around its eye. The other was a light brown with one swatch of white on its chest. "And did you name them yet?"

"Both boys. Brothers. They're eight weeks old, and I did name them. The gray one is Pitcher and the brown is Catcher."

Gumby laughed loud, making Catcher jump beneath his big hand. "You're ridiculous."

Screw just waggled his eyebrows as his truck ate up the miles to home. Gumby picked up the pups. Each fit in the palm of his hand. He cuddled their warm, wriggly bodies to his chest. Settling back in the seat, he watched his man drive with a smile on his face. In a short time, he'd be home and could focus on building a life with the two people who meant everything to him.

JAZZ SMOOTHED THE front of her form-fitted dress before glancing in the mirror. Over the past few months, she'd been working on feeling comfortable in short sleeves and tank tops. Scars were still there of course. Actually, she had a few new ones due to both Jeremy and Paul, but her men had helped her see that not only didn't they define her, they didn't draw stares of disgust and horror like she'd always feared. With the help of Screw, Gumby, and her amazing girlfriends, she'd taken a wild leap out of her comfort zone and began wearing short sleeves at work.

Not only did the world keep turning, but she'd been far more comfortable and less sweaty running around all day. Right now, she was looking pretty good if she did say so herself. The wine colored bodycon dress with a scooped neck hugged her in all the right places and actually gave her some curves.

Screw had texted about twenty-five minutes ago saying he was a half an hour out. She planned to surprise him, and hopefully they could cue Gumby up on FaceTime for a little three-way video sex.

The sound of the truck idling in the driveway had her running to the den. Jazz sat on the edge of the couch, positioning herself in what she hoped was a sexy pose. Luckily, Screw was easy and thought pretty much anything she did was sexy.

The door opened and Gumby strode into the room.

Jazz forgot all about being sexy. "Gumby!" she shrieked as she flew toward him, jumped in his arms and wrapped herself around him as tight as she could.

"Hey, baby," he said, holding her just as close. "Surprise."

"Oh, my God, are you really here?" She pulled back to look at his handsome, clean-shaven face.

"I really am," he said, before kissing her.

"For good?" she asked against his mouth.

She felt his lips curve. "For good, Jazzy."

This time she kissed him until she could no longer breathe or think. "I love you so much."

Pressing their foreheads together, he grinned.

"Hey, what am I? Chopped liver?"

Jazz giggled. She felt lighter than she had in weeks. Her men were under the same roof as her. Exactly where they were all meant to be.

"Love you, Screwball," Gumby said.

"And I love you too," said Jazz.

"Yeah, yeah, you guys are all right," he said which was pretty much a gushing declaration of love, especially since he sounded suspiciously choked up watching her love on Gumby.

"Hey, what's in that box?" Jazz jumped out of Gumby's arms. She felt giddy, so happy she could start flying around the room. "Oh, my God, Screw, they are so cute!"

"And I'm forgotten all ready," Gumby said.

Jazz swatted his arm as she giggled. "Oh, stop. Look at the puppies." They were the cutest little balls of squish and fur. Jazz knelt next to the box, crooning and babbling at the sweet puppies. She lifted the gray one, rubbing his soft little body against her cheek. "I'm in love. Are they ours? Please tell me we're keeping them."

"We're keeping them," Screw said a he shrugged out of his leather jacket and hung it in the closet. "But, babe, they're fierce guard dogs, so you can't go gaga all over them."

"What? Guard dogs? No, they're my cute little babies," she said in high-pitched baby talk.

Gumby laughed. "She's gonna turn your ferocious animals into little marshmallows."

Jazz looked up in time to see Screw sidle up next to Gumby. Gumby put his arm around Screw's waist, pulling him into his side as though it was as natural as breathing.

Being with them was as close to perfection as she'd ever encounter. Every night she went to bed warm, safe…satisfied and with a huge smile on her face. In the mornings, she practically hopped out of bed, ready to see what the day with her men would bring. And all those hours in between she floated on a cloud of blissful love. Or often orgasmic love.

"Hey, what are their names?"

Gumby snorted which earned him an elbow to the gut from Screw. "Ow! What was that for?"

"Making fun of my awesome names."

"Oh, Lord, what are they?"

"Well, these little guys are both boys, so I named them Pitcher and Catcher. You're holding Pitcher."

Wait? Huh? She frowned at the little puppy in her hands.

"Um, Screw?"

"Yeah, baby?"

"For someone who claims to have had as many encounters with both penises and vaginas as you, you should really be able to recognize anatomy better."

"Oh, shit," said Gumby as he cracked up laughing.

Jazz's shoulders began to shake as she suppressed her own hilarity.

"What do you mean?" Screw asked looking back and forth between them. "What's so funny?"

Gumby could barely speak he was laughing so hard.

Jazz lost the battle as well. A bark of laughter bubbled out. She held the little puppy up, stomach side out as her giggles turned to full-on belly laughter. "P-p-p-pitcher's a girl!"

Shock spread across Screw's face before he shifted his gaze to the puppy's nether region. "Oh, fuck me."

Jazz hooted with laugher, tipping to the side, until she landed on the carpet. Both puppies scrambled all over her, causing her to laugh even harder. "Oh, my stomach hurts."

Snickering along with her, Gumby walked over and dropped on his knees by her head. He leaned forward and captured her lips in a kiss that spoke of his intention to get naked in the next few minutes.

A second later, two strong thighs bracketed her sides. Screw had straddled her and set about working her dress up her hips. "Did we mention how sexy you look in this dress?"

"Actually, you did not."

Gumby caught her earlobe between his teeth. "Well consider that mistake remedied. You look hot as fuck in this thing."

"Wait, do you hear that?" She propped up on her elbows. "It sounds like running water."

"Oh, shit," Gumby yelled as he shifted to the side. Catcher squatted next to him leaving a sizable puddle on the rug.

"At least one of you has a cock," Screw grumbled which made Jazz laugh all over again.

If this was what the rest of her life was going to be like with these two men…this crazy, chaotic, sexy mess, she just might end up the happiest woman in the world.

Thank you so much for reading **SCREW**. If you enjoyed it, please consider leaving a review on Goodreads or your favorite retailer.

* * *

Other books by Lilly Atlas

No Prisoners MC
Hook: A No Prisoners Novella
Striker
Jester
Acer
Lucky
Snake

Trident Ink
Escapades

Hell's Handlers MC
Zach
Maverick
Jigsaw
Copper
Rocket
Little Jack
Joy
Screw

Join Lilly's mailing list for a **FREE** No Prisoners short story.
www.lillyatlas.com

Join my Facebook group, **Lilly's Ladies** for book previews, early cover reveals, contests and more!

About the Author

Lilly Atlas is an award-winning contemporary romance author. She's a proud Navy wife and mother of three spunky girls. Every time Lilly downloads a new eBook she expects her Kindle App to tell her it's exhausted and overworked, and to beg for some rest. Thankfully that hasn't happened yet so she can often be found absorbed in a good book.